PRAISE FOR WILBUR SMITH

'Wilbur Smith rarely misses a trick'
Sunday Times

'The world's leading adventure writer'
Daily Express

'Action is the name of Wilbur Smith's game and he's
a master'
Washington Post

'The pace would do credit to a Porsche, and the invention
is as bright and explosive as a fireworks display'
Sunday Telegraph

'A violent saga set in Boer War South Africa, told with
vigour and enthusiasm . . . Wilbur Smith spins a fine tale'
Evening Standard

'A bonanza of excitement'
New York Times

'A natural storyteller who moves confidently and
often splendidly in his period and sustains a flow of
convincing incident'
Scotsman

'Raw experience, grim realism, history and romance
welded with mystery and the bewilderment of life itself'
Library Journal

EAGLE IN THE SKY

Wilbur Smith was born in Central Africa in 1933. He was educated at Michaelhouse and Rhodes University. He became a full-time writer in 1964 after the successful publication of *When the Lion Feeds*, and has written over thirty novels, all meticulously researched on his numerous expeditions worldwide. His books are now translated into twenty-six languages.

Find out more about Wilbur Smith by
looking at his own author website,
www.wilbursmithbooks.com

THE NOVELS OF WILBUR SMITH

THE COURTNEYS

When the Lion Feeds   The Sound of Thunder
A Sparrow Falls   Birds of Prey   Monsoon
Blue Horizon   The Triumph of the Sun

THE COURTNEYS OF AFRICA

The Burning Shore   Power of the Sword   Rage
A Time to Die   Golden Fox   Assegai

THE BALLANTYNE NOVELS

A Falcon Flies   Men of Men   The Angels Weep
The Leopard Hunts in Darkness

THE EGYPTIAN NOVELS

River God   The Seventh Scroll
Warlock   The Quest

Also

The Dark of the Sun   Shout at the Devil
Gold Mine   The Diamond Hunters
The Sunbird   Eagle in the Sky
The Eye of the Tiger   Cry Wolf
Hungry as the Sea   Wild Justice
Elephant Song   Those in Peril

WILBUR SMITH

EAGLE IN THE SKY

PAN BOOKS

First published in Great Britain 1974 by William Heinemann Ltd

This edition published 2012 by Pan Books
an imprint of Pan Macmillan, a division of Macmillan Publishers Limited
Pan Macmillan, 20 New Wharf Road, London N1 9RR
Basingstoke and Oxford
Associated companies throughout the world
www.panmacmillan.com

ISBN 978-1-4472-6263-3

Copyright © Wilbur Smith 1974

1 3 5 7 9 8 6 4 2

A CIP catalogue record for this book is available from
the British Library.

Typeset by SetSystems Ltd, Saffron Walden, Essex
Printed and bound by CPI Group (UK) Ltd, Croydon, CR0 4YY

Visit www.panmacmillan.com to read more about all our books
and to buy them. You will also find features, author interviews and
news of any author events, and you can sign up for e-newsletters
so that you're always first to hear about our new releases.

This book is for my wife

MOKHINISO

who is the best thing
that has ever happened to me

ACKNOWLEDGEMENTS

While writing this story I had valuable help from a number of people. Major Dick Lord and Lieutenant Peter Cooke gave me advice on the technique and technicalities of modern fighter combat. Dr Robin Sandell and Dr David Davies provided me with the medical details. A brother angler, the Revd Bob Redrup, helped with the choice of the title. To them all I am sincerely grateful.

While in Israel many of the citizens of that state gave help and hospitality in generous measure. It grieves me that I may not mention their names.

'Three things are too wonderful for me,
four I do not understand,
The way of an eagle in the sky,
The way of a serpent on a rock,
The way of a ship on the high seas,
And the way of a man with a maiden.'

Proverbs 30: 18–20

There was snow on the mountains of the Hottentots' Holland and the wind came off it, whimpering like a lost animal. The instructor stood in the doorway of his tiny office and hunched down into his flight jacket, thrusting his fists deeply into the fleece-lined pockets.

He watched the black chauffeur-driven Cadillac coming down between the cavernous iron-clad hangars, and he frowned sourly. For the trappings of wealth Barney Venter had a deeply aching gut-envy.

The Cadillac swung in and parked in a visitors' slot against the hangar wall, and a boy sprang from the rear door with boyish enthusiasm, spoke briefly with the coloured chauffeur, then hurried towards Barney.

He moved with a lightness that was strange for an adolescent. There was no stumbling over feet too big for his body, and he carried himself tall. Barney's envy curdled as he watched the young princeling approach. He hated these pampered darlings, and it was his particular fate that he must spend so much of his working day in their company. Only the very rich could afford to instruct their children in the mysteries of flight.

He was reduced to this by the gradual running down of his body, the natural attrition of time. Two years previously, at the age of forty-five, he had failed the strict medical on which his position of senior airline captain depended, and now he was going down the other side of the hill, probably to end as a typical fly-bum, steering tired and beaten-up heaps on unscheduled and shady routes for unlicensed and unprincipled charter companies.

1

The knowledge made him growl at the child who stood before him. 'Master Morgan, I presume?'

'Yes, sir, but you may call me David.' The boy offered his hand and instinctively Barney took it – immediately wishing he had not. The hand was slim and dry, but with a hard grip of bone and sinew.

'Thank you, David.' Barney was heavy on irony. 'And you may continue to call me "sir".'

He knew the boy was fourteen years old, but he stood almost level with Barney's five-foot-seven. David smiled at him and Barney was struck almost as by a physical force by the boy's beauty. It seemed as though each detail of his features had been wrought with infinite care by a supreme artist. The total effect was almost unreal, theatrical. It seemed indecent that hair should curl and glow so darkly, that skin should be so satiny and delicately tinted, or that eyes possess such depth and fire.

Barney became aware that he was staring at the boy, that he was falling under the spell that the child seemed so readily to weave – and he turned away abruptly.

'Come on.' He led the way through his office with its fly-blown nude calendars and handwritten notices carrying terse admonitions against asking for credit, or making right-hand circuits.

'What do you know about flying?' he asked the boy as they passed through the cool gloom of the hangar where gaudily coloured aircraft stood in long rows, and out again through the wide doors into the bright mild winter sunshine.

'Nothing, sir.' The admission was refreshing, and Barney felt his mood sweeten slightly.

'But you want to learn?'

'Oh, yes sir!' The reply was emphatic and Barney glanced at him. The boy's eyes were so dark as to be almost black, only in the sunlight did they turn deep indigo blue.

'All right then – let's begin.' The aircraft was waiting on the concrete apron.

'This is a Cessna 150 high-wing monoplane.' Barney began the walk-around check with David following attentively, but when he started a brief explanation of the control surfaces and the principle of lift and wing-loading, he became aware that the boy knew more than he had owned up to. His replies to Barney's rhetorical questions were precise and accurate.

'You've been reading,' Barney accused.

'Yes, sir,' David admitted, grinning. His teeth were of peculiar whiteness and symmetry and the smile was irresistible. Despite himself, Barney realized he was beginning to like the boy.

'Right, jump in.'

Strapped into the cramped cockpit shoulder to shoulder, Barney explained the controls and instruments, then led into the starting procedure.

'Master switch on.' He flipped the red button. 'Right, turn that key – same as in a car.'

David leaned forward and obeyed. The prop spun and the engine fired and kicked, surged, then settled into a satisfying healthy growl. They taxied down the apron with David quickly developing his touch on the rudders, and paused for the final checks and radio procedure before swinging wide on to the runway.

'Right, pick an object at the end of the runway. Aim for it and open the throttle gently.'

Around them the machine became urgent, and it buzzed busily towards the far-off fence markers.

'Ease back on the wheel.'

And they were airborne, climbing swiftly away from the earth.

'Gently,' said Barney. 'Don't freeze on to the controls. Treat her like—' he broke off. He had been about to liken the aircraft to a woman, but realized the unsuitability of the simile. 'Treat her like a horse. Ride her light.'

Instantly he felt David's death-grip on the wheel relax, the touch repeated through his own controls.

'That's it, David.' He glanced sideways at the boy, and felt a flare of disappointment. He had felt deep down in his being that this one might be bird, one of the very rare ones like himself whose natural element was the blue. Yet here in the first few moments of flight the child was wearing an expression of frozen terror. His lips and nostrils were trimmed with marble white and there were shadows in the dark blue eyes like the shape of sharks moving beneath the surface of a summer sea.

'Left wing up,' he snapped, disappointed, trying to shock him out of it. The wing came up and held rock steady, with no trace of over-correction.

'Level her out.' His own hands were off the controls as the nose sank to find the horizon.

'Throttle back.' The boy's right hand went unerringly to the throttle. Once more Barney glanced at him. His expression had not altered, and then with a sudden revelation Barney recognized it not as fear, but as ecstasy.

'He is a bird.' The thought gave him a vast satisfaction, and while they flew on through the basic instruction in trim and attitude, Barney's mind went back thirty years to a battered old yellow Tiger Moth and another child in his first raptures of flight.

They skirted the harsh blue mountains, wearing their mantles of sun-blazing snow, and rode the tail of the wild winds that came down off them.

'Wind is like the sea, David. It breaks and swirls around high ground. Watch for it.' David nodded as he listened to his first fragments of flying lore, but his eyes were fixed ahead savouring each instant of the experience.

They turned north over the bleak bare land, the earth

naked pink and smoky brown, stripped by the harvest of its robes of golden wheat.

'Wheel and rudder together, David,' Barney told him. 'Let's try a steep turn now.' Down went the wing and boldly the nose swept around holding its attitude to the horizon.

Ahead of them the sea broke in long lines of cream on the white beaches. The Atlantic was cold green and ruffled by the wind, flecked with dancing white.

South again, following the coastline where small figures on the white sand paused to look up at them from under shading hands, south towards the great flat mountain that marked the limit of the land, its shape unfamiliar from this approach. The shipping lay thick in the bay and the winter sunlight flashed from the windows of the white buildings huddling below the steep wooded sides of the mountain.

Another turn, confident and sure, Barney sitting with his hands in his lap and his feet off the rudder bars, and they ran in over the Tygerberg towards the airfield.

'Okay,' said Barney. 'I've got her.' And he took them in for the touchdown and taxied back to the concrete apron beside the hangars. He pulled the mixture control fully lean and let the engine starve and die.

They sat silent for a moment, neither of them moving or speaking, both of them unwinding but still aware that something important and significant had happened and that they had shared it.

'Okay?' Barney asked at last.

'Yes, sir,' David nodded, and they unstrapped and climbed down on to the concrete stiffly. Without speaking they walked side by side through the hangar and office. At the door they paused.

'Next Wednesday?' Barney asked.

'Yes, sir.' David left him and started towards the waiting Cadillac, but after a dozen steps he stopped, hesitated, then turned back.

'That was the most beautiful thing that has ever happened to me,' he said shyly. 'Thank you, sir.' And he hurried away leaving Barney staring after him.

The Cadillac pulled off, gathering speed, and disappeared round a bend amongst the trees beyond the last buildings. Barney chuckled, shook his head ruefully and turned back into his office. He dropped into the ancient swivel chair and crossed his ankles on the desk. He fished a crumpled cigarette from the pack, straightened and lit it.

'Beautiful?' he grunted, grinning. 'Crap!' He flicked the match at the waste bin and missed it.

The telephone woke Mitzi Morgan and she crept out from under her pillows groping blindly for it.
''Lo.'

'Mitzi?'

'Hi, Dad, are you coming up?' She came half-awake at her father's voice, remembering that this was the day he would fly up to join the family at their holiday home.

'Sorry, baby. Something has broken here. I won't be up until next week.'

'Oh, Dad!' Mitzi expressed her disappointment.

'Where's Davey?' her father went on quickly to forestall any recriminations.

'You want him to call you back?'

'No, I'll hold on. Call him, please, baby.'

Mitzi stumbled out of bed to the mirror, and with her fingers tried to comb some order into her hair. It was off-blonde and wiry, and fuzzed up tight at the first touch of sun or salt or wind. The freckles were even more humiliating, she decided, looking at herself disapprovingly.

'You look like a Pekinese,' she spoke aloud, 'a fat little Pekinese – with freckles,' and gave up the effort of trying to change it. David had seen her like this a zillion times.

She pulled a silk gown over her nudity and went out into the passage, past the door to her parents' suite where her mother slept alone, and into the living area of the house.

The house was stacked in a series of open planes and galleries, glass and steel and white pine, climbing out of the dunes along the beach, part of sea and sky, only glass separating it from the elements, and now the dawn filled it with a strange glowing light and made a feature of the massive headland of the Robberg that thrust out into the sea across the bay.

The playroom was scattered with the litter of last night's party, twenty house guests and as many others from the big holiday homes along the dunes had left their mark – spilled beer, choked ashtrays and records thrown carelessly from their covers.

Mitzi picked her way through the debris and climbed the circular staircase to the guest rooms. She checked David's door, found it open, and went in. The bed was untouched, but his denims and sweat shirt were thrown across the chair and his shoes had been kicked off carelessly.

Mitzi grinned, and went through on to the balcony. It hung high above the beach, level with the gulls which were already dawn-winging for the scraps that the sea had thrown up during the night.

Quickly Mitzi hoisted the gown up around her waist, climbed up onto the rail of the balcony and stepped over the drop to the rail of the next balcony in line. She jumped down, drew the curtains aside and went into Marion's bedroom.

Marion was her best friend. Secretly she knew that this happy state of affairs existed chiefly because she, Mitzi, provided a foil for Marion's petite little body and wide-eyed doll-like beauty – and was a source of never-ending gifts and parties, free holidays and other good things.

She looked so pretty now in sleep, her hair golden and

soft as it fanned out across David's chest. Mitzi transferred all her attention to her cousin, and felt that sliding sensation in her breast and the funny warm liquid sensation at the base of her belly as she looked at him. He was seventeen years old now, but already he had the body of a grown man.

He was her most favourite person in all the world, she thought. He's so beautiful, so tall and straight, and his eyes can break your heart.

The couple on the bed had thrown aside their covering in the warmth of the night, and there was hair on David's chest now, thick and dark and curly, there was muscle in arm and leg, and breadth across the shoulders.

'David,' she called softly, and touched his shoulder. 'Wake up.'

His eyes opened, and he was awake instantly, his gaze focused and aware.

'Mitz? What is it?'

'Get your pants on, warrior. My papa's on the line.'

'God.' David sat up, dropping Marion's head on to the pillow. 'What time is it?'

'Late,' Mitzi told him. 'You should set the alarm when you go visiting.'

Marion mumbled a protest and groped for the sheets as David jumped from the bed.

'Where's the phone?'

'In my room – but you can take it on the extension in yours.'

She followed him across the balcony railing, and curled up on David's bed while he picked up the receiver and with the extension cord trailing behind him began pacing the thick carpet restlessly.

'Uncle Paul?' David spoke. 'How are you?'

Mitzi groped in the pocket of her gown and found a Gauloise. She lit it with her gold Dunhill, but at the third puff David turned aside from his pacing, grinned at her,

8

took the cigarette from between her lips and drew deeply upon it.

Mitzi pulled a face at him to disguise the turmoil that his nakedness stirred within her, and selected another cigarette for herself.

'He'd die if he knew what I was thinking,' she told herself, and derived a little comfort from the thought.

David finished his conversation and cradled the receiver before turning to her.

'He's not coming.'

'I know.'

'But he is sending Barney up in the Lear to fetch me. Big pow-wow.'

'It figures,' Mitzi nodded, then began a convincing imitation of her father. 'We have to start thinking about your future now, my boy. We have to train you to meet the responsibilities with which destiny has entrusted you.'

David chuckled and rummaged for his running shorts in the drawer of his bureau.

'I suppose I'll have to tell him now.'

'Yes,' Mitzi agreed. 'You sure will have to do that.'

David pulled up his shorts and turned for the door.

'Pray for me, doll.'

'You'll need more than prayer, warrior,' said Mitzi comfortably.

The tide had swept the beach smooth and firm, and no other feet had marked it this early. David ran smoothly, long strides leaving damp footsteps in a chain behind him.

The sun came up casting a soft pink sheen on the sea, and touching the Outeniqua mountains with flame – but David ran unseeing. His thoughts were on the impending interview with his guardian.

It was a time of crisis in his life, high school completed and many roads open. He knew the one he had chosen would draw violent opposition, and he used these last few hours of solitude to gather and strengthen his resolve.

9

A conclave of gulls, gathered about the body of a stranded fish, rose in a cloud as he ran towards them, their wings catching the low sun as they hovered then dropped again when he passed.

He saw the Lear coming before he heard it. It was low against the dawn, rising and dropping over the towering bulk of the Robberg. Then swiftly, coming in on a muted shriek, it streaked low along the beach towards him.

David stopped, breathing lightly even after the long run, and raised both arms above his head in salute. He saw Barney's head through the Perspex canopy turned towards him, the flash of his teeth as he grinned and the hand raised, returning his salute as he went by.

The Lear turned out to sea, one wingtip almost touching the wave crests, and it came back at him. David stood on the exposed beach and steeled himself as the long sleek nose dropped lower and lower, aimed like a javelin at him.

Like some fearsome predatory bird it swooped at him and at the last possible instant David's nerve broke and he flung himself on to the wet sand. The jet blast lashed him as the Lear rose and turned inland for the airfield.

'Son of a bitch,' muttered David as he stood up brushing damp sand from his bare chest, and imagined Barney's amused chuckle.

'I taught him good,' thought Barney, sprawled in the co-pilot's seat of the Lear as he watched David ride the delicate line of altitude where skill gave way to chance.

Barney had put on weight since he had been eating Morgan bread, and his paunch peeked shyly over his belt. The beginning of jowls bracketed the wide downturned mouth that gave him the air of a disgruntled toad, and the cap of hair that covered his skull was sparser and speckled with salt.

Watching David fly, he felt the small warmth of his affection for him that his sour expression belied. Three years he had been chief pilot of the Morgan group and he knew well to whose intervention he owed the post. It was security he had now, and prestige. He flew great men in the most luxuriously fitted machines, and when the time came for him to go out to pasture he knew the grazing would be lush. The Morgan group looked after its own.

This knowledge sat comfortably on his stomach as he watched his protégé handle the jet.

Extended low flying like this required enormous concentration, and Barney watched in vain for any relaxation of it in his pupil.

The long golden beaches of Africa streamed steadily beneath them, punctuated by rock promontories and tiny resorts and fishing villages. Delicately the Lear followed the contours of the coastline, for they had spurned the direct route for the exhilaration of this flight.

Ahead of them stretched another strip of beach but as they howled low along it they saw that this one was occupied.

A pair of tiny feminine figures left the frothy surf and ran panic-stricken to where towels and discarded bikinis lay above the high-water mark. White buttocks contrasted sharply with a coffee-brown tan, and they laughed delightedly.

'Nice change for you to see them running away, David,' Barney grinned as they left the tiny figures far behind and bore onwards into the south.

From Cape Agulhas they turned inland, climbing steeply over the mountain ranges, then David eased back on the throttles and they sank down beyond the crests towards the city, nestling under its mountain.

As they walked side by side towards the hangar, Barney looked up at David who now topped him by six inches.

11

'Don't let him stampede you, boy,' he warned. 'You've made your decision. See you stick to it.'

David took his British racing green MG over De Waal Drive, and from the lower slopes of the mountain looked down to where the Morgan building stood four-square amongst the other tall monuments to power and wealth.

David enjoyed its appearance, clean and functional like an aircraft's wing – but he knew that the soaring freedom of its lines was deceptive. It was a prison and fortress.

He swung off the freeway at an interchange and rode down to the foreshore, glancing up at the towering bulk of the Morgan building again before entering the ramp that led to the underground garages beneath it.

When he entered the executive apartments on the top floor, he passed along the row of desks where the secretaries, hand-picked for their looks as well as their skill with a typewriter, sat in a long row. Their lovely faces opened into smiles like a garden of exotic blooms as David greeted each of them. Within the Morgan building he was treated with the respect due the heir apparent.

Martha Goodrich, in her own office that guarded the inner sanctum, looked up from her typewriter, severe and businesslike.

'Good morning, Mr David. Your uncle is waiting – and I do think you could have worn a suit.'

'You're looking good, Martha. You've lost weight and I like your hair like that.' It worked, as it always did. Her expression softened.

'Don't you try buttering me up,' she warned him primly. 'I'm not one of your floozies.'

Paul Morgan was at the picture window looking down over the city spread below him like a map, but he turned quickly to greet David.

'Hello, Uncle Paul. I'm sorry I didn't have time to change. I thought it best to come directly.'

'That's fine, David.' Paul Moran flicked his eyes over

12

David's floral shirt open to the navel, the wide tooled leather belt, white slacks and open sandals. On him they looked good, Paul admitted reluctantly. The boy wore even the most outlandish modern clothes with a furious grace.

'It's good to see you.' Paul smoothed the lapels of his own dark conservatively cut suit and looked up at his nephew. 'Come in. Sit down, there, the chair by the fireplace.' As always, he found that David standing emphasized his own lack of stature. Paul was short and heavily built in the shoulders, thick muscular neck and square thrusting head. Like his daughter, his hair was coarse and wiry and his features squashed and puglike.

All the Morgans were built that way. It was the proper course of things, and David's exotic appearance was outside the natural order. It was from his mother's side, of course. All that dark hair and flashing eyes, and the temperament that went with it.

'Well, David. First off, I want to congratulate you on your final results. I was most gratified,' Paul Morgan told him gravely, and he could have added ' – I was also mightily relieved.' David Morgan's scholastic career had been a tempestuous affair. Pinnacles of achievement followed immediately by depths of disgrace from which only the Morgan name and wealth had rescued him. There had been the business with the games master's young wife. Paul never did find out the truth of the matter, but had thought it sufficient to smooth it over by donating a new organ to the school chapel and arranging a teaching scholarship for the games master to a foreign university. Immediately thereafter David had won the coveted Wessels prize for mathematics, and all was forgiven – until he decided to test his housemaster's new sports car, without that gentleman's knowledge, and took it into a tight bend at ninety miles an hour. The car was unequal to the test, and David picked himself up out of the wreckage and limped away with a nasty scratch on his calf. It had taken all of Paul

Morgan's weight to have the housemaster agree not to cancel David's appointment as head of house. His prejudices had finally been overcome by the replacement of his wrecked car with a more expensive model, and the Morgan Group had made a grant to rebuild the ablution block of East House.

The boy was wild, Paul knew it well, but he knew also that he could tame him. Once he had done that he would have forged a razor-edged tool. He possessed all the attributes that Paul Morgan wanted in his successor. The verve and confidence, the bright quick mind and adventurous spirit – but above all he possessed the aggressive attitude, the urge to compete that Paul defined as the killer instinct.

'Thank you, Uncle Paul,' David accepted his uncle's congratulations warily. They were silent, each assessing the other. They had never been easy in the other's company, they were too different in many ways – and yet in others too much alike. Always it seemed that their interests were in conflict.

Paul Morgan moved across to the picture windows, so that the daylight back-lit him. It was an old trick of his to put the other person at a disadvantage.

'Not that we expected less of you, of course,' he laughed, and David smiled to acknowledge the fact that his uncle had come close to levity.

'And now we must consider your future.' David was silent.

'The choice open to you is wide,' said Paul Morgan, and then went on swiftly to narrow it. 'Though I do feel business science and law at an American university is what it should be. With this obvious goal in mind I have used my influence to have you enrolled in my old college—'

'Uncle Paul, I want to fly,' said David softly, and Paul Morgan paused. His expression changed fractionally.

'We are making a career decision, my boy, not expressing preferences for different types of recreation.'

'No, sir. I mean I want to fly – as a way of life.'

'Your life is here, within the Morgan Group. It is not something in which you have freedom of action.'

'I don't agree with you, sir.'

Paul Morgan left the window and crossed to the fireplace. He selected a cigar from the humidor on the mantel, and while he prepared it he spoke softly, without looking at David.

'Your father was a romantic, David. He got it out of his system by charging around the desert in a tank. It seems you have inherited this romanticism from him.' He made it sound like some disgusting disease. He came back to where David sat.

'Tell me what you propose.'

'I have enlisted in the air force, sir.'

'You've done it? You've signed?'

'Yes, sir.'

'How long?'

'Five years. Short service commission.'

'Five years—' Paul Morgan whispered, 'Well, David, I don't know what to say. You know that you are the last of the Morgans. I have no son. It will be sad to see this vast enterprise without one of us at the helm. I wonder what your father would have thought of this—'

'That's hitting low, Uncle Paul.'

'I don't think so, David. I think you are the one who is cheating. Your trust fund is a huge block of Morgan shares, and other assets given to you, on the unstated understanding that you assume your duties and responsibilities—'

'If only he would bawl me out,' thought David fiercely, knowing that he was being stampeded as Barney had warned him. 'If only he would order me to do it – so I could tell him to shove it.' But he knew he was being manipulated by a man skilled in the art, a man whose whole life was the manipulation of men and money, in whose hands a seventeen-year-old boy was as soft as dough.

'You see, David, you are born to it. Anything else is cowardice, self indulgence—' the Morgan Group reached out its tentacles, like some grotesque flesh-eating plant, to suck him in and digest him, ' – we can have your enlistment papers annulled. It will be the matter of a single phone call—'

'Uncle Paul,' David almost shouted, trying to shut out the all-pervasive flow of words. 'My father. He did it. He joined the army.'

'Yes, David. But it was different at that time. One of us had to go. He was the younger – and, of course, there were other personal considerations. Your mother—' he let the rest of it hang for a moment then went on, ' – and when it was over he came back and took his rightful place here. We miss him now, David. No one else has been able to fill the gap he left. I have always hoped that you might be the one.'

'But I don't want to.' David shook his head. 'I don't want to spend my life in here.' He gestured at the mammoth structure of glass and concrete that surrounded them. 'I don't want to spend each day poring over piles of paper—'

'It's not like that, David. It's exciting, challenging, endlessly variable—'

'Uncle Paul.' David raised his voice again. 'What do you call a man who fills his belly with rich food – and then goes on eating?'

'Come now, David.' The first edge of irritation showed in Paul Morgan's voice, and he brushed the question aside impatiently.

'What do you call him?' David insisted.

'I expect that you would call him a glutton,' Paul Morgan answered.

'And what do you call a man with many millions – who spends his life trying to make more?'

Paul Morgan froze into stillness. He stared at his ward for long seconds before he spoke.

'You become insolent,' he said at last.

'No, sir. I did not mean it so. You are not the glutton – but I would be.'

Paul Morgan turned away and went to his desk. He sat in the high-backed leather chair and lit the cigar at last. They were silent again for a long time until at last Paul Morgan sighed.

'You'll have to get it out of your system, the way your father did. But how I grudge you five wasted years.'

'Not wasted, Uncle Paul. I will come out with a Bachelor of Science degree in aeronautical engineering.'

'I suppose we'll just have to be thankful for little things like that.'

David went and stood beside his chair.

'Thank you. This is very important to me.'

'Five years, David. After that I want you.' Then he smiled slightly to signal a witticism. 'At least they will make you cut your hair.'

Four miles above the warm flesh-coloured earth, David Morgan rode the high heavens like a young god. The sun visor of his helmet was closed, masking with its dark cyclops eye the rapt, almost mystic expression with which he flew. Five years had not dulled the edge of his appetite for the sensation of power and isolation that flight in a Mirage interceptor awoke in him.

The unfiltered sunlight blazed ferociously upon the metal of his craft, clothing him in splendour – while far below the very clouds were insignificant against the earth, scattered and flying like a sheep flock before the wolf of the wind.

Today's flight was tempered by a melancholy, a sense of impending loss. The morrow was the last day of his enlistment. At noon his commission expired and if Paul Morgan prevailed he would become Mr David – new boy at Morgan Group.

He thrust the thought aside, and concentrated on the enjoyment of these last precious minutes; but too soon the spell was broken.

'Zulu Striker One, this is Range Control. Report your position.'

'Range Control, this is Zulu Striker One holding up range fifty miles.'

'Striker One, the range is clear. Your target-markers are figures eight and twelve. Commence your run.'

The horizon revolved abruptly across the nose of the Mirage, as the wings came over and he went down under power, falling from the heights, a controlled plunge, purposeful and precise as the stoop of a falcon.

David's right hand moved swiftly across the weapon selector panel, locking in the rocket circuit.

The earth flattened out ahead, immense and featureless, speckled with low bush that blurred past his wing-tips as he let the Mirage sink lower. At this height the awareness of speed was breathtaking, and as the first marker came up ahead it seemed at the same instant to flash away below the silvery nose.

Five, six, seven – the black numerals on their glaring white grounds flickered by.

A touch of left rudder and stick, both adjustments made without conscious effort – and ahead was the circular layout of the rocket range, the concentric rings shrinking in size around the central mound – the 'coke' of flight jargon, which was the bull's-eye of the target.

David brought the deadly machine in fast and low, his mach meter recording a speed that was barely subsonic. He was running off the direct line of track, judging his moment with frowning concentration. When it came he pulled the Mirage's nose in to the 'pitch up' and went over on to the target with his gloved right finger curled about the trigger lever.

The shrieking silver machine achieved her correct slightly nose-down attitude for rocket launch at the precise instant of time that the white blob of 'coke' was centred in the diamond patterns of the reflector sight.

It was an evolution executed with subtle mastery of many diverse skills, and David pressed against the spring-loaded resistance of the trigger. There was no change in the feel of the aircraft, and the hiss of the rocket launch was almost lost beneath the howl of the great jet, but from beneath his wings the brief smoke lines reached out ahead towards the target, and in certainty of a fair strike David pushed his throttle to the gate and waited for the rumbling ignition of his afterburners, giving him power for the climb out of range of enemy flak.

'What a way to go,' he grinned to himself as he lay on his back with the Mirage's nose pointed into the bright blue, and gravity pressing him into the padding of his seat.

'Hello, Striker One. This is Range Control. That was right on the nose. Give the man a coke. Nice shooting. Sorry to lose you, Davey.' The break in hallowed range discipline touched David. He was going to miss them – all of them. He pressed the transmit button on the moulded head of his joystick, and spoke into the microphone of his helmet. 'From Striker One, thanks and farewell,' David said. 'Over and out.'

His ground crew were waiting for him also. He shook hands with each of them, the awkward handshakes and rough jokes masking the genuine affection that the years had built between them. Then he left them and went down the vast metal-skinned cavern, redolent with the smell of grease and oil along which the gleaming rows of needle-nosed interceptors stood, even in repose their forward lines giving them speed and thrust.

David paused to pat the cold metal of one of them, and the orderly found him there peering up at the emblem of the Flying Cobra upon the towering tailplane.

'C.O.'s compliments, sir, and will you report to him right away.'

Colonel 'Rastus' Naude was a dried-out stick of a man, with a wizened monkey face, who wore his uniform and medal ribbons with a casually distracted air. He had flown Hurricanes in the Battle of Britain, Mustangs in Italy, Spitfires and Messerschmitt 109s in Palestine and Sabres in Korea – and he was too old for his present command – but nobody could muster the courage to tell him that, especially as he could out-fly and out-gun most of the young bucks on the squadron.

'So we are getting rid of you at last, Morgan,' he greeted David.

'Not until after the mess party, sir.'

'Ja,' Rastus nodded. 'You've given me enough hardship these last five years. You owe me a bucket of whisky.' He gestured to the hard-backed chair beside his desk. 'Sit down, David.'

It was the first time he had used David's given name, and David placed his flying helmet on the corner of the desk and lowered himself into the chair, clumsy in the constricting grip of his G-suit.

Rastus took his time filling his pipe with the evil black Magaliesberg shag and he studied the young man opposite him intently. He recognized the same qualities in him that Paul Morgan had prized, the aggressive and competitive drive that gave him a unique value as an interceptor pilot.

He lit the pipe at last, puffing thick rank clouds of blue smoke as he slid a sheath of documents across the desk to David.

'Read and sign,' he said. 'That's an order.' David glanced rapidly through the papers, then he looked up and grinned.

'You don't give in easily, sir,' he admitted.

One document was a renewal of his short service contract for an additional five years, the other was a warrant of promotion – from captain to major.

'We have spent a great deal of time and money in making you what you are. You have been given an exceptional talent, and we have developed it until now you are – I'll not mince words – one hell of a pilot.'

'I'm sorry, sir,' David told him sincerely.

'Damn it,' said Rastus angrily. 'Why the hell did you have to be born a Morgan. All that money – they'll clip your wings, and chain you to a desk.'

'It's not the money.' David denied it swiftly. He felt his own anger stir at the accusation.

Rastus nodded cynically. 'Ja!' he said. 'I hate the stuff also.' He picked up the documents David had rejected, and grunted. 'Not enough to tempt you, hey?'

'Colonel, it's hard to explain. I just feel that there is more to do, something important that I have to find out about – and it's not here. I have to go look for it.'

Rastus nodded heavily. 'All right then,' he said. 'I had a good try. Now you can take your long-suffering commanding officer down to the mess and spend some of the Morgan millions on filling him up with whisky.' He stood up and clapped his uniform cap at a rakish angle over his cropped grey head. 'You and I will get drunk together this night – for both of us are losing something, I perhaps more than you.'

It seemed that David had inherited his love of beautiful and powerful machines from his father. Clive Morgan had driven himself, his wife, and his brand new Ferrari sports car into the side of a moving goods train at an unlit level crossing. The traffic police estimated that the Ferrari was travelling at one hundred and fifty miles an hour at the moment of impact.

Clive Morgan's provision for his eleven-year-old son was detailed and elaborate. The child became a ward of his uncle Paul Morgan, and his inheritance was arranged in a series of trust funds.

On his majority he was given access to the first of the funds which provided an income equivalent to that of, say, a highly successful surgeon. On that day the old green MG had given way to a powder-blue Maserati, in true Morgan tradition.

On his twenty-third birthday, control of the sheep ranches in the Karroo, the cattle ranch in South-West Africa and Jabulani, the sprawling game ranch in the Sabi-Sand block, passed to him, their management handled smoothly by his trustees.

On his twenty-fifth birthday the number two fund interest would divert to him, in addition to a large block of negotiable paper and title in two massive urban holdings – office and supermarket complexes, and a high-rise housing project.

At age thirty the next fund opened for him, as large as the previous two combined, and transfer to him for the first of five blocks of Morgan stock would begin.

From then onwards, every five years until age fifty further funds opened, further blocks of Morgan stock would be transferred. It was a numbing procession of wealth that stretched ahead of him, daunting in its sheer magnitude; like a display of too much rich food, it seemed to depress appetite.

David drove fast southwards, with the Michelin metallics hissing savagely on the tarmac, and he thought about all that wealth, the great golden cage, the insatiable maw of Morgan Group yawning open to swallow him so that, like the cell of a jelly fish, he would become a part of the whole, a prisoner of his own abundance.

The prospect appalled him, adding a hollow sensation in his belly to the pulse of pain that beat steadily behind his eyes – testimony to the foolhardiness of trying to drink level with Colonel Rastus Naude.

He pushed the Maserati harder, seeking the twin opiates of power and speed, finding comfort and escape in the rhythms and precision of driving very fast, and the hours flew past as swiftly as the miles so it was still daylight when he let himself into Mitzi's apartment on the cliffs that overlooked Clifton beach and the clear green Atlantic.

Mitzi's apartment was chaos, that much had not changed. She kept open house for a string of transitory guests who drank her liquor, ate her food and vied with each other as to who could create the most spectacular shambles.

In the first bedroom that David tried there was a strange girl with dark hair curled on the bed in boys' pyjamas, sucking her thumb in sleep.

With the second room he was luckier, and he found it deserted, although the bed was unmade and someone had left breakfast dishes smeared with congealed egg upon the side table.

David slung his bag on the bed and fished out his bathing costume. He changed quickly and went out by the side stairs that spiralled down to the beach and began to run – a trot at first, and then suddenly he sprinted away, racing blindly as though from some terrible monster that pursued him. At the end of Fourth beach where the rocks began, he plunged into the icy surf and swam out to the edge of the kelp at Bakoven point, driving overarm through the water and the cold lanced him to the bone, so that when he came out he was blue and shuddering. But the hunted feeling was gone and he warmed a little as he jogged back to Mitzi's apartment.

He had to remove the forest of pantihose and feminine underwear that festooned the bathroom before he could draw himself a bath. He filled it to the overflow, and as he settled into it the front door burst open and Mitzi came in like the north wind.

'Where are you, warrior?' She was banging the doors. 'I saw your car in the garage – so I know you're here!'

'In here, doll,' he called, and she stood in the doorway and they grinned at each other. She had put on weight again, he saw, straining the seam of her skirt, and her bosom was bulky and amorphous under the scarlet sweater. She had finally given up her struggle with myopia and the metal-framed spectacles sat on the end of her little nose, while her hair fuzzed out at unexpected angles.

'You're beautiful,' she cried, coming to kiss him and getting soap down her sweater as she hugged him.

'Drink or coffee?' she asked, and David winced at the thought of alcohol.

'Coffee will be great, doll.'

She brought it to him in a mug, then perched on the toilet seat.

'Tell all!' she commanded and while they chatted the pretty dark-haired girl wandered in, still in her pyjamas and bug-eyed from sleep.

'This is my coz, David. Isn't he beautiful?' Mitzi introduced them. 'And this is Liz.'

The girl sat on the dirty linen basket in the corner and fixed David with such an awed and penetrating gaze that Mitzi warned her, 'Cool it, darling. Even from here I can hear your ovaries bouncing around like ping-pong balls.'

But she was such a silent, ethereal little thing that they soon forgot her and talked as if they were alone. It was Mitzi who said suddenly, without preliminaries, 'Papa is waiting for you, licking his lips like an ivy-league ogre. I ate with them Saturday night – he must have brought your name up one zillion times. It's going to be strange to have you sitting up there on Top Floor, in a charcoal suit, being bright at Monday morning conference—'

David stood up suddenly in the bath, cascading suds and steaming water, and began soaping his crotch vigorously. They watched him with interest, the dark-haired girl's eyes widening until they seemed to fill her face.

David sat down again, slopping water over the edge.

'I'm not going!' he said, and there was a long heavy silence.

'What you mean – you're not going?' Mitzi asked timorously.

'Just that,' said David. 'I'm not going to Morgan Group.'

'But you have to!'

'Why?' asked David.

'Well, I mean it's decided – you promised Daddy that when you finished with the air force.'

'No,' David said, 'I made no promise. He just took it. When you said a moment ago – being bright at Monday morning conference – I knew I couldn't do it. I guess I've known all along.'

'What are you going to do, then?' Mitzi had recovered from the first shock, and her plump cheeks were tinged pink with excitement.

'I don't know. I just know I am not going to be a caretaker for other men's achievements. Morgan Group isn't me. It's something that Gramps, and Dad and Uncle Paul made. It's too big and cold—'

Mitzi was flushed, bright-eyed, nodding her agreement, enchanted by this prospect of rebellion and open defiance.

David was warming to it also. 'I'll find my own road to go. There's more to it. There has to be something more than this.'

'Yes,' Mitzi nodded so that she almost shook her

spectacles from her nose. 'You're not like them. You would shrivel and die up there in the executive suite.'

'I've got to find it, Mitzi. It's got to be out there somewhere.'

David came out of the bath, his body glowing dull red-brown from the scalding water and steam rising from him in light tendrils. He pulled on a terry robe as he talked and the two girls followed him through to the bedroom and sat side by side on the edge of the bed, eagerly nodding their encouragement as David Morgan made his formal declaration of independence. Mitzi spoiled it, however.

'What are you going to tell Daddy?' she asked. The question halted David's flow of rhetoric, and he scratched the hair on his chest as he considered it. The girls waited attentively.

'He's not going to let you get away again,' Mitzi warned. 'Not without a stand-up, knock-down, drag-'em-out fight.'

In this moment of crisis David's courage deserted him. 'I've told him once, I don't have to tell him again.'

'You just going to cut and run?' Mitzi asked.

'I'm not running,' David replied with frosty dignity as he picked up the pigskin folder which held his thick sheaf of credit cards from the bedside table. 'I am merely reserving the right to determine my own future.' He crossed to the telephone and began dialling.

'Who are you calling?'

'The airline.'

'Where are you heading?'

'The same place as their first flight out.'

'I'll cover for you,' declared Mitzi loyally, 'you're doing the right thing, warrior.'

'You bet I am,' David agreed. 'My way – and screw the rest of them.'

'Do you have time for that?' Mitzi giggled, and the dark-haired girl spoke for the first time in a husky intense voice without once taking her eyes off David. 'I don't know about the rest of them, but may I be first, please?'

With the telephone receiver to his ear David glanced at her, and realized with only mild surprise that she was in deadly earnest.

D avid came out into the impersonal concrete and glass arrivals hall of Schiphol Airport, and he paused to gloat on his escape and to revel at this sense of anonymity in the uncaring crowd. There was a touch at his elbow, and he turned to find a tall, smiling Dutchman quizzing him through rimless spectacles.

'Mr David Morgan, I think?' and David gaped at him.

'I am Frederick van Gent of Holland and Indonesian Stevedoring. We have the honour to act on behalf of Morgan Shipping Lines in Holland. It is a great pleasure to make your acquaintance.'

'God, no!' David whispered wearily.

'Please?'

'No. I'm sorry. It's nice to meet you.' David shook the hand with resignation.

'I have two urgent telex messages for you, Mr Morgan.' Van Gent produced them with a flourish. 'I have driven out from Amsterdam especially to deliver same.'

The first was from Mitzi who had sworn to cover for him.

'Abject apologies your whereabouts extracted with rack and thumbscrew stop Be brave as a lion stop Be ferocious as an eagle Love Mitzi.'

David said, 'Traitorous bitch!' and opened the second envelope.

'Your doubts understood, your action condoned stop Confident your good sense will lead you eventually on to

27

path of duty stop Your place here always open Affection-
ately Paul Morgan.'

David said, 'Crafty old bastard,' and stuffed both messages into his pocket.

'Is there a reply?' Van Gent asked.

'Thank you, no. It was good of you to take this trouble.'

'No trouble, Mr Morgan. Can I help you in any way? Is
there anything you require?'

'Nothing, but thanks again.' They shook hands and Van
Gent bowed and left him. David went to the Avis counter
and the girl smiled brightly at him.

'Good evening, sir.'

David slipped his Avis card across the desk. 'I want
something with a little jump to it, please.'

'Let me see, we have a Mustang Mach I?' She was pure
blonde with a cream and pink unlined face.

'That will do admirably,' David assured her, and as she
began filling the form in, she asked, 'Your first visit to
Amsterdam, sir?'

'They tell me it's the city with the most action in
Europe, is that right?'

'If you know where to go,' she murmured.

'You could show me?' David asked and she looked up at
him with calculating eyes behind a neutral expression,
made a decision and resumed her writings.

'Please sign here, sir. Your account will be charged,'
then she dropped her voice. 'If you have any queries on
this contract, you can contact me at this number – after
hours. My name is Gilda.'

Gilda shared a walk-up over the outer canal with three
other girls who showed no surprise, and made no objection
when David carried his single Samsonite case up the steep
staircase. However, the action that Gilda provided was in
a series of discotheques and coffee bars where lost little
people gathered to talk revolution and guru-babble. In two
days David discovered that pot tasted terrible and made

him nauseous, and that Gilda's mind was as bland and unmarked as her exterior. He felt the stirrings of uneasiness when he studied the others that had been drawn to this city by the news that it was wide open, with the most understanding police force in the world. In them he saw symptoms of his own restlessness, and he recognized them as fellow seekers. Then the damp chill of the lowlands seemed to rise up out of the canals like the spirits of the dead on doomsday, and when you have been born under the sun of Africa the wintry effusions of the north are a pale substitute.

Gilda showed no visible emotion when she said good-bye, and with the heaters blasting hot air into the cab of the Mustang, David sent it booming southwards. On the outskirts of Namur there was a girl standing beside the road. In the cold her legs were bare and brown, protruding sweetly from the short faded blue denim pants she wore. She tilted her golden head and cocked a thumb.

David hit the stick down, and braked with the rubber squealing protest. He reversed back to where she stood. She had flat-planed Slavic features and her hair was white-blonde and hung in a thick plait down her back. He guessed her age at nineteen.

'You speak English?' he asked through the window. The cold was making her nipples stand out like marbles through the thin fabric of her shirt.

'No,' she said. 'But I speak American – will that do?'

'Right on!' David opened the passenger door, and she threw her pack and rolled sleeping bag into the back seat.

'I'm Philly,' she said.

'David.'

'You in show biz?'

'God, no – what makes you ask?'

'The car – the face – the clothes.'

'The car is hired, the clothes are stolen and I'm wearing a mask.'

29

'Funny man,' she said and curled up on the seat like a kitten and went to sleep.

He stopped in a village where the forests of the Ardennes begin and bought a long roll of crisp bread, a slab of smoked wild boar meat and a bottle of Möet Chandon. When he got back to the car Philly was awake.

'You hungry?' he asked.

'Sure.' She stretched and yawned.

He found a loggers' track going off into the forest and they followed it to a clearing where a long golden shaft of sunlight penetrated the green cathedral gloom.

Philly climbed out and looked around her. 'Keen, Davey, keen!' she said.

David poured the champagne into paper cups and sliced the meat with a penknife while Philly broke the bread into hunks. They sat side by side on a fallen log and ate.

'It's so quiet and peaceful – not at all like a killing ground. This is where the Germans made their last big effort – did you know that?'

Philly's mouth was full of bread and meat which didn't stop her reply. 'I saw the movie, Henry Fonda, Robert Ryan – it was a complete crock.'

'All that death and ugliness, we should do something beautiful in this place,' David said dreamily, and she swallowed the bread, took a sip of the wine, before she stood up languidly and went to the Mustang. She fetched her sleeping bag and spread it on the soft bed of leaf mould.

'Some things are for talking about – others are for doing,' she told him.

For a while in Paris it looked as though it might be significant, as though they might have something for each other of importance. They found a room with a shower in a clean and pleasant little *pension* near the Gare St Lazare, and they walked through the streets all that day, from Concorde to Étoile, then across to the Eiffel Tower and back to Notre Dame. They ate supper at a sidewalk café on the 'Boul Mich', but halfway through the meal they reached an emotional dead end. Suddenly they ran out of conversation, they sensed it at the same time, each aware that they were strangers in all but the flesh and the knowledge chilled them both. Still they stayed together that night, even going through the mechanical and empty motions of love, but in the morning, when David came out of the shower, she sat up in the bed and said, 'You are splitting.'

It was a statement and not a question, and it needed no reply.

'Are you all right for bread?' he asked, and she shook her head. He peeled off a pair of thousand-franc notes and put them on the side table.

'I'll pay the bill downstairs.' He picked up his bag. 'Stay loose,' he said.

Paris was spoiled for him now, so he took the road south again towards the sun for the sky was filled with swollen black cloud and it rained before he passed the turn-off to Fontainebleau. It rained as he believed was only possible in the tropics, a solid deluge that flooded the concrete of the highway and blurred his windscreen so that the flogging of the wipers could not clear it swiftly enough for safe vision.

David was alone and discomforted by his inability to sustain communication with another human being. Although the other traffic had moderated its pace in the rain, he drove fast, feeling the drift and skate of his tyres on the slick surface. This time the calming effect of speed was ineffective and when he ran out of the rain south of Beaune it seemed that the wolf pack of loneliness ran close behind him.

However, the first outpouring of sunshine lightened his mood, and then far over the stone walls and rigid green lines of the vineyards he saw a wind-sock floating like a soft white sausage from its pole. He found the exit from the

highway half a mile farther on, and the sign 'Club Aéro-
nautique de Provence'. He followed it to a neat little airfield
set among the vineyards, and one of the aircraft on the
hard-stand was a Marchetti Aerobatic type F260. David
climbed out of the Mustang and stared at it like a drunkard
contemplating his first whisky of the day.

The Frenchman in the club office looked like an
unsuccessful undertaker, and even when David showed him
his logbook and sheafs of licences, he resisted the temptation of hiring him the Marchetti. David could take his
pick from the others – but the Marchetti was not for hire.
David added a five hundred franc note to the pile of documents, and it disappeared miraculously into the Frenchman's
pocket. Still he would not let David take the Marchetti
solo, and he insisted on joining him in the instructor's seat.

David executed a slow and stately four-point roll before
they had crossed the boundary fence. It was an act of
defiance, and he made the stops crisp and exaggerated. The
Frenchman cried 'Sacré bleu!' with great feeling and froze
in his seat, but he had the good sense not to interfere with
the controls. David completed the manoeuvre and then
immediately rolled in the opposite direction with the wing-
tip a mere fifty feet above the tips of the vines. The
Frenchman relaxed visibly, recognizing the masterly touch,
and when David landed an hour later he grinned mournfully at him.

'Formidable!' he said, and shared his lunch with David –
garlic polony, bread and a bottle of rank red wine. The
good feeling of flight and the aroma of garlic lasted David
all the way to Madrid.

In Madrid suddenly it began to happen, almost as
though it had been arranged long before, as though his
frantic flight across half of Europe was a pre-knowledge
that something of importance awaited him in Madrid.

He reached the city in the evening, hurrying the last
day's journey to be in time for the first running of the bulls

that season. He had read Hemingway and Conrad and much of the other romantic literature of the bullring. He wondered if there might not be something for him in this way of life. It read so well in the books – the beauty, glamour and excitement – the courage and trial and the final moment of truth. He wanted to evaluate it, to see it here in the great Plaza Des Torros, and then, if it still intrigued him, go on to the festival at Pamplona later in the season.

David checked in at the Gran Via with its elegance faded to mere comfort, and the porter arranged tickets for the following day. He was tired from the long drive and he went to bed early, waking refreshed and eager for the day. He found his way out to the ring and parked the Mustang amongst the tourist buses that already crowded the parking lot so early in the season.

The exterior of the ring was a surprise, sinister as the temple of some pagan and barbaric religion, unrelieved by the fluted tiers of balconies and encrustations of ceramic tiles – but the interior was as he knew it would be from film and photograph. The sanded ring smooth and clean, the flags against the cloud-flecked sky, the orchestra pouring out its jerky, rousing refrain – and the excitement.

The excitement amongst the crowd was more intense than he had known at prize fights or football internationals, they hummed and swarmed, rank upon rank of white eager faces and the music goaded them on.

David was sitting amongst a group of young Australians who wore souvenir sombreros and passed goat-skins of bad wine about, the girls squealing and chittering like sparrows. One of them picked on David, leaning forward to tug his shoulder and offer him the wine-skin. She was pretty enough in a kittenish way and her eyes made it clear that the offer was for more than cheap wine, but he refused both invitations brusquely and went to fetch a can of beer from one of the vendors. His chilly experience with the girl in Paris was still too fresh. When he returned to his seat the Aussie girl eyed the beer he carried reproachfully and then turned brightly and smiling to her companions.

The late arrivals were finding their seats now and the excitement was escalating sharply. Two of them climbed the stairs of the aisle towards where David sat. A striking young couple in their early twenties, but what first drew David's attention was the good feeling of companionship and love that glowed around them, like an aura setting them apart.

They climbed arm in arm, passed where David sat, and took seats a row behind and across the aisle. The girl was tall with long legs clad in short black boots and dark pants over which she wore an apple-green suede jacket that was not expensive but of good cut and taste. In the sun her hair glittered like coal newly cut from the face and it hung to her shoulders in a sleek soft fall. Her face was broad and sun-browned, not beautiful for her mouth was too big and her eyes too widely spaced, but those eyes were the colour of wild honey, dark brown and flecked with gold. Like her, her companion was tall and straight, dark and strong-looking. He guided her to her seat with a brown, muscled arm and David felt a sharp stab of anger and envy for him.

'Big cocky son of a gun,' he thought. They leaned their heads together and spoke secretly, and David looked away, his own loneliness accentuated by their closeness.

The parade of the toreadors began, and they came out with the sunlight glittering on the sequins and embroidery of their suits, as though they were the scales of some flamboyant reptile. The orchestra blared, and the keys to the bull pens were thrown down on to the sand. The toreadors' capes were spread on the *barrera* below their favourites and they retired from the ring.

In the pause that followed David glanced at the couple again. He was startled to find that they were both watching him and the girl was discussing him. She was leaning on her companion's shoulder, her lips almost touching his ear as she spoke and David felt his stomach clench under the impact of those honey-golden eyes. For an instant they stared at each other and then the girl jerked away guiltily and dropped her gaze – but her companion held David's eyes openly, smiling easily, and it was David who looked away.

Below them in the ring the bull came out at full charge, head high, and hooves skidding in the sand.

He was beautiful and black and glossy, muscle in the neck and shoulder bunching as he swung his head from side to side and the crowd roared as he spun and burst into a gallop, pursuing an elusive flutter of pink across the ring. They took him on a circuit, passing him smoothly from cape to cape, letting him show off his bulk and high-stepping style, and the perfect sickle of his horns with their creamy points, before they brought in the horse.

The trumpets ushered in the horse, and they were a mockery – a brave greeting from the wretched nag, with scrawny neck and starting coat, one rheumy old eye blinkered so he could not see the fearsome creature he was going to meet.

Clownish in his padding, seeming too frail to carry the big armoured man on his back, they led him out and placed him in the path of the bull – and here any semblance of beauty ended.

The bull went into him head down, sending the gawky animal reeling against the *barrera* and the man leaned over the broad black back and ripped and tore into the hump with the lance, worrying the flesh, working in the steel with all his weight until the blood poured out in a slick tide, black as crude oil, and dripped from the bull's legs into the sand.

Raging at the agony of the steel the bull hooked and butted at the protective pads that covered the horse's flanks. They came up as readily as a theatre curtain and the bull was into the scrawny roan body, hacking with the terrible horns, and the horse screamed as its belly split open and the purple and pink entrails spilled out and dangled into the sand.

David was dry-mouthed with horror as around him the crowd blood-roared, and the horse went down in a welter of equipment and its own guts.

They drew the bull away and flogged the fallen horse, twisting its tail and prodding its testicles, forcing it to rise at last and stand quivering and forlorn. Then beating it to make it move again they led it from the ring stumbling over its own entrails.

Then they went to work on the bull, slowly, torturously, reducing it from a magnificent beast to a blundering hunk of sweating and bleeding flesh, splattered with the creamy froth blown from its agonized lungs.

David wanted to scream at them to stop it, but sick to the stomach, frozen by guilt for his own part in this obscene ritual, he sat through it in silence until the bull stood in the centre of the ring, the sand about him ploughed and riven by his dreadful struggles. He stood with his head down, muzzle almost touching the sand and the blood and froth dripped from his nostrils and gaping mouth. The hoarse sawing of his breathing carried to David even above the crazed roaring of the crowd. The bull's legs shuddered and he passed a dribble of loose liquid yellow dung that fouled his back legs. It seemed to David that this was the final humiliation, and he found he was whispering aloud.

'No! No! Stop it! Please, stop it!'

Then the man in the glittering suit and ballet shoes came to end it, and the point of the sword struck bone and the blade arced then spun away in the sunlight, and the bull heaved and threw thick droplets of blood, before he stood again.

They picked up the sword from the sand and gave it to the man and he sighted over the quiescent, dying beast and again the thrust was deflected by bone and David found that at last he had power in his voice, and he screamed:

'Stop it! You filthy bastards.'

Twelve times the man in the centre tried with the sword, and each time the sword flicked out of his hand, and then at last the bull fell of its own accord, weak from the slow loss of much blood and with its heart broken by the torture and the striving. It tried to rise, lunging weakly, but the strength was not there and they killed it where it lay, with a dagger in the back of the neck, and they dragged it out with a team of mules – its legs waggling ridiculously in the air and its blood leaving a long brown smudge across the sand.

Stunned with the monstrous cruelty of it, David turned slowly to look at the girl. Her companion was leaning over her solicitously, whispering to her, trying to comfort her.

She was shaking her head slowly, in a gesture of incomprehension, and her honey-coloured eyes were blinded with weeping. Her lips were apart, quivering with grief, and her cheeks were awash, shiny with her tears.

Her companion helped her to her feet, and gently took her down the steps, leading her away blindly like a new widow from her husband's grave.

Around him the crowd was laughing and exhilarated, high on the blood and the pain – and David felt himself rejected, cut off from them. His heart went out to the weeping girl, she of all of them was the only one who seemed real to him. He had seen enough also, and he knew he would never get to Pamplona. He stood up and followed the girl out of the ring, he wanted to speak to her, to tell her that he shared her desolation, but when he reached the parking lot they were already climbing into a battered old Citroën CV100, and although he broke into a run, the car pulled away – blowing blue smoke and clattering like a lawn-mower – and turned into the traffic heading east.

David watched it go with a sense of loss that effectively washed away the good feeling of the last few days, but he saw the old Citroën again two days later, when he had abandoned all idea of the Pamplona Festival and headed south. The Citroën looked even sicker than before, under a layer of pale dust and with the canvas showing on a rear tyre. The suspension seemed to have sagged on the one side, giving it a rakishly drunken aspect.

It was parked at a filling station on the outskirts of Zaragoza on the road to Barcelona, and David pulled off the road and parked beyond the gasoline pumps. An attendant in greasy overalls was filling the tank of the Citroën under the supervision of the muscular young man from the bullring. David looked quickly for the girl – but she was not in the car. Then he saw her.

She was in a *cantina* across the street, haggling with the elderly woman behind the counter. Her back was turned towards him, but David recognized the mass of dark hair now piled on top of her head. He crossed the road quickly and went into the shop behind her. He was not certain what he was going to do, acting only on impulse.

The girl wore a short floral dress which left her back and shoulders bare, and her feet were thrust into open sandals. But in concession to the ice in the air she wore a shawl over her shoulders. Close to, her skin had a plastic smoothness and elasticity, as though it had been lightly oiled and polished, and down the back of her naked neck the hair was fine and soft, growing in a whorl in the nape.

David moved closer to her as she completed her purchase of dried figs and counted her change. He smelt her, a light summery perfume that seemed to come from her hair. He resisted the temptation to press his face into the dense pile of it.

She turned smiling and saw him standing close behind her. She recognized him instantly, his was not a face a girl would readily forget. She was startled. The smile flickered

38

out on her face and she stood very still looking at him, her expression completely neutral, but her lips slightly parted and her eyes soft and glowing golden. This peculiar stillness of hers was a quality he would come to know so well in the time ahead.

'I saw you in Madrid,' he said, 'at the bulls.'

'Yes,' she nodded, her voice neither welcoming nor forbidding.

'You were crying.'

'So were you.' Her voice was low and clear, her enunciation flawless, too perfect not to be foreign.

'No,' David denied it.

'You were crying,' she insisted softly. 'You were crying inside.' And he inclined his head in agreement. Suddenly she proffered the paper bag of figs.

'Try one,' she said and smiled. It was a warm friendly smile. He took one of the fruits and bit into the sweet flesh as she moved towards the door, somehow conveying an invitation for him to join her. He walked with her and they looked across the street at the Citroën. The attendant had finished filling the tank, and the girl's companion was waiting for her, leaning against the bonnet of the weary old car. He was lighting a cigarette, but he looked up and saw them. He evidently recognized David also, and he straightened up quickly and flicked away the burning match.

There was a soft whooshing sound and the heavy thump of concussion in the air, as fire flashed low across the concrete from a puddle of spilled gasoline. In an instant the flames had closed over the rear of the Citroën, and were drumming hungrily at the coachwork.

David left the girl and sprinted across the road.

'Get it away from the pumps, you idiot,' he shouted, and the driver started out of frozen shock.

It was happy fifth of November, a spectacular pyrotechnic display — but David got the handbrake off and the gearbox into neutral, and he and the driver pushed it into an open parking area alongside the filling station while a crowd materialized, seeming to appear out of the very earth, to scream hysterical encouragement and suggestions while keeping at a discreet distance.

They even managed to rescue the baggage from the rear seat before the flames engulfed it entirely – and belatedly the petrol attendant arrived with an enormous scarlet fire extinguisher. To the delighted applause of the crowd, he drenched the pathetic little vehicle in a great cloud of foam, and the excitement was over. The crowd drifted away, still laughing and chattering and congratulating the amateur firefighter on his virtuoso performance with the extinguisher – while the three of them regarded the scorched and blackened shell of the Citroën ruefully.

'I suppose it was a kindness really – the poor old thing was very tired,' the girl said at last. 'It was like shooting a horse with a broken leg.'

'Are you insured?' David asked, and the girl's companion laughed.

'You're joking – who would insure that? I only paid a hundred US dollars for her.'

They assembled the small pile of rescued possessions, and the girl spoke quickly to her companion in foreign, slightly guttural language which touched a deep chord in David's memory. He understood what she was saying, so it was no surprise when she looked at him.

'We've got to meet somebody in Barcelona this evening. It's important.'

'Let's go,' said David.

They piled the luggage into the Mustang and the girl's companion folded up his long legs and piled into the back seat. His name was Joseph – but David was advised by the girl to call him Joe. She was Debra, and surnames didn't seem important at that stage. She sat in the seat beside David, with her knees pressed together primly and her

40

hands in her lap. With one sweeping glance, she assessed the Mustang and its contents. David watched her check the expensive luggage, the Nikon camera and Zeiss binoculars in the glove compartment and the cashmere jacket thrown over the seat. Then she glanced sideways at him, seeming to notice for the first time the raw silk shirt with the slim gold Piaget under the cuff.

'Blessed are the poor,' she murmured, 'but still it must be pleasant to be rich.'

David enjoyed that. He wanted her to be impressed, he wanted her to make a few comparisons between himself and the big muscular buck in the back seat.

'Let's go to Barcelona,' he laughed.

David drove quietly through the outskirts of the town, and Debra looked over her shoulder at Joe.

'Are you comfortable?' she asked in the guttural language she had used before.

'If he's not – he can run behind,' David told her in the same language, and she gawked at him a moment in surprise before she let out a small exclamation of pleasure.

'Hey! You speak Hebrew!'

'Not very well,' David admitted. 'I've forgotten most of it,' and he had a vivid picture of himself as a ten-year-old, wrestling unhappily with a strange and mysterious language with back-to-front writing, an alphabet that was squiggly tadpoles and in which most sounds were made in the back of the throat, like gargling.

'Are you Jewish?' she asked, turning in the seat to confront him. She was no longer smiling; the question was clearly of significance to her.

David shook his head. 'No,' he laughed at the notion. 'I'm a half-convinced non-practising monotheist, raised and reared in the Protestant Christian tradition.'

'Then why did you learn Hebrew?'

'My mother wanted it,' David explained, and felt again the stab of an old guilt. 'She was killed when I was still a kid. I just let it drop. It didn't seem important after she had gone.'

'Your mother—' Debra insisted, leaning towards him, ' – she was Jewish?'

'Yeah. Sure,' David agreed. 'But my father was a Protestant. There was all sorts of hell when Dad married her. Everyone was against it – but they went ahead and did it anyway.'

Debra turned in the seat to Joe. 'Did you hear that – he's one of us.'

'Oh, come on!' David protested, still laughing.

'Mazaltov,' said Joe. 'Come and see us in Jerusalem some time.'

'You're Israeli?' David asked, with new interest.

'Sabras, both of us,' said Debra, with a note of pride and deep satisfaction. 'We are only on holiday here.'

'It must be an interesting country,' David hazarded.

'Like Joe just said, why don't you come and find out some time?' she suggested offhandedly. 'You have the right of return.' Then she changed the subject. 'Is this the fastest this machine will go? We have to be in Barcelona by seven.'

There was a relaxed feeling between them now, as though some invisible barrier had been lowered, as though she had made some weighty judgement. They were out of the city and ahead the open road wound down into the valley of the Ebro towards the sea.

'Kindly extinguish cigarettes and fasten your seat belts,' David said, and let the Mustang go.

She sat very still beside him with her hands folded in her lap and she stared ahead when the bends leapt at them, and the straights streamed in a soft blue blur beneath the body of the Mustang. There was a small rapturous smile on her mouth and the golden lights danced in her eyes, and David was moved to know that speed affected her the way it did him.

42

He forgot everything else but the girl in the seat beside him and the need to keep the mighty roaring machine on the ribbon of tarmac.

Once when they went twisting down into a dry dusty valley in a series of tight curves and David snaked the Mustang down into it with his hands darting from wheel to gear leaver, and his feet dancing heel and toe on the foot pedals – she laughed aloud with the thrill of it.

They bought cheese and bread and a bottle of white wine at a village *cantina* and ate lunch sitting on the parapet of a stone bridge while the water swirled below them, milky with snow melt from the mountains.

David's thigh touched Debra's, as they sat side by side. He could feel the warmth and resilience of her flesh through the stuff of their clothing and she made no move to pull away. Her cheeks were flushed a little brighter than seemed natural, even in the chill little wind that nagged at them.

David was puzzled by Joe's attitude. He seemed to be completely oblivious of David's bird dogging his girl, and he was deriving a childlike pleasure out of tossing pebbles at the trout in the waters below them. Suddenly David wished he would put up a better resistance, it would make his conquest a lot more enjoyable – for conquest was what David had decided on.

He leaned across Debra for another chunk of the white, tangy cheese and he let his arm brush lightly against the tantalizing double bulge of her bosom. Joe seemed not to notice.

'Come on, you big ape,' David thought scornfully. 'Fight for it. Don't just sit there.'

He wanted to test himself against this buck. He was big, and strong, and David could tell from the way he moved and held himself that he was well co-ordinated and self-assured. His face was chunky and half ugly, but he knew that some women liked them that way, and he was not fooled by Joe's slow and lazy grin – the eyes were quick and sharp.

'You want to drive, Joe?' he asked suddenly, and the slow grin spread like a puddle of spilled oil on Joe's face – but the eyes glittered with anticipation.

'Don't mind if I do,' said Joe, and David regretted the gesture as he found himself hunched in the narrow back seat. For the first five minutes Joe drove sedately, touching the brakes to test for grab and pull, flicking through the gears to feel the travel and bite of the stick, taking a burst of power through a bend to establish stability and detect any tendency for the tail to break out.

'Don't be scared of her,' David told him, and Joe grunted with a little frown of concentration creasing his broad forehead. Then he nodded to himself and his hands settled firmly, taking a fresh grip, and Debra whooped as he changed down to get the revs peaking. He slid the car through the first bend and David's right foot stabbed instinctively at a non-existent brake pedal and he felt his breathing jam in his throat.

When Joe parked them in the lot outside the airport at Barcelona and switched off the engine, all of them were silent for a few seconds and then David said softly, 'Son of a gun!'

Then they were all laughing. David felt a tinge of regret that he was going to have to take the girl away from him, for he was beginning to like him, despite himself, beginning to enjoy the slow deliberation of his speech and movements that was so clearly a put-on and finding pleasure in the big slow smile that took so long to reach its full bloom. David had to harden his resolve.

They were an hour early for the plane they were meeting and they found a table in the restaurant overlooking the runways. David ordered an earthenware jug of Sangria, and Debra sat next to Joe and put her hand on his arm while she chatted, a gesture that tempered David's new-found liking for him.

A private flight landed as the waiter brought the Sangria, and Joe looked up.

'One of the new executive Gulfstreams. They tell me she is a little beauty.' And he went on to list the aircraft's specifications in technical language that Debra seemed to follow intelligently.

'You know anything about aircraft?' David challenged him.

'Some,' admitted Joe, but Debra took the question.

'Joe is in the air force,' she said proudly, and David stared at them.

'So is Debs,' Joe laughed, and David switched his attention to her. 'She's a lieutenant in signals.'

'Only the reserve,' Debra demurred, 'but Joe is a flier. A fighter pilot.'

'A flier,' David repeated stupidly. He should have known from Joe's clear and steady gaze that was the peculiar mark of the fighter pilot. He should have known by the way he handled the Mustang. If he was an Israeli flier – then he would have flown a formidable number of operations. Hell, every time they took off, they were operational. He felt a vast tide of respect rising within him.

'What squadron are you on – Phantoms?'

'Phantoms!' Joe curled his lip. 'That isn't flying. That's operating a computer. No, we really fly. You ever heard of a Mirage?'

David blinked, and then nodded.

'Yeah,' said David, 'I've heard of them.'

'Well, I fly a Mirage.'

David began to laugh, shaking his head.

'What's wrong?' Joe demanded, his smile fading. 'What's funny about that?'

'I do too,' said David. 'I fly a Mirage.' It was no use

trying to get hot against this buck, he decided. 'I've got over a thousand hours on Mirages.' And it was Joe's turn to stare, then suddenly they were both talking at once – Debra's head turning quickly from one to the other.

David ordered another jug of Sangria, but Joe would not let him pay. He repeated for the fiftieth time, 'Well, that beats all,' and punched David's shoulder. 'How about that, Debs?'

Halfway through the second jug, David interrupted the talk which had been exclusively on aviation.

'Who are we meeting, anyway? We've driven across half of Spain and I don't even know who the guy is.'

'This guy is a girl,' Joe laughed, and Debra filled in.

'Hannah,' and she grinned at Joe, 'his fiancée. She is a nursing sister at Hadassah Hospital, and she could only get away for a week.'

'Your fiancée?' David whispered.

'They are getting married in June.' Debra turned to Joe. 'It's taken him two years to make up his mind.'

Joe chuckled with embarrassment, and Debra squeezed his arm.

'Your fiancée?' asked David again.

'Why do you keep saying that?' Debra demanded. David pointed at Joe, and then at Debra.

'What,' he started, 'I mean, who – what the hell?'

Debra realized suddenly and gasped. She covered her mouth with both hands, her eyes sparkling. 'You mean – you thought—? Oh, no,' she giggled. She pointed at Joe and then at herself. 'Is that what you thought?' David nodded.

'He is my brother,' Debra hooted. 'Joe is my. brother, you idiot! Joseph Israel Mordecai and Debra Ruth Mordecai – brother and sister.'

Hannah was a rangy girl with bright copper hair and freckles like gold sovereigns. She was only an inch or two shorter than Joe but he lifted her as she came through the customs gate, swung her off her feet and then engulfed her in an enormous embrace.

It seemed completely natural that the four of them should stay together. By a miracle of packing they got all their luggage and themselves into the Mustang with Hannah perched on Joe's lap in the rear.

'We've got a week,' said Debra. 'A whole week! What are we going to do with it?'

They agreed that Torremolinos was out. It was far south, and since Michener had written *The Drifters*, it had become a hangout for all the bums and freaks.

'I was talking to someone on the plane. There is a place called Colera up the coast. Near the border.'

They reached it in the middle of the next morning and it was still so early in the season that they had no trouble finding pleasant rooms at a small hotel off the winding main street. The girls shared, but David insisted on a room of his own. He had certain plans for Debra that made privacy desirable.

Debra's bikini was blue and brief, hardly sufficient to restrain a bosom that was more exuberant than David had guessed. Her skin was satiny and tanned to a deep mahogany, although a strip of startling white peeped over the back of her costume when she stooped to pick up her towel. She was long in the waist, and leg, and a strong swimmer – pacing David steadily through the cool blue water when they set out for a rocky islet half a mile off shore.

They had the tiny island to themselves and they found a patch of flat smooth rock out of the wind and full in the sun. They lay side by side with their fingers entwined and the salt water had sleeked Debra's hair to her shoulders, like the coat of an otter.

They lay in the sun and they talked away the afternoon. There was so much they had to learn about each other.

Her father had been one of the youngest colonels in the American Air Force during World War II, but afterwards he had gone on to Israel. He had been there ever since, and was now a major-general. They lived in a house in an old part of Jerusalem which was five hundred years old, but was a lot of fun.

She was a senior lecturer in English at the Hebrew University in Jerusalem and, this shyly as though it was a rather special secret, she wanted to write. A small volume of her poetry had already been published. That impressed David, and he came up on one elbow and looked at her with new respect, and a twinge of envy, for someone who saw the way ahead clearly.

She lay with her eyes closed against the sun, and droplets of water sparkling like gems on her thick dark eyelashes. She wasn't beautiful, he decided carefully, but very handsome and very, very sexy. He was going to have her, of course. There was no doubt in David's mind about this, but there seemed little urgency in it now. He was enjoying listening to her talk, she had a quaint way of expressing herself, once she was in full flight, and her accent was strangely neutral – although there were faint echoes of her American background now he knew to look for them. She told him that the poetry was merely a beginning. She was going to write a novel about being young and living in Israel. She had the outline worked out, and it seemed like a pretty interesting story to David. Then she started to talk about her land and the people who lived in it. David felt something move within him as he listened – a nostalgia, a deep race memory. Again his envy stirred. She was so certain of where she was from and where she was going – she knew where she belonged, and what her destiny was, and this made her strong. Beside her he felt suddenly insignificant and without purpose.

She opened her eyes suddenly, squinting a little in the sunlight, and looked up at him.

'Oh dear,' she smiled. 'We are so sad, David. Do I talk too much?' He shook his head but did not answer her smile, and she became solemn also.

She studied his face carefully, with minute attention. The sun had dried his hair and fluffed it out, and it was soft and fine and very dark. The bone of his cheek and jaw was sculptured and finely balanced, the eyes very clear and slightly Asiatic in cast, the lips full and firm, and the nose delicately fluted with wide nostrils and a straight graceful line.

She reached up and touched his cheek.

'You are very beautiful, David. You are the most beautiful human being I have ever seen.'

He did not move, and she ran the finger down his neck on to his chest, twirling it slowly in the dark body hair.

Slowly he leaned forward and placed his mouth over hers. Her lips were warm and soft and tasted of sea salt. Her arms came up around the back of his head and folded around him. They kissed until he reached behind her and unfastened the clasp of her costume between the smooth brown shoulder blades. She stiffened immediately and tried to pull away from him.

David held her gently but firmly, murmuring little soothing noises as he kissed her again. Slowly she relaxed and he went on gentling her until her hands went to the back of his neck again, and she sighed and shuddered.

His hands were skilled and expert, masterful enough to prevent rebellion, not rough enough to panic her. He pushed up the thin material of her costume top and was surprised and enchanted with the firm rubbery weight of her breasts and the big dusky rose-brown nipples which were pebble-hard to his touch.

It was shocking, completely foreign to his experience, for David was not accustomed to check or denial, but Debra placed her hands on his shoulders and shoved him with such force that he lost his balance and slid down the rock, grazing his elbow and ending in a heap at the water's edge.

He scrambled angrily to his feet as Debra came up with a fluid explosive movement, fastening her costume as she did so. A single bound of her long brown legs carried her to the edge of the rocks and she dived outwards, hitting the water flat and surfacing to call back at him.

'I'll race you to the beach.'

David would not accept the challenge and followed her at his own dignified pace. When he emerged unsmilingly from the low surf, she studied his face a moment and then grinned.

'When you sulk you look about ten years old,' she told him, which was no great exercise of tact, and David stalked back to his room.

He was still being extremely dignified and aloof that evening when they discovered a discotheque named '2001 AD' run by a couple of English boys down on the sea-front. They crowded round a table at which there were already two BEA hostesses and a couple of raggedy-looking beards. The music was loud enough and the rhythm hard enough to jar the spine and loosen the bowels, and when the two hostesses gazed at David with almost religious awe Debra forsook her attitude of cool amusement and suggested to David that they dance. Mollified by this little feminine by-play, David dropped his impersonation of the Ice King.

They moved well together, sharing the gut rhythms of the harsh music, executing the primeval movements that reeked of Africa with a grace that drew the attention of the other dancers.

When the music changed Debra came to him and laid her body against his. David felt some force flowing from her that seemed to charge every nerve of his body – and he knew that no relationship he had with this woman would

50

ever run calmly. It was too deeply felt for that, too volatile and triggered for momentary explosion.

When the record ended they left Joe and Hannah huddled over a carafe of red wine and they went out into the silent street and down to the beach.

There was a moon in the sky that lit the dark cliffs crowding in above the beach, and reflected off the sea in multiple yellow images. The low surf hissed and coughed on the pebble beach and they took off their shoes and walked along it, letting the water wash around their ankles.

In an angle of the cliff, they found a hidden place amongst the rocks and they stopped to kiss again, and David mistakenly took her new soft mood as an invitation to continue from where he had left off that afternoon.

Debra pulled away again, but this time with determination and said angrily, 'Damn you! Don't you ever learn? I don't want to do that. Do we have to go through this every time we are alone?'

'What's the matter?' David was immediately stung by her tone, and furious with this fresh check. 'This is the twentieth century, darling. The simpering virgin is out of style this season – hadn't you heard?'

'And spoilt little boys should grow up before they come out on their own,' she flashed back at him.

'Thanks!' he snarled. 'I don't have to stay around taking insults from any professional virgin.'

'Well, why don't you move out then?' she challenged him.

'Hey, that's a great idea!' He turned his back on her and walked away up the beach. She had not expected that, and she started to run after him – but her pride checked her. She stopped and leaned against the rock.

He shouldn't have rushed me, she thought miserably. I want him, I want him very much, but he will be the first since Dudu. If he will just give me time it will be all right, but he mustn't rush me. If he could only go at my speed, help me to do it right.

It is funny, she thought, how little I remember about Dudu now. It's only three years, but his memory is fading so swiftly, I wonder if I really did love him. Even his face is hazy in my mind, while I know every detail of David's – every plane and line of it.

Perhaps I should go after him and tell him about Dudu, and ask him to be patient and to help me a little. Perhaps I should do that, she thought, but she did not and slowly she walked up the beach, through the silent town to the hotel.

Hannah's bed across the room was empty. She would be with Joe, lying with him, loving with him. I should be with David also, she thought. Dudu was dead, and I'm alive, and I want David and I should be with him – but she undressed slowly and climbed into the bed and lay without sleeping.

David stood in the doorway of '2001 AD' and peered through the weirdly flashing lights and the smog, the warm palpable emanation from a hundred straining bodies. The BEA hostesses were still at the table, but Joe and Hannah had gone.

David made his way through the dancers. The one hostess was tall and blonde, with high English colour and china-doll eyes. She looked up and saw David, glanced around for Debra, made sure she was missing before she smiled.

They danced one cut of the record without touching each other and then David leaned close to her and placed both hands on her hips. She strained towards him with her lips parting.

'Have you got a room?' he asked, and she nodded, running the tip of her tongue lewdly around her lips.

'Let's go,' said David.

It was light when David got back to his own room. He shaved and packed his bag, surprised at the strength of his residual anger. He lugged his bag down to the proprietor's office and paid his bill with his Diners Club card.

Debra came out of the breakfast room with Joe and Hannah. They were all dressed for the beach with terry robes over their bathing gear, and they were happy and laughing – until they saw David.

'Hey!' Joe challenged him. 'Where are you going?'

'I've had enough of Spain,' David told them. 'I'm taking some good advice, and I'm moving out,' and he felt a flare of savage triumph as he saw the quick shadow of pain in Debra's eyes. Both Joe and Hannah glanced at her, and quickly she controlled the quiver of her lips. She smiled then, a little too brightly and stepped forward, holding out her hand.

'Thank you for all your help, David. I'm sorry you have to go. It was fun.' Then her voice dropped slightly and there was a tiny quiver in it. 'I hope you find what you are looking for. Good luck.'

She turned quickly and hurried away to her room. Hannah's expression was steely, and she gave David a curt nod before following Debra.

'So long, Joe.'

'I'll carry your bag.'

'Don't bother.' David tried to stop him.

'No trouble.' Joe took it out of his hand and carried it out to the Mustang. He dumped it on the rear seat.

'I'll ride up to the top of the hills with you and walk back.' He climbed into the passenger seat and settled comfortably. 'I need the exercise.'

David drove swiftly, and they were silent as Joe deliberately lit a cigarette and flicked the match out the window.

'I don't know what went wrong, Davey, but I can guess.'

David didn't reply, he concentrated on the road.

'She's had a bad time. These last few days she has been different. Happy, I guess, and I thought it was going to work out.'

Still David was silent, not giving him any help. Why didn't the big bonehead mind his own business?

'She's a pretty special sort of person, Davey, not because she's my sister. She really is, and I think you should know about her – just so you don't think too badly about her.'

They had reached the top of the hills above the town and the bay. David pulled on to the verge but kept the engine running. He looked down on the brilliant blue of the sea, where it met the cliffs and the pine-covered headlands.

'She was going to be married,' said Joe softly. 'He was a nice guy, older than she was, they worked together at the University. He was a tank driver in the reserve and he took a hit in the Sinai and burned with his tank.'

David turned and looked at him, his expression softening a little.

'She took it badly,' Joe went on doggedly. 'These last few days were the first time I've seen her truly happy and relaxed.' He shrugged and grinned like a big St Bernard dog. 'Sorry to give you the family history, Davey. Just thought it might help.' He held out a huge brown hand. 'Come and see us. It's your country also, you know. I'd like to show it to you.'

David took the hand. 'I might do that,' he said.

'*Shalom*.'

'*Shalom*, Joe. Good luck.' Joe climbed out of the car and when David pulled away he watched him standing on the side of the road with his hands on his hips. He waved and the first bend in the road hid him.

There was a school for aspiring Formula One racing drivers on a neglected concrete circuit near Ostia, on the road from Rome. The course lasted three weeks and cost $500 US.

David stayed at the Excelsior in the Via Veneto, and commuted each day to the track. He completed the full course, but after the first week knew it was not what he wanted. The physical limitation of the track was constricting after flying the high heavens, and even the crackling, snarling power of a Tyrell Ford could not match the thrust from the engine of a jet interceptor. Although he lacked the dedication and motivation of others in his class his natural talent for speed and his co-ordination brought him out high in the finishing order – and he had an offer to drive on the works team of a new and struggling company that was building and fielding a production team of Formula One racing machines. Of course, the salary was starvation, and it was a measure of his desperation that he came close to signing a contract for the season, but at the last moment he changed his mind and went on.

In Athens he spent a week hanging around the yacht basins of Piraeus and Glyfada. He was investigating the prospects of buying a motor yacht and running it out on charter to the islands. The prospect of sun and sea and pretty girls seemed appealing and the craft themselves were beautiful in their snowy paint and varnished teakwork. In one week he learned that charter work was merely running a sea-going boarding house for a bunch of bored, sunburned and seasick tourists.

On the seventh day the American Sixth Fleet dropped anchor in the bay of Athens. David sat at a table of one of the beach-front cafés and drank *ouzo* in the sun, while he studied the anchored aircraft carriers through his binoculars. On the great flat tops the rows of Crusaders and Phantoms were grouped with their wings folded. Watching them he felt a consuming hunger, a need that was almost spiritual. He had searched the earth, it seemed, and there was nothing for him upon its face. He laid the binoculars aside, and he looked up into the sky. The clouds were high, a brilliant silver against the blue.

He picked up the glass of milky *ouzo* that the sun had warmed and rolled its sweet liquorice taste about his tongue.

'East, west, home is best.'

He spoke aloud, and had a mental image of Paul Morgan sitting in his high office of glass and steel. Like a patient fisherman he tended his lines laid across the world. Right now the one to Athens was beginning to twitch. He could imagine the quiet satisfaction as he began to reel it in, drawing David struggling feebly back to the centre. What the hell, I could still fly Impalas as a reserve officer, he thought, and there was always the Lear – if he could get it away from Barney.

David drained the glass and stood up abruptly, feeling the fading glow of his defiance. He flagged a cab and was driven back to his room at the Grande Bretagne on Syndagma Square.

His defiance was dying so swiftly that one of his companions for dinner that night was John Dinopoulos, Morgan Group's agent for Greece, a slim elegant sophisticate with an unlined sun-tanned face, silver wings in his hair and an elegantly casual way of dressing.

John had selected for David's table companion the female star of a number of Italian spaghetti westerns. A young lady of ample bosom and dark flashing eye whose breathing and bosom had become so agitated when John introduced David as a diamond millionaire from Africa.

Diamonds were the most glamorous, although not the most significant, of Morgan Group's interests.

They sat upon the terrace of Dionysius, for the evening was mild. The restaurant was carved into the living rock of the hill-top of Lycabettus, under the church of St Paul.

Down the zig-zag path from the church, the Easter procession of worshippers unwound in a flickering stream of candle flames through the pine forest below them, and the singing carried sweetly on the still night air. On its far hill-top the stately columns of the Acropolis were flood-lit so that they glowed as creamily as ancient ivory, and beyond that again on the midnight waters of the bay the American fleet wore gay garlands of fairy lights.

'The glory that was Greece—' murmured the star of Italian westerns, as though she voiced the wisdom of the ages, and placed one heavily jewelled hand on David's thigh while with the other she raised a glass of red Samos wine to him and cast him a look under thick eyelashes that was fraught with significance.

Her restraint was impressive, and it was only after they had eaten the main course of savoury meats wrapped in vine leaves and swimming in creamy lemon sauce that she suggested that David might like to finance her next movie.

'Let's find some place where we can talk about it—' she murmured, and what better place than her suite?

John Dinopoulos waved them away with a grin and a knowing wink, a gesture that annoyed David for it made him see the whole episode for the emptiness that it was.

The star's suite was pretentious, with thick white carpets and bulky black leather furniture. David poured himself a drink while she went to change into clothing more suitable for a discussion of high finance. David tasted the drink, realized that he did not want it and left it on the bar counter.

The star came out of the bedroom in a bedrobe of white satin which was cut back from arm and bosom, and was so sheer that her flesh gleamed with a pearly pink sheen through the material. Her hair was loose, a great wild mane of swirling curls – and suddenly David was sick of the whole business.

'I'm sorry,' he said. 'John was joking – I'm not a millionaire, and I really prefer boys.'

He heard his untouched glass shatter against the door of the suite as he closed it behind him.

Back at his own hotel he ordered coffee from room service, and then on an impulse he picked up the telephone again and placed a Cape Town call. It came through with surprising speed, and the girl's voice on the other end was thickened with sleep.

'Mitzi,' he laughed. 'How's the girl?'

'Where are you, warrior? Are you home?'

'I'm in Athens, doll.'

'Athens – God! How's the action?'

'It's a drag.'

'Yeah! I bet,' she scoffed. 'The Greek girls are never going to be the same again.'

'How are you, Mitzi?'

'I'm in love, Davey. I mean really in love, it's far out. We are going to be married. Isn't that just something else?' David felt a spur of anger, jealous of the happiness in her voice.

'That's great, doll. Do I know him?'

'Cecil Lawley, you know him. He's one of Daddy's accountants.' David recalled a large, pale-faced, bespectacled man with a serious manner.

'Congratulations,' said David. He felt very much alone again. Far from home, and aware that life there flowed on without his presence.

'You want to talk to him?' Mitzi asked. 'I'll wake him up.' There was a murmur and mutter on the other end, then Cecil came on.

'Nice work,' David told him, and it really was. Mitzi's share of Morgan Group would be considerably larger than David's. Cecil had drilled himself an oil well in a most unconventional manner.

'Thanks, Davey.' Cecil's embarrassment at being caught

58

tending his oil well carried clearly over five thousand miles of telephone cable.

'Listen, lover. You do anything to hurt that girl, I'll personally tear out your liver and stuff it down your throat, okay?'

'Okay,' said Cecil, and his alarm was brittle in his tone. 'I'll put you back to Mitzi.'

She prattled on for another fifty dollars' worth before hanging up. David lay on the bed with his hands behind his head and thought about his dumpy soft-hearted cousin and her new happiness. Then quite suddenly he made the decision which had been lurking at the edge of his consciousness all these weeks since leaving Spain. He picked up the phone again and asked for the porter's desk.

'I'm sorry to trouble you at this time in the morning,' he said, 'but I should like to get on a flight to Israel as soon as possible, will you please arrange that.'

The sky was filled with a soft golden haze that came off the desert. The gigantic TWA 747 came down through it, and David had a glimpse of dark green citrus orchards before the solid jolt of the touch-down. Lod was like any other airport in the world but beyond its doors was a land like no other he had ever known. The crowd who fought him for a seat in one of the big black *sheruts*, communal taxis plastered with stickers and hung with gewgaws, made even the Italians seem shining towers of restrained good manners.

Once aboard, however, it was as though they were on a family outing – and he a member of that family. On one side of him a paratrooper in beret and blouse with his winged insignia on the breast and an Uzi submachine-gun slung about his neck offered him a cigarette, on the other a big strapping lass also in khaki uniform and with the dark gazelle eyes of an Israeli, which became even darker and more soulful when she looked at David, which was often, shared a sandwich of unleaven bread and balls of fried chick-peas, the ubiquitous pitta and falafel, with him and practised her English upon him. All the occupants of the front seat turned around to join the conversation, and this included the driver who nevertheless did not allow his speed to diminish in the slightest and who punctuated his remarks with fierce blasts of his horn and cries of outrage at pedestrians and other drivers.

The perfume of orange blossom lay as heavily as sea mist upon the coastal lowlands, and always afterwards it would be for David the smell of Israel.

Then they climbed into the Judaean hills, and David felt a sense of nostalgia as they followed the winding highway through pine forests and across the pale shining slopes where the white stone gleamed like bone in the sunlight and the silver olive trees twisted their trunks in graceful agony upon the terraces which were the monuments to six thousand years of man's patient labour.

It was so familiar and yet subtly different from those fair and well-beloved hills of the southern cape he called home. There were flowers he did not recognize, crimson blooms like spilled blood, and bursts of sunshine-yellow blossoms upon the slopes – then suddenly a pang that was like a physical pain as he glimpsed the bright flight of chocolate and white wings amongst the trees, and he recognized the crested head of an African hoopoe – a bird which was a symbol of home.

He felt a sense of excitement building within him, unformed and undirected as yet but growing, as he drew closer to the woman he had come to see – and to something else of which he was as yet uncertain.

There was, at last, a sense of belonging. He felt in sympathy with the young persons who crowded close to him in the cab.

'See,' cried the girl, touching his arm and pointing to the wreckage of war still strewn along the roadside, the burned-out carapaces of trucks and armoured vehicles, preserved as a memorial to the men who died on the road to Jerusalem. 'There was fighting here.'

David turned in the seat to study her face, and he saw again the strength and certainty that he had so admired in Debra. These were a people who lived each day to its limit, and only at its close did they consider the next.

'Will there be more fighting?' he asked.

'Yes,' she answered him without hesitation.

'Why?'

'Because – if it is good – you must fight for it,' and she made a wide gesture that seemed to embrace the land and all its people, 'and this is ours, and it is good,' she said.

'Right on, doll,' David agreed with her, and they grinned at each other.

So they came to Jerusalem with its tall, severe apartment blocks of custard-yellow stone, standing like monuments upon the hills, grouped about the massive walled citadel that was its heart.

TWA had reserved a room at the Intercontinental Hotel for David while on board the inward flight. From his window he looked across the garden of Gethsemane at the old city, at its turrets and spires and the blazing golden Dome of the Rock – centre of Christianity and Judaism, holy place of the Moslems, battleground of two thousand years, ancient land reborn – and David felt a sense of awe. For the first time in his life, he recognized and examined that portion of himself that was Jewish, and he thought it was right that he should have come to this city.

'Perhaps,' he said aloud, 'it's just possible that this is where it's all at.'

It was early evening when David paid off the cab in the car park of the University and submitted to a perfunctory search by a guard at the main gate. Here body search was a routine that would soon become so familiar as to pass unnoticed. He was surprised to find the campus almost deserted, until he remembered it was Friday – and that the whole tempo was slowing for the Sabbath.

The red-bud trees were in full bloom around the main plaza and the ornamental pool, as David crossed to the admin block and asked for her at the inquiries desk where the porter was on the point of leaving his post.

'Miss Mordecai—' The porter checked his list. 'Yes. English Department. On the second floor of the Lauterman Building.' He pointed out through the glass doors. 'Third building on your right. Go right on in.'

Debra was in a students' tutorial, and while he waited for her, he found a seat on the terrace in the warmth of the sun. It was as well, for suddenly he felt a breath of uncertainty cooling his spine. For the first time since leaving Athens, he wondered if he had much cause to expect a hearty welcome from Debra Mordecai. Even at this remove in time, David had difficulty in judging his own behaviour towards her. Self-criticism was an art which David had never seriously practised; with a face and fortune such as his, it was seldom necessary. In this time of waiting he found it novel and uncomfortable to admit that it was just possible that his behaviour may have been, as Debra had told him, that of a spoiled child. He was still exploring this thought, when a burst of voices and the clatter of heels upon the flags distracted him and a group of students came out on to the terrace, hugging their books to their chests, and most of the girls glanced at him with quick speculative attention as they passed.

There was a pause then before Debra came. She carried books under her arm and a sling bag over one shoulder, and her hair was pulled back severely at the nape of her neck; she wore no make-up, but her skirt was brightly coloured in big summery whorls of orange. Her legs were bare and her feet were thrust into leather sandals. She was in deep conversation with the two students who flanked her, and she did not see David until he stood up from the parapet. Then she froze into that special stillness he had first noticed in the *cantina* at Zaragoza.

David was surprised to find how awkward he felt, as though his feet and hands had grown a dozen sizes. He grinned and made a shrugging, self-deprecatory gesture.

'Hello, Debs.' His voice sounded gruff in his own ears, and Debra stirred and made a panicky attempt to brush back the wisps of hair at her temples, but the books hampered her.

'David—' She started towards him, a pace before she hesitated and stopped, glancing at her students. They sensed her confusion and melted, and she swung back at him.

'David—' she repeated, and then her expression crumbled into utter desolation. 'Oh God, and I haven't even a shred of lipstick on.'

David laughed with relief and went towards her, spreading his arms, and she flew at him and it was all confusion with books and sling bag muddled, and Debra making breathless exclamations of frustration before she could divest herself of them. Then at last they embraced.

'David,' she murmured with both arms wound tightly around his neck. 'You beast – what on earth took you so long? I had almost given you up.'

Debra had a motor scooter which she drove with such murderous abandon that she frightened even the Jerusalem taxi-drivers who crossed her path – men with a reputation for steel nerves and disregard for danger.

Perched on the pillion David clung to her waist and

remonstrated with her gently as she overtook a solid line of traffic and then cut smartly across a stream coming in the opposite direction with her exhaust popping merrily.

'I'm happy,' she explained over her shoulder.

'Fine! Then let's live to enjoy it.'

'Joe will be surprised to see you.'

'If we ever get there.'

'What's happened to your nerve?'

'I've just this minute lost it.'

She went down the twisting road into the valley of Ein Karem as though she was driving a Mirage, and called a travelogue back to him as she went.

'That's the Monastery of Mary's Well where she met the mother of John the Baptist – according to the Christian tradition in which you are a professed expert.'

'Hold the history,' pleaded David. 'There's a bus around that bend.'

The village was timeless amongst the olive trees, dug into the slope with its churches and monasteries and high-walled gardens, an oasis of the picturesque, while the skyline above it was cluttered with the high-rise apartments of modern Jerusalem.

From the main street Debra scooted into the mouth of a narrow lane, where high walls of time-worn stone rose on each hand, and braked to a halt outside a forbidding iron gate.

'Home,' she said, and wheeled the scooter into the gatehouse and locked it away before letting them in through a side gate hidden in a corner of the wall.

They came out into a large garden court enclosed by the high rough plastered walls which were lime-washed to glaring white. There were olive trees growing in the court with thick twisted trunks. Vines climbed the walls and spread their boughs overhead; already there were bunches of green grapes forming upon them.

'The Brig is a crazy keen amateur archaeologist.' Debra

indicated the Roman and Greek statues that stood amongst the olive trees, the exhibits of pottery amphorae arranged around the walls, and the ancient mosaic tiles which paved the pathway to the house. 'It's strictly against the law, of course, but he spends all his spare time digging around in the old sites.'

The kitchen was cavernous with an enormous open fireplace in which a modern electric stove looked out of place, but the copper pots were burnished until they glowed and the tiled floor was polished and sweet-smelling.

Debra's mother was a tall slim woman with a quiet manner, who looked like Debra's older sister. The family resemblance was striking and, as she greeted them, David thought with pleasure that this was how Debra would look at the same age. Debra introduced them and announced that David was a guest for dinner, a fact of which he had been unaware until that moment.

'Please,' he protested quickly, 'I don't want to intrude.' He knew that Friday was a special night in the Jewish home.

'You don't intrude. We will be honoured,' she brushed aside his protest. 'This house is home for most of the boys in Joe's squadron, we enjoy it.'

Debra fetched David a Goldstar beer and they were sitting on the terrace together when her father arrived. He came in through the wicket gate, stooping his tall frame under the stone lintel and taking off his uniform cap as he entered the garden.

He wore uniform casually cut, and open at the throat with cloth insignia or rank and wings at the breast pocket. He was slightly round-shouldered, probably from cramming his lanky body into the cramped cockpits of fighter aircraft, and his head was brown and bald with a monk's fringe of hair and a fierce spiky moustache through which a gold tooth gleamed richly. His nose was big and hooked, the nose of a biblical warrior, and his eyes were dark and snapping with the same golden lights as Debra's. He was a man of such presence that he commanded David's instant respect. He stood to shake the General's hand and called him 'sir' completely naturally.

The Brig subjected David to a rapid, raking scrutiny and reserved his judgement, showing neither pleasure nor disdain.

Later David would learn that the nickname 'The Brig' was a shortened version of 'The Brigand', a name the British had given him before 1948 when he was smuggling warplanes and arms into Palestine for the *Haganah*. Everyone, even his children, called him that and only his wife used his given name, Joshua.

'David is sharing the Sabbath meal with us tonight,' Debra explained to him.

'You are welcome,' said the Brig, and turned to embrace his women with love and laughter, for he had seen neither of them since the previous Sabbath, his duties keeping him at air bases and control rooms scattered widely across the land.

When Joe arrived, he was also in uniform, the casual open-necked khaki of summer, and when he saw David he dropped his slow manner and hurried to him, laughing, and enfolded him in a bear hug, speaking over his shoulder to Debra.

'Was I right?'

'Joe said you would come,' Debra explained.

'It looks like I was the only one who didn't know,' David protested.

There were fifteen at dinner, and the candlelight gleamed on the polished wood of the huge refectory table and the silver Sabbath goblets. The Brig said a short prayer, the satin and gold embroidered yarmulke looking slightly out of place on his wicked bald head, then he filled the wine goblets with his own hand murmuring a greeting to each of his guests. Hannah was with Joe, her copper hair glowing handsomely in the candlelight, and she greeted David with reserve. There were two of the Brig's brothers with their wives and children and grandchildren, and the talk was loud and confusing as the children vied with their elders for a hearing and the language changed at random from Hebrew to English. The food was exotic and spicy, although the wine was too sweet for David's taste. He was content to sit quietly beside Debra and enjoy the sense of belonging to this happy group. He was startled then when one of Debra's cousins leaned across her to speak to him.

'This must be very confusing for you – your first day in such an unusual country as Israel, and not understanding Hebrew, you not being Jewish—'

The words were not meant unkindly, but all conversation stopped abruptly and the Brig looked up, frowning swiftly, quick to sense an unkindness to guest at his board.

David was aware of Debra staring at him intently, as if to will words from him, and suddenly he thought how three denials finalized any issue – in the New Testament, in Mohammedan law, and perhaps in that of Moses as well. He did not want to be excluded from this household, from these people. He didn't want to be alone again. It was good here.

He smiled at the cousin and shook his head. 'It's strange, yes – but not as bad as you would think. I understand Hebrew, though I don't speak it very well. You see, I am Jewish, also.'

Beside him Debra gave a soft gasp of pleasure and exchanged quick glances with Joe.

'Jewish?' the Brig demanded. 'You don't look it,' and David explained, and when he was through the Brig nodded. It seemed that his manner had thawed a little.

'Not only that, but he is a flier also,' Debra boasted, and the Brig's moustache twitched like a living thing so that he had to soothe it with his napkin while he reappraised David carefully.

67

'What experience?' he demanded brusquely.

'Twelve hundred hours, sir, almost a thousand on jets.'

'Jets?'

'Mirages.'

'Mirages!' The Brig's gold tooth gleamed secretly.

'What squadron?'

'Cobra Squadron.'

'Rastus Naude's bunch?' The Brig stared at David as he asked.

'Do you know Rastus?' David was startled.

'We flew in the first Spitfires from Czechoslovakia together – back in '48. We used to call him Butch Ben Yok – Son of a Gentile – in those days. How is he, he must be getting on now? He was no spring chicken even then.'

'He's as spry as ever, sir,' David answered tactfully.

'Well, if Rastus taught you to fly – you might be half good,' the Brig conceded.

As a general rule the Israeli Air Force would not use foreign pilots, but here was a Jew with all the marks of a first-class fighter pilot. The Brig had noticed the marvellous élan and thrust which that other consummate judge of young men, Paul Morgan, had recognized also and valued so highly. Unless he had read the signs wrongly, something he seldom did, then here was a rare one. Once more he appraised the young man in the candlelight and noticed that clear and steady gaze that seemed to seek a distant horizon. It was the eye of the gunfighter, and all his pilots were gunfighters.

To train an interceptor pilot took many years and nearly a million dollars. Time and money were matters of survival in his country's time of trial – and rules could be bent.

He picked up the wine bottle and carefully refilled David's goblet. 'I will place a telephone call to Rastus Naude,' he decided silently, 'and find out a bit more about this youngster.'

Debra watched her father as he began to question David searchingly on his reasons, or lack of them, for coming to Israel – and on his future plans.

She knew precisely how the Brig's mind was working, for she had anticipated it. Her reasons for inviting David to dinner and for exposing him to the Brig were devious and calculated.

She switched her attention back to David, feeling the tense warm sensation in the pit of her stomach and the electric prickle of the skin upon her forearms as she looked at him.

'Yes, you big cocky stallion,' she thought comfortably, 'you aren't going to find it so easy to escape again. This time I'm playing for keeps, and I've got the Brig on to you also.'

She lifted her goblet to him, smiling sweetly at him over the rim.

'You're going to get exactly what you are after, but in trumps and with bells on,' she threatened silently, and aloud she said, '*Lechaim!* To life!' and David echoed the toast.

'This time I'm not going to be put off so easily,' he promised himself firmly as he watched the candlelight explode in tiny golden sparks in her eyes. 'I'm going to have you, my raven-haired beauty, no matter how long it takes or what it costs.'

T he telephone beside his bed woke David in the dawn, and the Brig's voice was crisp and alert, as though he had already completed a day's work.

'If you have no urgent plans for today, I'm taking you to see something,' he said.

'Of course, sir.' David was taken off balance.

'I will fetch you from your hotel in forty-five minutes, that will give you time for breakfast. Please wait for me in the lobby.'

The Brig drove a small nondescript compact with civilian plates, and he drove it fast and efficiently. David was impressed with his reaction time and co-ordination – after all the Brig must be well into his fifties, and David allowed himself to contemplate such immense age with awe.

They took the main highway west towards Tel Aviv, and the Brig broke a long silence.

'I spoke with your old CO last night. He was surprised to hear where you were. He tells me that you were offered promotion to staff rank before you left—'

'It was a bribe,' said David, and the Brig nodded and began to talk. David listened to him quietly while he watched with pleasure the quickly changing landscape as they came down out of the hills and turned southwards through the low rolling plains towards Beersheba and the desert.

'I am taking you to an air force base, and I might add that I am flouting all sorts of security regulations to do so. Rastus assured me that you can fly, and I want to see if he was telling me the truth.'

David looked at him quickly.

'We are going to fly?' and he felt a deep and pleasurable excitement when the Brig nodded.

'We are at war here, so you will be flying a combat sortie, and breaking just about every regulation in the book. But you'll find we don't go by the book very much.'

He went on quietly, explaining his own particular view of Israel, its struggle and its chances of success, and David remembered odd phrases he used.

' – We are building a nation, and the blood we have been forced to mix into the foundations has strengthened them—'

' – We don't want to make this merely a sanctuary for all the beaten-up Jews of the world. We want the strong bright Jews also—'

' – There are three million of us, and one hundred and fifty million enemies, sworn to our total annihilation—'

' – If they lose a battle, they lose a few miles of desert, if we lose one we cease to exist—'

' – We'll have to give them one more beating. They won't accept the others. They believe their ammunition was faulty in 1948, after Suez the lines were restored so they lost nothing, and in '67 they think they were cheated. We'll have to beat them one more time before they'll leave us alone—'

He talked as to a friend or an ally and David was warmed by his trust, and enlivened by the prospect of flying again.

A plantation of eucalyptus trees grew as a heavy screen alongside the road, and the Brig slowed to a gate in the barbed wire fence and a sign that proclaimed in both languages: 'Chaim Weissmann Agricultural Experimental Centre.'

They turned on to the side road through the plantation, and there was a secondary fence and a guard post amongst the trees.

A guard at the gate checked the Brig's papers briefly, they clearly knew him well. Then they drove on, emerging from the plantation into neatly laid-out blocks of different cereal crops. David recognized oats, barley, wheat and maize – all of it flourishing in the warm spring sunshine. The roads between each field were surveyed long and straight and paved with concrete that had been tinted to the colour of the surrounding earth. There was something unnatural in these smooth two-mile long fairways bisecting each other at right angles, and to David they were familiar. The Brig saw his interest and nodded. 'Yes,' he said, 'runways. We are digging in – not to be taken by the same tactics we used in '67.'

71

David pondered it while they drove rapidly towards a giant concrete grain silo that stood tall in the distance. In the fields scarlet tractors were at work, and overhead irrigation equipment threw graceful glittering ostrich feathers of spray into the air.

They reached the concrete silo and the Brig drove the compact through the wide doors of the barn-like building that abutted it. David was startled to see the lines of buses and automobiles parked in neat lines along the length of the barn. There was transport here for many hundreds of men – and yet he had noticed less than a score of tractor-drivers.

There were guards here again, in paratrooper uniform, and when the Brig led David to the rounded bulk of the silo, he realized suddenly that it was a dummy. A massive bomb-proof structure of solid concrete, housing all the sophisticated communications and radar equipment of a modern fighter base. It was combined control tower and plot for four full squadrons of Mirage fighters, the Brig explained briefly as they entered an elevator and sank below the earth.

They emerged into a reception area where again the Brig's papers were examined, and a paratrooper major was called to pass David through, a duty he performed reluctantly and at the Brig's insistence. Then the Brig led David along a carpeted and air-conditioned underground tunnel to the pilots' dressing-room. It was tiled and spotless, with showers and toilets and lockers like a country club changing-room.

The Brig had ordered clothing for David, guessing his size and doing so accurately. The orderly corporal had no trouble fitting him out in overalls, boots, G-suit, gloves and helmet.

The Brig dressed from his own locker and both of them went through into the ready room, moving stiffly in the constricting grip of the G-suits and carrying their helmets under their arms.

The duty pilots looked up from chess games and magazines as they entered, recognized the general and stood to greet him, but the atmosphere was easy and informal. The Brig made a small witticism and they all laughed and relaxed, while he led David through into the briefing-room.

Swiftly, but without overlooking a detail, he outlined the patrol that they would fly, and checked David out on radio procedure, aircraft identification, and other parochial details.

'All clear?' he asked at last, and when David nodded, he went on, 'Remember what I told you, we are at war. Anything we find that doesn't belong to us we hit it, hard! All right?'

'Yes, sir.'

'It's been nice and quiet the last few weeks, but yesterday we had a little trouble down near Ein Yahav, a bit of nastiness with one of our border patrols. So things are a little sensitive at the moment.' He picked up his helmet and map case then turned to face David, leaning close to him and fixing him with those fierce brown and golden eyes.

'It will be clear up there today, and when we get to forty thousand, you will be able to see it all, every inch of it from Rosh Hanikra to Suez, from Mount Hermon to Eilat, and you will see how small it is and how vulnerable to the enemies that surround us. You said you were looking for something worthwhile – I want you to decide whether guarding the fate of three million people might not be a worthwhile job for a man.'

They rode on a small electric personnel carrier down one of the long underground passages, and they entered the concrete bunker dispersed at one point of a great star whose centre was the concrete silo, and they climbed down from the cart.

The Mirages stood in a row, six of them, sleek and needle-nosed, crouching like leashed and impatient animals, so well remembered in outline, but vaguely unfamiliar in their desert brown and drab green camouflage with the blue Star of David insignia on the fuselage.

The Brig signed for two machines, grinning as he wrote 'Butch Ben Yok' under David's numeral.

'As good a name as any to fly under,' he grunted. 'This is the land of the pseudonym and alias.'

David settled into the tiny cockpit with a sense of homecoming. In here it was all completely familiar and his hands moved over the massed array of switches, instruments and controls like those of a lover as he began his pre-flight check.

In the confined space of the bunkers the jet thunder assaulted the eardrums, their din only made bearable by the perforated steel baffles set into the rear of the structure.

The Brig looked across at David, his head enclosed in the garishly painted helmet, and gave him the high sign. David returned it and reached up to pull the Perspex canopy closed. Ahead of them, the steel blast doors rolled swiftly upwards, and the ready lamps above them switched from red to green.

There was no taxiing to take-off areas; no needless ground exposure. Wing-tip to wing-tip they came up the ramp out of the bunker into the sunlight. Ahead of them stretched one of the long brown runways, and David pushed open his throttle to the gate, and then ignited his afterburners, feeling the thrust of the mighty jet through the cushioning of his seat. Down between the fields of green corn they tore, and then up, with the swooping sensation in the guts and the rapier nose of the Mirage pointed at the sapphire of the sky that arched unbroken and unsullied above them, and once again David experienced the euphoria of jet-powered flight.

They levelled out at a little under forty thousand feet

avoiding even altitudes or orderly flight patterns, and David placed his machine under the Brig's tail and eased back on the throttles to cruising power, his hands delighting in the familiar rituals of flight while his helmeted head revolved restlessly in the search routine, sweeping every quarter of the sky about him, weaving the Mirage to clear the blind spot behind his own tail.

The air had an unreal quality of purity, a crystalline clarity that made even the most distant mountain ranges stand out in crisp silhouette, hardly shaded with the blue of distance. In the north the Mediterranean blazed like a pool of molten silver in the sunlight, while the sea of Galilee was soft cool green, and farther south the Dead Sea was darker, forbidding in its sunken bed of tortured desert.

They flew north over the ridge of Carmel and the flecked white buildings of Haifa with its orange-gold beaches on which the sea broke in soft ripples of creamy lacework. Then they turned together easing back on the power and sinking slowly to patrol altitude at twenty thousand feet as they passed the peak of Mount Hermon where the last snows still lingered in the gullies and upon the high places, streaking the great rounded mountain like an old man's pate.

The softly dreaming greens and pastels delighted David who was accustomed to the sepia monochromes of Africa. The villages clung to the hill-tops, their white walls shining like diadems above the terraced slopes and the darker areas of cultivated land.

They turned south again, booming down the valley of the Jordan, over the Sea of Galilee with its tranquil green waters enclosed by the thickets of date palm and the neatly tended fields of the Kibbutzim, losing altitude as the land forsook its gentle aspect and the hills were riven and tortured, rent by the wadis as though by the claws of a dreadful predator.

On the left hand rose the mountains of Edom, hostile

and implacable, and beneath them Jericho was a green oasis in the wilderness. Ahead lay the shimmering surface of the Dead Sea. The Brig dropped down, and they thundered so low across the salt-thickened water that the jet blast ruffled the surface behind them.

The Brig's voice chuckled in David's earphones. 'That's the lowest you are ever going to fly – twelve hundred feet below sea level.'

They were climbing again as they crossed the mineral works at the southern end of the sea, and faced the blasted and mountainous deserts of the south.

'Hello, Cactus One, this is Desert Flower.' Again the radio silence was broken, but this time David recognized the call sign of command net. They were being called directly from the Operations Centre of Air Force Command, situated in some secret underground bunker at a location that David would never learn. On the command plot their position was being accurately relayed by the radar repeaters.

'Hello, Desert Flower,' the Brig acked, and immediately the exchange became as informal as two old friends chatting, which was precisely what it was.

'Brig, this is Motti. We've just had a ground support request in your area,' he gave the co-ordinates quickly, 'a motorized patrol of border police is under sneak lowlevel attack by an unidentified aircraft. See to it, will you?'

'*Beseder*, Motti, okay.' The Brig switched to flight frequency. 'Cactus Two, I'm going to interception power, conform to me,' he told David, and they turned together on to the new heading.

'No point in trying a radar scan,' the Brig grumbled aloud. 'He'll be down in the ground clutter. We'll not pick the swine off amongst those mountains. Just keep your eyes open.'

'*Beseder*.' David had already picked up the word. The favourite Hebrew word in a land where very little was really 'okay'.

David spotted it first, a slim black column of smoke beginning to rise like a pencil line drawn slowly against the windless and dazzling cobalt blue of the horizon.

'Ground smoke,' he said into his helmet microphone. 'Eleven o'clock low.'

The Brig squinted ahead silently, searching for it and then saw it on the extreme limit of his vision range. He grunted; Rastus had been right in one thing at least. The youngster had eyes like a hawk.

'Going to attack speed now,' he said, and David acked and lit his afterburners. The upholstery of his seat smacked into his back under the mighty increase in thrust and David felt the drastic alteration in trim as the Mirage went shooting through the sonic barrier.

Near the base of the smoke column, something flashed briefly against the drab brown earth, and David narrowed his eyes and made out the tiny shape, flitting swiftly as a sunbird, its camouflage blending naturally into the backdrop of desert, so it was as ethereal as a shadow.

'Bandit turning to port of the smoke,' he called the sighting.

'I have him,' said the Brig, and switched to command net.

'Hello, Desert Flower, I'm on an intruder. Call strike, please.' The decision to engage must be made at command level, and the answering voice was laconic, and flat.

'Brig, this is Motti. Hit him!'

While they spoke they were rushing down so swiftly that the details of the little drama being played out below sprang into comprehension.

Along a dusty border track three patrol vehicles of the border police were halted. They were camouflaged half-tracks, tiny as children's toys in the vastness of the desert.

One of the half-tracks was burning. The smoke was greasy black and rose straight into the air, the beacon that had drawn them. Lying spread-eagled in the road was a human body, flung down carelessly in death, and the sight of it stirred in David a deeply bitter feeling of resentment such as he had last felt in the bullring at Madrid.

The other vehicles were pulled off the track at abandoned angles, and David could see their crews crouching amongst the scrub and rock. Some of them were firing with small arms at their attacker who was circling for his next run down upon them.

David had never seen the type before, but knew it instantly from the recognition charts that he had studied so often. It was a Russian MiG 17 of the Syrian Air Force. The high tailplane was unmistakable. The dappled brown desert camouflage was brightened by the red, white and black roundels with their starred green centres on the fuselage and the stubby swept wings.

The MiG completed its turn, settling swiftly down and levelling off for its next strafing run upon the parked vehicles. The pilot's attention was concentrated on the helpless men cowering amongst the rocks and he was unaware of the terrible vengeance bearing down upon him on high.

The Brig lined up for his pass, turning slightly to bring himself down on the Syrian's tail, attacking in classic style from behind and above, while David dropped back to weave across his rear, covering him and backing up to press in a supporting attack if the first failed.

The Syrian opened fire again and the cannon bursts twinkled like fairy lights amongst the men and trucks. Another truck exploded in a dragon's breath of smoke and flame.

'You bastard,' David whispered as he levelled out behind the Brig, and saw the havoc that was being wrought amongst his people. It was the first time he had thought of them as that, his people, and he felt the cold anger of the shepherd whose flock is under attack.

A line of poetry popped up in his mind, 'The Assyrian came down like a wolf on the fold', and his hands went purposefully to the chore of locking in his cannons-selectors and flicking the trigger forward out of its recess in the moulded grip of the joystick. The soft green glow lit his gunsight as it came alive and he squinted through it.

The Brig was pressing his attack in to close range, rapidly overhauling the slower clumsy-looking MiG, and at that moment he knew he would open fire David saw the Syrian's wing-shape alter. At the fatal instant he had become aware of his predicament, and he had done what was best in the circumstances. He had pulled on full flap and while his speed fell sharply he dropped one wing in a slide towards the earth a hundred feet below.

The Brig was committed and he loosed his salvo of cannon fire at the instant that the Syrian dropped, ducking under it like a boxer avoiding a heavy punch. David saw the blaze of shot pass high, rending the air above the sand-coloured aircraft. Then the Brig was through, missing with every shell, spiralling up and around in a great flashing circle, raging internally at his failure.

At the instant that David recognized the MiG's manoeuvre he reacted with a rapidity that was purely reflexive. He closed down his power, and hit his air brakes to punch a little speed off the Mirage.

The MiG turned steeply away to port, standing on one wing-tip that seemed to be pegged into the bleak desert earth. David released his air brakes, to give his wings lift for the next evolution, and then he dropped his own wing-tip and went sweeping round to follow the Syrian's desperate twists with the Mirage hovering on the edge of the stall.

The Syrian was turning inside him, slower and more manoeuverable; David could not bring his sights to bear, his right forefinger was curled around the trigger but always the dark shape of the MiG was out of centre in the illuminated circle of the sight as the aiming pipper dipped and rose to the pull of gravity.

Ahead of the two circling aircraft rose a steep and forbidding line of cliffs, rent by deep defiles and gullies.

The MiG made no attempt to climb above them, but selected a narrow pass through the hills and went into it like a ferret into its run, a desperate attempt to shake off the pursuit.

The Mirage was not designed for this type of flying, and David felt the urge to hit his afterburners and ride up over the jagged fangs of rock – but to do so was to let the MiG escape, and his anger was still strong upon him.

He followed the Syrian into the rock pass, and the walls of stone on either hand seemed to brush his wing-tips, the gully turned sharply to starboard and David dropped his wing and followed its course. Back upon itself the rock turned, and David swung the needle nose from maximum rate turn starboard to port, and the stall warning device winked amber and red at him as he abused the Mirage's delicate flying capabilities.

Ahead of him the MiG clawed its way through the tunnel of rock. The pilot looked back over his shoulder and he saw the Mirage following him, creeping slowly up on him, and he turned back to his controls and forced his machine lower still, hugging the rugged walls of stone.

The air in the hills was hot and turbulent, and the Mirage bucked and fought against restraint wanting to be free and high, while ahead of it the Syrian drifted tantalizingly off-centre in David's gunsight.

Now the valley turned again and narrowed, before climbing and ending abruptly against a solid dark purple wall of smooth rock.

The Syrian was trapped, he levelled out and climbed steeply upwards, his flight path dictated by the rocks on each side and ahead.

David pushed his throttle to the gate and lit his after-burners, and the mighty engine rumbled, thrusting him powerfully forward, up under the Syrian's stern.

The eternal micro-seconds of mortal combat dragged by, as the Syrian floated lazily into the circle of the gunsight, expanding to fill it as the Mirage's nose seemed to touch the other's tailplane and David felt the buffeting of the Syrian's slipstream.

He pressed the cannon trigger and the Mirage lurched as she hurled her deadly load into the other machine in a clattering double stream of cannon fire and an eruption of incendiary shells.

The Syrian disintegrated, evaporating in a gush of silvery smoke, rent through with bright white lightning, and the ejecting pilot's body was blown clear of the fuselage. For an instant it was outlined ahead of David's screen, cruciform in shape with arms and legs thrown wide, the helmet still on the head, and the clothing ballooning in the rush of air. Then it flickered past the Mirage's canopy as David climbed swiftly up out of the valley and into the open sky.

The soldiers were moving about amongst their vehicles, tending their wounded and covering their dead, but they all looked up as David flew back low along the road. He passed so close that he could see their faces clearly. They were sunbrowned, some with beards or moustaches, strong young faces, their mouths open as they cheered him, waving their thanks.

My people, he thought. He was still high on the adrenalin that had poured into his blood, and he felt a fierce elation. He grinned wolfishly at the men below him and lifted one gloved hand in salute before climbing up to where the Brig was circling, waiting for him.

The artificial lights of the bunker were dim after the brilliance of the sun. An engineer helped David from the cockpit as his mates swarmed over the Mirage to refuel and rearm it. This was one of the vital skills of this tiny air force, the ability to ready a warplane for combat in a fraction of the time usually required for the task. Thus in emergency the machine could return to the battle long before its adversary.

Moving stiffly from the confines of the cockpit, David crossed to where the Brig was already in conversation with the flight controller.

He stood with the gaudy helmet tucked under one arm as he stripped off his gloves, but as David came up he turned to him and his wintry smile exposed the gold tooth in its nest of fur.

Lightly he punched David's arm. '*Ken*! Yes!' said Major-General Joshua Mordecai. 'You'll do.'

D avid was late to fetch Debra for dinner that evening, but she had already learned the reason from her father.

They went to the Select behind David's Tower, inside the Jaffa Gate of the old city. Its unpretentious interior, decorated with patterns of rope upon the walls, did not fully prepare David for the excellent meal that the Arab proprietor served with the minimum of delay – mousakha chicken, with nuts and spices on a bed of kous-kous.

They ate almost in silence, Debra quickly recognizing and respecting David's mood. He was in the grip of post-combat *tristesse*, the adrenalin hangover of stress and excitement, but slowly the good food in his belly and the heavy Carmel wine relaxed him, until over the thimble-sized cups of Turkish coffee, black and powerfully reeking of cardamon seed, Debra could ask, 'What happened today, David?'

He sipped the coffee before replying.

'I killed a man.' She set down her cup and studied his

face solemnly, and he began to speak, telling her the detail of it, the chase and the kill, until he ended lamely, 'I felt only satisfaction at the time. A sense of achievement. I knew I had done what was right.'

'And now?' she prompted him.

'Now I am sad,' he shrugged. 'I am saddened that I had to do it.'

'My father, who has always been a soldier, says that only those who do the actual fighting can truly know what it is to hate war.'

David nodded. 'Yes, I understand that now. I love to fly, but I hate to destroy.'

They were silent again, both of them considering their own personal vision of war, both of them trying to find words to express it.

'And yet it is necessary,' Debra broke the silence. 'We must fight – there is no other way.'

'There is no other way – with the sea at our backs and the Arabs at our throats.'

'You speak like an Israeli,' Debra challenged him softly.

'I made a decision today – or rather I was press-ganged by your father. He has given me three weeks to brush up my Hebrew, and complete the immigration formalities.'

'And then?' Debra leaned towards him.

'A commission in the air force. That was the only point I scored on, I had just enough strength to hold out for the equivalent rank I would have had back home. He haggled like a secondhand clothes dealer, but I had him, and he knew it. So he gave in at last. Acting major, with confirmation of rank at the end of twelve months.'

'That's wonderful, Davey, you'll be one of the youngest majors in the service.'

'Yeah,' David agreed, 'and after I've paid my taxes I'll have a salary a little less than a bus-driver back home.'

'Never mind,' Debra smiled for the first time. 'I'll help you with your Hebrew.'

'I was going to talk to you about that,' he answered her smile. 'Come on, let's get out of here. I'm restless tonight – and I want to walk.'

They strolled through the Christian quarter. The open stalls on each side were loaded with garish and exotic clothes, and leather work and jewellery, and the smells of spices and food and drains and stale humanity was almost solid in the narrow lanes where the arches met overhead.

Debra drew him into one of the antique stores in the Via Dolorosa, and the proprietor came to them, almost wriggling with pleasure.

'Ah, Miss Mordecai – and how is your dearly esteemed father?' Then he rushed into the back room to brew more coffee for them.

'He's one of the half-honest ones, and he lives in mortal fear of the Brig.'

Debra selected an antique solid gold Star of David on a slim golden neck chain, and though he had never before worn personal jewellery, David bowed his head and let her place it about his neck. The golden star lay against the coarse dark curls of his chest.

'That's the only decoration you'll ever get – we don't usually give medals,' she told him laughingly. 'But welcome to Israel anyway.'

'It's beautiful,' David was touched and embarrassed by the gift, 'thank you.' And he buttoned his shirt over it and then reached awkwardly to kiss her – but she drew away and warned him.

'Not in here. He's a Moslem, and he'd be very offended.'

'All right,' said David. 'Let's go and find some place where we won't hurt anybody's sensibilities.'

They went out through the Lion Gate in the great wall and found a stone bench in a quiet place amongst the olive trees of the Moslem cemetery. There was a half moon in

·the sky, silver and mysterious, and the night was warm and waiting, seemingly as expectant as a new bride.

'You can't stay on at the Intercontinental,' Debra told him, and they both looked up at its arched and lighted silhouette across the valley.

'Why not?'

'Well, first of all it's too expensive. On your salary you just can't afford it.'

'You don't really expect me to live on my salary?' David protested, but Debra ignored him and went on.

'And what is more important, you aren't a tourist any more. So you can't live like one.'

'What do you suggest?'

'We could find you an apartment.'

'Who would do the housework, and the laundry, and the cooking?' he protested vehemently. 'I haven't had much practice at that sort of thing.'

'I would,' said Debra, and he froze for an instant and then turned slowly on the seat to look at her.

'What did you say?'

'I said, I would,' she repeated firmly, and then her voice quavered. 'That's if you want me to.' He was silent for a long moment.

'See here, Debs. Are you talking about living together? I mean, playing house-house on a full-time basis – the whole bit?'

'That's precisely what I am talking about.'

'But—' He could think of nothing further to say. The idea was novel, breathtaking, and alive with enchanting possibilities. All David's previous experiences with the opposite sex had been profuse rather than deep, and he found himself on the frontiers of unexplored territory.

'Well?' Debra asked at last.

'Do you want to get married?' His voice cracked on the word, and he cleared his throat.

'I'm not sure that you are the finest marriage material in the market, my darling David. You are as beautiful as the dawn, and fun to be with – but you are also selfish, immature and spoiled stupid.'

'Thank you kindly.'

'Well, there is no point in me mincing words now, David, not when I am about to throw all caution aside and become your mistress.'

'Wow!' he exclaimed, with all the frost thawing from his voice. 'When you say it straight out like that – it almost blows my mind.'

'Me too,' Debra confessed. 'But one condition is that we wait until we have our own special place, you may recall that I'm not so high on public beaches or rocky islands.'

'I'll never forget,' David agreed. 'Does this mean that you *don't* want to marry me?' He found his mortal terror of matrimony fading under this slur on his potential marriage worth.

'I didn't say that either,' Debra demurred. 'But let's make that decision when both of us are ready for it.'

'Right on, doll,' said David, with an almost idiot grin of happiness spreading over his face.

'And now, Major Morgan, you may kiss me,' she said. 'But do try and help me remember the conditions.'

A long while later, they drew a little apart to breathe and a sudden thought made David frown with worry.

'My God,' he exclaimed, 'what will the Brig say!'

'He won't be joining us,' she told him, and they both laughed together, excited by their own wickedness.

'Seriously, what will you tell your parents?'

'I'll lie to them graciously, and they'll pretend to believe me. Let me worry about that.'

'*Beseder*,' he agreed readily.

'You are learning,' she applauded. 'Let's just try that kiss again – but this in time in Hebrew, please.'

'I love you,' he said in that language.

'Good boy,' she murmured. 'You are going to make a prize pupil.'

There was one more doubt to be set at rest, and Debra voiced it at the iron gate to the garden, when at last he took her home.

'Do you know what the *Bris*, the Covenant, is?'

'Sure,' he grinned, and made scissors out of his first and second finger. It seemed in the uncertain light that she blushed, and her voice was only just audible.

'Well, what about you?'

'That,' David told her severely, 'is a highly personal question, the answer to which little girls should find out for themselves,' and his expression became lascivious, 'the hard way.'

'All knowledge is precious as gold,' she said in a small voice, 'and be sure that I will seek the answer diligently.'

David discovered that the acquisition of an apartment in Jerusalem was a task much like the quest for the Holy Grail. Although the high-rise blocks were being thrown up with almost reckless energy, the demand for accommodation far outweighed the supply.

The father of one of Debra's students was an estate agent and the poor man took their problem to his heart; the waiting-list for the new blocks was endless, but an occasional apartment in one of the older buildings fell vacant, and he used all his influence for them.

At unexpected moments of the day, Debra would send out an urgent signal, and David would fetch her in a taxi at the University and they would get the hell across town, urging on the driver, to inspect the latest offering.

The last of these reminded David of a movie set from *Lawrence of Arabia* complete with a dispirited palm tree out front, a spectacular display of bright laundry hanging from every balcony and window, and all the sounds and smells of an Arab camel market and a nursery-school playground at recess rising from the courtyard.

There were two rooms and an alleged bathroom. The roses and wreathes of the wallpaper had faded, except in patches where hangings had protected their original pristine virulent colouring.

David pushed open the door of the bathroom and, without entering, inspected the raggedy linoleum floor-covering and the stained and chipped bath tub; then pushing the door further he discovered the toilet bowl festering quietly in the gloom with its seat set at a rakish angle like the halo of a drunken angel.

'You and Joe could work on it,' Debra suggested uncertainly. 'It's not really *that* bad.'

David shuddered, and closed the door as though it were the lid of a coffin.

'You're joking – of course,' he said, and Debra's determinedly bright smile cracked and her lip quivered.

'Oh, David, we are never going to find a place!'

'And I can't wait much longer.'

'Nor can I,' admitted Debra.

'Right.' David rubbed his hands together briskly. 'It's time to send in the first team.'

He was not sure what form the presence of Morgan Group would take in Jerusalem, but he found it listed in the business directory under 'Morgan Industrial Finance' and the Managing Director was a large mournful-looking gentleman named Aaron Cohen who had a suite of offices in the Leumi Bank building opposite the main post office. He was overcome with emotion to discover that one of the Morgan family had been ten days in Jerusalem without his knowledge.

David told him what he wanted, and in twenty hours he had it signed and paid for. Paul Morgan picked his executives with care, and Cohen was an example of this

88

attention. The price David must pay for this service was that Paul Morgan would have a full report of David's transaction, present whereabouts and future plans on his desk the next morning – but it was worth it.

Above the Hinnom canyon, facing Mount Zion with its impressive array of spires, the Montefiore quarter was being rebuilt as an integrated whole by some entrepreneur. All of it was clad in the lovely golden Jerusalem stone, and the designs of the houses were traditional and ageless. However, the interiors were lavishly modernized with tall cool rooms, mosaic-tiled bathrooms, and ceilings arched like those of a crusader church. Most of them had their own walled and private terraces. The one that Aaron Cohen procured for David was the pick of those that fronted Malik Street. The price was astronomical. That was the first question that Debra asked, once she had recovered her voice. She stood stunned upon the terrace beneath the single olive tree. The stone of the terrace had been cut and polished until it resembled old ivory, and she ran her fingers lightly over the carved front door. Her voice was hushed and her expression bemused.

'David! David! How much is this going to cost?'

'That's not important. What is important is whether you like it.'

'It's too beautiful. It's too much, David. We can't afford this.'

'It's paid for already.'

'Paid for?' She stared at him. 'How much, David?'

'If I said half a million Israeli pounds or a million, what difference would it make? It's only money.'

She clapped her hands over her ears. 'No!' she cried. 'Don't tell me! I'd feel so guilty I wouldn't be able to live in it.'

'Oh, so you are actually consenting to live in it.'

'Try me,' she said with emphasis. 'You just try me, lover!'

They stood in the central room that opened on to the

terrace, and although it was light and airy enough for the savage heat of summer that was coming, it smelled now of new paint and varnished woodwork.

'What are we going to do about furniture?' David asked.

'Furniture?' Debra repeated. 'I hadn't thought that far ahead.'

'For what I have in mind, we'll need at least one king-size bed.'

'Sex-maniac,' she said, and kissed him.

No modern furniture looked at home under the domed roof, or upon the stone-flagged floors. So they began to furnish from the bazaars and antique shops.

Debra solved the main problem with the discovery in a junk yard of an enormous brass bedstead from which they scraped the accumulated dirt; they polished it until it glowed, fitted it with a new inner-spring mattress, and covered it with a cream-coloured lace bedspread from Debra's bottom drawer.

They purchased *kelim* and woven woollen rugs by the bale from the Arab dealers in the old city, and scattered them thickly upon the stone floors, with leather cushions to sit upon and a low olive-wood table, inlaid with ebony and mother-of-pearl, to eat off. The rest of the furniture would come when they could find it for sale, or, failing that, have it custom-made by an Arab cabinet-maker that Debra knew of. Both the bed and the table were enormously heavy, and they needed muscle to move them, so they called for Joe. He and Hannah arrived in his tiny Japanese compact, and after they had recovered from the impact of the Morgan palace they fell to work enthusiastically with David supervising. Joe grunted and heaved, while Hannah disappeared with Debra into the modern American kitchen to exclaim with envy and admiration over the washing-machine, dryer, dish-washer and all the other appliances that went with the house. She helped to cook the first meal.

David had laid in a case of Goldstar beer, and after their labours they all gathered about the olive-wood table to warm the house and wet the roof.

David had expected Joe to be a little reserved, after all it was his baby sister who was being set up in a fancy house; but Joe was as natural as ever and enjoyed the beer and the company so well that Hannah had to intervene at last.

'It's late,' she said firmly.

'Late?' asked Joe. 'It's only nine o'clock.'

'On a night like tonight, that's late.'

'What do you mean?' Joe looked puzzled.

'Joseph Mordecai, diplomat extraordinary,' Hannah said with heavy sarcasm, and suddenly Joe's expression changed as he glanced from Debra to David guiltily, swallowed his beer in a single gulp, and hoisted Hannah to her feet by one arm.

'Come on,' he said. 'What are we sitting here for?'

David left the terrace lights burning, and they shone through the slats of the shuttered windows, so the room was softly lit, and the sounds from the outside world were so muted by distance and stone walls as to be a mere murmur that drifted from afar, and seemed rather to accentuate their aloneness than to spoil it.

The brass of the bedstead gleamed softly in the gloom, and the ivory lacework of the bedspread smelled of lavender and moth balls.

He lay upon the bed and watched her undress slowly, conscious of his eyes upon her and shy now as she had never been before.

Her body was slim and with a flowing line of waist and leg, young and tender-looking, with a child's awkward grace, and yet with a womanly thrust of hip and bosom.

She came to sit upon the edge of the bed, and he marvelled once again at the lustre and plasticity of her skin, at the subtlety of colouring where the sun had darkened it from soft cream to burned honey, and at the contrast of her dusky rose-tipped breasts and the dark thick bush of curls at the base of her softly curving stomach.

She leaned over him, still shyly, and touched his cheek with one finger, running down his throat on to his chest where the gold star lay upon the hard muscle.

'You are beautiful,' she whispered, and she saw it was true. For he was tall and straight with muscled shoulders and lean flanks and belly. The planes of his face were pure and perfect, perhaps its only fault lying in its very perfection. It was almost unreal, as though she were lying with some angel or god from out of mythology.

She twisted her legs up on to the bed, stretching out beside him upon the lace cover, and they lay on their sides facing each other, not touching but so close that she could feel the warmth of his belly upon her own like a soft desert wind, and his breath stirred the dark soft hair upon her cheek.

She sighed then, with happiness and contentment, like a traveller reaching the end of a long lonely journey.

'I love you,' she said for the first time, and reaching out she took his head, her fingers twining in the thick springing hair at the nape of his neck, and drew it tenderly to her breast.

Long afterwards the chill of night oozed into the room, and they came half-awake and crept together beneath the covers.

As they began drifting back into sleep she murmured sleepily, 'I'm so glad that surgery won't be necessary, after all,' and he chuckled softly.

'Wasn't it better finding out for yourself?'

'Much better, lover. Much, much better,' she admitted.

D ebra spent one entire evening explaining to David that a high-performance sports car was not a necessity for travel between his base and the house on Malik Street, for she knew her man's tastes by then. She pointed out that this was a country of young pioneers, and that extravagance and ostentation were out of place. David agreed vehemently, secure in the knowledge that Aaron Cohen and his minions were scouring the country for him.

Debra suggested a Japanese compact similar to Joe's, and David told her that he would certainly give that his serious consideration.

Aaron Cohen's henchman tracked down a Mercedes Benz 350 SL belonging to the German Chargé d'Affaires in Tel Aviv. This gentleman was returning to Berlin and wished to dispose of his auto, for a suitable consideration in negotiable cash. A single phone call was sufficient to arrange payment through the Crédit Suisse in Zurich.

It was golden bronze in colour, with a little under twenty thousand kilometres on the clock, and it had clearly been maintained with the loving care of an enthusiast.

Debra, returning on her motor scooter from the University, found this glorious machine parked at the top end of Malik Street, where a heavy chain denied access by all motor-driven vehicles to the village.

She took one look at it, and knew beyond all reasonable doubt who it belonged to. She was really quite angry when she stormed on to the terrace, but she pretended to be angrier than that.

'David Morgan, you really are absolutely impossible.'

'You catch on fast,' David agreed amiably; he was sunbathing on the terrace.

'How much did you pay for it?'

'Ask me another question, doll. That one is becoming monotonous.'

'You are really—' Debra paused and searched frantically

for a word of sufficient force. She found it and delivered it with relish, 'decadent!'

'You don't know the meaning of the word,' David told her gently as he rose from the cushions in the sun and drifted lazily in her direction. Though she had been his lover for only a mere three days she recognized the look in his eye and she began backing away.

'I will teach you the meaning,' he said. 'I am about to give you a practical demonstration of decadence in such a sensitive spot that you are likely to remember it for a long time.'

She ducked behind the olive tree as he lunged, and her books spilled across the terrace.

'Leave me! Hands off, you beast.'

He feinted right, and caught her as she fell for it. He picked her up easily across his chest.

'David Morgan, I warn you, I shall scream if you don't put me down this instant.'

'Let's hear it. Go ahead!' and she did, but in a ladylike fashion so as not to alarm the neighbours.

Joe, on the other hand, was delighted with the 350. The four of them took it on a trial run down the twisting road through the Wilderness of Judaea to the shores of the Dead Sea. The road challenged the car's suspension and David's driving skill, and they whooped with excitement through the bends. Even Debra was able to overcome her initial disapproval, and finally admitted it was beautiful – but still decadent.

They swam in the cool green waters of the oasis of Ein Gedi where they formed a deep rock pool before overflowing and running down into the thick saline water of the sea itself.

Hannah had brought her camera and she photographed Debra and David sitting together on the rocks beside the pool.

They were in their bathing costumes, Debra's brief

bikini showing off her fine young body as she half-turned to laugh into David's face. He smiled back at her, his face in profile and the dark sweep of his hair falling on to his forehead. The desert light picked out the pure features and the boldly stated facets of his beauty.

Hannah had a print of the photograph made for each of them, and later those squares of glossy photographic paper were all they had left of it, all that remained of the joy and the laughter of those days, like a lovely flower taken from the growing tree of life and pressed and dried, flattened and desiccated, deprived of its colour and perfume.

But the future threw no shadow over their happiness on that bright day, and with Joe driving this time they ran back for Jerusalem. Debra insisted that they stop for a group of tank corp boys hitch-hiking home on leave, and although David protested it was impossible, they squeezed three of them into the small cab. It was Debra's sop to her feelings of guilt, and she sat in the back seat with her arms around David's neck and they all sang the song that was that year a favourite with the young people of Israel, 'Let There be Peace'.

In the last few days while David waited to enter the air force, he loafed shamelessly, frittering the time away in small chores like having his uniforms tailored. He resisted Debra's suggestion that if regulation issue were good enough for her father, a general officer, then they might be good enough for David. Aaron Cohen supplied him with an introduction to his own tailor. Aaron was beginning to develop a fine respect for David's style.

Debra had arranged membership for David at the University Athletic Club, and he worked out in the first-class modern gym every day, and finished with twenty lengths of the Olympic-size swimming pool to keep himself in shape.

However, at other times, David merely lay sunbathing on the terrace, or fiddled with electrical plugs or other small tasks Debra had asked him to see to about the house.

As he moved through the cool and pleasant rooms, he would find an item belonging to Debra, a book or a brooch perhaps, and he would pick it up and fondle it briefly. Once a robe of hers thrown carelessly across the foot of the bed and redolent of her particular perfume gave him a physical pang as it reminded him sharply of her, and he held the silkiness to his face and breathed the scent of her, and grudged the hours until her return.

However, it was amongst her books that he discovered more about her than years of study would have revealed. She had crates of these piled in the unfurnished second bedroom which they were using as a temporary storeroom until they could find shelves and cupboards. One afternoon David began digging around in the crates. It was a literary mixed grill – Gibbon and Vidal, Shakespeare and Mailer, Solzhenitsyn and Mary Stewart, amongst other strange bedfellows. There was fiction and biography, history and poetry, Hebrew and English, softbacks and leather-bound editions – and a thin green-jacketed volume which he almost discarded before the author's name caught his attention. It was by D. Mordecai and with a feeling of discovery he turned to the flyleaf. *This Year, in Jerusalem*, a collection of poems, by Debra Mordecai.

He carried the book through to the bedroom, remembering to kick off his shoes before lying on the lace cover – she was very strict about that – and he turned to the first page.

There were five poems. The first was the title piece, the two-thousand-year promise of Jewry. 'Next year in Jerusalem' had become reality. It was a patriotic tribute to her land and even David, whose taste in writing ran to Maclean and Robbins, recognized that it had a superior quality. There were lines of startling beauty, evocative phrasing and penetrative glimpses. It was good, really good, and

David felt a strange proprietary pride – and a sense of awe. He had not guessed at these depths within her, these hidden areas of the mind.

When he came to the last poem, he found it was the shortest of the five, and it was a love poem – or rather it was a poem to someone dearly loved who was gone – and suddenly David was aware of the difference between that which was good and that which was magic.

He found himself shivering to the music of her words, felt the hair on his forearms standing erect with the haunting beauty of it, and then at last he felt himself choking on the sadness of it, the devastation of total loss, and the words swam as his eyes flooded, and he had to blink rapidly as the last terrible cry of the poem pierced him to the heart.

He lowered the book on to his chest, remembering what Joe had told him about the soldier who had died in the desert. A movement attracted his attention and he made a guilty effort to hide the book as he sat up. It was such a private thing, this poetry, that he felt like a thief.

Debra stood in the doorway of the bedroom watching him, leaning against the jamb with her hands clasped in front of her, studying him quietly.

He sat up on the bed and weighed the book in his hands. 'It's lovely,' he said at last, his voice was gruff with the emotions that her words had evoked.

'I'm glad you like it,' she said, and he realized that she was shy.

'Why did you not show it to me before?'

'I was afraid you might not like it.'

'You must have loved him very much?' he asked softly.

'Yes, I did,' she said, 'but now I love you.'

Then, finally, his posting came through and the Brig's hand was evident in it all, though Joe admitted that he had used his own family connections to influence the orders.

He was ordered to report to Mirage squadron 'Lance' which was a crack interceptor outfit based at the same hidden airfield from which he had first flown. Joe Mordecai was on the same squadron, and when he called at Malik Street to tell David the news, he showed no resentment that David would out-rank him, but instead he was confident that they would be able to fly together as a regular team. He spent the evening briefing David on squadron personnel, from 'Le Dauphin' the commanding officer, a French immigrant, down to the lowest mechanic. In the weeks ahead David would find Joe's advice and help invaluable, as he settled into his niche amongst this tightly-knit team of fliers.

The following day the tailor delivered his uniforms, and he wore one to surprise Debra when she backed in through the kitchen door, laden with books and groceries, using her bottom as a door buffer, her hair down behind and her dark glasses pushed up on top of her head.

She dropped her load by the sink, and circled him with her hands on her hips, her head cocked at a critical angle.

'I should like you to wear that, and come to pick me up at the University tomorrow afternoon, please,' she said at last.

'Why?'

'Because there are a few little bitches that lurk around the Lauterman Building. Some of them my students and some my colleagues. I want them to get a good look at you – and eat their tiny hearts out.'

He laughed. 'So you aren't ashamed of me?'

'Morgan, you are too beautiful for one person, you should have been born twins.'

It was their last day together, so he indulged her whimsy and wore his uniform to fetch her at the English Literature Department, and he was surprised to find how the dress affected the strangers he passed on the street – the girls smiled at him, the old ladies called *shalom*, even the guard at the University gates waved him through with a grin and a joke. To them all he was a guardian angel, one of those that had swept death from the very sky above them.

Debra hurried to meet and kiss him, and then walked beside him, her hand tucked proudly and possessively into the crook of his elbow. She took him to eat an early dinner at the staff dining-room in the rounded glass Belgium Building.

While they ate, a casual question of his revealed the subterfuge she had used to protect her reputation.

'I'll probably not get off the base for the first few weeks, but I'll write to you at Malik Street—'

'No,' she said quickly, 'I won't be staying there. It would be too lonely without you in that huge bed.'

'Where then? At your parents' home?'

'That would be a dead give-away. Every time you arrive back in town, I leave home! No, they think I am staying at the hostel here at the University. I told them I wanted to be closer to the department—'

'You've got a room here?' He stared at her.

'Of course, Davey. I have to be a little discreet. I couldn't tell my relatives, friends and employers to contact me care of Major David Morgan. This may be the twentieth century, and modern Israel, but I am still a Jewess, with a tradition of chastity and modesty behind me.'

For the first time David began to appreciate the magnitude of Debra's decision to come to him. He had taken it lightly compared to her.

'I'm going to miss you,' he said.

'And I you,' she replied.

'Let's go home.'

'Yes,' she agreed, laying aside her knife and fork. 'I can eat any old time.'

However, as they left Belgium House she exclaimed with exasperation: 'Damn, I have to have these books back by today. Can we go by the library? I'm sorry, Davey, it won't take a minute.'

So they climbed again to the main terrace and passed the brightly-lit plate-glass windows of the Students' Union Restaurant, and went on towards the solid square tower of the library whose windows were lighted already against the swiftly falling darkness. They had climbed the library steps and reached the glass doors when a party of students came pouring out, and they were forced to stand aside.

They were facing back the way they had come, across the plaza with its terraces and red-bud trees, towards the restaurant.

Suddenly the dusk of evening was lit by the searing white furnace glare of an explosion, and the glass windows of the restaurant were blown out in a glittering cloud of flying glass. It was as though a storm surf had burst upon a rock cliff, flinging out its shining droplets of spray, but this was a lethal spray that scythed down two girl students who were passing the windows at that moment.

Immediately after the flash of the explosion the blast swept across the terrace, a draught of violence that shook the red-bud trees and sent David and Debra reeling against the pillars of the library veranda. The air was driven in upon them so that their eardrums ached with the blow, and the breath was sucked from their lungs.

David caught her to him and held her for the moments of dreadful silence that followed the blast. As they stared so, a soft white fog of phosphorus smoke billowed from the gutted windows of the restaurant and began to roll and drift across the terrace.

Then the sounds reached them through their ringing

eardrums, the small tinkle and crunch of glass, the patter and crack of falling plaster and shattered furniture. A woman began to scream, and it broke the spell of horror.

There were shouts and running feet. One of the students near them began in a high hysterical voice, 'A bomb. They've bombed the café.'

One of the girls who had fallen under the storm of glass fragments staggered up and began running in small aimless circles, screaming in a thin passionless tone. She was white with plaster dust through which the blood poured in dark rivulets, drenching her skirt.

In David's arms Debra began to tremble. 'The swine,' she whispered, 'oh, the filthy murdering swine.'

From the smoking destruction of the shattered building another figure shambled with slow deliberation. The blast had torn his clothing from his body, and it hung from him in tatters, making him a strange scarecrow figure. He reached the terrace and sat down slowly, removed from his face the spectacles that were miraculously still in place and began fumbling to clean them on the rags of his shirt. Blood dripped from his chin.

'Come on,' grated David, 'we must help.' And they ran down the steps together.

The explosion had brought down part of the roof, trapping and crushing twenty-three of the students who had come here to eat and talk over the evening meal.

Others had been hurled about the large low hall, like the toys of a child in tantrum, and their blood turned the interior into a reeking charnel house. Some of them were crawling, creeping, or moving spasmodically amongst the tumbled furniture, broken crockery and spilled food. Some lay contorted as though in silent laughter at death's crude joke.

Afterwards they would learn that two young female members of El Fatah had enrolled in the university under false papers, and they had daily smuggled small quantities

101

of explosive on to the campus until they had accumulated sufficient for this outrage. A suitcase with a timing device had been left under a table and the two terrorists had walked out and got clean away. A week later they were on Damascus television, gloating over their success.

Now, however, there was no reason or explanation for this sudden burst of violence. It was as undirected, and yet as dreadfully effective as some natural cataclysm. Chilling in its insensate enormity, so that they, the living, worked in a kind of terrified frenzy, to save the injured and to carry from the shambles the broken bodies of the dead.

They laid them upon the lawns beneath the red-bud trees and covered them with sheets brought hurriedly from the nearest hostel. The long white bundles in a neat row upon the green grass was a memory David knew he would have for ever.

The ambulances came, with their sirens pulsing and rooflights flashing, to carry away death's harvest and the police cordoned off the site of the blast before David and Debra left and walked slowly down to where the Mercedes was parked in the lot. Both of them were filthy with dust and blood, and wearied with the sights and sounds of pain and mutilation. They drove in silence to Malik Street and showered off the smell and the dirt. Debra soaked David's uniform in cold water to remove the blood. Then she made coffee for them and they drank it, sitting side by side in the brass bed.

'So much that was good and strong died there tonight,' Debra said.

'Death is not the worst of it. Death is natural, it's the logical conclusion to all things. It was the torn and broken flesh that still lived which appalled me. Death has a sort of dignity, but the maimed are obscene.'

She looked at him with almost fear in her eyes. 'That's cruel, David.'

'In Africa there is a beautiful and fierce animal called

the sable antelope. They run together in herds of up to a hundred, but when one of them is hurt – wounded by a hunter or mauled by a lion – the lead bulls turn upon him and drive him from the herd. I remember my father telling me about that, he would say that if you want to be a winner then you must avoid the company of the losers for their despair is contagious.'

'God, David, that's a terribly hard way to look at life.'

'Perhaps,' David agreed, 'but then, you see, life is hard.'

When they made love, there was for the first time a quality of desperation in it, for it was the eve of parting and they had been reminded of their mortality.

In the morning David went to join his squadron and Debra locked the house on Malik Street.

Each day for seventeen days David flew two, and sometimes three, sorties. In the evenings, if they were not flying night interceptions, there were lectures and training films, and after that not much desire for anything but a quick meal and then sleep.

The Colonel, Le Dauphin, had flown one sortie with David. He was a small man with a relaxed manner and quick, shrewd eyes. He had made his judgement quickly.

After that first day, David and Joe flew together, and David moved his gear into the locker across from Joe in the underground quarters that the crews on standby used.

In those seventeen days the last links in an iron friendship were forged. David's flair and dash balanced perfectly with Joe's rock-solid dependability.

David would always be the star while Joe seemed destined to be the accompanist, the straight guy who was a perfect foil, the wingman without personal ambition for glory whose talent was to put his number one into the position for the strike.

Quickly they developed into a truly formidable team, so perfectly in accord that communication in the air was almost extra-sensory, similar to the instantaneous reaction of the bird flock or the shoal of fish.

Joe sitting out there behind him was for David like a million dollars in insurance. His tail was secure and he could concentrate on the special task that his superior eyesight and lightning reactions were so suited to. David was the gunfighter, in a service where the gunfighter was supreme.

The IAF had been the first to appreciate the shortcomings of the-air-to-air missile, and relied heavily on the classic type of air combat. A missile could be induced to 'run stupid'. It was possible to make its computer think in a set pattern and then sucker it with a break in the pattern. For every three hundred missile launches in air-to-air combat, a single strike could be expected.

However, if you had a gunfighter coming up into your six o'clock position with his finger on the trigger of twin 30-mm cannons, capable of pouring twelve thousand shells a minute into you, then your chances were considerably lighter than three hundred to one.

Joe also had his own special talent. The forward scanning radar of the Mirage was a complicated and sophisticated body of electronics, that required firstly a high degree of manual dexterity. The mechanism was operated entirely by the left hand, and the fingers of that hand had to move like those of a concert pianist. However, more important was the 'feel' for the instrument, a lover's touch to draw the optimum results from it. Joe had the 'feel', David did not.

They flew training interceptions, day and night, against high-flying and low-altitude practice targets. They flew low-level training strikes, and at other times they went out high over the Mediterranean and engaged each other in plane-to-plane dogfights.

However, Desert Flower steered them tactfully away from any actual or potential combat situation. They were watching David.

At the end of the period, David's service dossier passed over Major-General Mordecai's desk. Personnel was the Brig's special responsibility and although each officer's dossier was reviewed by him regularly, he had asked particularly to see David's.

The dossier was still slim, compared to the bulky tomes of some of the old salts, and the Brig flicked quickly over his own initial recommendation and the documents of David's acting commission. Then he stopped to read the later reports and results. He grinned wolfishly as he saw the gunnery report. He could pick them out of a crowd, he thought with satisfaction.

At last he came to Le Dauphin's personal appraisal:

'Morgan is a pilot of exceptional ability. Recommended that acting rank be confirmed and that he be placed on fully operational basis forthwith.'

The Brig picked up the red pen that was his own special prerogative and scrawled 'I agree' at the foot of the report.

That took care of Morgan, the pilot. He could now consider Morgan, the man. His expression became bleak and severe. Debra's sudden desire to leave home almost immediately David arrived in Jerusalem had been too much of a coincidence for a man who was trained to search for underlying motives and meanings.

It had taken him two days and a few phone calls to learn that Debra was merely using the hostel room at the University as an accommodation address, and that her real domestic arrangements were more comfortable.

The Brig did not approve, very definitely not. Yet he knew that it was beyond his jurisdiction. He had learned that his daughter had inherited his own iron will. Confrontations between them were cataclysmic events that shook the family to its foundations and seldom ended in satisfactory results.

Although he spent much of his time with young people, still he found the new values hard to live with – let alone accept. He remembered the physical agony of his long and chaste engagement to Ruth with pride, like a veteran reviewing an old campaign.

'Well, at the least she has the sense not to flaunt it, not to bring shame on us all. She has spared her mother that.' The Brig closed the dossier firmly.

Le Dauphin called David into his office and told him of his change in status. He would go on regular 'green' standby, which meant four nights a week on base.

David would have to undergo his paratrooper training in unarmed combat and weapons. A downed pilot in Arab territory had a much better chance of survival if he was proficient in this type of fighting.

David went straight from Le Dauphin's office to the telephone in the crew-room. He caught Debra before she left the Lauterman Building for lunch.

'Warm the bed, wench,' he told her, 'I'll be home tomorrow night.'

He and Joe drove up to Jerusalem in the Mercedes, and he wasn't listening to Joe's low rumbling voice until a thumb like an oar prodded his ribs.

'Sorry, Joe, I was thinking.'

'Well, stop it. Your thoughts are misting up the windows.'

'What did you say?'

'I was talking about the wedding – Hannah and me.'

David realized it was only a month away now, and he expected the excitement amongst the women was heavy as static on a summer's day before the rain. Debra's letters had been filled with news of the arrangements.

'I would be happy if you will stand up with me, and be

my witness. You fly as wingman for a change, and I'll take on the target.'

David realized that he was being honoured by the request and he accepted with proper solemnity. Secretly he was amused. Like most young Israelis David had spoken to, both Debra and Joe claimed not to be religious. He had learned that this was a pose. All of them were very conscious of their religious heritage, and well versed in the history and practice of Judaism. They followed all the laws of living that were not oppressive, and which accorded with a modern and busy existence.

To them 'religious' meant dressing in the black robes and wide-brimmed hats of the ultra-orthodox Mea Shearim, or in following a routine for daily living that was crippling in its restrictions.

The wedding would be a traditional affair, complete with all the ceremony and the rich symbolism, complicated only by the security precautions which would have to be most rigorously enforced.

The ceremony was to take place in the Brig's garden, for Hannah was an orphan. Also the secluded garden and fortress-like walls about it were easier to protect.

Amongst the guests would be many prominent figures in the government and the military.

'At the last count we have five generals and eighteen colonels on the list,' Joe told him, 'to which add most of the cabinet, even Golda has promised to try and be there. So you see, it's going to make a nice juicy target for our friends in Black September.' Joe scowled and lit two cigarettes, passing one to David. 'If it wasn't for Hannah, you know how women feel about weddings, I would just as soon go down to a registry office.'

'You are fooling nobody,' David grinned. 'You are looking forward to it.'

'Sure.' Joe's scowl cleared. 'It's going to be good to have

our own place, like you and Debs. I wish Hannah had been sensible. A year of pretending.' He shook his head. 'Thank God it's nearly over.'

He dropped Joe in the lane outside the Brig's house in Ein Karem.

'I won't bother to invite you in,' Joe said. 'I guess you've got plans.'

'Good guess,' David smiled. 'Will we see you and Hannah? Come to dinner tomorrow night.'

Joe shook his head again. 'I'm taking Hannah down to Ashkelon to visit her parents' graves. It's traditional before a wedding. Perhaps we'll see you Saturday.'

'Right then, I'll try and make it. Debra will want to see you. *Shalom*, Joe.'

'*Shalom, shalom*,' said Joe and David pulled away, flicking the gears in a racing change as he put the Mercedes at the hill. Suddenly he was in a hurry.

The terrace door stood open in welcome, and she was waiting for him. Debra was vibrant and tense with expectation, sitting in one of the new leather chairs with her legs curled under her. Her hair was freshly washed and shimmering like a starling's wing. She was dressed in a billowing kaftan of light silk and subtle honey colours that picked out the gold in her eyes.

She came out of the chair in a swirl of silk, and ran barefooted across the rugs to meet him.

'David! David!' she cried and he caught her up and spun on his heels, laughing with her.

Afterwards she led him proudly about the rooms and showed him the changes and additions that had turned it into a real home during his absence. David had convinced her that cost was not fundamental and they had chosen the designs for the furniture together. These had been made and delivered by Debra's tame Arab and she had arranged them as they had planned it. It was all in soft leather and dark wood, lustrous copper and brass, set off by the bright rugs. However, there was one article he had never seen before – a large oil painting on canvas, and Debra had hung it unframed on the freshly painted white wall facing the terrace. It was the only decoration upon the wall, and any other would have been insignificant beside it. It was a harsh dominant landscape, a desert scene which captured the soul of the wilderness; the colours were hot and fierce and seemed to pour through the room like the rays of the desert sun itself.

Debra held his hand and watched David's face anxiously for a reaction as he studied it.

'Wow!' he said at last.

'You like it?' She was relieved.

'It's terrific. Where did you get it?'

'A gift from the artist. She's an old friend.'

'She?'

'That's right. We are driving up to Tiberias tomorrow to have lunch with her. I've told her all about you, and she wants to meet you.'

'What's she like?'

'She's one of our leading artists, and her name is Ella Kadesh, but apart from that I can't begin to describe her. All I can do is promise you an entertaining day.'

Debra had prepared a special dish of lamb and olives and they ate it on the terrace under the olive tree. Again the talk turned to Joe's wedding, and in the midst of it David asked abruptly, 'What made you decide to come with me – without marrying?'

She replied after a moment. 'I discovered that I loved you, and I knew that you were too impatient to play the waiting game. I knew that if I didn't, I might lose you again.'

'Until recently, I didn't realize what a big decision it was,' he mused, and she sipped her wine without replying.

'Let's get married, Debs,' he broke the silence.

'Yes,' she nodded. 'That's a splendid idea.'

'Soon,' he said. 'Soon as possible.'

'Not before Hannah. I don't want to steal her day from her.'

'Right,' David agreed, 'but immediately afterwards.'

'Morgan, you have got yourself a date,' she told him.

It was a three-hour drive to Tiberias so they rose as soon as the sun came through the shutters and tiger-striped the wall above the brass bed. To save time, they shared one bath, sitting facing each other, waist-deep in suds.

'Ella is the rudest person you'll ever meet,' Debra warned him. She looked like a little girl this morning with her hair piled on top of her head and secured with a pink ribbon. 'The greater the impression you make on her, the ruder she will be, and you are expected to retaliate in kind. So please, David, don't lose your temper.'

David scooped up a dab of suds with a finger and smeared it on the tip of her nose.

'I promise,' he said.

They drove down to Jericho, and then turned north along the valley of the Jordan, following the high barbed-wire fence of the border with its warning notice boards for the minefields, and the regular motorized patrols grinding deliberately along the winding road.

It was hot in the valley and they drove with the windows open and Debra pulled her skirt high around her waist to cool her long brown legs.

'Better not do that if you want to be in time for lunch,' David warned her, and she smoothed them down hurriedly.

'Nothing is safe with you around,' she protested.

They came at last out of the barren land into the fertile basin of the Kibbutzim below Galilee, and again the smell of orange blossom was so strong on the warm air that it was difficult to breathe.

At last they saw the waters of the lake flashing amongst the date palms and Debra touched his arm.

110

'Slow down, Davey. Ella's place is a few miles this side of Tiberias. That's the turn-off, up ahead.'

It was a track that led down to the lake shore and it ended against a wall of ancient stone blocks. Five other cars were parked there already.

'Ella's having one of her lunch parties,' Debra remarked and led him to a gate in the wall. Beyond was a small ruined castle. The tumbled walls formed weird shapes and the stone was black with age; over them grew flamboyant creepers of bougainvillaea and the tall palms clattered their fronds in the light breeze that came off the lake. Other exotic flowering shrubs grew upon the green lawns.

Part of the ruins had been restored and renovated into a picturesque and unusual lakeside home, with a wide patio and a stone jetty against which a motor-boat was moored. Across the green waters of the lake rose the dark smooth whale-back of the Golan Heights.

'It was a crusader fortress,' Debra explained. 'One of the guard posts for traffic across the lake and part of the series leading up to the great castle on the Horns of Hittem that the Moslems destroyed when they drove the crusaders out of the Holy Land. Ella's grandfather purchased it during the Allenby administration, but it was a ruin until she did it up after the War of Independence.'

The care with which the alterations had been made so as not to spoil the romantic beauty of the site was a tribute to Ella Kadesh's artistic vision, which was completely at odds with the woman herself.

She was enormous; not simply fat or tall, but big. Her hands and her feet were huge, her fingers clustered with rings and semi-precious stones and her toenails through the open sandals were painted a glaring crimson, as if to flaunt their size. She stood as tall as David, but the tent-like dress that billowed about her was covered with great explosive designs that enhanced her bulk until she seemed to make

111

up two of him. She wore a wig of tiered curls, flaming red in colour and dangling gold earrings. It seemed she must have applied her eye make-up with a spade, and her rouge with a spray gun. She removed the thin black cheroot from her mouth and kissed Debra before she turned to study David. Her voice was gravelly, hoarse with cheroot smoke and brandy.

'I had not expected you to be so beautiful,' she said, and Debra quailed at the expression in David's eyes. 'I do not like beauty. It is so often deceptive, or inconsequential. It usually hides something deadly – like the glittering beauty of the cobra – or like the pretty wrapper of a candy bar, it contains cloying sweetness and a soft centre.' She shook the stiffly lacquered curls of her wig, and fixed David with her shrewd little eyes. 'No, I prefer ugliness to beauty.'

David smiled at her with all his charms upon display. 'Yes,' he agreed, 'having met you, and seen some of your work, I can understand that.'

She let out a cackle of raucous laughter, and clapped the cheroot back in her mouth. 'Well now, at the very least we are not dealing with a chocolate soldier.' She placed a huge masculine arm about David's shoulders and led him to meet the company.

They were a mixed dozen, all intellectuals – artists, writers, teachers, journalists – and David was content to sit beside Debra in the mild sunshine and enjoy the beer and the amusing conversation. However, Ella would not let him relax for long and when they sat down to the gargantuan *alfresco* meal of cold fish and poultry, she attacked him again.

'Your martial airs and affectations, your pomp and finery. A plague on it I say, a pox on your patriotism, and courage – on your fearlessness and your orders of chivalry. It is all sham and pretence, an excuse for you to stink up the earth with piles of carrion.'

'I wonder if you will feel the same when a platoon of

112

Syrian infantry break in here to rape you,' David challenged her.

'My boy, I find it so difficult to get laid these days that I should pray for such a heaven-sent opportunity.' She let out a mighty hoot of laughter and her wig slipped forward at an abandoned angle. Nothing was safe from her, and she pushed the wig back into place and streamed straight into the attack again.

'Your male bombast, your selfish arrogance. To you this woman—' and she indicated Debra with a turkey leg, '– to you she is merely a receptacle for your seething careless sperm. It matters not to you that she is a promise for the future, that within her are the seeds of a great writing talent. No, to you she is a rubbing block, a convenient means to a—'

Debra interrupted her. 'That definitely is enough, I will not allow a public debate on my bedroom,' and Ella turned towards her with the battle lust lighting her eyes.

'Your gift is not yours to use as you wish. You hold it in trust for all mankind, and you have a duty to them. That duty is to exercise your gift, to allow it to grow and blossom and give forth fruit.' She used the turkey leg like a judge's gavel, banging the edge of her plate with it, to silence Debra's protests.

'Have you written a word since you took young Mars to your heart? What of the novel we discussed on this very terrace a year ago? Have your animal passions swamped all else? Has the screeching of your ovaries—'

'Stop it, Ella!' Debra was angry now, her cheeks flushed and her brown eyes snapping.

'Yes! Yes!' Ella tossed the bone aside and sucked her fingers noisily. 'Ashamed you should be, angry with your-self—'

'Damn you,' Debra flared at her.

'Damn me if you will – but you are damned yourself if you do not write! Write, woman, write!' She sat back and the wicker chair protested at the movement of her vast body. 'All right, now we will all go for a swim. David has not seen me in a bikini yet – much he will care for that skinny little wench when he does!'

They drove back to Jerusalem in the night, flushed with the sun, and although the Mercedes seats had not been designed for lovers, Debra managed to sit close up against him.

'She's right, you know,' David broke a long contented silence. 'You must write, Debs.'

'Oh, I will,' she answered lightly.

'When?' he persisted, and to distract him she snuggled a little closer.

'One of these days,' she whispered as she made her dark head comfortable on his shoulder.

'One of these days,' he mimicked her.

'Don't bug me, Morgan.' She was already half-asleep.

'Stop being evasive.' He stroked her hair with his free hand. 'And don't go to sleep while I'm talking to you.'

'David, my darling, we have a lifetime – and more,' she murmured. 'You have made me immortal. You and I shall live for a thousand years, and there will be time for everything.'

Perhaps the dark gods heard her boast, and they chuckled sardonically and nudged each other.

On Saturday Joe and Hannah came to the house on Malik Street, and after lunch they decided on a tourist excursion for David and the four of them climbed Mount Zion across the valley. They entered the labyrinth of corridors that led to David's tomb, covered with splendid embroidered cloth and silver crowns and Torah covers. From there it was a few steps to the room of Christ's last supper in the same building, so closely interwoven were the traditions of Judaism and Christianity in this citadel.

Afterwards they entered the old city through the Zion gate and followed the wall around to the centre of Judaism, the tall cliff of massive stone blocks, bevelled in the fashion of Herodian times, which was all that remained of the fabulous second temple of Herod, destroyed two thousand years before by the Romans.

They were searched at the gate and then joined the stream of worshippers flocking down towards the wall. At the barrier they stood for a long time in silence. David felt again the stirring of a deep race memory, a hollow feeling of the soul which longed to be filled.

The men prayed facing the wall, many of them in the long black coats of the Orthodox Jew with the ringlets dangling against their cheeks as they rocked and swayed in religious ecstasy. Within the enclosure of the right-hand side, the women seemed more reserved in their devotions.

Joe spoke at last, a little embarrassed and in a gruff tone. 'I think I'll just go say a *sh'ma*.'

'Yes,' Hannah agreed. 'Are you coming with me, Debra?'

'A moment.' Debra turned to David, and took something from her handbag. 'I made it for you for the wedding,' she said. 'But wear it now.'

It was a yarmulke, an embroidered prayer cap of black satin.

'Go with Joe,' she said. 'He will show you what to do.'

The girls moved off to the women's enclosure and David placed the cap upon his head and followed Joe down to the wall.

A *shamash* came to them, an old man with a long silver beard, and he helped David bind upon his right arm a tiny leather box containing a portion of the Torah.

'So you shall lay these words upon your heart and your soul, and you shall bind them upon your right arm—'

Then he spread a *tallit* across David's shoulders, a tasselled shawl of woven wool, and he led him to the wall, and he began to repeat after the *shamash*:

'Hear, O Israel, the Lord our God, the Lord is one—'

His voice grew surer as he remembered the words from

115

long ago, and he looked up at the wall of massive stone blocks that towered high above him. Thousands of previous worshippers had written down their prayers on scraps of paper and wedged them into the joints between the blocks, and around him rose the plaintive voices of spoken prayer. It seemed to David that in his imagination a golden beam of prayer rose from this holy place towards the heavens.

Afterwards they left the enclosure and climbed the stairs into the Jewish quarter, and the good feeling remained with David, glowing warmly in his belly.

That evening they sat together on the terrace drinking Goldstar beer and splitting sunflower seeds for the nutty kernels, and naturally the talk turned to God and religion.

Joe said, 'I'm an Israeli and then a Jew. First my country, and a long way behind that comes my religion.'

But David remembered the expression on his face as he prayed against the wailing wall.

The talk lasted until late, and David glimpsed the vast body of his religious heritage.

'I would like to learn a little more about it all,' he admitted, and Debra said nothing but when she packed for him to go on base that night she placed a copy of Herman Wouk's *This is My God* on top of his clean uniforms.

He read it and when next he returned to Malik Street, he asked for more. She picked them for him, English works at first but then Hebrew, as his grip upon the language became stronger. They were not religious works only, but histories and historical novels that excited his interest in this ancient centre of civilization which for three thousand years had been a crossroads and a battleground.

He read anything and everything that she put into his case, from Josephus Flavius to Leon Uris.

This led to a desire to see and inspect the ground. It became so that much of the time that they were free together was spent in these explorations. They began with the hill-top fortress of Herod at Masada where the zealots had killed each other rather than submit to Rome, and from there they moved off the tourist beat to the lesser-known historical sites.

In those long sunlit days they might eat their basket lunch sitting on the ruins of a Roman aqueduct and watching a falcon working the thermals that rose off the floor of the desert, after they had searched the bed of a dry wadi for coins and arrowheads brought down by the last rains.

Around them rose the tall cliffs of orange and golden stone, and the light was so clean and stark that it seemed they could see for ever, and the silence so vast that they were the only living things in the world.

They were the happiest days that David had ever known, and they gave point and meaning to the weary hours of squadron standby, and when the day had ended there was always the house on Malik Street with its warmth and laughter and love.

Joe and David arranged leave of absence from the base for the wedding. It was a time of quiet, and Le Dauphin let them go without protest, for he would be a guest.

They drove up to Jerusalem the day before and were immediately conscripted to assist with the arrangements. David laboured mightily as a taxi-driver and trucker. The Mercedes transported everything from flowers to musical instruments and distant relatives.

The Brig's garden was decorated with palm leaves and coloured bunting. In the centre stood the *huppah*, a canopy worked with religious symbols in blue and gold, the Star of David and the grapes and ears of wheat, the pomegranates and all the other symbols of fertility. Beneath it, the marriage ceremony would take place. Trestle tables covered with bright cloths and set with bowls of flowers and dishes of fruit were arranged beneath the olive trees. There were places for three hundred guests, an open space for the dancing, a raised timber stand hung with flags for the band.

The catering was contracted out to a professional firm and the menu had been carefully decided upon by the chef and the women. It would have two high points – an enormous stuffed tuna, again a symbol of fertility, and a lamb dish in the bedouin style served upon enormous copper salvers.

On the Sunday of the wedding, David drove Debra to the home of the chief surgeon of Hadassah Hospital. Hannah was one of his theatre sisters and he had insisted that she use his home to prepare for the wedding. Debra was to assist her, and David left them and drove on to Ein Karem. The lane leading to the house was cordoned off and thick with Secret Service men and paratroopers.

While he watched Joe dressing, losing and finding the ring, and sweating with nerves, David lay on Joe's bed and gave him bad advice. They could hear the guests gathering in the garden below, and David stood up and went to the window. He watched an air force colonel being carefully scrutinized and searched at the gates, but taking it all in good part.

'They are being pretty thorough,' David remarked.

'Hannah has asked to have as few as possible of the guards in the garden. So they are being damned careful about who they let in.' Joe had at last completed dressing and already he was beginning to sweat through the armpits of his uniform.

'How do I look?' he asked anxiously.

'God, you handsome beast,' David told him.

'Piss off, Morgan,' Joe grinned at him, crammed his cap on to his head and glanced at his watch. 'Let's go,' he said.

The Chief Rabbi of the army was waiting with the Brig and the others in the Brig's study. The Rabbi was the mild-mannered man who had personally liberated the Tomb of the Patriarchs in the war of '67. During the advance on Hebron, he had driven a jeep through the disintegrating Arab lines, shot open the door to the tomb with a submachine-gun and chased the Arab guards screaming over the rear wall.

Joe sat at the Brig's desk and signed the *ketubbah*, the marriage contract, then the Rabbi handed him a silken cloth which Joe lifted in a formal act of acquisition to a chorus of congratulatory '*Mazal tovs*' from the witnesses.

The bridegroom's party trooped out into the crowded garden now to await the arrival of the bride, and she came accompanied by the chief surgeon standing in for her dead father, and a party of festively dressed women, including Debra and her mother. They all carried lighted candles.

To David, Hannah had never been particularly attractive, she was too tall and severe in body and expression; however, in her white bridal dress and veil she was transformed.

She seemed to float cloudlike upon the billowing white skirts, and her face was softened by the veil and by the inner happiness that seemed to glow through her green eyes. Red-gold hair framed her cheeks, and the freckles were disguised under make-up applied by Debra's cunning hand. She had used it to mute the rather harsh lines of Hannah's bony nose, and the result was that Hannah was as near to beautiful as she would ever come.

Joe, looking big and handsome in his air force tans, went forward eagerly to meet her at the gate to the garden and to lower the veil over her face in the ceremony of *bedeken dikalle*.

Joe moved to the *chuppah* canopy where the Rabbi waited with a *tallit* over his shoulders. After Joe the women led Hannah, each of them still carrying a burning candle, and the Rabbi chanted a blessing as the women and the bride circled Joe seven times in a magical circle which in olden times would serve to ward off evil spirits. At last bride and groom stood side by side, facing towards the site of the Temple with the guests and witnesses pressed closely about them and the ceremony proper began.

The Rabbi spoke the benediction over a goblet of wine from which bride and groom both drank. Then Joe turned to Hannah, her face still veiled, and he placed the plain gold ring upon her right forefinger.

'Behold you are consecrated unto me by this ring, according to the law of Moses and Israel.'

Then Joe broke the glass under his heel and the sharp crunch was a signal for an outburst of music and song and gaiety. David left Joe's side and worked his way through the joyous crowd of guests to where Debra waited for him.

She wore a gown of yellow and she had fresh flowers in the dark sheen of her hair. David smelled their perfume as he hugged her surreptitiously about the waist and whispered in her ear, 'You next, my beauty!' and she whispered back, 'Yes, please!'

Joe took Hannah on his arm, and then went to the improvised dance floor. The band began with a light bouncy tune and all the younger ones flocked to join them – while the elders spread out at the tables beneath the palm-decked trellis.

Yet amongst all the laughter and the gaiety, the uniforms added a sombre touch; almost every second man was adorned with the trappings of war, and at the garden gate and the entrance to the kitchens were uniformed paratrooper guards each with an Uzi submachine-gun slung at his shoulder. It was easy to pick out the Secret Service men. They were the ones in civilian clothes who moved without smiling, alert and vigilant, amongst the guests.

David and Debra danced together, and she was so light and warm and strong in his arms that when the band paused for breath he resented it. He led her to a quiet corner, and they stood together, discussing the other guests

120

in the most disrespectful terms until Debra giggled at some particularly outrageous remark and struck his arm lightly.

'You are terrible.' She leaned against him. 'I'm dying of thirst, won't you get me something to drink?'

'A glass of cold white wine?' he suggested.

'Lovely,' she said, smiling up into his face. For a moment they studied each other, and suddenly David felt something dark welling up from within him, a terrible despair, a premonition of impending loss. It was a physical thing and he could feel the chill of it enclose his chest and squeeze out all the happiness and the joy.

'What is it, David?' Her own expression altered in sympathy with his, and she tightened her grip on his arm.

'Nothing.' Abruptly he pulled away from her, trying to fight off the feeling. 'It's nothing,' he repeated, but it was still strong in his belly and he felt a wave of nausea from it. 'I'll get you the wine,' he said and turned away.

He made his way towards the bar, pushing gently through the throng. The Brig caught his eye and smiled bleakly across the garden at him. Joe was with his father and he called to David, laughing, with one arm around his bride. Hannah had her veil pushed up and her freckles were beginning to emerge from under the make-up, glowing vividly against the snow-white lace. David waved at them but went on towards the open-air bar at the end of the garden, the mood of sadness was still on him and he didn't want to talk to Joe now.

So he was cut off from Debra at the moment when, with a flourish, a procession of white-jacketed waiters came in through the iron gate of the garden. Each of them carried a huge copper salver from which, even in the warm sun, rose tendrils of steam, and the odour of meat and fish and spices filled the garden. There were gasps and cries of appreciation from the guests.

A way opened for them towards the high table on the

raised terrace which led to the kitchen doors and the house.

The procession of waiters passed close to David, and suddenly his attention was drawn from the display of fine food to the face of the second waiter in line. He was a man of medium height and dark complexion, a mahogany face with a thickly drooping moustache.

He was sweating. That was what had drawn David's attention, his face was shiny with sweat. Droplets clung in his moustache and slid down his cheeks. The white jacket was sodden at the armpits as he lifted the gigantic platter on high.

At the moment that he drew level with David their eyes met for an instant. David realized that the man was in the grip of some deep emotion – fear, perhaps, or exhilaration. Then the waiter seemed to become aware of David's scrutiny and his eyes slid nervously away.

David felt suspicion begin to chill his arms as the three figures climbed the stone stairs, and filed behind the table.

The waiter glanced again at David, saw that his gaze was still locked upon his face, and then he said something out of the corner of his mouth to one of his companions. He also glanced at David, and caught his stare, and his expression was sufficient to send alarm flaring urgently through David's chest and brain. Something was happening, something dangerous and ugly, he was certain of it.

Wildly he looked about for the guards. There were two of them on the terrace behind the line of waiters, and one near David beside the gate.

David shoved his way desperately towards him, mindless of the outraged comments of those in his way. He was watching the three waiters and so he saw it begin to happen.

It had obviously been carefully rehearsed, for as the three waiters placed the salvers upon the table to the laughter and applause of the guests crowded in the garden below them, so they drew back the sheets of plastic on which a thin display of food had been arranged to cover the deadly load that each copper salver carried.

The brown-faced waiter lifted a machine-pistol from under the plastic sheet, and turned swiftly to fire a traversing burst into the two paratroopers behind him at point-blank range. The clattering thunder of automatic fire was deafening in the walled garden, and the stream of bullets slashed through the bellies of the two guards like a monstrous cleaver, almost cutting them in half.

The waiter on David's left was a wizened monkey-faced man, with bright black berries for eyes. He, too, lifted a machine pistol from his salver, and he crouched over it and fired a burst at the paratrooper by the gate.

They were going for the guards, taking them out first. The pistol shook and roared in his fists, and the bullets socked into human flesh with a rubbery thumping sound.

The guard had cleared his Uzi, and was trying to aim as a bullet hit him in the mouth and snapped his head back, his paratrooper beret spinning high into the air. The machine-gun flew from his arms as he fell, and it slid across the tiles towards David. David dropped flat below the stone steps of the terrace as the Arab gunners turned their pistols on the wedding crowd, hosing the courtyard with a triple stream of bullets, and unleashing a hurricane of screams and shouts and desperate cries to join the roar of the guns.

Across the yard, a security agent had the pistol out of his shoulder holster and he dropped into the marksman crouch, holding the pistol with both arms extended as he aimed. He fired twice and hit the monkey-faced gunman, sending him reeling back against the wall, but he stayed on his feet and returned the agent's fire with the machine-pistol, knocking him down and rolling him across the paving stones.

The yard was filled with a panic-stricken mob, a struggling mass of humanity, that screamed and fell and crawled and died beneath the flail of the guns.

Two bullets caught Hannah in the chest, smashing her backwards over a table of glasses and bottles that shattered about her. The bright blood spurted from the wounds, drenching the front of her white wedding gown.

The centre gunman dropped his pistol as it emptied, and he stooped quickly over the copper salver and came up with a grenade in each hand. He hurled them into the struggling, screaming throng and the double blast was devastating, twin bursts of brightest white flame and the terrible sweep of shrapnel. The screams of the women rose louder, seeming as deafening as the gunfire – and the gunman stooped once more and his hands held another load of grenades.

All this had taken only seconds, but a fleeting moment of time to turn festivity into shocking carnage and torn flesh.

David left the shelter of the stone steps. He rolled swiftly across the flags towards the abandoned Uzi, and he came up on his knees, holding it at the hip. His paratrooper training made his actions automatic.

The wounded gunman saw him, and turned towards him, staggering slightly, pushing himself weakly away from the wall. His one arm was shattered and hung loosely in the tattered, blood-soaked sleeve of his jacket, but he lifted the machine-pistol and aimed at David.

David fired first, the bullets struck bursts of plaster from the wall behind the Arab and David corrected his aim. The bullets drove the gunman backwards, pinning him to the wall, while his body jumped and shook and twitched. He slumped down leaving a glistening wet smear of blood down the white plaster.

David swivelled the gun on to the Arab beside the kitchen door. He was poised to throw his next grenade, right arm extended behind him, both fists filled with the deadly steel balls. He was shouting something, a challenge or a war cry, a harsh triumphant screech that carried clearly above the screams of his victims.

Before he could release the grenade, David hit him with a full burst, a dozen bullets that smashed into his chest and belly, and the Arab dropped both grenades at his feet and doubled over clutching at his broken body, trying to stem the flood of his life blood with his bare hands.

The grenades were short fused and they exploded almost immediately, engulfing the dying man in a net of fire and shredding his body from the waist down. The same explosion knocked down the third assassin at the end of the terrace, and David came to his feet and charged up the steps.

The third and last Arab was mortally wounded, his head and chest torn by grenade fragments, but he was still alive, thrashing about weakly as he groped for the machine-pistol that lay beside him in a puddle of his own blood.

David was consumed by a terrible rage. He found that he was screaming and raging like a maniac, and he crouched at the head of the stairs and aimed at the dying Arab.

The Arab had the machine-pistol and was lifting it with the grim concentration of a drunken man. David fired, a single shot that slapped into the Arab's body without apparent effect, and then suddenly the Uzi in David's hands was empty, the pin falling with a hollow click on an empty chamber.

Across the terrace, beyond range of a quick rush, the Arab's face was streaked with sweat and blood as he frowned heavily, trying to aim the machine-pistol as it wavered. He was dying swiftly, the flame fluttering towards extinction, but he was using the last of his strength.

David stood frozen with the empty weapon in his hand, and the blank eye of the pistol sought him out, and fastened upon him. He watched the Arab's eyes narrow, and his sudden murderous grin of achievement as he saw David in his sights, and his finger tightening on the trigger.

At that range the bullets would hit like the solid stream of a fire hose. He began to move, to throw himself down the stairs, but he knew it was too late. The Arab was at the instant of firing, and at the same instant a revolver shot crashed out at David's side.

Half the Arab's head was cut away by the heavy lead slug, and he was flung backwards with the yellow custard contents of his skull splattering the white-washed wall behind him, and his death grip on the trigger emptied the machine-pistol with a shattering roar harmlessly into the grape vines above him.

Dazedly David turned to find the Brig beside him, the dead security guard's pistol in his fist. For a moment they stared at each other, and then the Brig stepped past him and walked to the fallen bodies of the other two Arabs. Standing over each in turn he fired a single pistol shot into their heads.

David turned away and let the Uzi drop from his hands. He went down the stairs into the garden.

The dead and the wounded lay singly and in piles, pitiful fragments of humanity. The soft cries and the groans of the wounded, the bitter weeping of a child, the voice of a mother, were sounds more chilling than the screaming and the shouting.

The garden was drenched and painted with blood. There were splashes and gouts of it upon the white walls, there were puddles and snakes of it spreading and crawling across the paving, dark slicks of it sinking into the dust, ropes of it dribbling and pattering like rain from the body of a musician as he hung over the rail of the bandstand. The sickly sweetish reek of it mingled with the smell of spiced food and spilled wine, with the floury taste of plaster dust and the bitter stench of burned explosive.

The veils of smoke and dust that still drifted across the garden could not hide the terrible carnage. The bark of the olive trees was torn in slabs from the trunks by flying steel, exposing the white wet wood. The wounded and dazed survivors crawled over a field of broken glass and shattered crockery. They swore and prayed, and whispered and groaned and called for succour.

David went down the steps, his feet moving without his bidding; his muscles were numb, his body senseless and only his finger-tips tingled with life.

Joe was standing below one of the torn olive trees. He stood like a colossus, with his thick powerful legs astride, his head thrown back and his face turned to the sky, but his eyes were tight-closed and his mouth formed a silent cry of agony – for he held Hannah's body in his arms.

Her bridal veil had fallen from her head, and the bright copper mane of her hair hung back – almost to the ground. Her legs and one arm hung loosely also, slack and lifeless. The golden freckles stood out clearly on the milky-white skin of her face – and the bloody wounds bloomed like the petals of the poinsettia tree upon the bosom of her wedding-gown.

David averted his eyes. He could not watch Joe in his anguish, and he walked on slowly across the garden, in terrible dread of what he would find.

'Debra!' he tried to raise his voice, but it was a hoarse raven's croak. His feet slipped in a puddle of thick dark blood, and he stepped over the unconscious body of a woman who lay, face down, in a floral dress, with her arms thrown wide. He did not recognize her as Debra's mother.

'Debra!' He tried to hurry, but his legs would not respond. He saw her then, at the corner of the wall where he had left her.

'Debra!' He felt his heart soar. She seemed unhurt, kneeling below one of the marble Grecian statues, with the

127

flowers in her hair and the yellow silk of her dress bright and festive.

She knelt, facing the wall, and her head was bowed as though in prayer. The dark wing of her hair hung forward screening her and she held her cupped hands to her face.

'Debra.' He dropped to his knees beside her, and timidly he touched her shoulder.

'Are you all right, my darling?' And she lowered her hands slowly, but still holding them cupped together. A great coldness closed around David's chest as he saw that her cupped hands were filled with blood. Rich red blood, bright as wine in a crystal glass.

'David,' she whispered, turning her face towards him. 'Is that you, darling?'

David gave a small breathless moan of agony as he saw the blood-glutted eye sockets, the dark gelatinous mess that congealed in the thick dark eyelashes and turned the lovely face into a gory mask.

'Is that you, David?' she asked again, her head cocked at a blind listening angle.

'Oh God, Debra.' He stared into her face.

'I can't see, David.' She groped for him. 'Oh David – I can't see.'

And he took her sticky wet hands in his, and he thought that his heart would break.

The stark modern silhouette of Hadassah Hospital stood upon the skyline above the village of Ein Karem. The speed with which the ambulances arrived saved many of the victims whose lives were critically balanced, and the hospital was geared to sudden influxes of war casualties.

The three men – the Brig, Joe and David – kept their

vigil together all that night upon the hard wooden benches of the hospital waiting-room. When more was learned of the planning behind the attack, a security agent would come to whisper a report to the Brig.

One of the assassins was a long-term and trusted employee of the catering firm, and the other two were his 'cousins' who had been employed as temporary staff on his recommendation. It was certain that their papers were forged.

The Prime Minister and her cabinet had been delayed by an emergency session, but had been on their way to the wedding when the attack was made. A fortunate chance had saved them, and she sent her personal condolences to the relatives of the victims.

At ten o'clock, Damascus radio gave a report in which El Fatah claimed responsibility for the attack by members of a suicide squad.

A little before midnight, the chief surgeon came from the main theatre, still in his theatre greens and boots, with his mask pulled down to his throat. Ruth Mordecai was out of danger, he told the Brig. They had removed a bullet that had passed through her lung and lodged under her shoulder blade. They had saved the lung.

'Thank God,' murmured the Brig and closed his eyes for a moment, imagining life without his woman of twenty-five years. Then he looked up. 'My daughter?'

The surgeon shook his head. 'They are still working on her in the small casualty theatre.' He hesitated. 'Colonel Halman died in theatre a few minutes ago.'

The toll of the dead was eleven so far, with four others on the critical list.

In the early morning the undertakers arrived for the bodies with their long wicker baskets and black limousines. David gave Joe the keys of the Mercedes, that he might follow by the hearse bearing Hannah's body and arrange the details of the funeral.

David and the Brig sat side by side, haggard and with sleepless bruised eyes, drinking coffee from paper cups.

In the late morning the eye surgeon came out to them. He was a smooth-faced, young-looking man in his forties, the greying of his hair seeming incongruous against the unlined skin and clear blue eyes.

'General Mordecai?'

The Brig rose stiffly. He seemed to have aged ten years during the night.

'I am Doctor Edelman. Will you come with me, please?'

David rose to follow them, but the doctor paused and looked to the Brig.

'I am her fiancé,' said David.

'It might be best if we spoke alone first, General.' Edelman was clearly trying to pass a warning with his eyes, and the Brig nodded.

'Please, David.'

'But—' David began, and the Brig squeezed his shoulder briefly, the first gesture of affection that had ever passed between them.

'Please, my boy,' and David turned back to the hard bench.

In the tiny cubicle of his office Edelman hitched himself on to the corner of the desk and lit a cigarette. His hands were long and slim as a girl's, and he used the lighter with a surgeon's neat economical movements.

'You don't want it with a sugar coating, I imagine?' He had appraised the Brig carefully, and went on without waiting for a reply. 'Neither of your daughter's eyes are damaged,' but he held up a hand to forestall the rising expression of relief on the Brig's lips, and turned to the scanner on which hung a set of X-ray plates. He switched on the back light.

'The eyes were untouched, there is almost no damage to her facial features – however, the damage is here—' He touched a hard frosty outline in the smoky grey swirls and patterns of the X-ray plate. ' – That is a steel fragment, a tiny steel fragment, almost certainly from a grenade. It is no larger than the tip of a lead pencil. It entered the skull through the outer edge of the right temple, severing the large vein which accounted for the profuse haemorrhage, and it travelled obliquely behind the eyeballs without touching them or any other vital tissue. Then, however, it pierced the bony surrounds of the optic chiasma,' he traced the path of the fragment through Debra's head, 'and it seems to have cut through the canal and severed the chiasma, before lodging in the bone sponge beyond.' Edelman drew heavily on the cigarette while he looked for a reaction from the Brig. There was none.

'Do you understand the implications of this, General?' he asked, and the Brig shook his head wearily. The surgeon switched off the light of the X-ray scanner, and returned to the desk. He pulled a scrap pad towards the Brig and took a propelling pencil from his top pocket. Boldly he sketched an optical chart, eyeballs, brain, and optical nerves, as seen from above.

'The optical nerves, one from each eye, run back into this narrow tunnel of bone where they fuse, and then branch again to opposite lobes of the brain.'

The Brig nodded, and Edelman slashed the point of his pencil through the point where the nerves fused. Understanding began to show on the Brig's strained and tired features.

'Blind?' he asked, and Edelman nodded.

'Both eyes?'

'I'm afraid so.'

The Brig bowed his head and gently massaged his own eyes with thumb and forefinger. He spoke again without looking at Edelman.

'Permanently?' he asked.

'She has no recognition of shape, or colour, of light or darkness. The track of the fragment is through the optic

131

chiasma. All indications are that the nerve is severed. There is no technique known to medical science which will restore that.' Edelman paused to draw breath, before going on. 'In a word then, your daughter is permanently and totally blinded in both eyes.'

The Brig sighed, and looked up slowly. 'Have you told her?' and Edelman could not hold his gaze.

'I was rather hoping that you would do that.'

'Yes,' the Brig nodded, 'it would be best that way. Can I see her now? Is she awake?'

'She is under light sedation. No pain, only a small amount of discomfort, the external wound is insignificant – and we shall not attempt to remove the metal fragment. That would entail major neurosurgery.' He stood up and indicated the door. 'Yes, you may see her now. I will take you to her.'

The corridor outside the row of emergency theatres was lined along each wall with stretchers, and the Brig recognized many of his guests laid out upon them. He stopped briefly to speak with one or two of them, before following Edelman to the recovery room at the end of the corridor.

Debra lay on the tall bed below the window. She was very pale, dry blood was still clotted in her hair and a thick cotton wool and bandage dressing covered both her eyes.

'Your father is here, Miss Mordecai,' Edelman told her, and she rolled her head swiftly towards them.

'Daddy?'

'I am here, my child.'

The Brig took the hand she held out, and stooped to kiss her. Her lips were cold, and she smelled strongly of disinfectant and anaesthetic.

'Mama?' she asked anxiously.

'She is out of danger,' the Brig assured her, 'but Hannah—'

'Yes. They told me,' Debra stopped him, her voice choking. 'Is Joe all right?'

'He is strong,' the Brig said. 'He will be all right.'

'David?' she asked.

'He is here.'

Eagerly she struggled up on to one elbow, her face lighting with expectation, the heavily bound eyes turned blindly seeking.

'David,' she called, 'where are you? Damn this bandage. Don't worry, David, it's just to rest my eyes.'

'No,' the Brig restrained her with a hand on her arm. 'He is outside, waiting,' and she slumped with disappointment.

'Ask him to come to me, please,' she whispered.

'Yes,' said the Brig, 'in a while, but first there is something we must talk about – something I have to tell you.'

She must have guessed what it was, she must have been warned by the tone of his voice for she went very still. That peculiar stillness of hers, like a frightened animal of the veld.

He was a soldier, with a soldier's blunt ways, and although he tried to soften it, yet even his tone was roughened with his own sorrow, so that it came out brutally. Her hand in his was the only indication that she had heard him, it spasmed convulsively like a wounded thing and then lay still, a small tense hand in the circle of his big bony fist.

She asked no questions and when he had done they sat quietly together for a long time. He spoke first.

'I will send David to you now,' he said, and her response was swift and vehement.

'No.' She gripped his hand hard. 'No, I can't meet him now. I have to think about this first.'

The Brig went back to the waiting-room and David stood up expectantly, the pure lines of his face seemingly carved from pale polished marble, and the dark blue of his eyes in deep contrast.

The Brig forestalled him harshly. 'No visitors.' He took David's arm. 'You will not be allowed to see her until tomorrow.'

'Is something wrong? What is it?' David tried to pull away, but the Brig held him and steered him towards the door.

'Nothing is wrong. She will be all right – but she must have no excitement now. You'll be able to see her tomorrow.'

They buried Hannah that evening in the family plot on the Mountain of Olives. It was a small funeral party attended by the three men and a mere handful of relatives, many of whom had others to mourn from the previous day's slaughter.

There was an official car waiting to take the Brig to a meeting of the High Command, where retaliatory measures would certainly be discussed, another revolution in the relentless wheel of violence that rolled across the troubled land.

Joe and David climbed into the Mercedes and sat silently, David making no effort to start the engine. Joe lit cigarettes for them, and they both felt drained of purpose and direction.

'What are you going to do now?' David asked him.

'We had two weeks,' Joe answered him. 'We were going down to Ashkelon—' His voice trailed off. 'I don't know. There isn't anything to do now, is there?'

'Shall we go and have a drink somewhere?'

Joe shook his head. 'I don't feel like drinking,' he said. 'I think I'll go back to base. They are flying night interceptions tonight.'

'Yes,' David agreed quickly, 'I'll come with you.' He could not see Debra until tomorrow, and the house on

Malik Street would be lonely and cold. Suddenly he longed for the peace of the night heavens.

The moon was a brightly curved Saracen blade against the soft darkness of the sky, and the stars were fat and silver and gemlike in their clarity.

They flew high above the earth, remote from its grief and sorrow, wrapped in the isolation of flight and lost in the ritual and concentration of night interception.

The target was a Mirage of their own squadron, and they picked it up on the scanner far out over the Negev. Joe locked on to it and called the track and range while David searched for and at last spotted the moving star of the target's jet blast, burning redly against the velvety blackness of the night.

He took them in on a clean interception creeping up under the target's belly and then pulling steeply up past its wing-tip, the way a barracuda goes for the lure from below and explodes out through the surface of the sea. They shot past so close that the target Mirage broke wildly away to port, unaware of their presence until that moment.

Joe slept that night, exhausted with grief, but David lay in the bunk beneath him and listened to him. In the dawn he rose and showered and left Joe still asleep. He drove into Jerusalem and reached the hospital just as the sun came up and lit the hills with its rays of soft gold and pearly pink.

The night sister at the desk was brusque and preoccupied. 'You shouldn't be here until visiting hours this afternoon,' but David smiled at her with all the charm he could muster.

'I just wanted to know if she is doing well. I have to rejoin my squadron this morning.'

The sister was not immune either to his smile or the air force uniform, and she went to consult her lists.

'You must be mistaken,' she said at last. 'The only Mordecai we have is Mrs Ruth Mordecai.'

'That's her mother,' David told her, and the sister flipped the sheet on her clipboard.

'No wonder I couldn't find it,' she muttered irritably. 'She was discharged last night.'

'Discharged?' David stared at her uncomprehendingly.

'Yes, she went home last night. I remember her now. Her father came to fetch her just as I came on duty. Pretty girl with eye bandages—'

'Yes,' David nodded. 'Thank you. Thank you very much,' and he ran down the steps to the Mercedes, his feet light with relief, freed at last from the gnawing doubt and dread.

Debra had gone home. Debra was safe and well.

The Brig opened the door to him, and let him into the silent house. He was still in his uniform, and it was wilted and rumpled. The Brig's face was fine-drawn, the lines crudely chiselled around his mouth, and his eyes were swollen and bloodshot from worry and sorrow and lack of sleep.

'Where is Debra?' David demanded eagerly, and the Brig sighed and stood aside for him to enter.

'Where is she?' David repeated, and the Brig led him to his study and waved him to a chair.

'Why don't you answer me?' David was becoming angry, and the Brig slumped into a chair across the large bare room, with its severe monastic furnishings of books and archaeological relics.

'I couldn't tell you yesterday, David, she asked me not to. I'm sorry.'

'What is it?' David was fully alarmed now.

'She had to have time to think – to make up her mind.' The Brig stood up again and began to pace, his footsteps echoing hollowly on the bare wooden floor, pausing every now and then to touch one of the pieces of ancient statuary, caressing it absently as he talked, as though to draw comfort from it.

136

David listened quietly, occasionally shaking his head as though to deny that what he was hearing was the truth.

'So you see it is permanent, final, without hope. She is blind, David, totally blind. She has gone into a dark world of her own where nobody else can follow her.'

'Where is she? I want to go to her,' David whispered, but the Brig ignored the request and went on steadily.

'She wanted time to make her decision – and I gave it to her. Last night, after the funeral, I went back to her and she was ready. She had faced it, come to terms with it, and she had decided how it must be.'

'I want to see her,' David repeated. 'I want to talk to her.'

Now the Brig looked at him and the bleakness in his eyes faded, his voice dropped, becoming gruff with compassion.

'No, David. That was her decision. You will not see her again. For you she is dead. Those were her words. "Tell him I am dead, but he must only remember me when I was alive—" '

David interrupted him, jumping to his feet. 'Where is she, damn you?' His voice was shaking. 'I want to see her now.' He crossed swiftly to the door and jerked it open, but the Brig went on.

'She is not here.'

'Where is she?' David turned back.

'I cannot tell you. I swore a solemn oath to her.'

'I'll find her—'

'You might, if you search carefully – but you will forfeit any respect or love she may have for you,' the Brig went on remorselessly. 'Again I will give you her exact words. "Tell him that I charge him on our love, on all we have ever been to each other, that he will let me be, that he will not come looking for me." '

'Why, but why?' David demanded desperately. 'Why does she reject me?'

'She knows that she is altered beyond all hope or promise. She knows that what was before can never be again. She knows that she can never be to you again what you have a right to expect—' He stopped David's protest with an angry chopping gesture of his hand. 'Listen to me, she knows that it cannot endure. She can never be your wife now. You are too young, too vital, too arrogant—' David stared at him. ' – She knows that it will begin to spoil. In a week, a month, a year perhaps, it will have died. You will be trapped, tied to a blind woman. She doesn't want that. She wants it to die now, swiftly – mercifully, not to drag on—'

'Stop it,' David shouted. 'Stop it, damn you. That's enough.' He stumbled to the chair and fell into it. They were silent for a while, David crouched in the chair with his face buried in his hands. The Brig standing before the narrow window casement, the early morning light catching the fierce old warrior's face.

'She asked me to make you promise—' He hesitated, and David looked up at him. ' – To promise that you would not try to find her.'

'No.' David shook his head stubbornly.

The Brig sighed. 'If you refused, I was to tell you this – she said you would understand, although I don't – she said that in Africa there is a fierce and beautiful animal called the sable antelope, and sometimes one of them is wounded by a hunter or mauled by a lion.'

The words were as painful as the cut of a whiplash, and David remembered himself saying them to her once when they were both young and strong and invulnerable.

'Very well,' he murmured at last, 'if that's what she wants – then I promise not to try and find her, though I don't promise not to try and convince her she is wrong.'

'Perhaps it would be best if you left Israel,' the Brig told him. 'Perhaps you should go back to where you came from and forget all of this ever happened.'

David paused, considering this a moment, before he answered, 'No, all I have is here. I will stay here.'

'Good.' The Brig accepted the decision. 'You are always welcome in this house.'

'Thank you, sir,' said David and went out to where the Mercedes was parked. He let himself into the house on Malik Street, and saw instantly that someone had been there before him.

He walked slowly into the living-room; the books were gone from the olive-wood table, the Kadesh painting no longer hung above the leather couch. In the bathroom he opened the wall cabinet and all her toilet articles had been removed, the rows of exotic bottles, the tubes and pots, even the slot for her toothbrush beside his was empty.

Her cupboard was bare, the dresses gone, the shelves blank, every trace of her swept away, except for the lingering scent of her perfume on the air, and the ivory lace cover upon the bed.

He went to the bed and sat upon it, stroking the fine lace-work, remembering how it had been.

There was the hard outline of something thin and square upon the pillow, beneath the cover. He turned back the lace and picked up the thin green book.

This Year, in Jerusalem. It had been left there as a parting gift.

The title swam and went misty before his eyes. It was all he had left of her.

It seemed as though the slaughter at Ein Karem was the signal for a fresh upsurge of hostility and violence throughout the Middle East. A planned escalation of international tensions, as the Arab nations rattled their impressive, oil-purchased array of weaponry and swore once more to leave not a single Jew in the land they still called Palestine.

There were savage and merciless attacks on soft targets, ill-protected embassies and consulates around the world, letter bombs, and night ambushes on school buses in isolated areas.

Then the provocations grew bolder, more directly aimed at the heart of Israel. Border infringements, commando-style raids, violations of air space, shellings, and a threatening gathering and massing of armed might along the long vulnerable frontiers of the wedge-shaped territories of the tiny land.

The Israelis waited, praying for peace – but gird for war.

Day after day, month after month, David and Joe flew to maintain that degree of expertise, where instinct and instantaneous reaction superseded conscious thought and reasoned action.

At those searing speeds beyond sound, it was only this training that swung the advantage from one combat team to another. Even the superior reaction times of these carefully hand-picked young men were unequal to the tasks of bringing their mighty machines into effective action, where latitudes of error were measured in hundredths of a second, until they had attained this extra-sensory perfection.

To seek out, to recognize, to close, to destroy, and to disengage – it was a total preoccupation that blessedly left little time for brooding and sorrow.

Yet the sorrow and anger, that David and Joe shared, seemed doubly to arm them. Their vengeance was all-consuming.

Soon they joined that select half-dozen strike teams that Desert Flower called to undertake the most delicate of sorties. Again and again they were ordered into combat, and each time the confidence that Command had in them was strengthened.

As David sat in his cockpit, dressed from head to foot in the stiff constricting embrace of a full-pressure suit, breathing oxygen from his closed face mask, although the Mirage still crouched upon the ground, there were four black, red and white miniature roundels painted on the fuselage below his cockpit. The scalps of the enemy.

It was a mark of Desert Flower's trust that Bright Lance flight had been selected for high altitude 'Red' standby. With the starter lines plugged ready to blow compressed air into the compressors and whirl the great engines into life, and the ground crew lounging beside the motor, the Mirages were ready to be hurled aloft in a matter of seconds. Both David and Joe were suited to survive the almost pressureless altitudes above sixty thousand feet where an unprotected man's blood would fizzle like champagne.

David had lost count of the weary uncomfortable days and hours he had sat cramped in his cockpit on 'Red' standby with only the regular fifteen-minute checks to break the monotony.

'Checking 11.15 hours – fifteen minutes to stand-down.' David said into the microphone, and heard Joe's breathing in his ears before the reply.

'Two standing by. *Beseder*.'

Immediately after stand-down, when another crew would assume the arduous waiting of standby, David would change into a track suit and run for five or six miles to get the stiffness out of his body and to have his sweat wash away the staleness. He was looking forward to that, afterwards he would—

There was a sharp crackle in his earphones and a new voice.

'Red standby – Go! Go!'

The command was repeated over loudspeakers in the underground bunker, and the ground crew boiled into action. With all his pre-flight checks and routine long ago

141

completed, David merely pushed his throttle to starting position, and the whine of the starters showed immediate results. The engine caught and he ran up his power to one hundred per cent.

Ahead of him the blast doors were lifting.

'Bright Lance Two, this is Leader going to take off power.'

'Two conforming,' said Joe and they went screaming up the ramp and hurled themselves at the sky.

'Hallo, Desert Flower, this is Bright Lance airborne and climbing.'

'Bright Lance, this is the Brig,' David was not surprised to find that he was in charge of command plot. Distinctive voices and the use of personal names would prevent any chance of the enemy confusing the net with false messages. 'David, we have an intruder approach at high level that should enter our airspace in four minutes, if it continues on its present course. We are tracking him at seventy-five thousand feet which means it is either an American U2, which is highly unlikely, or that it is a Russian spy plane coming over to have a look at our latest dispersals.'

'*Beseder*, sir,' David acked.

'We are going to try for a storm-climb to intercept as soon as the target becomes hostile in our air space.'

'*Beseder*, sir.'

'Level at twenty thousand feet, turn to 186 and go to maximum speed for storm-climb.'

At twenty thousand, David went to straight and level flight and glanced into his mirror to see Joe's Mirage hanging out on his tail.

'Bright Lance Two, this is Leader. Commencing run now.'

'Two conforming.'

David lit his tail and pushed the throttle open to maximum afterburner position. The Mirage jumped away, and David let the nose drop slightly to allow the speed to build up quickly. They went blazing through the sound barrier without a check, and David retrimmed for supersonic flight, thumbing the little top-hat on the end of his stick.

Their speed rocketed swiftly through Mach 1.2, Mach 1.5.

The Mirages were stripped of all but their essentials, there were no missiles dangling beneath them, no auxiliary fuel tanks to create drag, the only weapons they carried were their two 30-mm cannons.

Flying lightly, they drove on up the Mach scale, streaking from Beersheba to Eilat in the time it would take a man to walk a city block. Their speed stabilized at Mach 1.9 just short of the heat barrier.

'David, this is the Brig. We are tracking you. You are on correct course and speed for interception. Prepare to commence climb in sixteen seconds.'

'*Beseder*, sir.'

'Counting now. Eight, seven, six . . . two, one. Go! Go!'

David tensed his body and as he pulled up the nose of the Mirage, he opened his mouth and screamed to fight off the effects of gravity. But despite these precautions and the constricting grip of his pressure suit, the abrupt change of direction crammed him down into his seat and the blood drained out of his head so that his vision went grey and then black.

The Mirage was standing on her tail still flying at very nearly twice the speed of sound and, as his vision returned, David glanced at the G-meter and saw that he had subjected his body to nearly nine times the force of gravity to achieve this attitude of climb without loss of speed.

Now he lay on his back and stared up at the empty sky while the needle of his altimeter raced upwards, and his speed gradually eroded away.

A quick sweep showed Joe's Mirage rock steady in position below him, climbing in concert with him, and his voice came through calm and reassuring.

'Leader, this is Two. I have contact with target.'

Even under the stress of storm-climb, Joe was busy manipulating his beloved radar, and he had picked up the spy plane high above them.

In this manoeuvre they were trading speed for height, and as one increased so the other drained away.

They were like a pair of arrows aimed directly upwards. The bowstring could throw them just so far and then they would hang there in space for a few moments, until they were drawn irresistibly back to earth. In those few moments they must find and kill the enemy.

David lay back in his seat and watched with fresh wonder as the sky turned darker blue and then slowly became the midnight black of space, shot through with the fiery prickings of the stars.

They were at the top edge of the stratosphere, high above the highest clouds or signs of weather as known to earth. Outside the cockpit the air was thin and weak, insufficient for life, hardly sufficient to keep the jets of the Mirage's engines burning – and the cold was a fearsome sixty degrees of frost.

The two aircraft slowly ran out of energy, and they came out together at the top of a mighty parabola. The sensation of flight was gone, they swam through the dark forbidding oceans of space and far below them the earth glowed strangely, with a weird unnatural light.

There was no time to admire the view, the Mirage was wallowing in the thin and treacherous air, her control surfaces skidding and sliding without bite.

Joe was on the target, tracking quietly and steadily and they came round carefully on to the heading, with the aircraft staggering mushily and beginning to fall away from these inhospitable heights.

David stared ahead, holding the Mirage's nose up for sustained altitude but already the stall warning device was flicking amber and red at him. He was running out of time and height.

Then suddenly he saw it, seeming startlingly close in the rare air, ghosting along on its immense wings, like a black manta-ray through the sable and silent sea of space – ahead and slightly below them – calmly and silently, it drifted along, its height giving it a false sense of invulnerability.

'Desert Flower, this is Bright Lance visual on the intruder and requesting permission for strike.' David's cool tone hid the sudden gust of his anger and hatred that the sighting had released.

'Report your target.' The Brig was hedging, it was a dangerous decision to call the strike on an unknown target.

'Desert Flower, it's an Ilyushin Mark 17–11. No apparent markings.'

It needed no marking, it could only belong to one nation. David was closing fast, he could fly no slower than this, and he was rapidly overhauling the other machine. Those huge wings were designed to float upon the feeble air of the stratosphere.

'Closing fast,' he warned Desert Flower. 'Opportunity for strike will pass in approximately ten seconds.'

The silence in his headphones hummed quickly, and he readied his cannons and watched the spy plane blowing up rapidly in size as he dropped down upon it.

Suddenly the Brig made the decision, perhaps committing his country to heavy retaliation, but knowing that the spy plane's cameras were steadily recording vital details of their ability to resist aggression, information that would be passed quickly to their enemies.

'David,' his voice was curt and harsh, 'this is the Brig. Hit him!'

'*Beseder.*' David let the Mirage's nose drop a fraction, and she responded gratefully.

'Two, this is Leader attacking.'

'Two conforming.'

He went down on the Ilyushin so fast, that as she came into his sights he knew he had time for only a few seconds of fire.

He pressed the trigger with the aiming pipper on the spy plane's wing roots, and he saw her rear up like a great fish struck by the steel of the harpoon.

For three seconds he poured his cannon shells into her, and watched them flash and twinkle against the massive black silhouette. Then he was through, falling away below the giant's belly, with his power spent, dropping away like the burned-out shell of a rocket.

Joe came down astern of him, backing up the attack, and in his sights the spy plane hung helplessly on its wide wings, its long rounded nose pointing to the black sky with its cold uncaring stars.

He pressed the trigger and the plane broke up amidst the bright flashes of exploding cannon shells. One wing snapped off at its roots and the carcass began its long slow tumble down the heavens.

'Hello, Desert Flower, this is Bright Lance Leader. Target destroyed.' David tried to keep his voice level, but he found his hands were trembling and his guts were aching cold from the spill-over of his hatred that not even the enemy's death could expunge.

Again he pressed the button to open the flight net. 'Joe, that's one more for Hannah,' he said, but for once there was no reply, and after he had listened in vain to the throb of the carrier beam for a few seconds he closed it, and activated his doppler gear for a homing signal, and silently Joe followed him back to base.

Debra had been a steadying and maturing influence, but now David reacted so wildly to her going that Joe had to continue his role of wingman, even when they were off base.

They spent much of their leisure time together, for although they seldom mentioned their loss, yet the sharing of it drew them closer.

Often Joe slept over at Malik Street, for his own home was a sad and depressing place now. The Brig was seldom there in these troubled times, Debra gone and his mother was so altered by her terrible experience that she was grey and broken, aged beyond her years. The bullet wound in her body had closed, but there was other damage that would never heal.

David's wildness was a craving for the forgetfulness of constant action. He was only truly at peace when he was in the air, and on the ground he was restless and mercurial. Joe moved, big and calm beside him, steering him tactfully out of trouble with a slow grin and an easy word.

As a consequence of the downed spy plane, the Syrians began a policy of provocative patrols, calculated infringement of Israeli airspace, which was discontinued as soon as retaliation was drawn. As the interceptors raced to engage they would swing away, declining combat, and move back within their own borders.

Twice David saw the greenish luminous blur of these hostile patrols on the screen of his scanning radar, and each time he had surprised himself with the icy feeling of anger and hatred that had lain heavy as a rock upon his heart and lungs as he led Joe in on the interception. Each time, however, the Syrians had been warned by their own radar and they had turned away, increasing speed, and withdrawn discreetly and mockingly.

'Bright Lance, this is Desert Flower. Target is no longer hostile. Discontinue attack pattern.' The Syrian MiG 21s had crossed their own frontier, and each time David had answered quietly, 'Two, this is Leader. Discontinuing attack pattern and resuming scan.'

The tactics were designed to wear on the nerves of the defenders, and in all the interceptor squadrons the tension was becoming explosive. The provocation was pushing them to the edge of restraint. Incidents were only narrowly being averted, as the hot-bloods crowded their interceptions to the very frontiers of war. Finally, however, there had to come intervention from above as Desert Flower tried to hold them on a tighter leash. They sent the Brig to talk to his crews and as he stood on the dais and looked about the crowded briefing room, he realized that it was unfair to train the hawk and then keep the hood over his eyes and the thong upon his leg, to hold him upon the wrist, when the wild duck were flighting overhead.

He started at a philosophical level, taking advantage of the regard that he knew his young pilots had for him.

' – the object of war is peace, the ultimate strategy of any commander is peace—' There was no response from his audience. The Brig caught the level scrutiny of his own son. How could he talk of placation to a trained warrior who had just buried the multilated body of his bride? The Brig ploughed on manfully.

'Only a fool allows himself to be drawn on to a field of the enemy's choosing,' he was reaching them now, 'I won't have one of you young pups pushing us into something we are not ready for. I don't want to give them an excuse. That is what they want—' They were thawing now, he saw a head nod thoughtfully and heard a murmur of agreement.

'Any of you looking for big trouble, you don't have to go to Damascus, you know my address.' He tried for his first laugh, and got it. They were chuckling now. 'All right, then. We don't want trouble. We are going to lean right over backwards to prevent it – but we are not going to fall on our arses. When the time comes, I'll give you the word and it won't be the soft word, or the other cheek—' they growled then, a fierce little sound, and he ended it, ' – but you wait for that word.'

Le Dauphin stood up and took over from the Brig.

'All right, while I've got you all together, I've a little news for you that may help to cool the hot-heads who want to follow the MiGs over the border.' He motioned to the projection box at the end of the briefing-room, the lights went down and there was a shuffling of feet, and an outburst of coughing. A voice protested resignedly.

'Not *another* film show!'

'Yes,' the colonel took it up. '*Another* film show.' Then as the images began to flash upon the screen he went on, 'This is a military intelligence film, and the subject is a new ground-to-air missile system that has been delivered by the Soviet Army to the armies of the Arab Union. The code name for the system is "Serpent" and it updates the existing "Sam III" system. As far as we know, the system has been installed and is operative in the Syrian defensive perimeter, and will shortly be installed by the Egyptians. It is manned at present by Russian instructors.' As the colonel went on talking, the Brig sat back in his chair and watched their faces in the silver reflection from the screen. They were intent and serious, men looking for the first time on the terrible machines that might be the instrument of their own deaths.

'The missile is fired from a tracked vehicle. Here you see aerial reconnaissance shots of a mobile column. Notice that each vehicle carries a pair of missiles, and you will realize that they constitute an enormous threat—'

The Brig picked out the marvellously pure profile of David Morgan as he leaned forward to study the screen, and he felt a pang of sympathy and sorrow for him – and yet this was underlined by a new respect, a realignment of judgement. The boy had proved himself to be constant, capable of embracing an ideal and remaining loyal to it.

'The improvements in design of the "Serpent" are not

certain, but it is believed that the missile is capable of greater speeds, probably in the order of Mach 2.5, and that the guidance system is a combination of both infra-red heat seeker and computerized radar control.'

Watching the handsome young face, he wondered if Debra had not misjudged his reserves. It was possible that he would have been capable of – no, the Brig shook his head and groped for a cigarette. He was too young, too greedy for life, spoiled by good looks and riches. He would not be capable of it. Debra was right, as so often was the case. She had chosen the correct course. She could never hold him, she must set him free.

'It is expected that the "Serpent" is capable of engaging targets at altitudes between 1,500 feet and 75,000 feet.'

There was a stir amongst the listeners, as they assessed the threat of this new weapon.

'The warhead delivers a quarter of a ton of explosive and it is armed with a proximity fuse which is set to fire if the target is passed at range less than 150 feet. Within these limits the "Serpent" is lethal.'

The Brig was still watching David. Ruth and he had not seen the boy at their home for many months. He had come with Joe to spend the Sabbath evening with them twice after the outrage. However, the atmosphere had been stiff and artificial, everybody carefully avoiding mention of Debra's name. He had not come again after the second time, nearly six months ago.

'Evasive tactics at this stage will be the same as for "Sam III".'

'Prayer and good luck!' someone interjected and that raised a laugh.

' – maximum-rate turn towards the missile, to screen the radiation from your jet blasts, and attempt to force the "Serpent" to overshoot. In the event that the missile continues to track, you should climb into the sun and then make another maximum-rate turn. The missile may then accept the sun's infra-red radiation as a more tempting target—'

'And if that doesn't work?' a voice called, and another answered flippantly, 'Repeat the following: "Hear O Israel, the Lord our God, the Lord is one."' But this time nobody laughed at the old blasphemy.

The Brig timed his departure from the briefing-room to fall in beside David.

'When are we going to see you, David? It's been a long time.'

'I'm sorry, sir. I hope Joe made my apologies.'

'Yes, of course. But why don't you come with Joe this evening? God knows, there will be enough food.'

'I'll be very busy tonight, sir,' David declined lamely.

'I understand.' And as they reached the door of the OC's office the Brig paused, 'Remember you are always welcome,' and he turned away.

'Sir!' The Brig stopped and looked back at him. David spoke rapidly – almost guiltily.

'How is she, sir?' and then again, 'how is Debra? Have you seen her – I mean, recently?'

'She is well,' the Brig answered heavily. 'As well as she can be.'

'Will you tell her I asked?'

'No,' answered the Brig, ignoring the pleading in the dark blue eyes. 'No. You know I can't do that.'

David nodded and turned away. For a moment the Brig looked after him and then with a frown he went on into the colonel's office.

David dropped Joe in Ein Karem, at the entrance to the lane, and then he drove on into the main shopping area of East Jerusalem and parked outside the big new supermarket in Melech George V to do his shopping for the weekend ahead.

He was hanging over the freezer tray pondering the delicate choice between lamb cutlets and steak, when he became aware that he was being watched.

David looked up quickly and saw that she was a statuesque woman with a thick mane of blond curls. She stood beside the shelves farther down the aisle. Her hair was dyed, he could see the dark shadow of the roots, and she was older than he was, with a womanly heaviness in her hips and bosom and tiny lines at the corners of her eyes. She was eyeing him, a steady appraisal so unashamedly sensual that he felt the check in his breathing and the quick stirring of his lions. He looked back at the meat in the freezer, guilty and angry with the treachery of his body. It had been so long, so very long since he had experienced sexual awareness. He had believed that he never would again. He wanted to throw the pack of steak back into the freezer and leave, but he stood rooted with the breathless feeling squeezing his lungs, and he was aware of the woman's presence at his side. He could feel the warmth of her on his arm, and smell her – the flowery perfume mingled with the natural musky odour of the sexually aroused female.

'The steak is very good,' she said. She had a light sweet voice and he recognized the same breathless quality as his own. He looked at her. Her eyes were green, and her teeth were a little crooked but white. She was even older than he had thought, almost forty. She wore her dress low in front, he could see the crêpe effect of the skin between her breasts. The breasts were big and motherly, and suddenly David wanted to lay his head against them. They looked so soft and warm and safe.

'You should cook it rare, with mushrooms and garlic and red wine,' she said. 'It's very good that way.'

'Is it?' he asked hoarsely.

'Yes,' she nodded, smiling. 'Who will cook it for you? Your wife? Your mother?'

'No,' said David. 'I will cook it myself. I live alone,' and she leaned a little closer to him, her breast touching his arm.

David was dizzy and hot with the brandy. He had bought a bottle of it at the supermarket, and he had drunk it mixed with ginger ale to mask the spiritous taste. He had drunk it fast, and now he leaned over the basin in the bathroom and felt the house rock and sway about him. He steadied himself, gripping the edge of the basin.

He splashed cold water on to his face and shook off the drops, then he grinned stupidly at himself in the mirror above the basin. His hair was damp and hung on to his forehead; he closed one eye and the wavering image in the mirror hardened and squinted back at him.

'Hi there, boy,' he muttered and reached for the towel. He had dripped water down his tunic and this annoyed him. He threw the towel over the toilet seat and went back into the living-room.

The woman was gone. The leather couch still carried the indentation of her backside, and the dirty plates were on the olive-wood table. The air was thick with cigarette smoke and her perfume.

'Where are you?' he called thickly, swaying slightly in the doorway.

'Here, big boy.' He went to the bedroom. She lay on the bed, naked, plump and white with huge soft breasts and swelling belly. He stared at her.

'Come on, Davey.' Her clothing was thrown across the dressing-table, and he saw that her corsets were grey and unwashed. Her hair was yellow against the soft ivory lacework.

'Come to Mama,' she whispered hoarsely, opening her limbs languidly in invitation. She was spread upon the brass bed, upon the lace cover which had been Debra's — and David felt his anger surge within him.

'Get up,' he said, slurring his words.

'Come on, baby.'

'Get off that bed,' his voice tightened and she heard the tone and sat up with mild alarm.

'What is it, Davey?'

'Get out of here,' his voice was rising sharply. 'Get out, you bitch. Get out of here!' He was shaking now, his face pale and his eyes savage blue.

Quivering with panic, she climbed hurriedly from the bed, the great white breasts and buttocks wobbling with ridiculous haste as she stuffed them into the grey corset.

When she had gone, David went through into the bathroom and vomited into the toilet bowl. Then he cleaned the house, scouring pans and plates, polishing the glasses until they shone, emptying the ashtrays, opening the shutters to blow out the stench of cigarette and perfume – and finally, going through into the bedroom, he stripped and remade the bed with fresh sheets and smoothed the lace cover carefully until not a crease or wrinkle showed.

He put on a clean tunic and his uniform cap, and drove to the Jaffa gate. He parked the car in the lot outside the gate and walked through the old city to the reconstructed Sephardic synagogue in the Jewish quarter.

It was very quiet and peaceful in the high-domed hall and he sat a long time on the hard wooden bench.

Joe sat opposite David with a worried expression creasing his deep forehead as he studied the board. Three or four of the other pilots had hiked their chairs up and were concentrating on the game also. These chessboard conflicts between David and Joe were usually epics and attracted a partisan audience.

David had been stalking Joe's rook for half a dozen moves and now he had it trapped. Two more moves would shatter the king-sized defence, and the third must force a resignation. David grinned smugly as Joe reached a decision and moved a knight out.

'That's not going to save you, dear boy.' David hardly glanced at the knight, and he hit the rook with a white bishop. 'Mate in five,' he predicted, as he dropped the castle into the box, and then – too late – he realized that Joe's theatrical expression of anguish had slowly faded into a beatific grin. Joseph Mordecai used any deception to bait his traps, and David looked with alarm at the innocuous-seeming knight, suddenly seeing the devious plotting in which the castle was merely bait.

'Oh, you bastard,' David moaned. 'You sneaky bastard.'

'Check!' Joe gloated as he put the knight into a forked attack, and David had to leave his queen exposed to the horseman.

'Check,' said Joe again with an ecstatic little sigh as he lifted the white queen off the board, and again the harassed king took the only escape route open to him.

'And mate,' sighed Joe again as his own queen left the back file to join the attack. 'Not in five, as you predicted, but in three.' There was a loud outburst of congratulation and applause from the onlookers and Joe cocked an eye at David.

'Again?' he asked, and David shook his head.

'Take on one of these other patsies,' he said. 'I'm going to sulk for an hour.' He vacated his seat and it was filled by another eager victim as Joe reset the board. David crossed to the coffee machine, moving awkwardly in the grip of his G-suit, and drew a mug of the thick black liquid, stirred in four spoons of sugar and found another seat in a quieter corner of the crew-room beside a slim curly-headed young kibbutznik, with whom David had become friendly. He was reading a thick novel.

'*Shalom*, Robert. How you been?'

Robert grunted without looking up from his book, and David sipped the sweet hot coffee. Beside him, Robert moved restlessly in his seat and coughed softly. David was lost in his own thoughts, for the first time in months thinking of home, wondering about Mitzi and Barney Venter, wondering if the yellowtail were running hot in False Bay this season, and remembering how the proteas looked upon the mountains of the Helderberg.

Again Robert stirred in his chair and cleared his throat. David glanced at him, realized that he was in the grip of a deep emotion as he read, his lips quivering, and his eyes too bright.

'What are you reading?' David was amused, and he leaned forward to read the title. The picture on the dust jacket of the book was instantly familiar. It was a deeply felt desert landscape of fierce colours and great space. Two distant figures, man and woman, walked hand in hand through the desert and the effect was mystic and haunting. David realized that only one person could have painted that – Ella Kadesh.

Robert lowered the book. 'This is uncanny,' his voice was muffled with emotion. 'I tell you, Davey, it's beautiful. It must be one of the most beautiful books ever written.'

With a strange feeling of pre-knowledge, with a sense of complete certainty, of what it would be, David took the book out of his hands and turned it to read the title, *A Place of Our Own*.

Robert was still talking. 'My sister made me read it. She works for the publisher. She cried all night when she read it. It is very new, only published last week, but it's got to be the biggest book ever written about this country.'

David hardly heard him, he was staring at the writer's name in small print below the title.

'Debra Mordecai.'

He ran his fingers lightly over the glossy paper of the jacket, stroking the name.

'I want to read it,' he said softly.

'I'll let you have it when I'm finished,' Robert promised.

156

'I want to read it now!'

'No way!' Robert exclaimed with evident alarm, and almost snatched the book out of David's hands.

'You wait your turn, comrade!'

David looked up. Joe was watching him from across the room, and David glared at him accusingly. Joe dropped his eyes quickly to the chessboard again, and David realized that he had known of the publication. He started to go up to him, to challenge him, but at the moment the tannoy echoed through the bunker.

'All flights Lance Squadron to Red standby,' and on the readiness board the red lamps lit beside the flight designations.

'Bright Lance.

'Red Lance.

'Fire Lance.'

David snatched up his flying helmet and joined the lumbering rush of G-suited bodies for the electric personnel carrier in the concrete tunnel outside the crew-room door. He forced a place for himself beside Joe.

'Why didn't you tell me?' he demanded.

'I was going to, Davey, I really was.'

'Yeah, I bet,' David snapped sarcastically. 'Have you read it?'

Joe nodded, and David went on, 'What's it about?'

'I couldn't begin to tell you. You'd have to read it yourself.'

'Don't worry about that,' David muttered grimly, 'I will,' and he jumped down as they reached their hangar and strode across to his Mirage.

Twenty minutes later they were airborne and Desert Flower sent them hastening out over the Mediterranean at interception speed to answer a Mayday call from an El Al Caravelle who reported that she was being buzzed by an Egyptian MiG 21 J.

The Egyptian sheered off and raced for the coast and

the protection of his own missile batteries as the Mirages approached. They let him go and picked up the airliner. They escorted her into the circuit over Lod before returning to base.

Still in his G-suit and overalls, David stopped off at Le Dauphin's office and got himself a twenty-four-hour pass.

Ten minutes before closing time he ran into one of the bookstores in the Jaffa Road.

There was a pyramid display of A *Place of Our Own* on the table in the centre of the store.

'It's a beautiful book,' said the salesgirl as she wrapped it.

He opened a Goldstar, and kicked off his shoes before stretching out on the lace cover of the bed.

He began to read, and paused only once to switch on the overhead lights and fetch another beer. It was a thick book, and he read slowly – savouring every word, sometimes going back to re-read a paragraph.

It was their story, his and Debra's, woven into the plot she had described to him that day on the island off the Costa Brava, and it was rich with the feeling of the land and its people. He recognized many of the secondary characters, and he laughed aloud with the pleasure and the joy of it. Then at the end, he choked on the sadness as the girl of the story lies dying in Hadassah Hospital, with half her face torn away by a terrorist's bomb, and she will not let the boy come to her. Wanting to spare him that, wanting him to remember her as she was.

It was dawn then, and David had not noticed the passage of the night. He rose from the bed, light-headed from lack of sleep, and filled with a sense of wonder that Debra had captured so clearly the way it had been – that she had seen so deeply into his soul, had described emotions for which he had believed there were no words.

He bathed and shaved and dressed in casual clothes and went back to where the book lay upon the bed. He studied the jacket again, and then turned to the flyleaf for confirmation. It was there. 'Jacket design by Ella Kadesh.'

So early in the morning he had the road almost to himself and he drove fast, into the rising morning sun. At Jericho he turned north along the frontier road, and he remembered her sitting in the seat beside him with her skirts drawn high around her long brown legs and her thick dark hair shaking in the wind.

The whisper of the wind against the body of the Mercedes seemed to urge him, 'Hurry, hurry.' And the urgent drumming of the tyres carried him up towards the lake.

He parked the Mercedes beside the ancient crusader wall and went through into the garden on the lake shore.

Ella sat upon the wide patio before her easel. She wore a huge straw hat the size of a wagon wheel adorned with plastic cherries and ostrich feathers, her vast overalls covered her like a circus tent and they were stiff with dried paint in all her typically vivid colours.

Calmly she looked up from her painting with her brush poised.

'Hail, young Mars!' she greeted him. 'Well met indeed, and why do you bring such honour on my humble little home?'

'Piss on it, Ella, you know damn well why I'm here.'

'So sweetly phrased.' She was shifty, he could see it in her bright little eyes. 'Shame on it that such vulgar words pass such fair lips. Would you like a beer, Davey?'

'No, I don't want a beer. I want to know where she is.'

'Just who are we discussing?'

'Come on, I read the book. I saw the cover. You know, damn you, you know.'

She was silent then, staring at him. Then slowly the ornate head-dress dipped in acquiescence.

'Yes,' she agreed. 'I know.'

'Tell me where she is.'

'I can't do that, Davey. You and I both made a promise. Yes, I know of yours, you see.'

She watched the bluster go out of him. The fine young body with the arrogant set of shoulders seemed to sag, and he stood uncertainly in the sunlight.

'How about that beer now, Davey?' She heaved herself up from her stool and crossed the terrace with her stately tread. She came back and gave him a tall glass with a head of froth and they took a seat together at the end of the terrace out of the wind, in the mild winter sunlight.

'I've been expecting you for a week now,' she told him. 'Ever since the book was published. I knew it would set you on fire. It's just too damned explosive – even I wept like a leaky faucet for a couple of days,' she giggled shyly. 'You'd hardly believe it possible, would you?'

'That book was us – Debra and me,' David told her. 'She was writing about us.'

'Yes,' Ella agreed, 'but it does not alter the decision she had made. A decision which I think is correct, by the way.'

'She described exactly how I felt, Ella. All the things I felt and still feel – but which I could never have put into words.'

'It's beautiful and it's true, but don't you see that it confirms her position?'

'But I love her, Ella – and she loves me,' he cried out violently.

'She wants it to stay that way. She doesn't want it to die, she doesn't want it to sicken.' He began to protest, but she gripped his arm in a surprisingly powerful grip to silence him. 'She knows that she can never keep pace with you now. Look at you, David, you are beautiful and vital and

160

swift – she must drag you back, and in time you must as certainly resent it.'

Again he tried to interrupt, but she shook his arm in her huge fist. 'You would be shackled, you could never leave her, she is helpless, she would be your charge for all your life – think on it, David.'

'I want her,' he muttered stubbornly. 'I had nothing before I met her, and I have nothing now.'

'That will change. Perhaps she has taught you something and young emotions heal as swiftly as young flesh. She wants happiness for you, David. She loves you so much that her gift to you is freedom. She loves you so much that for your sake she will deny that love.'

'Oh, God,' he groaned. 'If only I could see her, if I could touch her and talk to her for a few minutes.'

She shook her massive head, and her jowls wobbled dolefully.

'She would not agree to that.'

'Why, Ella, tell me why?' His voice was rising again, desperate with his anguish.

'She is not strong enough, she knows that if you came near her, she would waver and bring even greater disaster upon you both.'

They sat silently together then and looked out across the lake. High mountains of cloud rose up beyond the heights of Golan, brilliant white in the winter sunlight, shaded with blue and bruised grey, and range upon range they bore down upon the lake. David shivered as an icy little wind came ferreting across the terrace and sought them out.

He drank the rest of his beer, and then revolved the glass slowly through his fingers.

'Will you give her a message from me, then?' he asked.

'I don't think—'

'Please, Ella. Just this one message.'

161

She nodded.

'Tell her that what she wrote in the book is exactly how much I love her. Tell her that it is big enough to rise above this thing. Tell her that I want the chance to try.'

She listened quietly, and David made a groping gesture with his hands as though to pluck words from the air that might convince her.

'Tell her—' He paused, then shook his head. 'No, that's all. Just tell her I love her, and I want to be with her.'

'All right, David. I'll tell her.'

'And you will give me her answer?'

'Where can I reach you?'

He gave her the number of the telephone in the crew ready room at the base.

'You'll ring me soon, Ella? Don't keep me waiting.'

'Tomorrow,' she promised. 'In the morning.'

'Before ten o'clock. It must be before ten.'

He stood up, and then suddenly he leaned forward and kissed her sagging and raddled cheek.

'Thank you,' he said. 'You are not a bad old bag.'

'Away with you, you and your blarney. You'd have the sirens of the *Odyssey* themselves come a-running to your bidding.' She sniffed moistly. 'Get away with you now, I think I'm going to cry, and I want to be alone to enjoy it.'

She watched him go up across the lawns under the date palms and at the gate in the wall he paused and looked back. For a second they stared at each other and then he stepped through the gate.

She heard the engine of the Mercedes whirr and pull away slowly up the track, then the note of it rose as it hit the highway and went racing away southwards. Ella rose heavily and crossed the terrace, went down the steps towards the jetty and its stone boathouses screened from the house by part of the ancient wall.

Her speedboat rode at its mooring, restless in the wind and the chop of the lake. She went on down to the farthest

162

and largest of the boathouses and stood in the open doorway.

The interior had been stripped and repainted with clean white. The furniture was simple and functional. The rugs on the stone floor were for warmth, plain woven wool, thick and rough. The large bed was built into a curtained alcove in the wall beside the fireplace.

On the opposite wall was a gas stove with a double cooking ring above which a number of copper cooking pots hung. A door beyond led through to a bathroom and toilet which Ella had added very recently.

The only decoration was the Ella Kadesh painting from the house on Malik Street, which hung on the bare white wall, facing the door. It seemed to lighten and warm the whole room; below it the girl sat at a working table. She was listening intently to her own voice speaking in Hebrew from the tape recorder. Her expression was rapt and intent, and she stared at the blank wall before her.

Then she nodded her head, smiling at what she had just heard. She switched off the recorder and turned in the swivel chair to the second recorder and punched the record button. She held the microphone close to her lips as she began to translate the Hebrew into English.

Ella stood in the doorway and watched her work. An American publisher had purchased the English-language rights of A Place of Our Own. They had paid Debra an advance of thirty thousand American dollars for the book, and an additional five thousand for her services as translator. She had almost completed the task now.

From where she stood, Ella could see the scar on Debra's temple. It was a glazed pinkish white against the deeply tanned skin of her face, a dimple like a child's drawing of a seagull in flight; V-shaped and no bigger than a snowflake, it seemed to enhance her fine looks, almost like a beauty spot, a tiny blemish that gave a focus point for her strong regular features.

She had made no attempt to conceal it for her dark hair was drawn back to the nape of her neck and secured there with a leather thong. She wore no make-up, and her skin looked clean and glowing, tanned and smooth.

Despite the bulky fisherman's jersey and woollen slacks her body appeared firm and slim for she swam each day, even when the snow winds came down from the north.

Ella left the doorway and moved silently closer to the desk, studying Debra's eyes as she so often did. One day she would paint that expression. There was no hint of the damage that lay behind, no hint that the eyes could not see. Rather their calm level gaze seemed to penetrate deeper, to see all. They had a serenity that was almost mystic, a depth and understanding that Ella found strangely disquieting.

Debra pressed the switch of the microphone, ending the recording, and then she spoke again without turning her head.

'Is that you, Ella?'

'How do you do it?' Ella demanded with astonishment.

'I felt the air move when you walked in, and then I smelt you.'

'I'm big enough to blow up a storm, but do I smell so bad?' Ella protested, chuckling.

'You smell of turpentine, and garlic and beer,' Debra sniffed, and laughed with her.

'I've been painting, and I was chopping garlic for the roast, and I was drinking beer with a friend.' Ella dropped into one of the chairs. 'How does it go with the book?'

'Nearly finished. It can go to the typist tomorrow. Do you want some coffee?' Debra stood up and crossed to the gas stove. Ella knew better than to offer her help, even though she gritted her teeth every time she watched Debra working with fire and boiling water. The girl was fiercely independent, utterly determined to live her life without other people's pity or assistance.

The room was laid out precisely, each item in its place where Debra could put her hand to it without hesitation. She could move confidently through her little world, doing her own housework, preparing her own food and drink, working steadily, and paying her own way.

Once a week, a driver came up from her publisher's office in Jerusalem to collect her tapes and her writing was typed out along with her other correspondence.

Weekly also she would go with Ella in the speedboat up the lake to Tiberias to do their shopping together, and each day she swam for an hour from the stone jetty. Often an old fisherman with whom she had become friendly would row down the lake to fetch her and she would go out with him, baiting her own lines and taking her turn at the oars.

Across the lawns from the jetty, in the crusader castle, there was always Ella's companionship and intelligent conversation – and here in her little cottage there was quietness and safety and work to fill the long hours. And in the night there was the chill of terrible aloneness and silent bitter tears into her solitary pillow, tears which only she knew about.

Debra placed a mug of coffee beside Ella's chair and carried her own back to her work bench.

'Now,' she said, 'you can tell me what is keeping you fidgeting around in your seat, and drumming your fingers on the arm of the chair.' She smiled towards Ella, sensing the surprise. 'You have got something to tell me, and it's killing you.'

'Yes,' Ella spoke after a moment. 'Yes, you are right, my dear.' She took a deep breath and then went on. 'He came, Debra. He came to see me, as we knew he must.'

Debra set the mug down on the table, her hand was steady and her face expressionless.

'I didn't tell him where you were.'

'How is he, Ella? How does he look?'

165

'He is thinner, a little thinner, I think, and paler than when I last saw him, but it suits him. He is still the most beautiful man I have ever seen.'

'His hair,' Debra asked, 'has he let it grow a little?'

'Yes, I think so. It's soft and dark and thick around his ears and curly down the back.'

Debra nodded, smiling. 'I'm glad he didn't cut it.' They were silent again, and then almost timidly Debra asked, 'What did he say? What did he want?'

'He had a message for you.'

'What was it?'

And Ella repeated it faithfully in his exact words. When she had finished, Debra turned away to face the wall above her desk.

'Please go away now, Ella. I want to be alone.'

'He asked me to give him your reply. I promised to speak to him tomorrow morning.'

'I will come to you later – but please leave me now.' And Ella saw the drop of bright liquid that slid down the smooth brown curve of her cheek.

Mountainously Ella came to her feet and moved towards the door. Behind her she heard the girl sob, but she did not turn back. She went across the stone jetty and up to the terrace. She sat before her canvas and picked up her brush and began to paint. Her strokes were broad and crude and angry.

David was sweating in the stiff shiny skin of his full pressure suit and he waited anxiously beside the telephone, glancing every few minutes at the crew-room clock.

He and Joe would go on high-altitude 'Red' standby at ten o'clock, in seven minutes' time, and Ella had not called him.

David's depression was thunderous and there was black anger and despair in his heart. She had promised to call before ten o'clock.

'Come on, Davey,' Joe called from the doorway and he stood up heavily and followed Joe to the electric carrier. As he took his seat beside Joe he heard it ring in the crew-room.

'Hold it,' he told the driver, and he saw Robert answer the telephone and wave through the glass panel at him.

'It's for you, Davey,' and he ran back into the crew-room.

'I'm sorry, David,' Ella's voice was scratchy and far away. 'I tried earlier but the exchange here—'

'Sure, sure,' David cut her short, his anger was still strong. 'Did you speak to her?'

'Yes, Davey. Yes, I did. I gave her your message.'

'What was her reply?' he demanded.

'There was no reply.'

'What the hell, Ella. She must have said something.'

'She said—' Ella hesitated, ' – and these are her exact words – " the dead cannot speak with the living. For David, I died a year ago."'

He held the receiver with both hands but still it shook. After a while she spoke again.

'Are you still there?'

'Yes,' he whispered, 'I'm still here.'

They were silent again, but David broke it at last.

'That's it, then,' he said.

'Yes. I'm afraid that's it, Davey.'

Joe stuck his head around the door.

'Hey, Davey. Cut it short, will you. Time to go.'

'I have to go now, Ella. Thanks for everything.'

'Goodbye, David,' she said, and even over the scratchy connection he could hear the compassion in her tone. It heightened the black anger that gripped him as he rode beside Joe to the Mirage bunker.

For the first time ever, David felt uncomfortable in the cockpit of a Mirage. He felt trapped and restless, sweating and angry, and it seemed hours between each of the fifteen-minute readiness checks.

His ground crew were playing back-gammon on the concrete floor below him, and he could see them laughing and joshing each other. It made him angrier than ever to see others happy.

'Tubby!' he barked into his microphone, and his voice was repeated by the overhead loudspeakers. The plump, serious young man, who was chief engineer for Lance squadron, climbed quickly up beside his cockpit and peered anxiously through the canopy at him.

'There is dirt on my screen,' David snapped at him. 'How the hell do you expect me to pick up a MiG when I'm looking through a screen you ate your bloody breakfast off?'

The cause of David's distress was a speck of carbon that marred the glistening perfection of his canopy. Tubby himself had supervised the polishing and buffing of it, and the carbon speck was wind-carried since then. Carefully he removed the offending spot, and lovingly he polished the place where it had been with a chamois leather.

The reprimand had been public and unfair, very unlike their top boy Davey. However, they all made allowances for 'Red' standby nerves – and spots on a canopy played hell with a pilot's nerves. Every time it caught his eye it looked exactly like a pouncing MiG.

'That's better,' David gruffed at him, fully aware that he had been grossly unfair. Tubby grinned and gave him a high sign as he climbed down.

At that moment there was a click and throb in his earphones and the distinctive voice of the Brig.

'Red standby – Go! Go!'

Under full reheat and with the driving thrust of the

168

afterburners hurling him aloft David called, 'Hello, Desert Flower, Bright Lance airborne and climbing.'

'Hello, David, this is the Brig. We have a contact shaping up for intrusion on our airspace. It looks like another teaser from the Syrians. They are closing our border at twenty-six thousand and should be hostile in approximately three minutes. We are going to initiate attack plan Gideon. Your new heading is 42° and I want you right down on the deck.'

David acked and immediately rotated the Mirage's nose downwards. Plan Gideon called for a low-level stalk so that the ground clutter would obscure the enemy radar and conceal their approach until such time as they were in position to storm-climb up into an attack vector above and behind the target.

They dropped to within feet of the ground, lifting and falling over the undulating hills, so low that the herds of black Persian sheep scattered beneath them as they shrieked eastwards towards the Jordan.

'Hello, Bright Lance, this is Desert Flower – we are not tracking you.' Good, thought David, then neither is the enemy. 'Target is now hostile in sector' – the Brig gave the co-ordinates – 'scan for your own contact.'

Almost immediately Joe's voice came in. 'Leader, this is Two. I have a contact.'

David dropped his eyes to his own radar screen and manipulated his scan as Joe called range and bearing. It was a dangerous distraction when flying in the sticky phase of high subsonic drag at zero feet, and his own screen was clear of contact.

They raced onwards for many more seconds before David picked up the faint luminous fuzz at the extreme range of his set.

'Contact firming. Range figures nine six nautical miles. Parallel heading and track. Altitude 25,500 feet.'

David felt the first familiar tingle and slither of his anger and hatred, like the cold of a great snake uncoiling in his belly.

'*Beseder*, Two. Lock to target and go to interception speed.'

They went supersonic and David looked up ahead at the crests of the thunderheads that reared up from the solid banks of cumulo nimbus lower down. These mountainous upthrusts of silver and pale blue were sculptured into wonderful shapes that teased the imagination – towers and turrets embattled and emblazoned, heroic human shapes standing proud or hunched in the attitude of mourning, the rearing horsemen of the chessboard, a great fleecy pack of wolves, and other animal shapes of fantasy – with the deep crevasses between them bridged in splendour by the rainbows. There were hundreds of these, great blazes of colour, that turned and followed their progress across the sky, keeping majestic station upon them. Above them, the sky was a dark unnatural blue, dappled like a Windsor grey by the thin striation of the cirrocumulus, and the sunlight poured down to shimmer upon the two speeding warplanes. As yet there was no sight of the target. It was up there somewhere amongst the cloud mountains. He looked back at his radar screen. He had taken his radar out of scan and locked it into the target, and now as they closed rapidly he could appraise their relative positions.

The target was flying parallel to them, twenty miles out on their starboard side, and it was high above them and moving at a little more than half their speed. The sun was beyond the target, just short of its zenith, and David calculated his approach path to bring him into an attack vector from above and into the target's starboard quarter.

'Turning to starboard now,' he warned Joe, and they came around together, crossing the target's rear to put themselves in the sun. Joe was calling the range and bearing, it showed a leisurely patrol pattern. There was no indication as yet that the target was aware of the hunters behind and far below.

'Two, this is Leader. Arm your circuits.'

Without taking his eyes from the radar screen, David pressed the master switch on his weapon console. He activated the two air-to-air Sidewinder missiles that hung under each wing-tip, and immediately heard the soft electronic tone cycling in his earphones. That tone indicated that the missiles were dormant, they had not yet detected an infra-red source to excite them. When they did they would increase the volume and rate of cycle, growling with anticipation, clamouring like hunting dogs on the leash. He turned them down so he could no longer hear them.

Now he selected his cannon switch, readying the twin 30-mm weapons in their pods just below his seat. The trigger flicked forward out of its recess in the head of the joystick and he curled his forefinger about it to familiarize himself with the feel of it.

'Two, this is Leader. I am commencing visual.' It was a warning to Joe to concentrate all his attention on the screen and feed David with directional data.

'Target is now ten o'clock high, range figures two seven nautical miles.'

David searched carefully, raking the billowing walls of blinding white, breaking off the search to look away at a ground point or a pinnacle of cloud to prevent his eyes focusing short, and to sweep the blind spot behind them, lest the hunters become the hunted.

Then he saw them. There were five of them, and they appeared suddenly out of cloud high above and were immediately outlined against it like tiny black fleas on a newly ironed bedsheet. Just then Joe called the range again.

'Figures one three nautical miles,' but the targets were outlined so crisply against their background that David

171

could make out the delta-winged dart shape, and the high tailplane that identified them beyond all doubt as MiG 21 J.

'I have target visual,' he told Joe. 'Five MiG 21 Js.' His tone was flat and neutral, but it was a lie, for now at last his anger had something on which to fasten, and it changed its shape and colour, it was no longer black and aching but cold and bright and keen as a rapier's blade.

'Target is still hostile,' Joe confirmed that they were within Israeli territory, but his tone was not as well guarded as David's. David could detect the huskiness in it, and knew that Joe was feeling that anger also.

It would be another fifteen seconds before they had completed their turn across the enemy's stern, and David assessed the relative positions and saw that so far it had been a perfect approach. The formation sailed on serenely, unaware of the enemy beneath their tail, creeping up in the blind spot where the forward scanning radar could not discover them and rapidly moving into a position up toward the sun. Once there, David would go to attack speed and climb steeply up into a position of superior height and tactical advantage over the enemy formation. Looking ahead now, he realized that chance had given him an added bonus; one of the huge tower blocks of cloud was perfectly placed to screen his climb into the sun. He would use it to cover his stalk, the way the Boer huntsman of Africa stalked wild buffalo from behind a herd of domestic oxen.

'Target is altering course to starboard,' Joe warned him, the MiGs were turning away, edging back towards the Syrian border. They had completed their taunting gesture, they had flaunted the colours of Islam in the face of the infidel, and were making for safety.

David felt the blade of anger in his guts burn colder, sting sharper, and with an effort of restraint he waited out the last few seconds before making his climb. The moment came and his voice was still flat and without passion as he called to Joe, 'Two, this is Leader, commencing storm-climb.'

'Two conforming.'

David eased back on the controls and they went up in a climb so vicious that it seemed to tear their bowels from their bellies.

Almost immediately, Desert Flower picked up the radar images as they emerged from the ground clutter.

'Hullo both units Bright Lance. We are now tracking you. Show friend or foe.'

Both David and Joe were lying on their backs in the thrust of storm-climb, but at the order they punched in their IFF systems. Identification Friend or Foe would show a distinctive pattern, a bright halo, around their radar images on command plot identifying them positively even while they were locked with the enemy in the close proximity of the dogfight.

'*Beseder* – we are tracking you in IFF,' said the Brig, and they went plunging into the pillar of cloud and raked upwards through it. David's eyes darted between the boulé that contained his blind-flying instruments and the radar screen on which the enemy images shone bright and with hard outline, so close now that the individual aircraft in the enemy formation stood out clearly.

'Target is increasing speed and tightening starboard turn,' Joe intoned and David compensated for the enemy's manoeuvre.

David was certain that they had not detected his approach, the turn away was coincidental. Another glance at the screen showed that he had achieved his height advantage. He was now two miles off their quarter above them, with the sun at his back. It was the ideal approach.

'Turning now into final leg of attack pattern.' He alerted Joe to his intention and they began to pitch in. The last-second strike which would send their speed rocketing as they closed.

The target centred dead ahead, and the gunsight lit up, glowing softly on the screen ahead of him. The Sidewinder missiles caught the first emanations of infra-red rays from their victims, and they began to growl softly in David's earphones.

Still blinded by thick grey cloud they raced in, and suddenly they burst out into the clear. Ahead and below them opened a deep trough of space, a valley between cloud ranges and close below them the five MiGs sparkled silvery in the sunlight, pretty and toylike, their red, white and green markings festive and gay, the clean geometrical sweeps of wing and tail nicely balanced and the shark-like mouths of the jet intakes gaping, as they sucked in air.

They were in loose V-formation, two stacked back on each flank of the leader and in the fleeting seconds that David had to study them, he had assessed them. The four wingmen were Syrians, there was an indefinable sloppiness in their flying, a looseness of control. They flew with that lack of polish and confidence of the pupil. They were soft targets, easy pickings.

However, it did not need the three red rings about the leader's fuselage to identify him as a Russian instructor. Some leery old veteran with hawk's blood in his veins, tough and canny, and dangerous as an angry black mamba.

'Engage two port targets,' David ordered Joe, reserving the MiG leader and the starboard echelon for his attack. In David's headphones the missiles were growling their anxiety, they had sniffed out the massed jet blasts below them and already they were tracking, howling their eagerness to kill.

David switched to command net. 'Hello, Desert Flower, this is Bright Lance on target and requesting strike.'

Almost instantly the voice came back, 'David, this is the Brig—' he was speaking, rapidly, urgently, ' – discontinue attack pattern. I repeat, disengage target. They are no longer hostile. Break off attack.'

Shocked by the command, David glanced down the deep valley of cloud and saw the long brown valley of the Jordan falling away behind them. They had crossed over a line on the earth and immediately their roles had changed from defender to aggressor. But they were closing the target rapidly. It was a fair bounce, they were still unaware.

'We are going to hit them,' David made the decision through the cold bright thing that burned within him and he closed command net and spoke to Joe.

'Two, this is Leader attacking.'

'Negative! I say again negative!' Joe called urgently. 'Target is no longer hostile!'

'Remember, Hannah!' David shouted into his mask. 'Conform to me!' and he curled his finger about the trigger and touched left rudder, yawing fractionally to bring the nearest MiG into the field of his sights. It seemed to balloon in size as he shrieked towards it.

There was a heart-beat of silence from Joe, and then his voice strangled and rough.

'Two conforming.'

'Kill them, Joe,' David yelled and pressed against the spring-loaded tension of the trigger. There was a soft double hiss, hardly discernible above the jet din, and from under each wing-tip the missiles unleashed, they skidded and twisted as they aligned themselves on the targets, leaving darkly etched trails of vapour across David's front, and at that moment the MiGs became aware.

At a shouted warning from their leader, the entire formation burst into its five separate parts, splintering silvery swift like a shoal of sardines before the driving charge of the barracuda.

The rearmost Syrian was slow, he had only just begun to turn away when one of the Sidewinders flicked its tail, followed his turn and united with him in an embrace of death.

The shock wave of the explosion jarred David's

machine, but the sound of it was muted as the MiG was enveloped in the greenish-tinted cloud of the strike and it shattered into fragments. A wing snapped off and went whirling high and the brief blooming flower of smoke blew swiftly past David's head.

The second missile had chosen the machine with the red ring, the formation leader, but the Russian reacted so swiftly and pulled his turn so tight that the missile slid past him in an overshoot, and it lost the scent, unable to follow the MiG around. As David hauled the Mirage round after the Russian, he saw the missile destroy itself in a burst of greenish smoke, far out across the valley of clouds.

The Russian was in a hard right-hand turn, and David followed him. Staring across the imaginary circle that separated them, he could see every detail of the enemy machine; the scarlet helmet of the pilot, the gaudy colours of its roundels, the squiggle of Arabic script that was its identification markings – even the individual rivets that stitched the polished metal skin of the MiG.

David pulled back with all his strength against his joystick, for gravity was tightening the loading of his controls, opposing his efforts to place additional stress on the Mirage lest he tear its wings off the fuselage.

Gravity had hold of David also, its insidious force sucked the blood away from his brain so that his vision dimmed, the colour of the enemy pilot's helmet faded to dull brown, and David felt himself crushed down into his seat.

About his waist and legs his G-suit tightened its coils, squeezing brutally like a hungry python, attempting to prevent the drainage of blood from his upper torso.

David tensed every muscle in his body, straining to resist the loss of blood, and he took the Mirage up in a sliding, soaring yo-yo, up the side of an imaginary barrel. Like a motor-cyclist on a wall of death he whirled aloft, trying once more for the advantage of height.

His vision narrowed, greyed out, until his field was

reduced to the limits of his cockpit, and he was pinned heavily to his seat, his mouth sagging open, his eyelids dragging downwards; the effort of holding his right hand on the control column was Herculean.

In the corner of his vision the stall indicator blinked its little eye at him, changing from amber to red, warning him that he was on the verge of catastrophe, courting the disaster of supersonic stall.

David filled his lungs and screamed with all his strength, his own voice echoing through the grey mist. The effort forced a little blood back to his brain and his vision cleared briefly, enough to let him see that the MiG had anticipated his yo-yo and had come up under him, sliding up the wall of death towards his unprotected flank and belly.

David had no alternative but to break out of the turn before the MiG's cannons could bear. He rolled the Mirage out, and went instantly into a tight climbing left-hander, his afterburners still thundering at full power, consuming fuel at a prodigious rate, and placing a limit upon these desperate manoeuvres.

Neatly and gracefully as a ballet dancer, the Russian followed him out of the turn and locked into his next manoeuvre. David saw him coming up into an attack position in his rear-view mirror and he rolled out again and went up and right, blacking out with the rate of turn.

Roll and turn, turn for life, David had judged the Russian fairly. He was a deadly opponent, quick and hard, anticipating each of David's turns and twists, riding always within an ace of strike. Turn, and turn again, in great winging parabolas, climbing always, turning always, vapour trails spinning out from their wing-tips in silky arabesque patterns against the hard blue of the sky.

David's arms and shoulders ached as he fought the control dampers and the weight of gravity, sickened by the drainage of blood and the adrenalin in his system. His cold battle rage turned gradually to icy despair as each of his efforts to dislodge the Russian were met and countered, and always the gaping shark's maw of the MiG hung and twisted a point off his shoulder or belly. All David's expertise, all the brilliance of his natural flying gifts were slowly being discounted by the store of combat experience upon which his enemy could draw.

At one stage, when for an instant they flew wing-tip to wing-tip, David glanced across the gap and saw the man's face. Just the eyes and forehead above the oxygen mask; the skin was pale as bone and the eyes were deeply socketed like those of a skull – and then David was turning again, turning and screaming and straining against gravity, screaming also against the first enfolding coils of fear.

He rolled half out of the turn and then, without conscious thought, reversed the roll. The Mirage shuddered with protest and his speed bled off. The Russian saw it and came down on him from high on his starboard quarter. As David pushed the stick fully forward and left he kicked on full left rudder, ducking under the blast of cannon fire, and the Mirage went down in a spiralling dive. The blood which gravity had sucked from his head was now flung upwards through his body, filling his head and his vision with bright redness, the red-out of inverted gravitational force. A vein in his nose popped under the pressure and suddenly his oxygen mask was filled with a flood of warm choking blood.

The Russian was after him, following him into the dive, lining him up for his second burst.

David screamed with the metallic salty taste of blood in his mouth and hauled back on the stick with all his strength, the nose came up and over, climbing out of the dive, and again the blood drained from his head – going from red-out to black-out in the fraction of a second and he saw the Russian following him up, drawn up by the ploy. At the top David kicked it out in a breakaway roll. It caught the Russian, he was one-hundredth of a second slow in countering and he swung giddily through David's gunsight, an almost impossible deflection shot that sluiced cannon fire wildly across the sky, spraying it like water from a garden hose. The MiG was in David's sight for perhaps one-tenth of a second, but in that time David saw a flash of light, a bright wink of it below the pilot's canopy, and then David rolled and turned out, coming around hard and finding the Russian still hanging in the circuit, but losing air space, swaying out with a feather of white vapour streaming back from below his cockpit canopy.

I've hit him, David exulted, and his fear was gone, become anger again, a fierce triumphant anger. He took the Mirage up in another soaring yo-yo and this time the MiG could not hold station on him and David flickrolled off the top and came out with the Russian centred in his gunsight.

He fired a one-second burst and saw the incendiary shells lace in and burst in quick little stabbing stars in the silver fuselage of the MiG.

The Russian came out of his turn, in a gentle dive, flying straight, no longer taking evasive action, probably dead at his controls, and David sat on his tail, and settled the pipper of his gunsight.

He fired another one-second burst and the MiG began to break up. Small unidentifiable pieces of wreckage flew back at David, but the Russian stayed with his machine.

Again David hit him with a two-second burst, and now the MiG's nose sank until she was in a vertical dive still under full power and she went down like a silver javelin. David could not follow her without tearing off his own wings. He pulled out and watched the Russian fly into the earth at a speed that must have exceeded Mach 2. He burst like a bomb in a tall tower of dust and smoke that stood for long seconds on the brown plains of Syria.

David shut down his afterburners and looked to his fuel gauges. They were all showing only a narrow strip above the empty notch, and David realized that the last screaming dive after the MiG had taken him down to an altitude of five thousand, he was over enemy territory and too low – much too low.

Expending precious fuel he came around on a westerly heading and went to interception speed, climbing swiftly out of range of flak and searching the heavens about him for sign of either Joe or the other MiGs – although he guessed that the Syrians were either with Allah in the garden of the Houris, or back home with mother by this time.

'Bright Lance Two, this is Leader. Do you read me?'

'Leader, this is Two,' Joe's voice answered him immediately. 'I have you visual. In the name of God, get out of there!'

'What is my position?'

'We are fifty miles within Syrian territory, our course for base is 250°.'

'How did you go?'

'I took out one of mine. The other one ran for it, after that I was too busy keeping an eye on you—'

David blinked his eyes and was surprised to find that sweat was pouring down his forehead from under his helmet and his mask was slick and sticky with blood from his nosebleed. His arms and shoulders still ached, and he felt drunken and light-headed from the effects of gravity and combat and his hands on the control column were shaky and weak.

'I got two,' he said, 'two of the swines – one for Debra, and one for Hannah.'

'Shut up, Davey.' Joe's voice was stiff with tension. 'Concentrate on getting out of here. You are within range of both flak and ground missiles. Light your tail – and let's go.'

'Negative,' David answered him. 'I'm low on fuel. Where are you?'

'Six o'clock high at 25,000.' As he answered, Joe sat up in his seat, leaning forward against his shoulder straps to watch the tiny wedge shape of David's machine far below. It was climbing slowly up to meet him, slowly – too slowly, and low – too low. David was vulnerable and Joe was afraid for him, frowning heavily into his face mask and searching restlessly, sweeping heaven and earth for the first hint of danger. Two minutes would see them clear, but they would be two long, slow minutes.

He almost missed the first missile. The ground crew must have allowed David to overfly their launch pad before they put it up in pursuit – for Joe picked up its vapour trail as it streaked in from behind David, closing rapidly with him.

'Missile, break left,' Joe yelled into his mask. 'Go! Go! Go!' and he saw David begin his turn instantly, steeply, side-stepping the sizzling attack of the missile.

'It's lost you!' Joe called, as the missile continued its crazy career through space, beginning to yaw from side to side as it hunted for a target and at last bursting in self-destruction.

'Keep going, Davey,' Joe encouraged him, 'but keep awake, there will be more.'

They both saw the next one leave the ground from its camouflaged vehicle. There was a nest of them on a rocky ridge above a sun-blasted plain. The Serpent slid off the rock and lifted into the sky, climbing rapidly towards David's little machine.

'Light your tail,' Joe told him, 'and wait for it!' He watched the missile boring in, converging with dazzling speed on David's Mirage.

'Break right! Go! Go! Go!' Joe yelled and David twisted violently aside. Again the Serpent slid past him, over-shooting, but this time not losing contact and coming around to attack again, its seekers locked to David's machine.

'He's still on you,' Joe was screaming now. 'Go for the sun, Davey. Try for the sun,' and the Mirage pointed its nose at the great blazing orb that burned above the mountain ranges of dark cloud. The Serpent followed him upwards, hunting him with the dreadful single-mindedness of the automaton.

'He's on to you, Davey. Flip out now! Go! Go! Go!'

David flicked the Mirage out of her vertical climb, and fell like a stone – while the Serpent fastened its attention upon the vast infra-red output from the sun and streaked on towards it, losing the Mirage.

'You've lost it. Get out, Davey, get out!' Joe pleaded with him, but for the moment the Mirage was helpless. In her desperate climb for the sun she had lost manoeuvring speed and was wallowing clumsily now. It would be many seconds before she became agile and lithe once more – and by then it would be too late – for Joe saw the third missile become airborne and dart upwards on its feather of flame and smoke aiming at David's Mirage.

Joe did not consciously realize what he was going to do until he had winged over and commenced his dive under full power. He came down with his Mach meter indicating twice the speed of sound, and he levelled across David's tail, cutting obliquely across his track under the nose of the oncoming Serpent.

The Serpent saw him with its little cyclops radar eye, and it sensed the heat of his exhausts – fresher, more tantalizing than David's, and it accepted him as an alternative target and swung away after him, leaving David to fly on unscathed.

David saw Joe's aircraft flash past his wing-tip at searing speed, and but an instant behind him followed the Serpent. It took him only a second to realize that Joe had deliberately pulled the missile off him, had accepted the attack that must surely have destroyed David.

He watched with fascinated horror as Joe pulled out of

182

his dive, and used his speed to climb into the sun. The missile followed him smoothly, angling upwards, overhauling Joe's Mirage with effortless ease. Joe was watching the missile in his mirror, and at the last instant he flipped out of the climb – but this time the Serpent was not deceived; as Joe dropped so it swivelled also, and as earlier David had wallowed helplessly now Joe was in the same predicament. He had taken his chance and it had not worked for him. The missile found him, and in a brusque burst of flame, Joe and his Mirage died together.

David flew on alone, his Mirage once more at manoeuvring speed and his throat dry with horror and fear and grief. He found himself talking aloud.

'Joe, no, Joe. Oh God no! You shouldn't have done it.'

Ahead of him through the gaps in the massive cloud bases he saw the Jordan.

'It should be you that's going home, Joe,' he said. 'It should be you, Joe,' and felt the hard ball of sorrow in his throat.

But the instinct of survival was still strong and David yawned and glanced back to clear his blind spot – and he saw the last missile coming in on him. It was just a small black speck far behind, with a little frill of dark smoke around it, but it was watching him hungrily with its wicked little eye.

As he saw it, he knew beyond doubt that this one was his, the one that the fates had reserved for him. The attacks he had evaded so far had worn his nerves and strained his judgement, he felt a sense of fatalistic dismay as he watched the attacking missile gaining on him; nevertheless he gathered his scattered reserves for one more supreme effort.

His eyes narrowed to slits, the sweat sliding down his face and drenching his mask, his left hand holding the throttle fully open and his right gripping the control column with the strength of despair, he judged his moment.

The missile was almost upon him and he screamed with

all his might and hurled the Mirage into the turn, but he had misjudged it by the smallest part of a second. As he turned away the missile slid past him and it was close enough to pick up the shadow of the Mirage in the photo-electric eye of its fusing device. The eye winked at him and the missile exploded.

The Mirage was in the critical attitude of its turn, and the cockpit canopy was exposed entirely to the centre of the blast. It hit the plane with a blow that sent it tumbling; like a running man tripping it went over, and it lost life and flying capability.

The canopy was penetrated by flying steel. A piece struck David's armoured seat with a clang and then it glanced off and struck his arm above the elbow, snapping the bone cleanly so that the arm dropped uselessly and hung into his lap.

An icy wind raged through the torn canopy as the Mirage hurled itself through space with suicidal force, whipping its nose through the vicious motions and flat plane of high-speed spin. David was thrown against his straps, his ribs bruised and his skin smeared from his shoulders, and the broken arm flailing agonizingly.

He tried to hold himself upright in his seat as he reached up over his head, caught hold of the handle of the ejector mechanism and hauled the blind down over his face. He expected to have the charge explode beneath his seat and hurl him free of the doomed Mirage – but nothing happened.

Desperately he released the handle and strained forward to reach the secondary firing mechanism under his seat between his feet. He wrenched it and felt despair as there was no response. The seat was not working, the blast had damaged some vital part of it. He had to fly the Mirage out of it, with one arm and very little altitude left to him. He fastened his right fist on to the moulded grip of the stick, and in the crazy fall and flutter and whirl, David began to fight for control, flying now by instinct alone, for he was badly hurt, and sky and horizon, earth and cloud spun giddily across his vision.

He was aware that he was losing height rapidly, for every time the earth swayed through his line of vision it was closer and more menacing, but doggedly he continued his attempts to roll against the direction of spin.

The earth was very close before he felt the first hint of response, and the ferocity of her gyrations abated slightly. Stick and rudder together, he tried again and the Mirage showed herself willing at last. Gently, with the touch of a lover, he wooed her and suddenly she came out and he was flying straight and level, but she was hard hit. The blast of the missile had done mortal damage, and she was heavy and sick in his hands. He could feel the rough vibration of the engine shaking her, and he guessed that the compressor had thrown a blade and was now out of balance. Within minutes or seconds she would begin to tear herself to pieces. He could not try for climbing power on her.

David looked quickly about him and realized with a shock how far he had fallen in that terrible tumble down the sky. He was only two or three hundred feet above the earth. He was not sure of his direction, but when he glanced at his doppler compass, he found with mild surprise that he was still heading in the general direction of home.

The engine vibration increased, and he could hear the shrill screech of rending metal. He wasn't going to make it home – that was certain – and there was insufficient height to jettison the canopy, release his straps and attempt to scramble out of the cockpit. There was only one course still remaining, he must fly the Mirage in.

Even as he made the decision his one good hand was busy implementing it. Holding the stick between his knees, he let down his landing gear; the nose wheel might hold him up long enough to take some of the speed off her and prevent her cartwheeling.

He looked ahead, and saw a low ridge of rocky ground and sparse green vegetation. Disaster lurked for him there – but beyond it were open fields, ploughed land, orderly blocks of orchards, neatly laid-out buildings. That in itself was cheering. Such order and industry could only mean that he had returned across the border to Israel.

David skimmed over the ridge of broken rocks, sucking in his own belly as though to lift the Mirage bodily over the hungry teeth of granite, and ahead of him lay the fields. He could see women working in one of the orchards, stopping and turning to look at him. So close that he could clearly see the expressions of surprise and apprehension on their faces.

There was a man on a blue tractor and he jumped from his seat and fell to the earth as David passed only feet above his head.

All fuel cocks closed, all switches off, master switch off – David went into the final ritual for crash-landing.

Ahead of him lay the smooth brown field, open and clear. He might just be lucky enough, it might just come off.

The Mirage was losing flying speed, her nose coming up, the airspeed needle sinking back, 200 miles per hour, 190, 180, dropping back to her stalling speed of 150.

Then suddenly David realized that the field ahead of him was latticed with deep concrete irrigation channels. They were twenty feet wide, and ten deep, a deadly hazard – enough to destroy a Centurion tank.

There was nothing David could do now to avoid their gaping jaws. He flew the Mirage in, touching down smoothly.

'Smooth as a tomcat pissing on a sheet of velvet,' he thought bitterly, aware that all his skill was unavailing now. 'Even Barney would have been proud of me.' The field was rough, but the Mirage settled to it, pitching and lurking, shaking David ruthlessly about the cockpit, but

186

she was up on all three wheels, losing speed handily, her undercart taking the strain. However, she was still travelling at ninety miles an hour when she went into the irrigation ditch.

It snapped her undercart off like pretzel sticks and she nosed in, struck the far bank of concrete that sheered through metal like a scythe, and sent the fuselage cartwheeling across the field with David still strapped within it. The wings broke away and the body slid on across the soft earth to come to rest at last, right way up like a stranded whale.

The whole of David's left side was numb, no feeling in his arm or leg, the straps had mauled him with their rude grasp, and he was stunned and bewildered in the sudden engrossing silence.

For many seconds he sat still, unable to move or think. Then he smelled, it, the pervasive reek of Avtur jet fuel from the ruptured tanks and lines. The smell of it galvanized him with the pilot's deadly fear of fire.

With his right hand he grabbed the canopy release lever and heaved at it. He wasted ten precious seconds with it, for it was jammed solid. Then he turned his attention to the steel canopy breaker in its niche below the lever. This was a tool specially designed for this type of emergency. He lifted it, lay back in his seat and attacked the Perspex dome above his head. The stink of jet fuel was overpowering, filling the cockpit, and he could hear the little pinging and tinkling sound made by white-hot metal.

His left arm hampered him, he had no feeling or use in it. The straps bound him tightly to his seat and he had to pause in his assault upon the canopy to loosen them.

Then he began again. He tore an opening in the Perspex, the size of a hand, and as he worked to enlarge it, a ruptured fuel-pressure line somewhere in the shattered fuselage sprayed a jet of Avtur high in the air. It fell in a heavy drizzle upon the canopy like a garden sprinkler, poured down the curved sides and dribbled through the hole David was cutting. It fell into his face, icy cold on his cheeks and stinging his eyes, it drenched his shoulders and the front of his pressure suit, and David began to pray. For the first time ever in his life the words took on meaning and he felt his terror receding.

'Hear O Israel, the Lord our God, the Lord is one.'

He prayed aloud, striking up at the softly yielding Perspex and feeling the soft rain of death in his face. He tore at the opening with his hands, bringing away slabs of transparent material, but ripping his gloves and leaving his blood smearing the jagged edges of the opening.

'Blessed be His name, whose glorious kingdom is for ever—'

The opening was large enough. He hauled himself up in the seat, and found himself caught by the oxygen and radio lines attached to his helmet. He could not reach them with his crippled left arm. He stared down at the offending limb, and saw the blood welling out of the torn sleeve of the suit. There was no pain but it was twisted at a comical angle from the elbow.

'You shall love the Lord your God with all your heart—' he whispered, and with his right hand he tore loose the chin strap and let his helmet drop to the floor-boards. The Avtur soaked into the soft dark mop of his hair and ran down his neck behind his ears, and he thought about the flames of hell.

Painfully he dragged himself out through the opening in the canopy, and now not even prayer could hold off the dark hordes of terror that assaulted his soul.

'For the anger of God will kindle against you—'

Laboriously he crawled across the slippery sleek metal of the wing root and fell to the ground. He fell face down and lay for a moment, exhausted by fear and effort.

' – remember all the commands of God—'

He heard voices then as he lay with his face against the

dusty earth, and he lifted his head and saw the women from the orchard running towards him across the open field. The voices were shrill but faint and the words were in Hebrew. He knew that he was home.

Steadying himself against the shattered body of the Mirage, he came to his feet with the broken arm dangling at his side, and he tried to shout to them.

'Go back! Beware!' but his voice was a throaty croak, and they ran on towards him. Their dresses and aprons were gay spots of colour against the dry brown earth.

He pushed himself away from the aircraft and staggered to meet the running women.

'Go back!' he croaked in his own terrible distress, with the grip of his G-suit strangling his movements and the evaporating fuel cold as ice in his air and down his face.

Within the battered hull of the Mirage a puddle of Avtur had been heated by the white-hot shell of the jet compressor. Its low volatility at last was raised to flash point and a dying spark from the electronic equipment was enough to ignite it.

With a dull but awful roar, the Mirage bloomed with dark crimson flame and sooty black smoke, the wind ripped the flames outwards in great streamers and pennants that engulfed all around them, and David staggered onwards in the midsts of the roaring furnace that seemed to consume the very air.

He held his breath – if he had not, the flame would have scorched his lungs. He closed his eyes tightly against the agony and ran on blindly. His body and his limbs were protected by the fireproof pressure suit and boots and gloves – but his head was bare and soaked with jet fuel.

As he ran his head burned like a torch. His hair frizzled off in a stinking puff of flame and the skin of his scalp and neck and face were exposed. The flames burnt his ears off and most of his nose, they flayed off his skin in a blistering sheet and then they ate into the raw flesh, they burnt away his lips and exposed his teeth and part of the bone of his jaw. They ate through his eyelids and stripped the living meat from his cheeks.

David ran on through the burning air and smoke, and he did not believe that such pain was possible. It exceeded all his imaginings and swamped all the senses of his body and mind – but he knew he must not scream. The pain was a blackness and the vivid colours of flame in his tightly closed eyes, it was a roaring in his ears like all the winds of the world, and in his flesh it was the goads and whips and burning hooks of hell itself. But he knew he could not let this terrible fire enter his body and he ran on without screaming.

The women from the orchard were brought up short by the sudden forest of flame and black smoke that rose up in front of them, engulfing the squashed-insect body of the aircraft, and closing around the running figure of the pilot.

It was a solid impenetrable wall of heat and smoke that blotted out all ahead of them, and forced them to draw back, awed and horrified, before its raging hot breath. They stood in a small group, panting and wild-eyed.

Then abruptly a freak gust of wind opened the heavy oily curtains of smoke, and out of them stumbled a dreadful thing with a scorched and smoking body and a head of flame.

Blindly it came out of the smoke, one arm hanging and its feet dragging and staggering in the soft earth. They stared at this thing in horror, frozen in silence, and it came towards them.

Then a strapping girl, with a strong brown body and a man of dark hair, uttered a cry of compassion – and raced to meet him.

As she ran, she stripped off her heavy voluminous skirt of thick wool, leaving her strong brown legs bare. She reached David and she swirled the skirt over his head, smothering the flames that still ate into his flesh. The other women followed her, using their clothing to wrap him as he fell and rolled on the earth.

Only then did David begin to scream, from that lipless mouth with the exposed teeth. It was a sound that none of them would ever forget. As he screamed the eyes were open, with the lashes and brow and most of the lids burned away. The eyes were dark indigo blue in the glistening mask of wet scorched meat, and the little blood vessels, sealed by the heat, popped open and dribbled and spurted. As he screamed, the blood and lymph bubbled from the nostril holes where his nose had been, and his body writhed and heaved and convulsed as spasm after spasm of unbearable agony hit him.

The women had to hold him down to control his struggles, and to prevent him tearing with clawed fingers at the ruins of his face.

He was still screaming when the doctor from the kibbutz slashed open the sleeve of his pressure suit with a scalpel and pressed the morphine needle into the twitching, jumping muscles of his arm.

The Brig saw the last bright radar image fade from the plot and heard the young radar officer report formally, 'No further contact.' And a great silence fell on the command bunker.

They were all watching him. He stood hunched over the plot and his big bony fists were clasped at his sides. His face was stiff and expressionless, but his eyes were terrible.

It seemed that the frantic voices of his two pilots still echoed from the speakers above his head, as they called to each other in the extremes of mortal conflict.

They had all heard David's voice, hoarse with sorrow and fear.

'Joe! No, Joe! Oh God, no!' and they knew what that

meant. They had lost them both, and the Brig was still stunned by the sudden incalculable turn that the sortie had taken.

At the moment he had lost control of his fighters he had known that disaster was unavoidable – and now his son was dead. He wanted to cry out aloud, to protest against the futility of it. He closed his eyes tightly for a few seconds, and when he opened them, he was in control again.

'General alert,' he snapped. 'All squadrons to "Red" standby—' he knew they faced an international crisis. 'I want air cover over the area they went down. They may have ejected. Put up two Phantom flights and keep an umbrella over them. I want helicopters sent in immediately, with paratrooper guards and medical teams—'

Command bunker moved swiftly into general alert procedure.

'Get me the Prime Minister,' he said. He was going to have to do a lot of explaining, and he spared a few vital seconds to damn David Morgan roundly and bitterly.

T he air force doctor took one look at David's charred and scorched head and he swore softly.

'We'll be lucky to save this one.'

Loosely he swathed the head in Vaseline bandages and they hurried with David's blanket-wrapped body on the stretcher to the Bell 205 helicopter waiting in the orchard.

The Bell touched down on the helipad at Hadassah Hospital and a medical team was ready for him. One hour and fifty-three minutes after the Mirage hit the irrigation canal David had passed through the sterile lock into the special burns unit on the third floor of the hospital – into a quiet and secluded little world where everybody wore masks and long green sterile robes and the only contact with the outside world was through the double-glazed windows and even the air he breathed was scrubbed and cleaned and filtered.

However, David was enfolded in the soft dark clouds of morphine and he did not hear the quiet voices of the masked figures as they worked over him.

'It's third degree over the entire area—'

'No attempt to clean it or touch it, Sister, not until it stabilizes. I am going to spray with Epigard, and we'll go to intra-muscular Tetracycline four-hourly against infection—

'It will be two weeks before we dare touch it.'

'Very well, Doctor.'

'Oh, and Sister, fifteen milligrams of morphine six-hourly. We are going to have a lot of pain with this one.'

Pain was infinity, an endless ocean across which the wave-patterns marched relentlessly to burst up the beaches of his soul. There were times when the surf of pain ran high and each burst of it threatened to shatter his reason. Again there were times when it was low, almost gentle in its throbbing rhythm and he drifted far out upon the ocean of pain to where the morphine mists enfolded him. Then the mists parted and a brazen sun beat down upon his head, and he squirmed and writhed and cried out. His skull seemed to bloat and swell until it must burst, and the open nerve-ends screamed for surcease.

Then suddenly there was the sharply beloved sting of the needle in his flesh, and the mists closed about him once more.

'I don't like the look of this at all. Have we taken a culture, Sister?'

'Yes, Doctor.'

'What are we growing?'

'I'm afraid it's strep.'

'Yes. I thought so. I think we'll change to Cloxacillin – see if we get a better response with that.'

With the pain, David became aware of a smell. It was the smell of carrion and things long dead, the smell of vermin in dirty blankets, of vomit and excreta, and the odour of wet garbage festering in dark alleys – and at last he came to know that the smell was the rotting of his own flesh as the bacteria of Streptococcus infection attacked the exposed tissue.

They fought it with the drugs, but now the pain was underlined with the fevers of infection and the terrible burning thirsts which no amount of liquids could slake.

With the fever came the nightmares and the fantasies to plague and goad him even further beyond the limits of his endurance.

'Joe—' he cried out in his agony, 'try for the sun, Joe. Break left now – Go! Go!' And then he was sobbing from the ruined and broken mouth. 'Oh, Joe! Oh God, no! Joe.'

Until the night-sister could no longer bear it and she came hurrying with the syringe, and his screams turned into babbling and then into the low whimper and moan of the drug sleep.

'We'll start with the acriflavin dressings now, Sister.'

When they changed the dressings every forty-eight hours it was under general anaesthetic for the entire head was of raw flesh, a bland expressionless head, a head like a child's drawing, crude lines and harsh colours, hairless, earless, streaked and mottled with yellow runs and patches of soft pus and corruption.

'We are getting a response from the Cloxacillin, it's looking a lot healthier, Sister.'

The naked flesh of his eyelids had contracted, pulling back like the glistening petals of a pink rose, exposing the eyeballs to the air without respite. They had filled the eyes' sockets with a yellow ointment to soothe and moisten them, to keep out the loathsome infection that covered his head. The ointment prevented vision.

'I think we'll go for an abdominal pedicel now. Will you prep for afternoon theatre, please, Sister?'

Now it was time for the knife, and David was to learn that the pain and the knife lived together in terrible sin. They lifted a long flap of skin and flesh from his belly, leaving it still attached at one end, and they rolled it into a fat sausage, then they strapped his good arm, the one without the plaster cast, to his side and they stitched the free end of the sausage to his forearm, training it to draw its blood supply from there. Then they brought him back from theatre and left him trussed and helpless and blind with the pedicel fastened to his arm, like a remora to the belly of a shark.

'Well, we have saved both eyes.' The voice was proud, fond almost, and David looked up and saw them for the first time. They were gathered around his cot, a circle of craning heads, mouths and noses covered by surgical masks, but his vision was still smeary with ointment and distorted by the drip irrigation that had replaced it.

'Now we will go for the eyelids.'

It was the knife again, the contracted and bunched-up eyelids split and re-shaped and stitched, the knife and pain and the familiar sickly taste and stink of anaesthetic that saturated his body and seemed to exude from the very pores of his skin.

'Beautiful, really lovely – we have cleaned up the infection nicely. Now we can begin.'

The head was cleansed of its running rivers of pus, and now it was glistening and wet, bald and bright red, the colour of a cocktail cherry as granulation tissue formed. There were two gnarled and twisted flaps for ears, the double row of teeth startlingly white and perfect where the lips had been eaten away, a long white blade of exposed bone outlined the point of the jaw, the nose was a stump with the nostrils like the double muzzles of a shotgun, and only the eyes were still beautiful – dark indigo and flawlessly white between lids of shocking crimson and neatly laid back stitches.

'We'll begin at the back of the neck. Will you prep for this afternoon's theatre, please, Sister?'

It was a variation on the theme of the knife. They planed sheets of live skin from his thighs and meshed them to allow a wider spread, then they laid them over the exposed flesh, covering a little at each session, and evaluating each attempt while David lay in his cot and rode the long swells of pain.

'That one is no good. I'm afraid we will have to scrap it and try again.'

While his thighs grew a new crop of skin, they planed fresh sheets from his calves, so that each donor-site became a new source of pain.

'Lovely! An edge-to-edge take with that graft.'

Slowly the cap of skin extended up across the nape of his neck and over his scalp. The meshing of the skin grafts gave them a patterned effect, regular as the scales of a fish, and the new grafts were hard-looking and raised.

'We can move the pedicel up now.'

'This afternoon's theatre, Doctor?'

'Yes, please, Sister.'

David came to know that they operated every Thursday in the burns unit. He came to dread the Thursday morning rounds when the consultant and his staff crowded around his cot and touched and prodded and discussed the restructuring of his flesh with an impersonal candour that chilled him.

They freed the fat sausage of flesh from his belly and it dangled from his arm like some grotesque white leech, seeming to have a life of its own, drawing blood and sustenance from its grip upon his forearm.

They lifted his arm and strapped it across his chest, and

the raw end of the pedicel they split and stitched to his jaw and to the stump of his nose.

'It's taken very nicely. We will begin shaping it this afternoon. We'll have him at the head of the theatre list. Will you see to that please, Sister?'

With the living flesh that they had stolen from his belly they fashioned a crude lump of a nose, taut, narrow lips and a new covering for his jawbone.

'The oedema has settled. This afternoon I will go for the bone-graft on the jaw.'

They opened his chest and split his fourth rib laterally, robbing it of a long sliver of bone, and they grafted this to the damaged jaw-bone, then they spread the flesh of the pedicel over it and stitched it all into place.

On Thursdays it was the knife and the stink of anaesthetic, and for the days in between it was the ache and pain of abused and healing flesh.

They fined down the new nose, piercing it with nostrils, they finished the reconstruction of his eyelids. They laid the last grafts behind his ears, they cut a double zig-zag incision around the base of his jaw where the contracting scar tissue was trying to draw his chin down on to his chest. The new lips took firm hold on the existing muscles and David gained control of them so he could form his words again and speak clearly.

The last area of raw flesh was closed beneath the patchwork of skin grafts, flesh grafts and stitches. David was no longer a high-infection risk and he was moved from a sterile environment. Once again he saw human faces, not merely eyes peering over white surgical masks. The faces were friendly, cheerful faces. Men and women proud of their achievement in saving him from death and refleshing his ravaged head.

'You'll be allowed visitors now, and I expect you'll welcome that,' said the consultant. He was a distinguished-looking young surgeon who had left a highly paid post at a Swiss clinic to head this burns and plastic surgery unit.

'I don't think I will be having any visitors,' David had lost contact with the reality of the outside world during the nine months in the burns unit.

'Oh, yes, you will,' the surgeon told him. 'We've had regular enquiries on your progress from a number of people. Isn't that correct, Sister?'

'That's right, Doctor.'

'You can let them know that he is allowed visitors now.'

The consultant and his group began to move on.

'Doctor,' David called him back. 'I want a look at a mirror,' and they were all silent, immediately embarrassed. This request of his had been denied many times over the last months.

'Damn it,' David became angry. 'You can't protect me from it for ever.'

The consultant gestured for the others to leave and they filed out of the ward, while he came back to David's bed.

'All right, David,' he agreed gently. 'We'll find you a mirror – though we don't have much use for them around here.' For the first time in the many months he had known him, David glimpsed the depths of his compassion, and he wondered at it. That a man who lived constantly amongst great pain and terrible disfigurement could still be moved by it.

'You must understand that how you are now is not how you will always be. All I have been able to do, so far, is heal your exposed flesh and make you functional again. You are once more a viable human being. You have not experienced the loss of any of your faculties – but I will not pretend that you are beautiful. However, there remains much that I can still do to change that. Your ears, for example, can be reconstructed with the material I have

198

reserved for that purpose—' He indicated the stump of the pedicel that still hung from David's forearm. ' – There is much fine work still to be done about the nose and mouth and eyes.' He paced slowly the length of the ward and looked out into the sunlight for a moment before turning back again and coming forward to face David.

'But let me be truthful with you. There are limitations to what I can do. The muscles of expression, those delicate little muscles around the eyes and mouth, have been destroyed. I cannot replace those. The hair follicles of your lashes and brows and scalp have been burned away. You will be able to wear a wig, but—'

David turned to his bedside locker and took from the drawer his wallet. He opened it and drew out a photograph. It was the one which Hannah had taken so long ago of Debra and David sitting at the rock-pool in the oasis of Ein Gedi and smiling at each other. He handed it to the surgeon.

'Is that what you looked like, David? I never knew.' The regret showed like a quick shadow in his eyes.

'Can you make me look like that again?'

The surgeon studied the photograph a moment longer, the young god's face with the dark mop of hair and the clean pure lines of the profile.

'No,' he said. 'I could not even come close.'

'That's all I wanted to know.' David took the photograph back from him. 'You say I'm functional now. Let's leave it at that, shall we?'

'You don't want further cosmetic surgery? We can still do a lot—'

'Doctor, I've lived under the knife for nine months. I've had the taste of antibiotics and anaesthetic in my mouth, and the stink of it in my nostrils for all that time. Now all I want is a little escape from pain – a little peace and the taste of clean air.'

'Very well,' the surgeon agreed readily. 'It is not important that we do it now. You could come back at any time in the future.' He walked to the door of the ward. 'Come on. Let's go find a mirror.'

There was one in the nurses' room beyond the double doors at the end of the passage. The room itself was empty and the mirror was set into the wall above the wash basin.

The surgeon stood in the doorway and leaned against the jamb. He lit a cigarette and watched as David crossed towards the mirror and then halted abruptly as he saw his own image.

He wore the blue hospital dressing-gown over his pyjamas. He was tall and finely proportioned. His shoulders were wide, his hips narrow, and he had the same lithe and beautiful man's body.

However, the head that topped it was something from a nightmare. Involuntarily he gasped out aloud and the gash of a mouth parted in sympathy. It was a tight lipless mouth, like that of a cobra, white-rimmed and harsh.

Drawn by the awful fascination of the horror, David drew closer to the mirror. The thick mane of his dark hair had concealed the peculiar elongation of his skull. He had never realized that it jutted out behind like that, for now the hair was gone and the bald curve was covered with meshed skin, thickened and raised.

The skin and flesh of his face was a patchwork, joined by seams of scar tissue drawn tightly over his cheekbones, giving him a vaguely Asiatic appearance, but the eyes were round and startled, with clumsy lids and puffed dead-looking flesh beneath.

His nose was a shapeless blob, out of balance with his other coarsened features, and his ears were gnarled excrescences, seemingly fastened haphazardly to the sides of his head. The whole of it was bland and bald and boiled-looking.

The gash of a mouth twisted briefly in a horrid rictus, and then regained its frozen shape.

200

'I can't smile,' said David.

'No,' agreed the surgeon. 'You will have no control of your expressions.'

That was the truly horrifying aspect of it. It was not the twisted and tortured flesh, with the scarring and stitch marks still so evident – it was the expressionlessness of this mask. The frozen features seemed long dead, incapable of human warmth or feeling.

'Yeah! But you should have seen the other guy!' David said softly, and the surgeon chuckled without mirth.

'We'll have those last few stitches behind your ears out tomorrow – I shall remove what remains of the pedicel from your arm – and then you can be discharged. Come back to us when you are ready.'

David ran his hand gingerly over the bald patterned skull.

'I'm going to save a fortune in haircuts and razor blades,' he said, and the surgeon turned quickly away and walked down the passage, leaving David to get to know his new head.

The clothes that they had found for him were cheap and ill-fitting – slacks and open-neck shirt, a light jacket and sandals – and he asked for some head covering, anything to conceal the weird new shape of his scalp. One of the nurses found him a cloth cap, and then told him that a visitor was waiting for him in the hospital superintendent's department.

He was a major from the military provost marshal's office, a lean grey-haired man with cold grey eyes and a tight hard mouth. He introduced himself without offering to shake hands and then opened the file on the desk in front of him.

'I have been instructed by my office to ask for the formal resignation of your commission in the Israeli Air Force,' he started, and David stared at him. In the long pain-filled, fever-hot nights, the thought of flying once more had seemed like a prospect of paradise.

'I don't understand,' he mumbled, and reached for a cigarette, breaking the first match and then puffing quickly as the second flared. 'You want my resignation – and if I refuse?'

'Then we shall have no alternative other than to convene a court martial and to try you for dereliction of duty, and refusing in the face of the enemy to obey the lawful orders of your superior officer.'

'I see,' David nodded heavily, and drew on the cigarette. The smoke stung his eyes.

'It doesn't seem I have any choice.'

'I have prepared the necessary documents. Please sign here, and here, and I shall sign as witness.'

David bowed over the papers and signed. The pen scratched loudly in the silent room.

'Thank you.' The major gathered his papers, and placed them in his briefcase. He nodded at David and started for the door.

'So now I am an outcast,' said David softly, and the man stopped. They stared at each other for a moment, and then the major's expression altered slightly, and the cold grey eyes became ferocious.

'You are responsible for the destruction of two warplanes that are irreplaceable and whose loss has caused us incalculable harm. You are responsible for the death of a brother officer, and for bringing your country to the very brink of open war which would have cost many thousands more of our young people's lives – and possibly our very existence. You have embarrassed our international friends – and given strength to our enemies.' He paused and drew a deep breath. 'The recommendation of my office was that you be brought to trial and that the prosecution be instructed to ask for the death penalty. It was only the personal intervention of the Prime Minister and of Major-General Mordecai that saved you from that. In my view, instead of bemoaning your fate, you should consider yourself highly fortunate.'

He turned away and his footsteps cracked on the stone floor as he strode from the room.

In the bleak impersonal lobby of the hospital, David was suddenly struck by a reluctance to walk on out into the spring sunshine through the glass swing doors. He had heard that long-term prisoners felt this way when the time came for their release.

Before he reached the doors he turned aside and went down to the hospital synagogue. In a corner of the quiet square hall he sat for a long time. The stained-glass windows, set high in the nave, filled the air with shafts of coloured lights when the sun came through, and a little of the peace and beauty of that place stayed with him and gave him courage when at last he walked out into the square and boarded a bus for Jerusalem.

He found a seat at the rear, and beside a window. The bus pulled away and ground slowly up the hill towards the city.

He became aware that he was being watched, and he lifted his head to find that a woman with two young children had taken the seat in front of him. She was a poorly dressed, harassed-looking woman, prematurely aged and she held the grubby young infant on her lap and fed it from the plastic bottle. However, the second child was an angelic little girl of four or five years. She had huge dark eyes and a head of thick curls. She stood on the seat facing backwards, with one thumb thrust deeply into her mouth. She was watching David steadily over the back of the seat, studying his face with that total absorption and candour of the child. David felt a sudden warmth of emotion for the child, a longing for the comfort of human contact, of which he had been deprived all these months.

He leaned forward in his seat, trying to smile, reaching out a gentle hand to touch the child's arm.

She removed her thumb from her mouth and shrank away from him, turning to her mother and clinging to her arm, hiding her face in the woman's blouse.

At the next stop David stepped down from the bus and left the road to climb the stony hillside.

The day was warm and drowsy, with the bee murmur and the smell of the blossoms from the peach orchards. He climbed the terraces and rested at the crest, for he found he was breathless and shaky. Months in hospital had left him unaccustomed to walking far, but it was not that alone. The episode with the child had distressed him terribly.

He looked longingly towards the sky. It was clear and brilliant blue, with high silver cloud in the north. He wished he could ascend beyond those clouds. He knew he would find peace up there.

A taxi dropped him off at the top of Malik Street. The front door was unlocked, swinging open before he could fit his key in the lock.

Puzzled and alarmed he stepped into the living-room. It was as he had left it so many months before, but somebody had cleaned and swept, and there were fresh flowers in a vase upon the olive-wood table – a huge bouquet of gaily coloured dahlias, yellow and scarlet.

David smelled food, hot and spicy and tantalizing after the bland hospital fare.

'Hello,' he called. 'Who is there?'

'Welcome home!' There was a familiar bellow from behind the closed bathroom door. 'I didn't expect you so soon – and you've caught me with my skirts up and pants down.'

There was a scuffling sound and then the toilet flushed thunderously and the door was flung open. Ella Kadesh appeared majestically through it. She wore one of her huge kaftans, it was a blaze of primary colours. Her hat was apple-green in colour, the brim pinned up at the side like an Australian bush hat by an enormous jade brooch and a bunch of ostrich feathers.

Her heavy arms were flung wide in a gesture of welcome, and the face was split in a huge grin of anticipation. She came towards him, and the grin persisted long after the horror had dawned in her bright little eyes. Her steps slowed.

'David?' Her voice was uncertain. 'It is you, David?'

'Hello, Ella.'

'Oh God. Oh, sweet holy name of God. What have they done to you, my beautiful young Mars—'

'Listen, you old bag,' he said sharply, 'if you start blubbering I'm going to throw you down the steps.'

She made a huge effort to control it, fighting back the tears that flooded into her eyes, but her jowls wobbled and her voice was thick and nasal as she enfolded him in her huge arms and hugged him to her bosom.

'I've got a case of cold beers in the refrigerator – and I made a pot of curry for us. You'll love my curry, it's the thing I do best—'

David ate with enormous appetite, washing down the fiery food with cold beer, and he listened to Ella talk. She spouted words like a fountain, using their flow to cover her pity and embarrassment.

'They would not let me visit you, but I telephoned every week and kept in touch that way. The sister and I got very friendly, she let me know you were coming today. So I drove up to make sure you had a welcome—'

She tried to avoid looking directly at his face, but when she did the shadows appeared in her eyes, even though she made a convincing effort at gaiety. When he finished eating at last, she asked, 'What will you do now, David?'

'I would have liked to go back and fly. It's the thing I like to do best – but they have forced me to resign my commission. I disobeyed orders, Joe and I followed them across the border, and they don't want me any more.'

'There was nearly open war, David. It was a crazy thing that you and Joe did.'

David nodded. 'I was mad. I wasn't thinking straight – after Debra—'

Ellen interrupted quickly. 'Yes, I know. Share another beer?'

David nodded distractedly. 'How is she, Ella?' It was the question he had wanted to ask all along.

'She is just fine, Davey. She has begun the new book, and if anything it's better than the first. I think she will become a very important writer—'

'Her eyes? Is there any improvement?'

Ella shook her head. 'She had come to terms with that now. It doesn't seem to bother her any longer, just as you will come to accept what has happened—'

David was not listening. 'Ella, in all that time, when I was in hospital, every day I hoped – I knew it was useless, but I hoped to hear from her. A card, a word—'

'She didn't know, Davey.'

'Didn't know?' David demanded and leaned across the table to grip Ella's wrist. 'What do you mean?'

'After Joe – was killed, Debra's father was very angry. He believed that you were responsible.'

David nodded, the blank mask of his face concealing his guilt.

'Well, he told Debra that you had left Israel, and gone back to your home. We were all sworn to silence – and that's what Debra believes now.'

David released Ella's wrist, picked up his beer glass and sipped at the head of froth.

'You still haven't answered my question, David. What are you going to do now?'

'I don't know, Ella. I guess I'll have to think about that.'

A harsh warm wind came off the hills and ruffled the surface of the lake, darkening it to black and flecking it with white crests. The fishing boats along the curve of the shore tugged restlessly at their mooring ropes, and the fishing nets upon their drying racks billowed like bridal veils.

The wind caught Debra's hair and shook it out in a loose cloud. It pressed the silk dress she wore against her body, emphasizing the heavy roundness of her breasts and the length of her legs.

She stood on the battlements of the crusader castle, leaning both hands lightly on the head of her cane, and she stared out across the water, almost as though she could see beyond it.

Ella sat near her, on a fallen block of masonry out of the wind, but she pinned her hat down with one hand as she spoke, watching Debra's face intently to judge her reactions.

'At the time it seemed the kindest thing to do. I agreed to keep the truth from you, because I did not want you to torture yourself—'

Debra spoke sharply. 'Don't ever do that again.'

Ella made a moue of resignation and went on. 'I had no way of knowing how bad he was, they would not let me see him, and so I suppose I was a coward and let it drift.'

Debra shook her head angrily, but she remained silent. Ella wondered again that sightless eyes could contain so much expression, for Debra's emotions blazed clearly in the honey-coloured sparks as she turned her head towards Ella.

'It was not the time to distract you. Don't you see, my dear? You were adjusting so nicely – working so well on your book. I did not see that we could gain anything by telling you. I decided to co-operate with your father – and see how things turned out later.'

'Then why are you telling me all this now?' Debra

demanded. 'What has happened to change your mind – what has happened to David?'

'Yesterday at noon David was discharged from Hadassah Hospital.'

'Hospital?' Debra was puzzled. 'You don't mean he has been in hospital all this time, Ella? Nine months – it's impossible!'

'It's the truth.'

'He must have been terribly hurt,' Debra's anger had changed to concern. 'How is he, Ella? What happened? Is he healed now?'

Ella was silent a moment, and Debra took a pace towards her. 'Well?' she asked.

'David's plane flamed out and he was very badly burned about the head. He has recovered completely now. His burns have healed – but—'

Ella hesitated again, and Debra groped for her hand and found it. 'Go on, Ella! But—'

'David is no longer the most beautiful man I have ever seen.'

'I don't understand?'

'He is no longer swift and vital and – any woman who sees him now will find it difficult to be near him, let alone love him.'

Debra was listening intently, her expression rapt and her eyes soft-focused.

'He is very conscious of the way he looks now. He is searching for some place to hide, I think. He talks of wanting to fly as though it is some form of escape. He knows he is alone now, cut off from the world by the mask he wears—'

Debra's eyes had misted, and Ella made her gravelly voice gentler and she went on.

'But there is someone who will never see that mask.' Ella drew the girl closer to her. 'Somebody who remembers only the way he was before.' Debra's grip tightened on

Ella's hand, and she began to smile – it was an expression that seemed to radiate from deep within her.

'He needs you now, Debra,' Ella said softly. 'That is all there is left for him. Will you change your decision now?'

'Fetch him to me, Ella,' Debra's voice shook. 'Fetch him to me as soon as you can.'

David climbed the long line of stairs towards Ella's studio. It was a day of bright sunlight and he wore open sandals and light silk slacks of a bronze colour and a short-sleeved shirt with a wide V-neck. His arms were pale from lack of sun, the dark hair of his chest contrasting strongly against the soft cream – and upon his head he wore a wide-brimmed white straw hat to guard the cicatrice from the sun and to soften his face with shadow.

He paused, and he could feel the break of sweat under the shirt and the pumping of his lungs. He despised the weakness of his body and the quivering of his legs as he came out on the terrace. It was deserted, and he crossed to the shuttered doors and went into the gloom.

Ella Kadesh sitting on a Samarkand carpet in the centre of the paved floor was an astonishing sight. For she was dressed in a brief bikini costume adorned with pink roses that almost disappeared under the rolls of ponderous flesh that hung over it from belly and breast. She was in the yoga position of Padmasana, the sitting lotus, and her massive legs were twisted and entwined like mating pythons. Her hands were held before her palm to palm and her eyes were closed in meditation; upon her head her ginger wig was set four square like that of a judge.

David leaned in the doorway and before he could recover his breath he began to laugh. It began as a wheezy little chuckle, and then suddenly he was really laughing, from deep down – great gusts of it that shook his helpless body, and flogged his lungs. It was not mirth but a catharsis of the last dregs of suffering, it was the moment of accepting life again, a taking up once more of the challenge of living.

Ella must have recognized it as such, for she did not move, squatting like some cheerful Buddha on the brilliant carpet, and she opened one little eye. The effect was even more startlingly comic, and David reeled away from the door, and fell into one of the chairs.

'Your soul is a desert, David Morgan,' said Ella. 'You have no recognition of beauty, all loveliness would wither on the dung heap which—' But the rest of it was lost as she also began to giggle and the yoga pose broke down, melting like a jelly on a hot day, and she traded him hoot for hoot and bellow for bellow of laughter.

'I'm stuck,' she gasped at last. 'Help me, Davey, you oaf—' And he staggered to her, knelt and struggled to help her unlock her interwoven legs. They came apart with little creaking and popping sounds and Ella collapsed face down on the carpet groaning and giggling at the same time.

'Get out of here,' she moaned. 'Leave me to die in peace. Go and find your woman, she is down on the jetty.'

She watched him go quickly, and then she dragged herself up and went to the door. The laughter dried up and she whispered aloud, 'My two poor little crippled kittens – I wonder if I have done the right thing.' The shadows of doubt crossed her face, and then faded. 'Well, it's too damn late for worry now, Kadesh, you interfering old bag, you should have thought about that before.'

A gaudily coloured towel and beach jacket were spread upon the jetty and a transistor radio, with its volume turned high, blared out a heavy rock tune. Far out in the bay Debra was swimming alone, a steady powerful overarm crawl. Her brown arms flashed wetly in the sun at each stroke and the water churned to froth at the beat of her legs.

She stopped to tread water. Her bathing cap was plain white, and he could see that she was listening for the sound of the radio for she began to swim again, heading directly in towards the jetty.

She came out of the water, pulling off the cap and shaking out her hair. Her body was dark, sun-browned and bejewelled with drops, the muscles looked firm and hard and her tread was confident and sure as she came up the stone steps and picked up her towel.

As she dried herself David stood near and watched her avidly, seeming to devour her with his eyes, trying to make up in that first minute for all those many months. He had pictured her so clearly, and yet there was much he had forgotten. Her hair was softer, cloudier than he remembered. He had forgotten the plasticity and lustre of her skin, it was darker also than it had been before – almost the colour of her eyes – she must have spent many hours each day in the sun. Suddenly and unaffectedly she threw her towel down and adjusted the top of her brief costume, pulling open the thin fabric and cupping one fat breast in her hand to settle it more comfortably, David felt his need for her so strongly that it seemed he could not contain it all within the physical bounds of his chest. He moved slightly and the gravel crunched softly under his shoes.

Instantly the lovely head turned towards him and froze in the attitude of listening. The eyes were wide open, intelligent and expressive, they seemed to look slightly to one side of him – and David had a powerful impulse to turn and glance behind him, following their steady gaze.

'David?' she asked softly. 'Is that you, David?'

He tried to answer her, but his voice failed him and his reply was a small choking sound. She ran to him, swiftly and long-legged as a roused foal, with her arms reaching out and her face lighting with joy.

He caught her up, and she clung to him fiercely, almost angrily – as though she had been too long denied.

'I've missed you, David.' Her voice was fierce also. 'Oh, God, you'll never know how I have missed you,' and she pressed her mouth to the stark gash in his mask of flesh.

This was the first human being who had treated him without reserve – without pity or revulsion – in all those months, and David felt his heart swell harder and his embrace was as fierce as hers.

She broke at last, leaning back to press her hips unashamedly against his, exulting in the hard thrustingness of his arousal, proud to have evoked it – and quickly, questioningly she ran her hands over his face, feeling the new contours and the unexpected planes and angles.

She felt him begin to pull away, but she stopped him and continued her examination.

'My fingers tell me that you are still beautiful—'

'You have lying fingers,' he whispered, but she ignored his words, and pushed forward teasingly with her hips.

'And I'm getting another very powerful message from further south.' She gave a breathless little laugh. 'Come with me, please, sir.'

Holding his hand, she ran lightly up the steps, dragging him after her. He was amazed at the agility and confidence with which she negotiated the climb. She drew him into the cottage and as he looked about him, quickly taking it all in, she closed and bolted the door. Immediately the room was cool and dim and intimate.

On the bed her body was still damp and cold from the lake, but her lips were hot as she strained against him urgently. The two beautiful young bodies meshed hungrily, almost as if they were attempting to find sanctuary within each other, desperately flesh sought haven within flesh, within each other's encircling arms and legs they searched for and found surcease from the loneliness and the darkness.

The physical act of love, no matter how often repeated, was insufficient for their needs; even in the intervals between they clung desperately to each other; sleeping pressed together, they groped drowsily but anxiously for each other if the movements of sleep separated them for even an instant. They talked holding hands, she reaching up to touch his face at intervals, he staring into her golden eyes. Even when she prepared their simple meals, he stood close beside or behind her so that she could sway against him and feel him there. It was as though they lived in momentary dread of being once more separated.

It was two days before they left the sanctuary of the cottage and walked together along the lake shore or swam from the jetty and lay in the warm sun. But even when Ella looked down at them from the terrace and waved, David asked, 'Shall we go up to her?'

'No,' Debra answered quickly. 'Not yet. I'm not ready to share you with anybody else yet. Just a little while more, please, David.'

And it was another three days before they climbed the path to the studio. Ella had laid on one of her gargantuan lunches, but she had invited no other guests and they were grateful to her for that.

'I thought I'd have to send down a party of stretcher-bearers to carry you up, Davey,' Ella greeted him, with a lecherous chuckle.

'Don't be crude, Ella,' Debra told her primly, flushing to a dark rose brown, and Ella let fly with one of her explosive bursts of mirth that was so contagious they must follow it.

They sat beneath the palm trees and drank wine from the earthenware jugs, and ate hugely, laughing and talking without restraint, David and Debra so involved with each other that they were not aware of Ella's shrewdly veiled appraisal.

The change in Debra was dramatic, all the coolness and reserve were gone now, the armour in which she had clad her emotions was stripped away. She was vital and eager and blooming with love.

She sat close beside David, laughing with delight at his sallies, and leaning to touch and caress him, as though to reassure herself of his presence.

Ella glanced again at David, trying to smile naturally at him, but guiltily aware of the sneaking sensation of repulsion she still felt – repulsion and aching pity – when she looked at that monstrous head. She knew that if she saw it every day for twenty years, it would still disturb her.

Debra laughed again at something David had said and turned her face to him, offering her mouth with a touching innocence.

'What a terrible thing to say,' she laughed. 'I think a gesture of contrition is called for,' and responded eagerly as the great ravaged head bent to her and the thin slit of a mouth touched hers.

It was disquieting to see the lovely dark face against that mask of ruined flesh, and yet it was also strangely moving.

'It was the right thing. For once I did the right thing,' Ella decided, watching them, and feeling a vague envy. These two were bound together completely, made strong by their separate afflictions. Before it had been a mutual itching of the flesh, a chance spark struck from two minds meeting, but now it was something that transcended that.

Ella recalled regretfully a long line of lovers stretching back to the shadowy edges of her memory, receding images which seemed unreal now. If only there had been something to bind her to one of those, if only she had been left with something more valuable than half-remembered words and faded memories of brief mountings and furtive couplings. She sighed, and they looked at her questioningly.

'A sad sound, Ella, darling,' Debra said. 'We are selfish, please forgive us.'

'Not sad, my children,' Ella denied hotly, scattering the old phantoms of her memory. 'I am happy for you. You have something very wonderful – strong and bright and wonderful. Protect it as you would your life.'

She took up her wine glass. 'I give you a toast. I give you David and Debra – and a love made invincible by suffering.' And they were serious for a moment while they drank the toast together in golden yellow wine, sitting in golden yellow sunlight, then the mood resumed and they were gay once more.

Once the first desperate demands of their bodies had been met, once they had drawn as close together as physical limits would allow, then they began a coupling of the spirit. They had never really spoken before, even when they had shared the house on Malik Street they had used only the superficial word symbols.

Now they began learning really to talk. Some nights they did not sleep but spent the fleeting hours of darkness in exploring each other's minds and bodies, and they delighted to realize that this exploration would never be completed – for the areas of their minds were boundless.

During the day the blind girl taught David to see. He found that he had never truly used his eyes before, and now that he must see for both of them he had to learn to make the fullest use of his sight. He must learn to describe colour and shape and movement accurately and incisively, for Debra's demands were insatiable.

In turn, David, whose own confidence had been shattered by his disfigurement, taught confidence to the girl. She learned to trust him implicitly as he grew to anticipate her needs. She learned to step out boldly beside him, knowing that he would guide or caution her with a light touch or a word. Her world had shrunk to the small area about the cottage and the jetty within which she could find her way surely. Now with David beside her, her frontiers fell back and she was free to move wherever she chose.

Yet they ventured out together only cautiously at first, wandering along the lakeside together or climbing the hills towards Nazareth, and each day they swam in the green lake waters and each night they made love in the curtained alcove.

David grew hard and lean and sun-tanned again, and it seemed they were complete for when Ella asked, 'Debra, when are you going to make a start on the new book?' she laughed and answered lightly:

'Sometime within the next hundred years.'

A week later she asked of David this time.

'Have you decided what you are going to do yet, Davey?'

'Just what I'm doing now,' he said, and Debra backed him up quickly. 'For ever!' she said. 'Just like this for ever.'

Then without thinking about it, without really steeling themselves to it, they went to where they would meet other people in the mass.

David borrowed the speedboat, picked up a shopping list from Ella, and they planed down along the lake shore to Tiberias, with the white wake churning out behind them and the wind and drops of spray in their faces.

They moored in the tiny harbour of the marina at Lido Beach and walked up into the town. David was so engrossed with Debra that the crowds around him were unreal, and although he noticed a few curious glances they meant very little to him.

Although it was early in the season, the town was filled with visitors, and the buses were parked in the square at the foot of the hill and along the lake front, for this was full on the tourist route.

David carried a plastic bag that grew steadily heavier until it was ready to overflow.

'Bread, and that's the lot,' Debra mentally ticked off the list.

They went down the hill under the eucalyptus trees and found a table on the harbour wall, beneath the gaily coloured umbrella.

They sat touching each other and drank cold beer and ate pistachio nuts, oblivious of everything and everybody about them even though the other tables were crowded with tourists. The lake sparkled and the softly rounded hills seemed very close in the bright light. Once a flight of Phantoms went booming down the valley, flying low on some mysterious errand, and David watched them dwindle southward without regrets.

When the sun was low they went to where the speed-boat was moored, and David handed Debra down into it. On the wall above them sat a party of tourists, probably on some package pilgrimage, and they were talking animatedly – their accents were Limehouse, Golders Green and Merseyside, although the subtleties of pronunciation were lost on David.

He started the motor and pushed off from the wall, steering for the harbour mouth with Debra sitting close beside him and the motor burbling softly.

A big red-faced tourist looked down from the wall and, supposing that the motor covered his voice, nudged his wife.

'Get a look at those two, Mavis. Beauty and the beast, isn't it?'

'Cork it, Bert. They might understand.'

'Go on, luv! They only talk Yiddish or whatever.'

Debra felt David's arm go rigid under her hand, felt him begin to pull away, sensing his outrage and anger – but she gripped his forearm tightly and restrained him.

'Let's go, Davey, darling. Leave them, please.'

Even when they were alone in the safety of the cottage, David was silent and she could feel the tension in his body and the air was charged with it.

They ate the evening meal of bread and cheese and fish and figs in the same strained silence. Debra could think of nothing to say to distract him for the careless words had wounded her as deeply. Afterwards she lay unsleeping beside him. He lay on his back, not touching her, with his arms at his sides and his fists clenched. When at last she could bear it no longer, she turned to him and stroked his face, still not knowing what to say. It was David who broke the silence at last.

'I want to go away from people. We don't need people – do we?'

'No,' she whispered. 'We don't need them.'

'There is a place called Jabulani. It is deep in the African bushveld, far from the nearest town. My father bought it as a hunting lodge thirty years ago – and now it belongs to me.'

'Tell me about it.' Debra laid her head on his chest, and he began stroking her hair, relaxing as he talked.

'There is a wide plain on which grow open forests of mopani and mohobahoba, with some fat old baobabs and a few ivory palms. In the open glades the grass is yellow gold and the fronds of the ilala palms look like beggars' fingers. At the end of the plain is a line of hills, they turn blue at a distance and the peaks are shaped like the turrets of a fairy castle with tumbled blocks of granite. Between the hills rises a spring of water, a strong spring that has never dried and the water is very clear and sweet—'

'What does Jabulani mean?' Debra asked when he had described it to her.

'It means the "place of rejoicing",' David told her.

'I want to go there with you,' she said.

'What about Israel?' he asked. 'Will you not miss it?'

218

'No,' she shook her head. 'You see, I will take it with me – in my heart.'

Ella went up to Jerusalem with them, filling the back seat of the Mercedes. She would help Debra select the furniture they would take with them from the house and have it crated and shipped. The rest of it she would sell for them. Aaron Cohen would negotiate the sale of the house, and both David and Debra felt a chill of sadness at the thought of other people living in their home.

David left the women to it and he drove out to Ein Karem and parked the Mercedes beside the iron gate in the garden wall.

The Brig was waiting for him in that bleak and forbidding room above the courtyard. When David greeted him from the doorway he looked up coldly, and there was no relaxation of the iron features, no warmth or pity in the fierce warrior eyes.

'You come to me with the blood of my son on your hands,' he said, and David froze at the words and held his gaze. After a few moments the Brig indicated the tall-backed chair against the far wall, and David crossed stiffly to it and sat down.

'If you had suffered less, I would have made you answer for more,' said the Brig. 'But vengeance and hatred are barren things – as you have discovered.'

David dropped his eyes to the floor.

'I will not pursue them further, despite the dictates of my heart, for that is what I am condemning in you. You are a violent young man, and violence is the pleasure of fools and only the last resort of wise men. The only excuse for it is to protect what is rightfully yours – any other display of violence is abuse. You abused the power I gave you – and in doing it you killed my son, and brought my country to the verge of war.'

The Brig stood up from his desk, and he crossed to the window and looked down into the garden. They were both

219

silent while he stroked his moustache and remembered his son.

At last the Brig sighed heavily and turned back into the room.

'Why do you come to me?' he asked.

'I wish to marry your daughter, sir.'

'You are asking me – or telling me?' the Brig demanded, and then without waiting for an answer returned to his desk and sat down. 'If you abuse this also – if you bring her pain or unhappiness, I will seek you out. Depend upon it.'

David stood up and settled the cloth cap over his gross head, pulling the brim well down.

'We would like you to be at the wedding. Debra asked that particularly – for you and her mother.'

The Brig nodded. 'You may tell her that we will be there.'

The synagogue at Jerusalem University is a gleaming white structure, shaped like the tent of a desert wanderer, with the same billowing lines.

The red-bud trees were in full bloom and the wedding party was larger than they had planned, for apart from the immediate family there were Debra's colleagues from the university, Robert and some of the other boys from the squadron, Ella Kadesh, Doctor Edelman the baby-faced eye surgeon who had worked on Debra, Aaron Cohen and a dozen others.

After the simple ceremony, they walked through the university grounds to one of the reception rooms that David had hired. It was a quiet gathering with little laughter or joking. The young pilots from David's old squadron had to leave early to return to base, and with them went any pretence of jollity.

Debra's mother was still not yet fully recovered, and the

prospect of Debra's departure reduced her to quiet grey weeping. Debra tried without success to comfort her.

Before he left, Dr Edelman drew David aside.

'Watch for any sign of atrophy in her eyes, any cloudiness, excessive redness – any complaints of pain, headaches—'

'I will watch for it.'

'Any indications, no matter how trivial – if you have any doubts, you must write to me.'

'Thank you, Doctor.'

They shook hands. 'Good luck in your new life,' said Edelman.

Through it all Debra showed iron control, but even she at last succumbed and she, her mother, and Ella Kadesh all broke down simultaneously at the departure barrier of Lod airport and hung around each other's necks, weeping bitterly.

The Brig and David stood by, stiff and awkward, trying to look as though they were not associated with the weeping trio, until the first warning broadcast gave them an excuse for a brief handshake and David took Debra's arm and drew her gently away.

They climbed the boarding ladder into the waiting Boeing without looking back. The giant aircraft took off and turned away southwards, and as always the sensation of flight soothed David; all the cares and tensions of these last few days left on the earth behind and below, he felt a new lightness of the spirit – excitement for what lay ahead.

He reached across and squeezed Debra's arm.

'Hello there, Morgan,' he said, and she turned towards him and smiled happily – blindly.

It was necessary to spend some time in Cape Town before they could escape to the sanctuary of Jabulani in the north.

David took a suite at the Mount Nelson Hotel, and from there he was able to settle the numerous issues that had piled up in his absence.

The accountants who managed his trust funds demanded ten days of his time and they spent it in the sitting-room of the suite, poring over trust documents and accounts.

In two years his income had grossly exceeded his spending, and the unused portion of his income had to be re-invested. In addition the third trust fund would soon pass to him and there were formalities to be completed.

Debra was hugely impressed by the extent of David's wealth.

'You must be almost a millionaire,' she said in a truly awed voice, for that was as rich as Debra could imagine.

'I'm not just a pretty face,' David agreed, and she was relieved that he could talk so lightly about his appearance.

Mitzi and her new husband came to visit them in their suite. However, the evening was not a success. Although Mitzi tried to act as though nothing had changed, and though she still called him 'warrior', yet it was apparent that she and her feelings had altered.

She was heavily pregnant and more shapeless than David would have thought possible. It was halfway through the evening before David realized the true reason for all the reserve. At first he thought that his disfigurement was worrying them, but after Mitzi had given a half-hour eulogy of the strides that Cecil was making at Morgan Group and the immense trust that Paul Morgan had placed in him, Cecil had asked innocently, 'Are you thinking of joining us at the Group? I'm sure we could find something useful for you to do – ha, ha!'

David could assure them quietly.

'No, thank you. You won't have to worry about me,

Cecil, old boy. You take over from Uncle Paul with my blessing.'

'Good Lord, I didn't mean that.' Cecil was shocked, but Mitzi was less devious.

'He really will be very good, warrior, and you never were interested, were you?'

After that evening they did not see the couple again, and Paul Morgan was in Europe, so David fulfilled his family obligations without much pain or suffering and he could concentrate on the preparations for the move to Jabulani.

Barney Venter spent a week with them in choosing a suitable aircraft to handle the bush airstrip and yet give David the type of performance he enjoyed. At last they decided on a twin-engined Piper Navajo, a six-seater with two big 300-hp Lycoming engines and a tricycle under-cart, and Barney walked around it with his hands on his hips.

'Well, she's no Mirage.' He kicked the landing-wheel and then checked himself and glanced quickly at David's face.

'I've had enough of Mirages,' David told him. 'They bite!'

On the last day David drove out with Debra to a farm near Paarl. The owner's wife was a dog breeder and when they went down to the kennels one of her Labrador pups walked directly to Debra and placed a cold nose on her leg as he inhaled her scent. Debra squatted and groped for his head and after fondling for a few moments she in her turn leaned forward and sniffed the pup's fur.

'He smells like old leather,' she said. 'What colour is he?'

'Black,' said David. 'Black as a Zulu.'

'That's what we'll call him,' said Debra. 'Zulu.'

'You want to choose this one?' David asked.

'No,' Debra laughed. 'He chose us.'

When they flew northwards the next morning the pup was indignant at being placed in the back seat and with a flying scrambling leap he came over Debra's shoulder and took up position in her lap, which seemed to suit them both very well.

'It looks like I have competition,' David muttered ruefully.

From the brown plateau of the high veld, the land dropped away steeply down the escarpment to the bush veld of southern Africa.

David picked up his landmark on the little village of Bush Buck Ridge and the long slim snake of the Sabi River as it twisted through the open forests of the plain. He altered course slightly northwards and within ten minutes he saw the low line of blue hills which rose abruptly out of the flat land.

'There it is, ahead of us,' David told Debra and his tone was infectious. She hugged the dog closer to her and leaned towards David.

'What does it look like?'

The hills were forested with big timber, and turreted with grey rock. At their base the bush was thick and dark. The pools glinted softly through the dark foliage. He described them to her.

'My father named them "The String of Pearls", and that's what they look like. They rise out of the run-off of rain water from the sloping ground beyond the hills. They disappear just as suddenly again into the sandy earth of the plain,' David explained as he circled the hills, slowly losing height. 'They are what give Jabulani its special character, for they provide water for all the wild life of the plain. Birds and animals are drawn from hundreds of miles to the Pearls.' He levelled out and throttled back, letting the aircraft sink lower. 'There is the homestead, white walls and thatch to keep it cool in the hot weather, deep shaded verandas and high rooms – you will love it.'

The airstrip seemed clear and safe, although the wind-sock hung in dirty tatters from its pole. David circled it carefully before lining up for the landing, and they taxied towards the small brick hangar set amongst the trees. David kicked on the wheel brakes and cut the engines.

'This is it,' he said.

J abulani was one of a block of estates that bounded the Kruger National Park – the most spectacular nature reserve on earth. These estates were not productive, in that they were unsuitable for the growth of crops and few of them were used for grazing of domestic animals; their immense value lay in the unspoiled bush veld and the wild life – in the peace and space upon which wealthy men placed such a premium that they would pay large fortunes for a piece of this *Lebensraum*.

When David's grandfather had purchased Jabulani he had paid a few·shillings an acre, for in those days the wilderness was still intact.

It had been used as a family hunting estate down the years, and as Paul Morgan had never shown interest in the veld, it had passed to David's father and so to David.

Now the eighteen thousand acres of African bush and plain, held as freehold land, was a possession beyond price.

Yet the Morgan family had made little use of it these last fifteen years. David's father had been an enthusiastic huntsman, and with him most of David's school holidays had been spent here. However, after his father's death, the visits to Jabulani had become shorter and further apart.

It was seven years since the last visit, when he had brought up a party of brother officers from Cobra Squadron.

Then it had been immaculately run by Sam, the black overseer, butler and game ranger.

Under Sam's management there had always been fresh

crisp linen on the beds, highly polished floors, the exterior walls of the buildings had been snowy white and the thatch neat and well-tended. The deep-freeze had been well stocked with steak and the liquor cupboard filled – with every bottle accounted for.

Sam ran a tight camp, with half a dozen willing and cheerful helpers.

'Where is Sam?' was the first question David asked of the two servants who hurried down from the homestead to meet the aircraft.

'Sam gone.'

'Where to?' And the answer was the eloquent shrug of Africa. Their uniforms were dirty and needed mending, and their manners disinterested.

'Where is the Land-Rover?'

'She is dead.'

They walked up to the homestead and there David had another series of unpleasant surprises.

The buildings were dilapidated, looking forlorn and neglected under their rotting black thatch. The walls were dingy, grey-brown with the plaster falling away in patches.

The interiors were filthy with dust, and sprinkled with the droppings of the birds and reptiles that had made their homes in the thatch.

The mosquito gauze, that was intended to keep the wide verandas insect-free, was rusted through and breaking away in tatters.

The vegetable gardens were overgrown, the fences about them falling to pieces. The grounds of the homestead itself were thick with rank weed, and not only the Land-Rover had died. No single piece of machinery on the estate – water pump, toilet cistern, electricity generator, motor vehicle – was in working order.

'It's a mess, a frightful mess,' David told Debra as they sat on the front step and drank mugs of sweet tea.

Fortunately David had thought to bring emergency supplies with them.

'Oh, Davey. I am so sorry, because I like it here. It's peaceful, so quiet. I can just feel my nerves untying themselves.'

'Don't be sorry. I'm not. These old huts were built by Gramps back in the twenties – and they weren't very well built even then.' David's voice was full of a new purpose, a determination that she had not heard for so long. 'It's a fine excuse to tear the whole lot down, and build again.'

'A place of our own?' she asked.

'Yes,' said David delightedly. 'That's it. That's just it!'

They flew into Nelspruit, the nearest large town, the following day. In the week of bustle and planning that followed they forgot their greater problems. With an architect they planned the new homestead with care, taking into consideration all their special requirements – a large airy study for Debra, workshop and office for David, a kitchen laid out to make it safe and easy for a blind cook, rooms without dangerous split levels and with regular easily learned shapes, and finally a nursery section. When David described this addition Debra asked cautiously, 'You making some plans that I should know about?'

'You'll know about it, all right,' he assured her.

The guest house was to be separate and self-contained and well away from the main homestead, and the small hutment for the servants was a quarter of a mile beyond that, screened by trees and the shoulder of the rocky kopje that rose behind the homestead.

David bribed a building contractor from Nelspruit to postpone all his other work, load his workmen on four heavy trucks and bring them out to Jabulani.

They began on the main house, and while they worked, David was busy resurfacing the airstrip, repairing the water pumps and such other machinery as still had life left in it.

However, the Land-Rover and the electricity generator had to be replaced.

Within two months the new homestead was habitable, and they could move. Debra set up her tape recorders beneath the big windows overlooking the shaded front garden, where the afternoon breeze could cool the room and waft in the perfume of the frangipani and poinsettia blooms.

While David was completely absorbed in making Jabulani into a comfortable home, Debra made her own arrangements.

Swiftly she explored and mapped in her mind all her immediate surroundings. Within weeks she could move about the new house with all the confidence of a person with normal sight and she had trained the servants to replace each item of furniture in its exact position. Always Zulu, the Labrador pup, moved like a glossy black shadow beside her. Early on he had decided that Debra needed his constant care, and had made her his life's work.

Quickly he learned that it was useless staring at her or wagging his tail, to attract her attention he must whine or pant. In other respects she was also slightly feeble-minded, the only way to prevent her doing stupid things like falling down the front steps or tripping over a bucket left in the passage by a careless servant was to bump her with his shoulder, or with his nose.

She had fallen readily into a pattern of work that kept her in her workroom until noon each day, with Zulu curled at her feet.

David set up a large bird bath under the trees outside her window, so the tapes she made had as a background the chatter and warble of half a dozen varieties of wild birds. She had discovered a typist in Nelspruit who could speak Hebrew, and David took the tapes in to her whenever he flew to town for supplies and to collect the mail, and he brought each batch of typing back with him for checking.

They worked together on this task, David reading each batch of writing or correspondence aloud to her and making the alterations she asked for. He made it a habit of reading almost everything, from newspapers to novels, aloud.

'Who needs braille with you around,' Debra remarked, but it was more than just the written word she needed to hear from him. It was each facet and dimension of her new surroundings. She had never seen any of the myriad of birds that flocked to drink and bathe below her window, though she soon recognized each individual call and would pick out a stranger immediately.

'David, there's a new one, what it is? What does he look like?'

And he must describe not only its plumage, but its mannerisms and its habits. At other times he must describe to her exactly how the new buildings fitted into their surroundings, the antics of Zulu the Labrador, and supply accurate descriptions of the servants, the view from the window of her workroom – and a hundred other aspects of her new life.

In time the building was completed and the strangers left Jabulani, but it was not until the crates from Israel containing their furniture and other possessions from Malik Street arrived that Jabulani started truly to become their home.

The olive-wood table was placed under the window in the workroom.

'I haven't been able to work properly, there was something missing—' and Debra ran her fingers caressingly across the inlaid ivory and ebony top ' – until now.'

Her books were in shelves on the wall beside the table, and the leather suite in the new lounge looked very well with the animal-skin rugs and woven wool carpets.

David hung the Ella Kadesh painting above the fireplace, Debra determining the precise position for him by sense of touch.

'Are you sure it shouldn't be a sixteenth of an inch higher?' David asked seriously.

'Let's have no more lip from you, Morgan, I have to know exactly where it is.'

Then the great brass bedstead was set up in the bedroom, and covered with the ivory-coloured bedspread. Debra bounced up and down on it happily.

'Now, there is only one thing more that is missing,' she declared.

'What's that?' he asked with mock anxiety. 'Is it something important?'

'Come here.' She crooked a finger in his general direction. 'And I'll show you just how important it is.'

D uring the months of preparation they had not left the immediate neighbourhood of the homestead, but now quite suddenly the rush and bustle was over.

'We have eighteen thousand acres and plenty of four-footed neighbours – let's go check it all out,' David suggested.

They packed a cold lunch and the three of them climbed into the new Land-Rover with Zulu relegated to the back seat. The road led naturally down to the String of Pearls for this was the focal point of all life upon the estate.

They left the Land-Rover amongst the fever trees and went down to the ruins of the thatched summer house on the bank of the main pool.

The water aroused all Zulu's instincts and he plunged into it, paddling out into the centre with obvious enjoyment. The water was clear as air, but shaded to black in the depths.

David scratched in the muddy bank and turned out a thick pink earthworm. He threw it into the shallows and a dark shape half as long as his arm rushed silently out of the depths and swirled the surface.

'Wow!' David laughed. 'There are still a few fat ones around. We will have to bring down the rods. I used to spend days down here when I was a kid.'

The forest was filled with memories and as they wandered along the edge of the reed banks he reminisced about his childhood, until gradually he fell into silence, and she asked:

'Is something wrong, David?' She had grown that sensitive to his moods.

'There are no animals.' His tone was puzzled. 'Birds, yes. But we haven't seen a single animal, not even a duiker, since we left the homestead.' He stopped at a place that was clear of reeds, where the bank shelved gently. 'This used to be a favourite drinking place. It was busy day and night – the herds virtually lining up for a chance to drink.' He left Debra and went down to the edge, stooping to examine the ground carefully. 'No spoor even, just a few kudu and a small troop of baboon. There has not been a herd here for months, or possibly years.'

When he came back to her she asked gently, 'You are upset?'

'Jabulani without its animals is nothing,' he muttered. 'Come on, let's go and see the rest of it. There is something very odd here.'

The leisurely outing became a desperate hunt, as David scoured the thickets and the open glades, followed the dried water courses and stopped the Land-Rover to examine the sand beds for signs of life.

'Not even an impala.' He was worried and anxious. 'There used to be thousands of them. I remember herds of them, silky brown and graceful as ballet dancers, under nearly every tree.'

He turned the Land-Rover northwards, following an overgrown track through the trees.

'There is grazing here that hasn't been touched. It's lush as a cultivated garden.'

A little before noon they reached the dusty, corrugated public road that ran along the north boundary of Jabulani. The fence that followed the edge of the road was ruinous, with sagging and broken wire and many of the uprights snapped off at ground level.

'Hell, it's a mess,' David told her, as he turned through a gap in the wire on to the road, and followed the boundary for two miles until they reached the turn-off to the Jabulani homestead.

Even the signboard hanging above the stone pillars of the gateway, which David's father had fashioned in bronze and of which he had been so proud, was now dilapidated and hung askew.

'Well, there's plenty of work to keep us going,' said David with a certain relish.

Half a mile beyond the gates the road turned sharply, hedged on each side by tall grass, and standing full in the sandy track was a magnificent kudu bull, ghostly grey and striped with pale chalky lines across the deep powerful body. His head was held high, armed with the long corkscrew black horns, and his huge ears were spread in an intent listening attitude.

For only part of a second he posed like that, then, although the Land-Rover was still two hundred yards off, he exploded into a smoky blur of frantic flight. His great horns laid along his back as he fled through the open bush in a series of long, lithe bounds, disappearing so swiftly it seemed he had been only a fantasy, and David described it to Debra.

'He took off the very instant he spotted us. I remember when they were so tame around here that we had to chase them out of the vegetable garden with sticks.'

Again he swung off the main track and on to another overgrown path, on which the new growth of saplings was already thick and tall. He drove straight over them in the tough little vehicle.

'What on earth are you doing?' Debra shouted above the crash and swish of branches.

'In this country, when you run out of road, you just make your own.'

Four miles farther on, they emerged abruptly on to the fire-break track that marked the eastern boundary of Jabulani, the dividing line between them and the National Park which was larger than the entire land area of the state of Israel, five million acres of virgin wilderness, three hundred and eighty-five kilometres long and eighty wide, home of more than a million wild animals, the most important reservoir of wildlife left in Africa.

David stopped the Land-Rover, cut the engine and jumped down. After a moment of shocked and angry silence he began to swear.

'What's made you so happy?' Debra demanded.

'Look at that – just look at that!' David ranted.

'I wish I could.'

'Sorry, Debs. It's a fence. A game fence!'

It stood eight feet high and the uprights were hardwood poles thick as a man's thigh, while the mesh of the fence was heavy gauge wire. 'They have fenced us off. The National Park's people have cut us off. No wonder there are no animals.'

As they drove back to the homestead David explained to her how there had always been an open boundary with the Kruger National Park. It had suited everybody well enough, for Jabulani's sweet grazing and the perennial water of the pools helped to carry the herds through times of drought and scarcity.

'It's becoming very important to you, this business of the wild animals.' Debra had listened silently, fondling the Labrador's head, as David spoke.

'Yes, suddenly it's important. When they were here, I

guess I just took them for granted – but now they are gone it's suddenly important.'

They drove on for a mile or two without speaking and then David said with determination, 'I'm going to tell them to pull that fence down. They can't cut us off like that. I'm going to get hold of the head warden, now, right away.'

David remembered Conrad Berg from his childhood when he had been the warden in charge of the southern portion of the park, but not yet the chief. There was a body of legend about the man that had been built up over the years, and two of these stories showed clearly the type of man he was.

Caught out in a lonely area of the reserve after dark with a broken-down truck, he was walking home when he was attacked by a full-grown male lion. In the struggle he had been terribly mauled, half the flesh torn from his back and the bone of his shoulder and arm bitten through. Yet he had managed to kill the animal with a small sheath knife, stabbing it repeatedly in the throat until he hit the jugular. He had then stood up and walked five miles through the night with the hyena pack following him expectantly, waiting for him to drop.

On another occasion one of the estate owners bounding the park had poached one of Berg's lions, shooting it down half a mile inside the boundary. The poacher was a man high in government, wielding massive influence, and he had laughed at Conrad Berg.

'What are you going to do about it, my friend? Don't you like your job?'

Doggedly, ignoring the pressure from above, Berg had collected his evidence and issued a summons. The pressure had become less subtle as the court date approached, but he had never wavered. The important personage finally stood in the dock, and was convicted. He was sentenced to a thousand pounds fine or six months at hard labour.

Afterwards he had shaken Berg's hand and said to him,

'Thank you for a lesson in courage,' and perhaps this was one of the reasons Berg was now chief warden.

He stood beside his game fence where he had arranged over the telephone to meet David. He was a big man, broad and tall and beefy, with thick heavily muscled arms still scarred from the lion attack, and a red sunburned face.

He wore the suntans and slouch hat of the Park's service, with the green cloth badges on his epaulettes.

Behind him was parked his brown Chevy truck with the Park Board's emblem on the door, and two of his black game rangers seated in the back. One of them was holding a heavy rifle.

Berg stood with his clenched fists on his hips, his hat pushed back and a forbidding expression on his face. He so epitomized the truculent male animal guarding his territory that David muttered to Debra, 'Here comes trouble.'

He parked close beside the fence and he and Debra climbed down and went to the wire.

'Mr Berg. I am David Morgan. I remember you from when my father owned Jabulani. I'd like you to meet my wife.'

Berg's expression wavered. Naturally he had heard all the rumours about the new owner of Jabulani; it was a lonely isolated area and it was his job to know about these things. Yet he was unprepared for this dreadfully mutilated young man, and his blind but beautiful wife.

With an awkward gallantry Berg doffed his hat, then realized she would not see the gesture. He murmured a greeting and when David thrust his hand through the fence he shook it cautiously.

Debra and David were working as a team and they turned their combined charm upon Berg, who was a simple and direct man. Slowly his defences softened as they chatted. He admired Zulu, he also kept Labradors and it served as a talking-point while Debra unpacked a Thermos of coffee and David filled mugs for all of them.

'Isn't that Sam?' David pointed to the game ranger in the truck who held Berg's rifle.

'*Ja*.' Berg was guarded.

'He used to work on Jabulani.'

'He came to me of his own accord,' Berg explained, turning aside any implied rebuke.

'He wouldn't remember me, of course, not the way I look now. But he was a fine ranger, and the place certainly went to the bad without him to look after it,' David admitted before he went into a frontal assault. 'The other thing which has ruined us is this fence of yours.' David kicked one of the uprights.

'You don't say?' Berg swished the grounds of his coffee around the mug and flicked it out.

'Why did you do it?'

'For good reason.'

'My father had a gentleman's agreement with the Board, the boundary was open at all times. We have got water and grazing that you need.'

'With all respects to the late Mr Morgan,' Conrad Berg spoke heavily, 'I was never in favour of the open boundary.'

'Why not?'

'Your daddy was a *sportsman*.' He spat the word out, as though it were a mouthful of rotten meat. 'When my lions got to know him and learned to stay this side of the line – then he used to bring down a couple of donkeys and parade them along the boundary – to tempt them out.'

David opened his mouth to protest, and then closed it slowly. He felt the seamed scars of his face mottling and staining with a flush of shame. It was true, he remembered the donkeys and the soft wet lion skins being pegged out to dry behind the homestead.

'He never poached,' David defended him. 'He had an owner's licence and they were all shot on our land.'

'No, he never poached,' Berg admitted. 'He was too damned clever for that. He knew I would have put a rocket

236

up him that would have made him the first man on the moon.'

'So that's why you put up the fence.'

'No.'

'Why then?'

'Because for fourteen years Jabulani has been under the care of an absentee landlord who didn't give a good damn what happened to it. Old Sam here—' he motioned at the game ranger in the truck ' – did his best, but still it became a poachers' paradise. As fast as the grazing and water you boast of pulled my game out of the Park, so they were cut down by every sportsman with an itchy trigger finger. When Sam tried to do something about it, he got badly beaten up, and when that didn't stop him somebody put fire into his hut at night. They burned two of his kids to death—'

David felt his very soul quail at the thought of the flames on flesh, his cheeks itched at the memory.

'I didn't know,' he said gruffly.

'No, you were too busy making money or whatever is your particular form of pleasure.' Berg was angry. 'So at last Sam came to me and I gave him a job. Then I strung this fence.'

'There is nothing left on Jabulani – a few kudu, and a duiker or two – but otherwise it's all gone.'

'You are so right. It didn't take them long to clean it out.'

'I want it back.'

'Why?' Berg scoffed. 'So you can be a sportsman like your daddy? So you can fly your pals down from Jo'burg for the weekend to shoot the shit out of my lions?' Berg glanced at Debra, and immediately his red face flushed a deep port-wine colour. 'I'm sorry, Mrs Morgan, I did not mean to say that.'

'That's perfectly all right, Mr Berg. I think it was very expressive.'

'Thank you, ma'am.' Then he turned furiously back to David. 'Morgan's Private Safari Service, is that what you are after?'

'I would not allow a shot fired on Jabulani,' said David.

'I bet – except for the pot. That's the usual story. Except for the pot, and you've got the Battle of Waterloo being fought all over again.'

'No,' said David. 'Not even for the pot.'

'You'd eat butcher's beef?' Berg asked incredulously.

'Look here, Mr Berg. If you pull your fence out, I'll have Jabulani declared a private nature reserve—'

Berg had been about to say something, but David's declaration dried the words, and his mouth remained hanging open. He closed it slowly.

'You know what that means?' he asked at last. 'You place yourself under our jurisdiction, completely. We'd tie you up properly with a lawyer's paper and all that stuff: no owner's licence, no shooting lions because they are in a cattle area.'

'Yes. I know. I've studied the act. But there is something more. I'd undertake to fence the other three boundaries to your satisfaction, and maintain a force of private game rangers that you considered adequate – all at my own expense.'

Conrad Berg lifted his hat and scratched pensively at the long sparse grey hairs that covered his pate.

'Man,' he said mournfully, 'how can I say no to that?' Then he began to smile, the first smile of the meeting. 'It looks like you are really serious about this then.'

'My wife and I are going to be living here permanently. We don't want to live in a desert.'

'Ja,' he nodded, understanding completely that a man should feel that way. The strong revulsion that he had originally felt for the fantastic face before him was fading.

'I think the first thing we should work on is these

238

poachers you tell me about. Let's snatch a couple of those and make a few examples,' David went on.

Berg's big red face split into a happy grin.

'I think I'm going to enjoy having you as a neighbour,' he said, and again he thrust his hand through the fence. David winced as he felt his knuckles cracking in the huge fist.

'Won't you come to dinner with us tomorrow night? You and your wife?' Debra asked with relief.

'It will be a mighty great pleasure, ma'am.'

'I'll get out the whisky bottle,' said David.

'That's kind of you—' said Conrad Berg seriously, 'but the missus and I only drink Old Buck dry gin, with a little water.'

'I'll see to it,' said David just as seriously.

J ane Berg was slim woman of about Conrad's age. She had a dried-out face, lined and browned by the sun. Her hair was sunbleached and streaked with grey, and, as Debra remarked, she was probably the only thing in the world that Conrad was afraid of.

'I'm talking, Connie,' was enough to halt any flow of eloquence from her huge spouse, or a significant glance at her empty glass sent him with elephantine haste for a refill. Conrad had a great deal of trouble finishing any story or statement, for Jane had to correct the details during the telling, while he waited patiently for an opportunity to resume.

Debra chose the main course with care so as not to give offence, beefsteaks from the deep freeze, and Conrad ate four of them with unreserved pleasure although he spurned the wine that David served.

'That stuff is poison. Killed one of my uncles,' and stayed with Old Buck gin, even through the dessert.

Afterwards they sat about the cavernous fireplace with its logs blazing cheerfully and Conrad explained, with Jane's assistance, the problems that David would face on Jabulani.

'You get a few of the blacks from the tribal areas coming in from the north—'

'Or across the river,' Jane added.

'Or across the river, but they are no big sweat. They set wire snares mostly, and they don't kill that much—'

'But it's a terribly cruel way, the poor animals linger on for days with the wire cutting down to the bone,' Jane elaborated.

'As I was saying, once we have a few rangers busy that will stop almost immediately. It's the white poachers with modern rifles and hunting lamps—'

'Killing lamps,' Jane corrected.

' – killing lamps, that do the real damage. They finished off all your game on Jabulani in a couple of seasons.'

'Where do they come from?' David asked. His anger was rising again, the same protective anger of the shepherd that he had felt as he flew the skies of Israel.

'There is a big copper mine fifty miles north of here at Phalabora, hundreds of bored miners with a taste for venison. They would come down here and blaze away at every living thing – but now it's not worth the trip for them. Anyway they were just the amateurs, the weekend poachers.'

'Who are the professionals?'

'Where the dirt road from Jabulani meets the big national highway, about thirty miles from here—'

'At a place called Bandolier Hill,' Jane supplied the name.

' – there is a general dealer's store. It's just one of those trading posts that gets a little of the passing trade from the main road, but relies on the natives from the tribal areas. The person who owns and runs it has been there eight years now, and I have been after him all that time, but he's the craftiest bastard – I'm sorry, Mrs Morgan – I have ever run into.'

'He's the one?' David asked.

'He's the one,' Conrad nodded. 'Catch him, and half your worries are over.'

'What's his name?'

'Akkers. Johan Akkers,' Jane gave her assistance; the Old Buck was making her slightly owl-eyed, and she was having a little difficulty with her enunciation.

'How are we going to get him?' David mused. 'There isn't anything left on Jabulani to tempt him – the few kudu we have got are so wild, it wouldn't be worth the effort.'

'No, you haven't got anything to tempt him right now, but about the middle of September—'

'More like the first week in September,' Jane said firmly with strings of hair starting to hang down her temples.

' – the first week in September the marula trees down by your pools will come into fruit, and my elephants are going to visit you. The one thing they just can't resist is marula berries, and they are going to flatten my fence to get at them. Before I can repair it a lot of other game are going to follow the jumbo over to your side. You can lay any type of odds you like that our friend Akkers is oiling his guns and drooling at the mouth right this minute. He will know within an hour when the fence goes.'

'This time he may get a surprise.'

'Let's hope so.'

'I think—' David said softly ' – that we might run down to Bandolier Hill tomorrow to have a look at this gentleman.'

'One thing is for sure—' said Jane Berg indistinctly, ' – a gentleman, he is not.'

The road down to Bandolier Hill was heavily corrugated and thick with white dust that rose in a banner behind the Land-Rover and hung in the air long after they had passed. The hill was rounded and thickly timbered and stood over the main metalled highway.

The trading post was four or five hundred yards from the road junction, set back amidst a grove of mango trees with their deep green and glistening foliage. It was a type found all over Africa – an unlovely building of mud brick with a naked corrugated-iron roof, the walls plastered thickly with posters advertising goods from tea to flashlight batteries.

David parked the Land-Rover in the dusty yard beneath the raised stoep. There was a faded sign above the front steps:

'Bandolier Hill General Dealers'.

At the side of the building was parked an old green Ford one-ton truck with local licence plates. In the shade of the stoep squatted a dozen or so potential customers, African women from the tribal area, dressed in long cotton print dresses, timeless in their patience and their expressions showing no curiosity about the occupants of the Land-Rover. One of the women was suckling her infant with an enormously elongated breast that allowed the child to stand beside her and watch the newcomers without removing the puckered black nipple from his mouth.

Set in the centre of the yard was a thick straight pole, fifteen feet tall, and on top of the pole was a wooden structure like a dog kennel. David exclaimed as from the kennel emerged a big brown furry animal. It descended the pole in one swift falling action, seemingly as lightly as a bird, and the chain that was fastened to the pole at one end was, at the other, buckled about the animal's waist by a thick leather strap.

'It's one of the biggest old bull baboons I've ever seen.' Quickly he described it to Debra, as the baboon moved out to the chain's limit, and knuckled the ground as he made a leisurely circle about his pole, the chain clinking as it swung behind him. It was an arrogant display, and he ruffled out the thick mane of hair upon his shoulders. When he had completed the circle, he sat down facing the Land-Rover, in a repellently humanoid attitude, and thrust out his lower jaw as he regarded them through the small brown, close-set eyes.

'A nasty beast,' David told Debra. He would weigh ninety pounds, with a long dog-like muzzle and a jaw full of yellow fangs. After the hyena, he was the most hated animal of the veld – cunning, cruel and avaricious, all the vices of man and none of his graces. His stare was unblinking and, every few seconds, he ducked his head in a quick aggressive gesture.

While all David's attention was on the baboon, a man had come out of the store and now leaned on one of the pillars of the veranda.

'What can I do for you, Mr Morgan?' he asked in a thick accent. He was tall and spare, dressed in slightly rumpled and not entirely clean khaki slacks and open-neck shirt, with heavy boots on his feet and braces hooked into his pants, crossing his shoulders.

'How did you know my name?' David looked up at him, and saw he was of middle age with close-cropped greying hair over a domed skull. His teeth were badly fitting with bright pink plastic gums and his skin was drawn over the bones of the cheeks, and his deep-set eyes gave him a skull-like look. He grinned at David's question.

'Could only be you, scarred face and blind wife – you the new owner of Jabulani. Heard you built a new house and all set to live there now.'

The man's hands were huge, out of proportion to the rest of his rangy body, they were clearly very powerful and the lean muscles of his forearms were as tough as rope.

He slouched easily against the pillar and took from his

pocket a clasp knife and a stick of black wind-dried meat –
the jerky of North America, boucan of the Caribbean, or
the biltong of Africa – and he cut a slice as though it were
a plug of tobacco, popping it into his mouth.

'Like I asked – what can we do for you?' He chewed
noisily, his teeth squelching at each bite.

'I need nails and paint.' David climbed out of the Land-
Rover.

'Heard you did all your buying in Nelspruit.' Akkers
looked him over with a calculated insolence, studying
David's ruined face with attention. David saw that his
deep-set eyes were a muddy green in colour.

'I thought there was a law against caging or chaining
wild animals.' Akkers had roused David's resentment
almost immediately, and the needle showed in his tone.
Akkers began to grin again easily, still chewing.

'You a lawyer – are you?'

'Just asking.'

'I got a permit – you want to see it?'

David shook his head, and turned to speak to Debra in
Hebrew. Quickly he described the man.

'I think he can guess why we are here, and he's looking
for trouble.'

'I'll stay by the car,' said Debra.

'Good.' David climbed the steps to the veranda.

'What about the nails and paint?' he asked Akkers.

'Go on in,' he was still grinning. 'I got a nigger helper
behind the counter. He will look after you.'

David hesitated and then walked on into the building.
It smelled of carbolic soap and kerosene and maize meal.
The shelves were loaded with cheap groceries, patent
medicines, blankets and bolts of printed cotton cloth. From
the roof hung bunches of army surplus boots and greatcoats,
axe-heads and storm lanterns. The floor was stacked with
tin trunks, pick handles, bins of flour and maize meal and
the hundreds of other items that traditionally make up the

stock of the country dealer. David found the African assistant and began his purchase.

Outside in the sunlight Debra climbed from the Land-Rover and leaned lightly against the door. The Labrador scrambled down after her and began sniffing the concrete pillars of the veranda with interest where other dogs before him had spurted jets of yellow urine against the white-washed plaster.

'Nice dog,' said Akkers.

'Thank you.' Debra nodded politely.

Akkers glanced quickly across at his pet baboon, and his expression was suddenly cunning. A flash of understanding passed between man and animal. The baboon ducked its head again in that nervous gesture, then it rose from its haunches and drifted back to the pole. With a leap and bound it shot up the pole and disappeared into the opening of its kennel.

Akkers grinned and carefully cut another slice of the black biltong.

'You like it out at Jabulani?' he asked Debra, and at the same time he offered the scrap of dried meat to the dog.

'We are very happy there,' Debra replied stiffly, not wanting to be drawn. Zulu sniffed the proffered titbit, and his tail beat like a metronome. No dog can resist the concentrated meat smell and taste of biltong. He gulped it eagerly. Twice more Akkers fed him the scraps, and Zulu's eyes glistened and his soft silky muzzle was damp with saliva.

The waiting women in the shade of the veranda were watching with lively interest now. They had seen this happen before with a dog, and they waited expectantly. David was in the building, out of sight. Debra stood blind and unsuspecting.

Akkers cut a larger piece of the dried meat and offered it to Zulu, but when he reached for it he pulled his hand away, teasing the dog. With his taste for biltong now firmly

245

established, Zulu tried again for the meat as it was offered. Again it was pulled away at the last moment. Zulu's black wet nose quivered with anxiety, and the soft ears were cocked.

Akkers walked down the steps with Zulu following him eagerly, and at the bottom he showed the dog the biltong once more, letting him sniff it. Then he spoke softly but urgently, 'Get it, boy,' and threw the scrap of biltong at the base of the baboon's pole. Zulu bounded forward, still slightly clumsy on his big puppy paws, into the circle of the chain where the baboon's paws had beaten the earth hard. He ran on under the pole and grubbed hungrily for the biltong in the dust.

The bull baboon came out of his kennel like a tawny grey blur and dropped the fifteen feet through the air; his limbs were spread and his jaws were open in a snarl like a great red trap, and the fangs were vicious, long and yellow and spiked. He hit the ground silently, and his muscles bunched as they absorbed the shock and hurled the long lithe body feet first at the unsuspecting pup. The baboon crashed into him, taking him on the shoulder with all the weight of his ninety pounds.

Zulu went down and over, rolling on his back with a startled yelp, but before he could find his feet or his wits, the baboon was after him.

Debra heard the pup cry, and started forward, surprised but not yet alarmed.

As he lay on his back, Zulu's belly was unprotected, sparsely covered with the silken black hair, the immature penis protruding pathetically, and the baboon went onto him in a crouching leap, pinning him with powerful furry legs as he bowed his head and buried the long yellow fangs deep into the pup's belly.

Zulu screamed in dreadful agony, and Debra screamed in sympathy and ran forward.

Akkers shot out a foot as she passed him and tripped her, sending her sprawling on her hands and knees.

'Leave it, lady,' he warned her, still grinning. 'You'll get hurt if you interfere.'

The baboon locked its long curved eye teeth into the tender belly, and then hurled the pup away from it with all the fierce strength of its four limbs. The thin wall of the stomach was ripped through, and the purple ropes of the entrails came out, hanging festooned in the baboon's jaws.

Again the disembowelled pup screamed, and Debra rolled blindly to her feet.

'David!' she cried wildly. 'David – help me!'

David came out of the building running; pausing in the doorway he took in the scene at a glance and snatched up a pick handle from the pile by the door. He jumped off the veranda, and in three quick strides he had reached the pup.

The baboon saw him coming and released Zulu. With uncanny speed, he whirled and leapt for the pole, racing upwards to perch on the roof of the kennel, his jowls red with blood, as he shrieked and jabbered, bouncing up and down with excitement and triumph.

David dropped the pick and gently lifted the crawling crippled black body. He carried Zulu to the Land-Rover and ripped his bush jacket into strips as he tried to bind up the torn belly, pushing the hanging entrails back into the hole with his fist.

'David, what is it?' Debra pleaded with him, and as he worked he explained it in a few terse Hebrew sentences.

'Get in,' he told her and she clambered into the passenger seat of the Land-Rover. He laid the injured Labrador in her lap, and ran around to the driver's seat.

Akkers was back at the doorway of his shop, standing with his thumbs hooked into his braces, and he was laughing. The false teeth clucked in the open mouth as he laughed, rocking back and forth on his heels.

On its kennel the baboons shrieked and cavorted, sharing its master's mirth.

'Hey, Mr Morgan,' Akkers giggled, 'don't forget your nails!'

David swung round to face him, his face felt tight and hot, the cicatrice that covered his cheeks and forehead were inflamed and the dark blue eyes blazed with a terrible anger. He started up the steps. His mouth was a pale hard slit, and his fists were clenched at his sides.

Akkers stepped backwards swiftly and reached behind the shop counter. He lifted out an old double-barrelled shotgun, and cocked both hammers with a sweep of his thick bony thumb.

'Self defence, Mr Morgan, with witnesses,' he giggled with sadistic relish. 'Come one step closer and we will get a look at your guts also.'

David paused at the top of the steps, and the gun – held in one huge fist – pointed at his belly.

'David, hurry – oh, please hurry,' Debra called anxiously from the Land-Rover, with the weak squirming body of the pup in her lap.

'We'll meet again.' David's anger had thickened his tongue.

'That will be fun,' said Akkers, and David turned away and ran down the steps.

Akkers watched the Land-Rover pull away and swing into the road in a cloud of dust, before he set the shotgun aside. He went out into the sunlight, and the baboon scrambled down from its pole and rushed to meet him. It jumped up on to his hip and clung to him like a child.

Akkers took a boiled sweet from his pocket and placed it tenderly between the terrible yellow fangs.

'You lovely old thing,' he chuckled, scratching the high cranium with its thick cap of grey fur and the baboon squinted up at his face with narrow brown eyes, chattering softly.

D espite the rough surface, David covered the thirty miles back to Jabulani in twenty-five minutes. He skidded the vehicle to a halt beside the hangar, and ran with the pup in his arms to the aircraft.

During the flight Debra nursed him gently in her lap, and her skirts were sodden with his dark blood. The pup had quieted, and except for an occasional whimper now lay still. Over the W/T David arranged for a car to meet them at Nelspruit airfield and forty-five minutes after take-off they had Zulu on the theatre table in the veterinary surgeon's clinic.

The veterinary surgeon worked with complete concentration for over two hours at repairing the torn entrails and suturing the layers of abdominal muscle.

The pup was so critically injured, and infection was such a real danger, that they dared not return to Jabulani until it had passed. Five days later, when they flew home with Zulu still weak and heavily strapped but out of danger, David altered his flight path to bring them in over the trading store at Bandolier Hill.

The iron roof shone like a mirror in the sun, and David felt his anger very cold and hard and determined.

'The man is a threat to us,' he said aloud. 'A real threat to each of us, and to what we are trying to build at Jabulani.'

Debra nodded her agreement, stroking the pup's head and not trusting herself to speak. Her own anger was as fierce as David's.'

'I'm going to get him,' he said softly, and he heard the Brig's voice in his memory.

'The only excuse for violence is to protect what is rightfully yours.'

He banked steeply away and lined up for his approach to the landing-strip at Jabulani.

Conrad Berg called again to sample the Old Buck gin, and to tell David that his application to have Jabulani declared a private nature reserve had been approved by the Board and that the necessary documentation would soon be ready for signature.

'Do you want me to pull the fence out now?'

'No,' David answered grimly. 'Let it stand. I don't want Akkers frightened off.'

'Ja,' Conrad agreed heavily. 'We have got to get him.' He called Zulu to him and examined the scar that was ridged and shaped like forked lightning across the pup's belly. 'The bastard,' he muttered, and then glanced guiltily at Debra. 'Sorry, Mrs Morgan.'

'I couldn't agree more, Mr Berg,' she said softly, and Zulu watched her lips attentively when she spoke – his head cocked to one side.

Like all young things, he had healed cleanly and quickly.

The marula grove that ran thickly along the base of the hills about the String of Pearls came into flower.

The boles were straight and sturdy, each crowned with a fully rounded, many-branched head of dense foliage, and the red flowers made a royal show.

Almost daily David and Debra would wander together through the groves, down the rude track to the pools, and Zulu regained his strength on these leisurely strolls which always culminated in a swim and a lusty shaking off of water droplets, usually on to the nearest bystander.

Then the green plum-shaped fruits that covered the female marulas thickly began to turn yellow as they ripened, and their yeasty smell was heavy on the warm evening breeze.

The herd came up from the Sabi, forsaking the lush reed beds for the promise of the marula harvest. They were led by two old bulls, who for forty years had made the annual pilgrimage to the String of Pearls, and there were fifteen breeding cows with calves running at heel and as many adolescents.

They moved up slowly from the south, feeding spread out, sailing like ghostly grey galleons through the open bush, overloaded bellies rumbling. Occasionally a tall tree would catch the attention of one of the bulls and he would place his forehead upon the thick trunk and, swaying rhythmically as he built up momentum, he would strain suddenly and bring it crackling and crashing down. A few mouthfuls of the tender tip leaves would satisfy him, or he might strip the bark and stuff it untidily into his mouth before moving on northwards.

When they reached Conrad Berg's fence the two bulls moved forward and examined it, standing shoulder to shoulder as though in consultation, fanning their great grey ears, and every few minutes picking up a large pinch of sand in their trunks to throw over their own backs against the worrisome attention of the stinging flies.

In forty years they had travelled, and knew exactly all the boundaries of their reserve. As they stood there contemplating the game fence, it was as though they were fully aware that its destruction would be a criminal act, and injurious to their reputations and good standing.

Conrad Berg was deadly serious when he discussed 'his' elephants' sense of right and wrong with David. He spoke of them like schoolboys who had to be placed on good behaviour, and disciplined when they transgressed. Discipline might take the form of driving, darting with drugs, or formal execution with a heavy rifle. This ultimate punishment was reserved for the incorrigibles who raided cultivated crops, chased motor-cars or otherwise endangered human life.

Sorely tempted, the two old bulls left the fence and ambled back to the breeding herd that waited patiently for their decision amongst the thorn trees. For three days the herd drifted back and forth along the fence, feeding and resting and waiting – then suddenly the wind turned westerly and it came to them laden with the thick, cloyingly sweet smell of the marula berries.

David parked the Land-Rover on the fire-break road and laughed with delight.

'So much for Connie's fence!'

For reasons of pachyderm prestige, or perhaps merely for the mischievous delight of destruction, no adult elephant would accept the breach made by another.

Each of them had selected his own fence pole, hard wood uprights embedded in concrete, and had effortlessly snapped it off level with the ground. Over a length of a mile the fence was flattened, and the wire mesh lay across the firebreak.

Each elephant had used his broken pole like a tightrope, to avoid treading on the sharp points of the barbed wire. Then once across the fence they had streamed in a tight bunch down to the pools to spend a night in feasting, an elephantine gorge on the yellow berries, which ended at dawn when they had bunched up into close order and dashed back across the ruined fence into the safety of the Park – perhaps pursued by guilt and remorse and hoping that Conrad Berg would lay the blame on some other herd.

However, the downed fence provided ready access for many others who had long hankered after the sweet untouched grazing and deep water holes.

Ugly little blue wildebeest with monstrous heads, absurdly warlike manes and curved horns in imitation of the mighty buffalo. Clowns of the bush, they capered with glee and chased each other in circles. Their companions the zebra were more dignified, ignoring their antics, and trotted in businesslike fashion down to the pools. Their rumps were striped and glossy and plump, their heads up and ears pricked.

Conrad Berg met David at the remains of his fence,

climbing out of his own truck and picking his way carefully over the wire. Sam, the African ranger, followed him.

Conrad shook his head as he surveyed the destruction, chuckling ruefully.

'It's old Mahommed and his pal One-Eye, I'd know that spoor anywhere. They just couldn't help themselves – the bastards—' He glanced quickly at Debra in the Land-Rover.

'That's perfectly all right, Mr Berg,' she forestalled his apology.

Sam had been casting back and forth along the soft break road and now he came to where they stood.

'Hello, Sam,' David greeted him. It had taken a lot of persuasion to get Sam to accept that this terribly disfigured face belonged to the young *nkosi* David who he had taught to track, and shoot and rob a wild beehive without destroying the bees.

Sam saluted David with a flourish. He took his uniform very seriously and conducted himself like a guardsman now. It was difficult to tell his age, for he had the broad smooth moonface of the Nguni – the aristocratic warrior tribes of Africa – but there was a frosting of purest white on the close-curled hair of his temples under the slouch hat, and David knew he had worked at Jabulani for forty years before leaving. The man must be approaching sixty years of age.

Quickly he made his report to Conrad, describing the animals and the numbers which had crossed into Jabulani.

'There is also a herd of buffalo, forty-three of them.' Sam spoke in simple Zulu that David could still follow. 'They are the ones who drank before Ripape Dam near Hlangulene.'

'That will bring Akkers running – the sirloin of a young buffalo makes the finest biltong there is,' Conrad observed dryly.

'How long will it be before he knows the fence is down?'

David asked, and Conrad fell into a long rapid-fire discussion with Sam that lost David after the first few sentences. However, Conrad translated at the end.

'Sam says he knows already, all your servants and their wives buy at his store and he pays them for that sort of information. It turns out that there is bad blood between Sam and Akkers. Sam suspects him of arranging to have him beaten, on a lonely road on a dark night. Sam was in hospital three months – he also accused Akkers of having his hut fired to drive him off Jabulani.'

'It adds up, doesn't it?' David agreed.

'Old Sam is dead keen to help us grab Akkers – and he has a plan of action all worked out.'

'Let's hear it.'

'Well, as long as you are in residence at Jabulani Akkers is going to restrict his activities to night poaching with a killing lamp. He knows every trick there is and we will never get him.'

'So?'

'You must tell your servants that you are leaving for two weeks, going to Cape Town on business. Akkers will know as soon as you leave and he will believe he has the whole of Jabulani to himself—' For an hour more they discussed the details of the plan, then they shook hands and parted.

As they drove back to the homestead they emerged from the open forest into one of the glades of tall grass, and David saw the brilliant white egrets floating like snowflakes over the swaying tops of golden grass.

'Something in there,' he said and cut the engine. They waited quietly until David saw the movement in the grass, the opening and closing at the passage of heavy bodies. Then three egrets, sitting in row, moved slowly towards him, borne on the back of a concealed beast as it grazed steadily forward.

'Ah, the buffalo!' David exclaimed as the first of them appeared, a great black bovine shape. It stopped as it saw the Land-Rover on the edge of the trees and it regarded them intently from beneath the wide spread of its horns, with its muzzle lifted high. It showed no alarm for these were Park animals, almost as tame as domestic cattle.

Gradually the rest of the herd emerged from the tall grass. Each in turn scrutinized the vehicle and then resumed feeding once more. There were forty-three of them, as Sam had predicted, and amongst them were some fine old bulls standing five and a half feet tall at the shoulder and weighing little less than 2,000 lb. Their horns were massively bossed, meeting in the centre of the head and curving downwards and up to blunt points, with a rugged surface that became polished black at the tips.

Crawling over their heavy trunks and thick short legs were numbers of ox-peckers, dull-plumaged birds with scarlet beaks and bright beady eyes. Sometimes head down they scavenged for the ticks and other blood-sucking body vermin in the folds of skin between the limbs. Occasionally one of the huge beasts would snort and leap, shaking and swishing its tail, as a sharp beak pried into a delicate portion of its anatomy, under the tail or around the heavy dangling black scrotum. The birds fluttered up with hissing cries, waited for the buffalo to calm down and then settled again to their scurrying and searching.

David photographed the herd until the light failed, and they drove home in the dark.

Before dinner David opened a bottle of wine and they drank it together on the stoep, sitting close and listening to the night sounds of the bush – the cries of the night birds, the tap of flying insects against the wire screen and the other secret scurrying and rustling of small animals.

'Do you remember once I told you that you were spoiled, and not very good marriage material?' Debra asked softly, nestling her dark head against his shoulder.

'I'll never forget it.'

'I'd like to withdraw that remark formally,' she went on,

and he moved her gently away so that he could study her face. Sensing his eyes upon her she smiled, that shy little smile of hers. 'I fell in love with a little boy, a spoiled little boy, who thought only of fast cars and the nearest skirt—' she said, ' – but now I have a man, a grown man,' she smiled again, 'and I like it better this way.'

He drew her back to him and kissed her, their lips melded in a lingering embrace before she sighed happily and laid her head back upon his shoulder. They were silent for a while before Debra spoke again.

'These wild animals – that mean so much to you—'

'Yes?' he encouraged her.

'I am beginning to understand. Although I have never seen them, they are becoming important to me also.'

'I'm glad.'

'David, this place of ours – it's so peaceful, so perfect. It's a little Eden before the fall.'

'We will make it so,' he promised, but in the night the gunfire woke him. He rose quickly, leaving her lying warm and quietly sleeping, and he went out on the stoop.

It came again, faintly on the still night, distance muting it to a small unwarlike popping. He felt his anger stirring again, as he imagined the long white shaft of the killing lamp, questing relentlessly through the forest until it settled suddenly upon the puzzled animal, holding it mesmerized in the beam, the blinded eyes glowing like jewels, making a perfect aiming point in the field of the telescopic rifle sight.

Then suddenly the rifle blast, shocking in the silence, and the long licking flame of the muzzle flash. The beautiful head snapping back at the punch of the bullet and the soft thump of the falling body on the hard earth, the last spasmodic kicking of hooves and again the silence.

He knew it was useless to attempt pursuit now, the gunman would have an accomplice in the hills above them ready to flash a warning if any of the homestead lights came on, or if an auto engine whirred into life. Then the killing lamp would be doused and the poacher would creep away. David would search the midnight expanse of Jabulani in vain. His quarry was cunning and experienced in his craft of killing, and would only be taken by greater cunning.

David could not sleep again. He lay awake beside Debra, and listened to her soft breathing – and at intervals to the distant rifle fire. The game was tame and easily approached, innocent after the safety of the Park. It would run only a short distance after each shot, and then it would stand again staring without comprehension at the mysterious and dazzling light that floated towards it out of the darkness.

David's anger burned on through the night, and in the dawn the vultures were up. Black specks against the pink dawn sky, they appeared in ever-increasing numbers, sailing high on wide pinions, tracing wide swinging circles before beginning to drop towards the earth.

David telephoned Conrad Berg at Skukuza Camp, then he and Debra and the dog climbed into the Land-Rover, warmly dressed against the dawn chill. They followed the descent of the birds to where the poacher had come on the buffalo herd.

As they approached the first carcass, the animal scavengers scattered – slope-backed hyena cantering away into the trees, hideous and cowardly, looking back over their misshapen shoulders, grinning apologetically – little red jackal with silvery backs and alert ears, trotting to a respectful distance before standing and staring back anxiously.

The vultures were less timid, seething like fat brown maggots over the carcass as they squawled and squabbled, fouling everything with their stinking droppings and loose feathers, leaving the kill only when the Land-Rover was very close and then flapping heavily up into the trees to crouch there grotesquely with their bald scaly heads out-thrust.

There were sixteen dead buffalo, lying strung out along the line of the herd's flight. On each carcass the belly had been split open to let the vultures in, and the sirloin and fillet had been expertly removed.

'He killed them just for a few pounds of meat?' Debra asked incredulously.

'That's all,' David confirmed grimly. 'But that's not bad – sometimes they'll kill a wildebeest simply to make a fly whisk of its tail, or they'll shoot a giraffe for the marrow in its bones.'

'I don't understand,' Debra's voice was hopeless. 'What makes a man do it? He can't need the meat that badly.'

'No,' David agreed. 'It's deeper than that. This type of killing is a gut thing. This man kills for the thrill of it, he kills to see an animal fall, to hear the death cry, to smell the reek of fresh blood—' his voice choked off, 'this is one time you can be thankful you cannot see,' he said softly.

Conrad Berg found them waiting beside the corpses, and he set his rangers to work butchering the carcasses.

'No point in wasting all that meat. Food there for a lot of people.'

Then he put Sam to the spoor. There had been four men in the poaching party, one wearing light rubber-soled shoes and the others bare-footed.

'One white man, big man, long legs. Three black men, carry meat, blood drip here and here.'

They followed Sam slowly through the open forest as he patted the grass with his long thin tracking staff, and moved towards the unsurfaced public road.

'Here they walk backwards,' Sam observed, and Conrad explained grimly.

'Old poacher's trick. They walk backwards when they cross a boundary. If you cut the spoor while patrolling the fence you think they have gone the other way – leaving instead of entering – and you don't bother following them.'

The spoor went through a gap in the fence, crossed the

road and entered the tribal land beyond. It ended where a motor vehicle had been parked amongst a screening thicket of wild ebony. The tracks bumped away across the sandy earth and rejoined the public road.

'Plaster casts of the tyre tracks?' David asked.

'Waste of time.' Conrad shook his head. 'You can be sure they are changed before each expedition, he keeps this set especially and hides it when it's not in use.'

'What about spent cartridge shells?' David persisted.

Conrad laughed briefly. 'They are in his pocket, this is a fly bird. He's not going to scatter evidence all over the country. He picks up as he goes along. No – we'll have to sucker him into it.' And his manner became businesslike. 'Right, have you selected a place to stake old Sam out?'

'I thought we would put him up on one of the kopjes, near the String of Pearls. He'll be able to cover the whole estate from there, spot any dust on the road, and the height will give the two-way radio sufficient range.'

After lunch David loaded their bags into the luggage compartment of the Navajo. He paid the servants two weeks' wages in advance.

'Take good care,' he told them. 'I shall return before the end of the month.'

He parked the Land-Rover in the open hangar with the key in the ignition facing the open doorway, ready for a quick start. He took off and kept on a westerly heading, passing directly over Bandolier Hill and the buildings amongst the mango trees. They saw no sign of life, but David held his course until the hill sank from view below the horizon, then he came around on a wide circle to the south and lined up for Skukuza, the main camp of the Kruger National Park.

Conrad Berg was at the airstrip in his truck to meet the Cessna, and Jane had placed fresh flowers in the guest room. Jabulani lay fifty miles away to the north-west.

It was like squadron 'Red' standby again, with the Navajo parked under one of the big shade trees at the end of the Skukuza airstrip, and the radio set switched on, crackling faintly on the frequency tuned to that of Sam's transmitter, as he waited patiently on the hill-top above the pools.

The day was oppressively hot, with the threat of a rainstorm looming up out of the east, great cumulus thunderheads striding like giants across the bushveld.

Debra and David and Conrad Berg sat in the shade of the aircraft's wing, for it was too hot in the cockpit. They chatted in desultory fashion, but always listening to the radio crackle, and they were tense and distracted.

'He is not going to come,' said Debra a little before noon.

'He'll come,' Conrad contradicted her. 'Those buffalo are too much temptation. Perhaps not today – but tomorrow or the next day he'll come.'

David stood up and climbed in through the open door of the cabin. He went forward to the cockpit.

'Sam,' he spoke into the microphone. 'Can you hear me?'

There was a long pause, presumably while Sam struggled with radio procedure, then his voice, faint but clear: 'I hear you, *Nkosi*.'

'Have you seen anything?'

'There is nothing.'

'Keep good watch.'

'*Yebho, Nkosi.*'

Jane brought a cold picnic lunch down to the airstrip. They ate heartily despite the tension, and they were about to start on the milk tart, when suddenly the radio set throbbed and hummed. Sam's voice carried clearly to where they sat.

'He has come!'

'Red standby – Go! Go!' shouted David, and they rushed

for the cabin door, Debra treading squarely in the centre of Jane's milk tart before David grabbed her arm and guided her to her seat.

'Bright Lance, airborne and climbing.' David laughed with excitement and then memory stabbed him with a sharp blade. He remembered Joe hanging out there at six o'clock but he shut his mind to it and he banked steeply on to his heading, not wasting time in grabbing for altitude but staying right down at tree-top level.

Conrad Berg was hunched in the seat behind them, and his face was redder than usual – seeming about to burst like an over-ripe tomato.

'Where is the Land-Rover key?' he demanded anxiously.

'It's in the ignition – and the tank is full.'

'Can't you go faster?' Conrad growled.

'Have you got your walkie-talkie?' David checked him.

'Here!' It was gripped in one of his huge paws, and his double-barrelled .450 magnum was in the other.

David was hopping the taller trees, and sliding over the crests of higher ground with feet to spare. They flashed over the boundary fence and ahead of them lay the hills of Jabulani.

'Get ready,' he told Conrad, and flew the Navajo into the airstrip, taxiing up to the hangar where the Land-Rover waited.

Conrad jumped down at the instant that David braked to a halt, then he slammed the cabin door behind him and raced to the Land-Rover. Immediately David opened the throttle and swung the aircraft around, lining up for his take-off before the Navajo had gathered full momentum.

As he climbed, he saw the Land-Rover racing across the airstrip, dragging a cloak of dust behind it.

'Do you read me, Conrad?'

'Loud and clear,' Conrad's voice boomed out of the speaker, and David turned for the grey ribbon of the public road that showed through the trees, beyond the hills.

He followed it, flying five hundred feet above it, and he searched the open parkland.

The green Ford truck had been concealed from observation at ground level, again in a thicket of wild ebony, but it was open from the sky. For Akkers had never thought of discovery coming from there.

'Connie, I've got the truck. He's stashed it in a clump of ebony about half a mile down the bank of the Luzane stream. Your best route is to follow the road to the bridge, then go down into the dry river bed and try and cut him off before he gets to the truck.'

'Okay, David.'

'Move it, man.'

'I'm moving.' David saw the Land-Rover's dust above the trees, Conrad must have his foot down hard.

'I'm going to try and spot the man himself – chase him into your arms.'

'You do that!'

David started a long climbing turn towards the hills, sweeping and searching, up and around. Below him the pools glinted and he opened the throttles slightly, seeking altitude to clear the crests.

From the highest peak, a tiny figure waved frantically.

'Sam,' he grunted. 'Doing a war dance.' He altered course slightly to pass him closely, and Sam stopped his imitation of a windmill and stabbed with an extended arm towards the west. David acknowledged with a wave, and turned again, dropping down the western slopes.

Ahead of him the plain spread, dappled like a leopard's back with dark bush and golden glades of grass. He flew for a minute before he saw a black mass, moving slowly ahead of him, dark and amorphous against the pale grass. The remains of the buffalo herd had bunched up and were running without direction, desperate from the harrying they had received.

'Buffalo,' he told Debra. 'On the run. Something has alarmed them.' She sat still and intent beside him, hands in her lap, staring unseeingly ahead.

'Ah!' David shouted. 'Got him – with blood on his hands!'

In the centre of one of the larger clearings lay the black beetle-like body of a dead buffalo, its belly swollen and its legs sticking out stiffly as it lay on its side.

Four men stood around it in a circle, obviously just about to begin butchering the carcass. Three of them were Africans, one with a knife in his hand.

The fourth man was Johan Akkers. There was no mistaking the tall gaunt frame. He wore an old black fedora hat on his head, strangely formal attire for the work in which he was engaged, and his braces criss-crossed his tan-coloured shirt. He carried a rifle at the trail in his right hand, and at the sound of the aircraft engines he swung round and stared into the sky, frozen with the shock of discovery.

'You swine. Oh, you bloody swine,' whispered David, and his anger was strong and bright against the despoilers.

'Hold on!' he warned Debra, and flew straight at the man, dropping steeply on to him.

The group around the dead buffalo scattered, as the aircraft bore down on them, each man picking his own course and racing away on it, but David selected the lanky galloping frame with the black hat jammed down over the ears and sank down behind him. The tips of the propellers clipped the dry grass, as he swiftly overtook the running Akkers.

He was set to fly into him, driven by the unreasoning anger of the male animal protecting his own, and he lined up to cut him down with the spinning propeller blades.

As David braced himself for the impact Akkers glanced back over his shoulder, and his face was muddy grey with fright, the skull eyes dark and deeply set. He saw the murderous blades merely feet from him, and he threw himself flat into the grass.

The Navajo roared inches over his prone body, and David pulled it round in a steep turn, with the wing-tip brushing the grass. As he came round he saw that Akkers was up and running, and that he was only fifty paces from the edge of the trees.

David levelled out, aimed for the fugitive again but realized that he could not reach him before he was into the trees. Swiftly he sped across the clearing, but the lumbering figure drew slowly closer to the timber line and as he reached the sanctuary of a big leadwood trunk, Akkers whirled and raised the rifle to his shoulder. He aimed at the approaching aircraft; although the rifle was unsteady in his hands the range was short.

'Down,' shouted David, pushing Debra's head below the level of the windshield, and he pulled open the throttles and climbed steeply away.

Even above the bellow of the engines David heard the heavy bullet clang into the fuselage of the aircraft.

'What's happening, David?' Debra pleaded.

'He fired at us, but we've got him on the run. He'll head back for his truck now, and Conrad should be there waiting for him.'

Akkers kept under cover of the trees, and circling above him David caught glimpses of the tall figure trotting purposefully along his escape route.

'David, can you hear me?' Conrad's voice boomed suddenly in the tense cockpit.

'What is it, Connie?'

'We've got trouble. I've hit a rock in your Land-Rover and knocked out the sump. She's had it, pouring oil all over the place.'

'How the hell did you do that?' David demanded.

'I was trying a short cut.' Conrad's chagrin carried clearly over the ether.

'How far are you from the Luzane stream?'

'About three miles.'

'God, he'll beat you to it,' David swore. 'He's two miles from the truck and going like he's got a tax collector after him.'

'You have not seen old Connie move yet. I'll be there waiting for him,' Berg promised.

'Good luck,' David called, and the transmission went dead.

Below them Akkers was skirting the base of the hills, his black hat bobbing along steadily amongst the trees. David kept his starboard wing pointed at him and the Navajo turned steadily, holding station above him.

Other movement caught David's eye on the open slope of the hill above Akkers. For a moment he thought it was an animal, then with an intake of breath he realized that he was mistaken.

'What is it?' Debra demanded, sensing his concern.

'It's Sam, the damned fool. Connie told him not to leave his post – he's unarmed – but he's haring down the slope to try and cut Akkers off.'

'Can't you stop him?' Debra asked anxiously, and David didn't bother to answer.

He called Conrad four times before there was a reply. Conrad's voice was thick and wheezing with the effort of running.

'Sam is on to Akkers. I think he's going to confront him.'

'Oh God damn him,' groaned Conrad. 'I'll kick his black ass for him.'

'Hold on,' David told him, 'I'm going around for a closer look.'

David saw it all quite plainly, he was only three hundred

feet above them when Akkers became aware of the running figure on the slope above him. He stopped dead, and half-lifted the rifle; perhaps he shouted a warning but Sam kept on down, bounding over the rocky ground towards the man who had burned his children to death.

Akkers lifted the rifle to his shoulder and aimed deliberately, the rifle jumped sharply, the barrel kicking upwards at the recoil and Sam's legs kept on running while his upper torso was flung violently backwards by the strike of the heavy soft-nosed bullet.

The tiny brown-clad body bounced and rolled down the slope, before coming to a sprawling halt in a clump of scrub.

David watched Akkers reload the rifle, stooping to pick up the empty cartridge shell. Then he looked up at the circling aircraft above him, David may have been mistaken but it seemed the man was laughing – that obscene tooth-clucking giggle of his – then he started off again at a trot towards the truck.

'Connie,' David spoke hoarsely into his handset, 'he just killed Sam.'

Conrad Berg ran heavily over the broken sandy ground. He had lost his hat and sweat poured down his big red face, stinging his eyes and plastering the lank grey hair down his forehead. The walkie-talkie set bounced on his back, and the butt of the rifle thumped rhythmically against his hip.

He ran with grim concentration, trying to ignore the swollen pounding of his heart and the torture of breath that scalded his lungs. A thorn branch clawed at his upper arms, raking thin bloody lines through his skin, but he did not break the pattern of his run.

He turned his red and streaming face to the sky and saw

David's aircraft, circling ahead of him and slightly to his left. That marked for him Akkers' position – and it was clear that Conrad was losing ground in his desperate race to head off the escape.

The radio set on his back buzzed, but he ignored the call, he could not halt now. To break his run would mean he would only slump down exhausted. He was a big, heavy man, the air was hot and enervating, and he had run three miles through loose and difficult going – he was almost finished. He was burning the last of his reserves now.

Suddenly the earth seemed to fall away under him, and he pitched forward and half-slid – half-rolled – down the steep bank of the Luzane stream, to finish lying on his back in the white river sand, clean and grainy as sugar. The radio was digging painfully into his flesh and he dragged it out from under him.

Still lying in the sand he panted like a dog, blinded by sweat, and he fumbled the transmit button of the set.

'David—' he croaked thickly, 'I am in the bed of the stream – can you see me?'

The aircraft was arcing directly overhead now, and David's answer came back immediately.

'I see you, Connie, you are a hundred yards downstream from the truck. Akkers is there, Connie, he has just reached the truck, he'll be coming back down the river bed at any moment.'

Painfully, gasping, choking for breath, Conrad Berg dragged himself to his knees – and at that moment he heard the whirr and catch and purr of an engine. He unstrapped the heavy radio and laid it aside, then he unslung his rifle, snapped open the breech to check the load, and pulled himself to his feet.

Surprised at the weakness of his own massive body, he staggered into the centre of the river bed.

The dry river bed was eight feet deep with banks cut sheer by flood water, and it was fifteen feet wide at this

267

point, and the floor was of smooth white sand, scattered with small water-rounded stones no bigger than a baseball. It made a good illegal access road into Jabulani, and the tracks of Akkers' truck were clearly etched in the soft sand.

Around a bed in the stream Conrad heard the truck revving and roaring as it came down a low place in the bank into the smooth bed.

Conrad stood squarely in the middle of the river bed with the rifle held across his hip, and he fought to control his breathing. The approaching roar of the truck reached a crescendo as it came skidding wildly around the bend in the stream, and raced down towards him. Showers of loose sand were thrown out from under the spinning rear wheels.

Johan Akkers crouched over the steering wheel, with the black hat pulled down to his eyebrows, and his face was grey and glistening with sweat, and he saw Conrad blocking the river bed.

'Stop!' Conrad shouted, hefting the rifle. 'Stop or I shoot!'

The truck was swaying and sliding, the engine screamed in tortured protest. Akkers began to laugh, Conrad could see the open mouth and the shaking shoulders. There was no slackening in the truck's roaring, rocking charge.

Conrad lifted the rifle and sighted down the stubby double barrels. At that range he could have put a bullet through each of Johan Akkers' deep-set eyes, and the man made no effort to duck or otherwise avoid the menace of the levelled rifle. He was still laughing, and Conrad could clearly see the teeth lying loosely on his gums. He steeled himself with the truck fifty feet away, and racing down upon him.

It takes a peculiar state of mind before one man deliberately and cold-bloodedly shoots down another. It must either be the conditioned reflex of the soldier or law-enforcement officer, or it must be the terror of the hunted, or again it must be the unbalanced frenzy of the criminal lunatic.

None of these was Conrad Berg. Like most big, strong men, he was essentially a gentle person. His whole thinking was centred on protecting and cherishing life – he could not pull the trigger.

With the truck fifteen feet away, he threw himself aside, and Johan Akkers swung the wheel wildly, deliberately driving for him.

He caught Berg a glancing blow with the side of the truck, hurling him into the earthen bank of the stream. The truck went past him, slewing out of control. It hit the bank farther down the stream in a burst of earth and loose pebbles, swaying wildly as Akkers fought the bucking wheel. He got it under control again, jammed his foot down on the accelerator and went roaring on down the river bed, leaving Conrad lying in the soft sand below the bank.

As the truck hit him, Conrad felt the bone in his hip shatter like glass, and the breath driven from his lungs by the heavy blow of metal against his rib cage.

He lay in the sand on his side and felt the blood well slowly into his mouth. It had a bitter salt taste, and he knew that one of the broken ribs had pierced his lung like a lance and that the blood sprang from deep within his body.

He turned his head and saw the radio set lying ten paces away across the river bed. He began to drag himself towards it and his shattered leg slithered after him, twisted at a grotesque angle.

'David,' he whispered into the microphone. 'I couldn't stop him. He got away,' and he spat a mouthful of blood into the white sand.

David picked the truck up as it came charging up the river bank below the concrete bridge of the Luzane, bounced and bumped over the drainage ditch and swung on to the road. It gathered speed swiftly and raced west-wards towards Bandolier Hill and the highway. Dust boiled out from behind the green chassis, marking its position clearly for David as he turned two miles ahead of it.

After crossing the Luzane the road turned sharply to avoid a rocky outcrop, and then ran arrow-straight for two miles, hedged in with thick timber and undulating like a switchback, striking across the water shed and the grain of the land.

As David completed his turn he lowered his landing gear, and throttled back. The Navajo sank down, lined up on the dusty road as though it was a landing-strip.

Directly ahead was the dust column of the speeding truck. They were on a head-on course, but David concen-trated coldly on bringing the Navajo down into the narrow lane between the high walls of timber. He was speaking quietly to Debra, reassuring her and explaining what he was going to attempt.

He touched down lightly on the narrow road, letting her float in easily, and when she was down he opened the throttles again, taking her along the centre of the road under power but holding her down. He had speed enough to lift the Navajo off, if Akkers chose a collision rather than surrender.

Ahead of them was another hump in the road, and as they rolled swiftly towards it the green truck suddenly burst over the crest, not more than a hundred yards ahead.

Both vehicles were moving fast, coming together at a combined speed of almost two hundred miles an hour, and the shock of it was too much for Johan Akkers.

The appearance of the aircraft dead in the centre of the road, bearing down on him with the terrible spinning discs of the propellers was too much for nerves already run raw and ragged.

He wrenched the wheel hard over, and the truck went

into a broadside dry skid. It missed the port wing-tip of the Navajo as it went rocketing off the narrow road.

The front wheels caught the drainage ditch and the truck went over, cartwheeling twice in vicious slamming revolutions that smashed the glass from her windows and burst the doors open. The truck ended on its side against one of the trees.

David shut the throttles and thrust his feet hard down on the wheel brakes, bringing the Navajo up short.

'Wait here,' he shouted at Debra, and jumped down into the road. His face was a frozen mask of scar tissue, but his eyes were ablaze as he sprinted back along the road towards the wreckage of the green truck.

Akkers saw him coming, and he dragged himself shakily to his feet. He had been thrown clear and now he staggered to the truck. He could see his rifle lying in the cab, and he tried to scramble up on to the body to reach down through the open door. Blood from a deep scratch in his forehead was running into his eyes blinding him, he wiped it away with the back of his hand and glanced around.

David was close, hurdling the irrigation ditch and running towards him. Akkers scrambled down from the battered green body, and groped for the hunting knife on his belt. It was eight inches of Sheffield steel with a bone handle, and it had been honed to a razor edge.

He hefted it under-handed, in the classic grip of the knife-fighter, and wiped the blood from his face with the palm of his free hand.

He was crouching slightly, facing David, and the haft of the knife was completely covered by the huge bony fist.

David stopped short of him, his eyes fastened on the knife, and Akkers began to laugh again. It was a cracked falsetto giggle, the hysterical laughter of a man driven to the very frontiers of sanity.

The point of the knife weaved in the slow mesmeric movement of an erect cobra, and it caught the sunlight in bright points of light. David watched it, circling and crouching, steeling himself, summoning all the training of paratrooper school, screwing up his nerve to go in against the naked steel.

Akkers feinted swiftly, leaping in, and when David broke away, he let out a fresh burst of high laughter.

Again they circled, Akkers mouthing his teeth loosely, sucking at them, giggling, watching with those muddy green eyes from their deep, close-set sockets. David moved back slowly ahead of him, and Akkers drove him back against the body of the truck, cornering him there.

He came then, flashing like the charge of a wounded leopard. His speed and strength were shocking, and the knife hissed upwards for David's belly.

David caught the knife hand at the wrist, blocking the thrust and trapping the knife low down. They were chest to chest now, face to face, like lovers, and Akkers' breath stank of unwashed teeth.

They strained silently, shifting like dancers to balance each other's heaves and thrusts.

David felt the knife hand twisting in his grip. The man had hands and arms like steel, he could not hold him much longer. In seconds it would be free, and the steel would be probing into his belly.

David braced his legs and twisted sideways. The move caught Akkers off-balance and he could not resist it. David was able to get his other hand on to the knife arm, but even with both hands he was hard put to hold on.

They swayed and shuffled together, panting, grunting, straining, until they fell, still locked together, against the bonnet of the truck. The metal was hot and smelled of oil.

David was concentrating all his strength on the knife, but he felt Akkers' free hand groping for his throat. He ducked his head down on his shoulders, pressing his chin against his chest, but the fingers were steel hard and powerful as machinery. They probed mercilessly into his flesh, forcing his chin up, and settling on his throat, beginning to squeeze the life out of him.

Desperately David hauled at the knife arm, and found it more manageable now that Akkers was concentrating his strength on strangling him.

The open windscreen of the truck was beside David's shoulder, the glass had been smashed out of it, but jagged shards of it still stood in the metal rim, forming a crude but ferocious line of saw-teeth.

David felt the fingers digging deep into his throat, crushing the gristle of his larynx and blocking off the arteries that fed his brain. His vision starred and then began to fade darkly, as though he were pulling eight Gs in a dogfight.

With one last explosive effort David pulled the knife arm around on to the line of broken glass, and he dragged it down, sawing it desperately across the edge.

Akkers screamed and his strangling grip relaxed. Back and forth David sawed the arm, slashing and ripping through skin and fat and flesh, opening a wound like a ragged-petalled rose, hacking down into the nerves and arteries and sinews so that the knife dropped from the lifeless fingers and Akkers screamed like a woman.

David broke from him and shoved him away. Akkers fell to his knees still screaming and David clutched at his own throat massaging the bruised flesh, gasping for breath and feeling the flow of fresh blood to his brain.

'God Jesus, I'm dying. I'm bleeding to death. Oh sweet Jesus, help me!' screamed Akkers, holding the mutilated arm to his belly. 'Help me, oh God, don't let me die. Save me, Jesus, save me!'

Blood was streaming and spurting from the arm, flooding the front of his trousers. As he screamed his teeth fell from his mouth, leaving it a dark and empty cave in the palely glistening face.

'You've killed me. I'll bleed to death!' he screamed at

David, thrusting his face towards David. 'You've got to save me – don't let me die.'

David pushed himself away from the truck and took two running steps towards the kneeling man, then he swung his right leg and his whole body into a flying kick that took Akkers cleanly under the chin and snapped his head back.

He went over backwards and lay still and quiet, and David stood over him, sobbing and gasping for breath.

For purposes of sentence Mr Justice Barnard of the Transvaal division of the Supreme Court took into consideration four previous convictions – two under the Wildlife Conservation Act, one for aggravated assault, and the fourth for assault with intent to do grievous bodily harm.

He found Johan Akkers guilty of twelve counts under the Wildlife Conservation Act, but considered these as one when sentencing him to three years at hard labour without option of a fine, and confiscation of firearms and motor vehicles used in commission of these offences.

He found him guilty of one count of aggravated assault, and sentenced him to three years at hard labour without option.

The prosecutor altered one charge from attempted murder to assault with intent to do grievous bodily harm. He was found guilty as charged on this count, and the sentence was five years' imprisonment without option.

On the final charge of murder he was found guilty and Justice Barnard said in open court:

'In considering sentence of death on this charge, I was obliged to take into account the fact that the accused was acting like an animal in a trap, and I am satisfied that there was no element of premeditation—'

The sentence was eighteen years' imprisonment, and all

sentences were to run consecutively. They were all con-firmed on appeal.

As Conrad Berg said from his hospital bed with one heavily plastered leg in traction, and a glass of Old Buck gin in his hand, 'Well, for the next twenty-eight years we don't have to worry about that bastard – I beg your pardon, Mrs Morgan.'

'Twenty-nine years, dear,' Jane Berg corrected him firmly.

I n July the American edition of A *Place of Our Own* was published, and it dropped immediately into that hungry and bottomless pool of indifference wherein so many good books drown. It left not a sign, not a ripple of its passing.

Bobby Dugan, Debra's new literary agent in America, wrote to say how sorry he was – and how disappointed. He had expected at least some sort of critical notice to be taken of the publication.

David took it as a personal and direct insult. He ranted and stormed about the estate for a week, and it seemed that at one stage he might actually journey to America to commit a physical violence upon that country – a sort of one-man Vietnam in reverse.

'They must be stupid,' he protested. 'It's the finest book ever written.'

'Oh, David!' Debra protested modestly.

'It is! And I'd love to go over there and rub their noses in it,' and Debra imagined the doors of editorial offices all over New York being kicked open, and literary reviewers fleeing panic-stricken, jumping out of skyscraper windows or locking themselves in the women's toilets to evade David's wrath.

'David, my darling, you are wonderful for me,' she

giggled with delight, but it had hurt. It had hurt very badly. She felt the flame of her urge to write wane and flutter in the chill winds of rejection.

Now when she sat at her desk with the microphone at her lips, the words no longer tumbled and fought to escape, and the ideas no longer jostled each other. Where before she had seen things happening as though she were watching a play, seen her characters laugh and cry and sing, now there was only the dark cloud banks rolling across her eyes – unrelieved by colour or form.

For hours at a time she might sit at her desk and listen to the birds in the garden below the window.

David sensed her despair, and he tried to help her through it. When the hours at the desk proved fruitless he would insist she leave it and come with him along the new fence lines, or to fish for the big blue Mozambique bream in the deep water of the pools.

Now that she had completely learned the layout of the house and its immediate environs, David began to teach her to find her way at large. Each day they would walk down to the pools and Debra learned her landmarks along the track; she would grope for them with the carved walking-stick David had given her. Zulu soon realized his role in these expeditions, and it was David's idea to clip a tiny silver bell on to his collar so that Debra could follow him more readily. Soon she could venture out without David, merely calling her destination to Zulu and checking him against her own landmarks.

David was busy at this time with the removal of Conrad's game fence, as he was still laid up with the leg, and with building his own fences to enclose the three vulnerable boundaries of Jabulani. In addition there was a force of African rangers to recruit and train in their duties. David designed uniforms for them, and built outposts for them at all the main access points to the estate. He flew into Nelspruit at regular intervals to consult Conrad Berg on these arrangements, and it was at his suggestion that David began a water survey of the estate. He wanted surface water on the areas of Jabulani that were remote from the pools, and he began studying the feasibility of building catchment dams or sinking bore-holes. His days were full and active, and he became hard and lean and sunbrowned. Yet always there were many hours spent in Debra's company.

The 35-mm colour slides that David had taken of the buffalo herd before Johan Akkers had decimated it, were returned by the processing laboratory and they were hopelessly inadequate. The huge animals seemed to be standing on the horizon, and the ox-peckers on their bodies were tiny grey specks. This failure spurred David, and he returned from one trip to Nelspruit with a 600-mm telescopic lens.

While Debra was meant to be working, David set up his camera beside her and photographed the birds through her open window. The first results were mixed. Out of thirty-six exposures, thirty-five could be thrown away, but one was beautiful, a grey-headed bush shrike at the moment of flight, poised on spread wings with the sunlight catching his vivid plumage and his sparkling eye.

David was hooked by the photography bug, and there were more lenses and cameras and tripods, until Debra protested that it was a hobby which was completely visual, and from which she was excluded.

David had one of his inspirations of genius. He sent away for pressings of June Stannard's bird song recordings – and Debra was enchanted. She listened to them intently, her whole face lighting with pleasure when she recognized a familiar call.

From there it was a natural step for her to attempt to make her own bird recordings, which included the tinkle of Zulu's silver bell, the buzz of David's Land-Rover, the voices of the servants arguing in the kitchen yard – and faintly, very faintly, the chatter of a glossy starling.

'It's no damned good,' Debra complained bitterly. 'I wonder how she got hers so clear and close.'

David did some reading, and built a parabolic reflector for her. It did not look particularly lovely, but it worked. Aimed at a sound source it gathered and directed the sound waves into the microphone.

From the window of Debra's study they became more adventurous and moved out. He built permanent and comfortable hides beside the drinking places at the pools, and when his rangers reported a nesting site of an interesting bird species, they would build temporary blinds of thatch and canvas – sometimes on tall stilts – where David and Debra spent many silent and enjoyable hours together, shooting film and catching sound. Even Zulu learned to lie still and silent with his bell removed on these occasions.

Slowly they had begun to build up a library of photographs and recordings of a professional standard – until at last David plucked up sufficient courage to send to *African Wild Life Magazine* a selection of a dozen of his best slides. Two weeks later, he received a letter of acceptance, with a cheque for a hundred dollars. This payment represented a return of approximately one-twentieth of one per cent of his capital outlay on equipment. David was ecstatic, and Debra's pleasure almost as great as his. They drank two bottles of Veuve Clicquot for dinner, and under the spell of excitement and champagne their love-making that night was particularly inventive.

When David's photographs were published in *Wild Life* accompanied with Debra's text they reaped an unexpected harvest of letters from persons of similar interest all over the world, and a request from the editors for a full-length, illustrated article on Jabulani, and the Morgans' plans for turning it into a game sanctuary.

Debra made a lovely model for David's photographs that he compiled for the article, and she also worked with care on the text – while David fed her ideas and criticism.

Debra's new book lay abandoned, but her disappointment was forgotten in the pleasure of working together.

Their correspondence with other conservationists provided them with sufficient intellectual stimulus, and the occasional company of Conrad Berg and Jane satisfied their need for human contact. They were still both sensitive about being with other people, and this way they could avoid it.

The *Wild Life* article was almost complete and ready for posting, when a letter arrived from Bobby Dugan in New York. The editor of *Cosmopolitan* magazine had chanced upon one of the few copies of *A Place of Our Own* in circulation. She had liked it, and the magazine was considering serialization of the book – possibly linked with a feature article on Debra. Bobby wanted Debra to let him have a selection of photographs of herself, and four thousand words of autobiographical notes.

The photographs were there, ready to go to *Cosmopolitan*, and Debra ran through the four thousand words in three hours with David making suggestions, some helpful and some bawdy.

They sent off the tape and pictures in the same post as the article to *Wild Life*. For nearly a month they heard nothing more about it and then something happened to drive it from their minds.

They were in the small thatch and daub hide beside the main pool, sitting quietly and companionably during a lull in the evening activity. David had his camera tripod set up in one of the viewing windows and Debra's reflector was raised above the roof of the hide, daubed with camouflage paint and operated by a handle above her head.

The water was still and black, except where a surface-feeding bream was rising near the far reed banks. A flock of laughing doves was lining up with a chittering troop of spotted guinea fowl at the water's edge, sipping water and then pointing their beaks to the sky as they let it run down their throats.

Suddenly David took her wrist as a cautionary signal, and by the intensity of his grip she knew that he had seen something unusual and she leaned close against him so that she could hear his whispered descriptions, and with her right hand she switched on the recorder and then reached up to aim the reflector.

A herd of the rare and shy nyala antelope were approaching the drinking place timidly, clinging until the last possible moment to the security of the forest. Their ears were spread, and their nostrils quivered and sucked at the air, huge dark eyes glowing like lamps in the gloom.

There were nine hornless females, delicate chestnut in colour, striped with white, dainty-stepping and suspicious, as they followed the two herd bulls. These were so dissimilar from their females as though to belong to a different species. Purplish black, and shaggy with a rough mane extending from between the ears to the crupper, their horns were thick and corkscrewed, tipped with cream, and between their eyes was a vivid white chevron marking.

Advancing only a step at a time, and then pausing to stare with the limitless patience of the wild, searching for a hint of danger, they came slowly down the bank.

They passed the hide so closely that David was afraid to press the trigger of his camera lest the click of the shutter frighten them away.

He and Debra sat frozen as they reached the water; Debra smiled happily as she picked up the soft snort with which the lead bull blew the surface before drinking, and the liquid slurping with which he drew his first mouthful.

Once they were all drinking, David aimed and focused with care, but at the click of the shutter the bull nearest him leapt about and uttered a hoarse, throbbing alarm bark. Instantly the entire herd whirled and raced away like pale ghosts through the dark trees.

'I got it! I got it!' exulted Debra. 'Wow! He was so close, he nearly burst my eardrums.'

The excitement on Jabulani was feverish. Nyala antelope had never been seen on the estate before, not even in David's father's time, and all steps were taken to encourage them to remain. The pools were immediately placed out of bounds to all the rangers and servants, lest the human presence frighten the herd off before they had a chance to settle down and stabilize their territory.

Conrad Berg arrived, still using a stick and limping heavily as he would for the rest of his life. From the hide he watched the herd with David and Debra, and then back at the homestead he sat before the log fire, eating prime beef steak and drinking Old Buck while he gave his opinion.

'They aren't from the Park, I shouldn't think. I would have recognized a big old bull like that if I'd ever seen him before – they have probably sneaked in from one of the other estates – you haven't got the south fence up yet, have you?'

'Not yet.'

'Well, that's where they have moved from – probably sick of being stared at by all the tourists. Come up here for a bit of peace.' He took a swallow of his gin. 'You're getting a nice bit of stuff together here, Davey – another few years and it will be real show-place. Have you got any plans for visitors – you could make a good thing out of this place, like they have at Mala-Mala. Five-star safaris at economy prices—'

'Connie, I'm just too damn selfish to want to share this with anybody else.'

The distractions and the time had given Debra an opportunity to recover from the American failure of *A Place of Our Own*, and one morning she sat down at her desk and began working again on her second novel. That evening she told David:

'One of the blocks I have had is that I hadn't a name for it. It's like a baby – you have to give it a name or it's not really a person.'

'You have got a name for it?' he asked.

'Yes.'

'Would you like to tell me?'

She hesitated, shy at saying it to some other person for the first time. 'I thought I'd call it – A *Bright and Holy Thing*,' she said, and he thought about it for a few moments, repeating it softly.

'You like it?' she asked anxiously.

'It's great,' he said. 'I like it. I really do.'

With Debra once more busy on her novel it seemed each day was too short for the love and laughter and industry which filled it.

T he call came through while David and Debra were sitting around the barbecue in the front garden. David ran up to the house when the telephone bell insisted.

'Miss Mordecai?' David was puzzled, the name was vaguely familiar.

'Yes. I have a person-to-person call from New York, for Miss Debra Mordecai,' the operator repeated impatiently, and David realized who she was talking about.

'She'll take it,' he said, and yelled for Debra. It was Bobby Dugan, and the first time she had heard his voice.

'Wonder girl,' he shouted over the line. 'Sit down, so you don't fall down. Big Daddy has got news for you that will blow your mind! *Cosmopolitan* ran the article on you two weeks ago. They did you real proud, darling, full-page photograph – God, you looked good enough to eat—'

Debra laughed nervously and signalled David to put his ear against hers to listen.

'– the mag hit the stands Saturday, and Monday morning was a riot at the book stores. They were beating the doors down. You've caught the imagination of everybody here, darling. They sold seventeen thousand hardback in five days, you jumped straight into the number five slot on the *New York Times* bestseller list – it's a freak, a phenomenon, a mad crazy runner – darling, we are going to sell half a million copies of this book standing on our heads. All the big papers and mags are screaming for review copies – they've lost the ones we sent them three months ago. Doubleday are reprinting fifty thousand – and I told them they were crazy – it should have been a hundred thousand – it's only just starting – next week will see the West Coast catch fire and they'll be screaming for copies across the whole country—' There was much more, Bobby Dugan riding high, shouting his plans and his hopes, while Debra laughed weakly and kept saying, 'No! I can't believe it!' and 'It's not true!'

They drank three bottles of Veuve Clicquot that night, and a little before midnight Debra fell pregnant to David Morgan.

'Miss Mordecai combines superb use of language and a sure literary touch with the readability of a popular bestseller,' said the *New York Times*.

'Who says good literature has to be dull?' asked *Time*. 'Debra Mordecai's talent burns like a clean white flame.'

'Miss Mordecai takes you by the throat, slams you against the wall, throws you on the floor and kicks you in the guts. She leaves you as shaken and weak as if you had been in a car smash,' added the *Free Press*.

Proudly David presented Conrad Berg with a signed

copy of *A Place of Our Own*. Conrad had finally been prevailed upon to drop the 'Mrs Morgan' and call Debra by her given name. He was so impressed with the book that he had an immediate relapse.

'How do you think of those things, Mrs Morgan?' he asked with awe.

'Debra,' Debra prompted him.

'She doesn't think of them,' Jane Berg explained help-fully. 'It just comes to her – it's called *inspiration*.'

Bobby Dugan was correct, they had to reprint another fifty thousand copies.

It seemed as though the fates, ashamed of the cruel pranks they had played upon them, were determined to shower Debra and David with gifts.

As Debra sat at her olive-wood table, growing daily bigger with her child, once again the words flowed as strongly and as clearly as the spring waters of the String of Pearls. However, there was still time to help David with the illustrated publication he was compiling on the birds of prey of the bushveld, and to accompany him on the daily expeditions to different areas of Jabulani, and to plan the furnishings and the layout of the empty nursery.

Conrad Berg came to her secretly to enlist her aid in his plan to have David nominated to the Board of the National Parks Committee. They discussed it in length and great detail. A seat on the Board carried prestige and was usually reserved for men of greater age and influence than David. However, Conrad was confident that the dignity of the Morgan name combined with David's wealth, ownership of Jabulani, demonstrated interest in conservation and his ability to devote much time to the affairs of the Board would prevail.

'Yes,' Debra decided. 'It will be good for him to meet

people and get out a little more. We are in danger of becoming recluses here.'

'Will he do it?'

'Don't worry,' Debra assured him. 'I'll see to it.'

Debra was right. After the initial uneasiness of the first meeting of the Board, and once the other members became accustomed to that dreadful face and realized that behind it was a warm and forceful person, David gathered increasing confidence with each subsequent journey to Pretoria where the Board met. Debra would fly up with him and while they were at their deliberations she and Jane Berg shopped for the baby and the other items of luxury and necessity that were not readily come by in Nelspruit.

However, by November Debra was carrying low and she felt too big and uncomfortable to make the long flight in the cockpit of the Navajo, especially as the rains were about to break and the air was turbulent with storm cloud and static and heavy thermals. It would be a bumpy trip, and she was deeply involved in the last chapters of the new book.

'I'll be perfectly all right here,' she insisted. 'I've got a telephone and I have also got six game rangers, four servants and a fierce hound to guard me.'

David argued and protested for five days before the meeting and agreed only after he had worked out a timetable.

'If I leave here before dawn I'll be at the meeting by nine, we'll be finished by three and I can be back here by six-thirty at the latest,' he muttered. 'If it wasn't the budget and financial affairs vote, I would cut it – tell them I was sick.'

'It's important, darling. You go.'

'You sure now?'

'I won't even notice you're not here.'

'Don't get too carried away by it,' he told her ruefully. 'I might stay just to punish you.'

In the dawn the thunderheads were the colour of wine and flame and ripe fruit, fuming and magnificent, towering high above the tiny aircraft, high above the utmost ceiling of which it was capable.

David flew the corridors of open sky alone and at peace, wrapped in the euphoria of flight which never failed for him. He altered course at intervals to avoid the mountainous upsurges of cloud; within them lurked death and disaster, great winds that would tear the wings from his machine and send the pieces whirling on high, up into the heights where a man would perish from lack of oxygen.

He landed at Grand Central where a hire car was waiting for him, and spent the journey into Pretoria reading through the morning papers. It was only when he saw the meteorological prediction of a storm front moving in steadily from the Mozambique channel that he felt a little uneasy.

Before he entered the conference-room he asked the receptionist to place a telephone call to Jabulani.

'Two-hour delay, Mr Morgan.'

'Okay, call me when it comes through.'

When they broke for lunch he asked her again.

'What happened to my call?'

'I'm sorry, Mr Morgan. I was going tell you. The lines are down. They are having very heavy rainfull in the low veld.'

His vague uneasiness became mild alarm.

'Would you call the meteorological office for me, please?'

The weather was down solid. From Barberton to Mpunda Milia and from Lourenço Marques to Machado-dorp, the rain was heavy and unrelenting. The cloud ceiling was above twenty thousand feet and it was right down on the ground. The Navajo had no oxygen or electronic navigational equipment.

'How long?' David demanded of the meteorological officer. 'How long until it clears?'

286

'Hard to tell, sir. Two or three days.'

'Damn! Damn!' said David bitterly, and went down to the canteen on the ground floor of the government building. Conrad Berg was at a corner table with two other members of the Board, but when he saw David he jumped up and limped heavily but urgently across the room.

'David,' he took his arm, and his round face was deadly serious. 'I've just heard – Johann Akkers broke jail last night. He killed a guard and got clean away. He's been loose for seventeen hours.'

David stared at him, unable to speak with the shock of it.

'Is Debra alone?'

David nodded, his face stiff with scar tissue, but his eyes dark and afraid.

'You'd better fly down right away to be with her.'

'The weather – they've grounded all aircraft in the area.'

'Use my truck!' said Conrad urgently.

'I need something faster than that.'

'Do you want me to come with you?'

'No,' said David. 'If you aren't there this afternoon, they won't approve the new fencing allocations. I'll go on my own.'

D ebra was working at her desk when she heard the wind coming. She switched off her tape recorder and went out on to the veranda with the dog following her closely.

She stood listening, not sure of what she was hearing. It was a soughing and sighing, a far-off rushing like that of a wave upon a pebble beach.

The dog pressed against her leg and she squatted beside him, placing one arm around his neck, listening to the gathering rush of the wind, hearing the roar of it building

287

up swiftly, the branches of the marula forest beginning to thrash and rattle.

Zulu whimpered, and she hugged him a little closer.

'There, boy. Gently. Gently,' she whispered and the wind struck in a mighty squalling blast, crashing through the tree-tops, tearing and cracking the upper branches.

It banged into the insect screen of the veranda with a snap like a mainsail filling, and unsecured windows and doors slammed like cannon shots.

Debra sprang up and ran back into her workroom, the window was swinging and slamming, dust and debris boiling in through it. She put her shoulder to it, closing it and securing the latch, then she ran to do the same to the other windows and bumped into one of the house servants.

Between them they battened down all the doors and windows.

'Madam, the rain will come now. Very much rain.'

'Go to your families now,' Debra told them.

'The dinner, madam?'

'Don't worry, I'll make that,' and thankfully they streamed away through the swirling dust to their hutments beyond the kopje.

The wind blew for fifteen minutes, and Debra stood by the wire screen and felt it tugging and whipping her body. Its wildness was infectious, and she laughed aloud, elated and excited.

Then suddenly the wind was passed, as swiftly as it had come, and she heard it tearing and clawing its way over the hills above the pools.

In the utter silence that followed the whole world waited, tensed for the next onslaught of the elements. Debra felt the cold, the sudden fall in temperature as though the door to a great ice-box had opened, and she hugged her arms and shivered; she could not see the dark cloud banks that rolled across Jabulani, but somehow she

288

sensed their menace and their majesty in the coldness that swamped her.

The first lightning bolt struck with a crackling electric explosion that seemed to singe the air about her, and Debra was taken so unawares that she cried out aloud. The thunder broke, and seemed to shake the sky and rock the earth's very foundations.

Debra turned and groped her way back into the house, locking herself into her room, but walls could not diminish the fury of the rain when it came. It drummed and roared and deafened, battering the window panes, and striking the walls and doors, pouring through the screen to flood the veranda.

As overpowering as was the rainstorm, yet it was the lightning and the thunder that racked Debra's nerves. She could not steel herself for each mighty crack and roar. Each one caught her off-balance, and it seemed that they were aimed directly at her.

She crouched on her day bed, clinging to the soft warm body of the dog for a little comfort. She wished she had not allowed the servants to leave, and she thought that her nerve might crack altogether under the bombardment.

Finally she could stand it no longer. She groped her way into the living-room. In her distress she had almost lost her way about her own home, but she found the telephone and lifted it to her ear.

Immediately she knew that it was dead, there was no tone to it, but she cranked the handle wildly, calling desperately into the mouthpiece, until finally she let it fall and dangle on its cord.

She began to sob as she stumbled back to her workroom, hugging the child in her big belly, and she fell upon the day bed and covered her ears with both hands.

'Stop it,' she screamed. 'Stop it, oh please God, make it stop.'

The new national highway as far as the coal-mining town of Witbank was broad and smooth, six lanes of traffic, and David eased the hired Pontiac into the fast lane and went flat, keeping his foot pressed down hard. She peaked out at a hundred and thirty miles an hour, and she sat so solid upon the road that he hardly needed to drive her. His mind was free to play with horror stories, and to remember Johan Akkers' face as he stood in the dock glaring across the Court Room at them. The deep-set muddy eyes, and the mouth working as though he were about to spit. As the warders had led him to the stairs down to the cells he had pulled free and shouted back.

'I'm going to get you, Scarface,' he giggled. 'If I have to wait twenty-nine years – I'm going to get you,' and they took him away.

After Witbank the road narrowed. There was heavy traffic and the bends had dangerous camber and deceptive gradients. David was able to concentrate on keeping the big car on the road, and to drive the phantoms from his mind.

He took the Lyndenburg turn off, cutting the corner of the triangle, and the traffic thinned out to an occasional truck. He was able to go flat out again, and race along the edge of the high escarpment. Then suddenly the road turned and began its plunge down into the low veld.

When he emerged from the Erasmus tunnel David ran into the rain. It was a solid grey bank of water that filled the air and buffeted the body of the Pontiac. It flooded the road, so David had difficulty following its verge beneath the standing sheets of water, and it swamped the windshield, so that the efforts of the wipers to clear it were defeated.

David switched on his headlights and drove as fast as he dared, craning forward in his seat to peer into the impenetrable blue-grey curtains of rain.

Darkness came early in the rain, beneath the lowering

black clouds, and the wet road dazzled him with the reflections of his own headlights, while the fat falling drops seemed as big as hailstones. He was forced to moderate his speed a little more, creeping down the highway towards Bandolier Hill.

In the darkness he almost missed the turning, and he reversed back to it, swinging on to the unmade surface.

It was slushy with mud, puddled and swampy, slippery as grease. Again he was forced to lower his speed. Once he lost it, and slid broadside into the drainage ditch. By packing loose stones under the wheels and racing the engine he pulled the Pontiac out and drove on.

By the time he reached the bridge over the Luzane stream, he had been six hours at the wheel of the Pontiac, and it was a few minutes after eight o'clock in the evening.

As he reached the bridge the rain stopped abruptly, a freak hole in the weather. Directly overhead the stars showed mistily, while around them the cloud banks swirled, turning slowly, as though upon the axis of a great wheel.

David's headlights cut through the darkness, out across the mad brown waters to the far bank a hundred yards away. The bridge was submerged under fifteen feet of flood water, and the water was moving so swiftly that its waves and whirlpools seemed sculpted in polished brown marble, and the trunks of uprooted trees dashed downstream upon the flood.

It seemed impossible that the bed of this raging torrent had been the narrow sandy bed in which Johan Akkers had run down Conrad with the green Ford truck.

David climbed out of the Pontiac and walked down to the edge of the water. As he stood there he saw the level creeping up perceptibly towards his feet. It was still rising.

He looked up at the sky, and judged that the respite in the weather would not last much longer.

He reached his decision and ran back to the Pontiac. He reversed well back onto the highest ground and parked it off the verge with the headlights still directed at the river edge. Then, standing beside the door, he stripped down to his shirt and underpants. He pulled his belt from the loops of his trousers and buckled it about his waist, then he tied his shoes to the belt by their laces.

Barefooted he ran to the edge of the water, and began to feel his way slowly down the bank. It shelved quickly and within a few paces he was knee-deep and the current plucked at him, viciously trying to drag him off-balance.

He posed like that, braced against the current, and waited, staring upstream. He saw the tree trunk coming down fast on the flood, with its roots sticking up like beseeching arms. It was swinging across the current and would pass him closely.

He judged his moment and lunged for it. Half a dozen strong strokes carried him to it and he grasped one of the roots. Instantly he was whisked out of the beams of the headlight into the roaring fury of the river. The tree rolled and bucked, carrying him under and bringing him up coughing and gasping.

Something struck him a glancing blow and he felt his shirt tear and the skin beneath it rip. Then he was under water again, swirling end over end and clinging desperately to his log.

All about him the darkness was filled with the rush and threat of crazy water, and he was buffeted and flogged by its raw strength, grazed and bruised by rocks and driftwood.

Suddenly he felt the log check and bump against an obstruction, turning and swinging out into the current again.

David was blinded with muddy water and he knew there was a limit to how much more of this treatment he could survive. Already he was weakening quickly. He could feel his mind and his movements slowing, like a battered prize fighter in the tenth round.

He gambled it all on the obstruction which the log had

encountered being the far bank, and he released his death-grip on the root and stuck out sideways across the current with desperate strength.

His overarm stroke ended in the trailing branches of a thorn tree hanging over the storm waters. Thorns tore the flesh of his palm as his grip closed over them, and he cried out at the pain but held on.

Slowly he dragged himself out of the flood and crawled up the bank, hacking and coughing at the water in his lungs. Clear of the river, he fell on his face in the mud and vomited a gush of swallowed water that shot out of his nose and mouth.

He lay exhausted for a long while, until his coughing slowed and he could breathe again. His shoes had been torn from his belt by the current. He dragged himself to his feet and staggered forward into the darkness. As he ran, he held his hand to his face, pulling the broken thorns from the flesh of his palm with his teeth.

Stars were still showing overhead and by their feeble light he made out the road, and he began to run along it, gathering strength with each pace. It was very still now, with only the dripping of the trees and the occasional far-off murmur of thunder to break the silence.

Two miles from the homestead, David made out the dark bulk of something on the side of the road, and it was only when he was a few paces from it that he realized it was an automobile – a late model Chevy. It had been abandoned, bogged down in one of the greasy mudholes that the rains had opened.

The doors were unlocked and David switched on the interior and parking lights. There was dried blood on the seat, a dark smear of it, and on the back seat was a bundle of clothing. David untied it quickly and recognized immediately the coarse canvas suiting as regulation prison garb. He stared at it stupidly for a moment, until the impact of it struck him.

The car was stolen, the blood probably belonging to the unfortunate owner. The prison garb had been exchanged for other clothing, probably taken from the body of the owner of the Chevy.

David knew then beyond all possible doubt that Johan Akkers was at Jabulani, and that he had arrived before the bridge over the Luzane stream had become impassable – probably three or four hours previously.

David threw the prison suiting back into the car, and he began to run.

J ohan Akkers drove the Chevy across the Luzane bridge with the rising waters swirling over the guard rail, and with the rain teeming down in blinding white sheets.

The muddy water shoved at the body of the car, making steering difficult, and it seeped in under the doors, flooding the floorboards and swirling about Akkers' feet; but he reached the safety of the far bank and raced the engine as he shot up it. The wheels spun on the soft mud, and the Chevy skidded and swayed drunkenly in the loose footing.

The closer he drew to Jabulani the more reckless he became in his haste.

Before his conviction and imprisonment, Akkers had been a twisted and blighted creature, a man of deep moods and passionate temper. Feeling himself rejected and spurned by his fellow men he had lived in a world of swift defensive violence, but always he had kept within the bounds of reason.

However, during the two years that he had laboured and languished within prison walls, his anger and his lust for vengeance had driven him over that narrow boundary.

Vengeance had become the sole reason for his existence,